DEMON
POPE

A DOCTOR ORIENT THRILLER

DEMON POPE

by Frank Lauria

Rothco Press • Los Angeles, California

'For John Douglas, a fine editor, a better friend...'

Published by
Rothco Press
5500 Hollywood Blvd., 3rd Floor
Los Angeles, CA 90028

Copyright © 2014 by Frank Lauria

Cover design by Rob Cohen
Cover image by Barrand/iStock Photo

Rothco Press is a division of Over Easy Media Inc.

ISBN: 978-1-941519-22-6

"Marched into Russia, murdered the Jews, strangled the women, killed children...everyone knows what we bring."

Willie Peter Reese, A Stranger To Myself

Prologue

The blond priest was on his way to church.

He ambled casually, ignoring the occasional stares that trailed his passing. It was a sunny autumn morning and he was enjoying the crisp weather. Tall and erect, he had an air of benign authority. Despite a set smile his pale blue eyes mirrored cold contempt, as if able to see one's secret vices. And the zigzag scar that ran from eye to ear suggested a warrior rather than a cleric. If asked he would say he took shrapnel while helping Christians in Iraq.

But no one ever asked.

It was a typical blue collar neighborhood in Bay Ridge. Predominantly third generation Italian, it had neat rows of two family houses, and tree lined streets. The only reason a priest caused any stir walking past was because most of their local clergy was dark haired. Still, fair, Irish priests were a common sight in other sections of Brooklyn—Save for the scar.

The priest checked his Rolex. He was running a bit late. He quickened his pace for a few blocks. When he reached the Church of the Holy Virgin Mary he slowed to a more clerical saunter.

As expected, there was a great deal of activity on and around the stone steps leading to the great metal doors of the church. It was Confirmation Day and proud families swarmed over the stairway and sidewalk, shooting videos and snapshots of their thirteen year olds who were about to be confirmed as young Catholic men and women.

The church could have qualified as a cathedral. Built in the early twentieth century, by stone workers and masons imported from Italy, its marble pillars supported a grand domed ceiling alight with celestial murals of Mary surrounded by renaissance angels. The altar, too, was impressive, made of gilded ivory. It had always been a rich parish, due to the generosity of certain trustees. This in turn washed them with new world respectability

The church had a generous number of confessional boxes. *In response to the heavy traffic in sin, no doubt,* the priest observed with amusement. *This parish might even set some sort of record.*

Many of the pews were already filled with parents and relatives in anticipation of the procession down center aisle. Although Holy Mass was in progress there was a constant buzz of excited whispers among the worshippers who kept shifting in their pews to see if their children were coming.

Attached to the large church was an old fashioned chantry which was used for minor services. The priest entered this chapel unnoticed. There were two confessional boxes near the entrance and the pews were deserted.

In the main church the priest at the altar was consecrating the sacred host, the body and blood of Christ.

Showtime, hey zus, the priest chuckled. Whistling quietly, he checked the confessional box for some stray penitent or passed out wino. Satisfied he had the chantry to himself he went out to the hall where the children where gathered, the nuns prodding them into neat files, girls on one side, boys on the other. The girls were dressed as mini brides in white ruffled dresses and shoes, the boys as bridegrooms in blue suits and red carnations.

The priest hummed the opening notes of Mendelssohn's Wedding March as they slowly filed inside the church. He looked about the hall for his nun.

She found him. The nun moved toward the chantry, adjusting her habit as she came to make sure he saw her in the crowd.

"Is everything in order?" he asked.

"It's all there."

"Go fetch our little lamb."

Still humming the priest walked back inside the chantry and went to the altar. Everything was in order. There was the vestment, a simple purple stole, the ciborium, a gold cup containing the consecrated host, a chalice for the wine, and even a monstrance, the ornate holder for the Eucharist on hand, strictly for effect. He put on the stole, picked up the gold ciborium, and began to chant.

Outside the nun was completing her assignment. Heavy-set but agile, she moved purposefully through the scattered bystanders and arrived at the main entrance as the last section of children, the tallest, were filing inside. Without hesitation she tapped the last girl in the procession on the shoulder.

"Hurry dear. Come with me. The good father has a special gift for you."

The girl, Angela Cassenta, a thirteen year old with a stuffed animal collection and a crush on Justin Beiber, knew better than to question a nun. She followed, glancing back as the last of her classmates disappeared inside. *The line's moving slowly,* Angela thought, *I'll get back in time.*

When she entered the small chapel Angela saw a tall, blond priest at the altar, saying mass. His back was to her but as she neared she saw him elevate the chalice and drink. To her surprise he turned, beckoned her closer and offered her the chalice. Startled by his proximity and by his scar, she numbly knelt at the altar rail, but made no move to take the chalice.

"Drink blessed child of the blood of our Lord," he said fervently.

Obediently, Angela accepted the chalice and sipped. She had drunk sacred wine before but this tasted different. Thicker somehow, and sweeter.

"All of it child," the priest urged, "and I'll give you Communion." His blue eyes seemed to see into her soul. You are without sin, aren't you?"

"Yes, Father, but..."

"Then drink, and accept your Savior."

It tasted better the second time. The priest took the chalice and put it on the altar. Angela knelt at the altar, still confused by the ceremony.

"Father, why did you choose me?" She asked, suddenly emboldened by the wine.

The priest put a finger to his lips, and began to pray over the ciborium. As Angela listened she thought she heard the priest chanting in a language other than Latin. Still chanting the priest turned. With his two consecrated fingers he took the holy wafer from the gold cup and placed it on Angela's waiting tongue. As he bent over her, she noticed that his dangling crucifix was upside down.

Christ's head was pointing to the floor.

He continued chanting as she let the wafer dissolve then swallowed the remnants, anxious to leave, despite a torpid heaviness in her legs and arms.

"Now, child, what was it you asked me?"

It took Angela a few seconds to recall.

The priest bent closer.

"Because you're a virgin."

He kept her from falling to one side when she passed out. Certain she would remain propped up, he quickly went to work. Idly humming the wedding march, he went about gathering all the altar gear, including the chalice, and dumped them into the gym bag left at the side of the altar.

Then he bent over the rail and hefted Angela's unconscious body over his shoulder. He went into the sacristy behind the altar, where a thin rug had been placed on the floor. He rolled Angela into the rug then walked out through the back door.

Anyone passing would have seen a priest, carrying a small rug under one arm, gym bag in the other hand, leave the church, and enter a waiting van—driven by a nun.

+ + +

When Angela opened her eyes, she thought she was in a hospital—until the white robed nurses and doctors gathered around her began chanting, then she knew it was someplace else.

It seemed like a dream, except there was something she had to remember... something the priest had said. It was important. Too drowsy to speak, she fell back. Deep inside she knew she should be frightened, but a thick, warm blanket smothered her emotions. She closed her eyes.

The chanting roused her. It was becoming more intense, rising in pitch. She looked around and saw the nun. Except now she wasn't dressed like a nun. She wore the same white robe as the others in the hot, stifling room. Only the strange, red symbols on her robe set her apart from the others.

Angela's vision blurred. When she managed to focus she saw the priest. He was holding the gold chalice aloft. His black robe had the same red symbols, the nun wore, a double S that resembled twin electric bolts. Almost like his scar.

The priest came closer and cradled her in his arms. Just then, Angela remembered what it was she had to tell the father. Tall for her age and slightly overweight she had always felt she was ugly. So when Vinnie Castellano wanted to touch her breasts, she let him, even though she knew it was a mortal sin. Angela had to tell the priest that she lied—she wasn't a virgin anymore. She had to confess.

"Father..."

As the words tried to slowly crawl past Angela's dry tongue, the priest slit her throat.

He caught the spurting red liquid in his chalice, raised high the golden goblet, and drank her innocent blood.

"Agnus Dei," he whispered.

Lamb of God.

Chapter 1

Do you believe in magic?

Owen Orient did.

After becoming an MD at age twenty he had devoted much of his life to the pursuit of enlightenment. He had become adept at everything from Tibetan yoga to the most arcane of occult rituals. Along the way he had evolved a technique to awaken man's natural telepathic facilities. He once employed that same technique to regenerate a young girl's damaged spine, enabling her to walk.

It was his proudest achievement.

Yesterday's news. Orient brooded, now you're just another relic, like the Walkman. At the moment, he was out of work and nearly broke. His options had shrunk to one—an interview for a spot on St. Luke's Hospital elite trauma unit.

Elite was the operative word. Once considered one of the most skilled physicians in medicine—these days he was considered a wild card. He'd been turned away the last three times out.

Maybe it was time to cash in and head for India, Orient speculated. He still had a vintage Rolls Royce Ghost in storage, and a small collection of Egyptian artifacts. The proceeds would probably keep him afloat for three or four years in Goa or somewhere equally remote.

He made a note to contact a few auction houses for an appraisal.

Negative thinking he told himself, focus on acing the interview.

Orient turned off his phone and sat on the mat in the middle of his living room. As he began to stretch his body he took long, measured breaths. He deepened his breathing focusing his consciousness until self merged with infinity and time dissolved...

It was dusk when he emerged. He'd been meditating for two hours. And he was hungry.

The text message on the screen solved his problem. *Owen, please meet me at Mezzaluna 7ish.*

Orient smiled. Only Sybelle would text 7ish. His reply was terse: *ok 7.*

Sybelle Lean was one of a few close friends. A professional psychic, she maintained a lucrative practice. Orient's spiritual beliefs precluded the use of his own psychic skills for profit. However Sybelle had every right to make her own choices— Except when it came to telepathy. Before teaching her the technique Orient had extracted an oath of secrecy.

So far she had only broken it once, Orient noted ruefully. But in Sybelle's case you had to make an exception. She wasn't like other people.

He took a quick a shower and dressed, still wondering why she had asked to meet after weeks of silence. It could be something as simple as catching up with a friend, or it could be urgent. He changed shoes from Nike to Gucci and swapped his worn leather jacket for a dark blue blazer. Whatever the occasion, dinner with Sybelle was always an event.

The restaurant she had chosen was located on the Upper East Side. Orient decided to walk across Central Park. Although pushing fifty he was lean and fit from years of yoga.

Lately he had resumed the martial art of *QiGong* and he could feel the new strength and balance in his stride.

He exited the park at Seventy Second Street and crossed Fifth Avenue, strolling past the town houses and apartment buildings that formed the golden canyons of the east side. Since 9/11 Manhattan had changed, if not evolved, into a fortress for the rich. All the young authors, actors and artists had found sanctuary in Brooklyn.

Mezzaluna was a trendy Italian restaurant with walls covered over by small paintings and graphics arranged in a glossy collage. When he arrived Sybelle was already ensconced at a prime table and had a drink standing at attention in front of his chair.

"You're so prompt,' she said with a hint of disappointment. "I haven't even had my second Bellini."

"You probably ordered three to start with." He sat down and picked up his glass.

"To your health."

He immediately regretted his choice of toast. Sybelle looked decidedly unhealthy. Not sick exactly, but worn. Always full figured she had lost weight and her skin was sallow beneath the artful cosmetics. Her green eyes were dull and her cherubic features sagged despite her smile. Even her frizzy red hair seemed limp.

Orient sipped his drink. "Been a while since we got together."

"Too long," she sniffed, "but it's not entirely my fault. You are a bit of a hermit."

"I plead no contest. Did you order?"

"Salad, is that all right?"

"Sounds good.. So what brings us here?"

Her dazzling smile washed the shadows from her face. "The ravioli darling. I thought you could use a proper meal in civilized surroundings. Although I must admit you look quite dashing. "

Orient knew he was being set up but his perception was tempered by concern. They both shared a real connection and he sensed something disquieting around her like an aura, something dark and... *unclean*...

Over the years Orient had learned to wait her out, so he went with the flow.

"Everything okay at the office?" he ventured for want of a better term. Sybelle was New York's leading psychic, specializing in Tarot reading, crystal skrying, and the occasional séance.

"Actually, business is booming. I have to turn clients away."

Orient nodded. He didn't approve of Sybelle's professional choice but admittedly she was the best. He had been her mentor and respected the enormous occult power she was able to channel, if not always control.

She was right, the ravioli was excellent. Orient limited his wine intake but Sybelle was a woman of generous appetites. Their conversation over dinner was lighthearted enough, ranging from film to general gossip, but by dessert she still hadn't mentioned why she wanted to get together.

"Too many hours with clients could be draining," he ventured diplomatically.

She fluttered her lashes in annoyance. "Of course you would say something like that but I find my work quite stimulating these days—energizing actually. Shall we share the Italian cheesecake?"

So much for diplomacy, Orient thought. He decided to let it lay.

The restaurant had filled and the sleek couples standing at the door were being served complimentary champagne. The noise level lifted and for the next fifteen minutes Sybelle's animated banter almost convinced Orient he might have misdiagnosed her problem.

When the check came she snatched it with a flourish. "*I* invited *you*. But you can buy me an after dinner drink."

Perhaps it was the night air but once outside all the strength seemed to drain from Sybelle and she slumped heavily against him. "I think I really need that cognac," she said, steadying herself.

Fortunately JG Melons' was literally next door. Inside the air was warmer and thick with noise yet it seemed to revive Sybelle like a blast of pure oxygen. She recovered her poise as well as her zest for cognac. "You might be right about working too many hours," she conceded, scanning the crowd. "Well I'm ready for another. How about you?"

"How many clients on your list these days?" he asked casually, signaling the bartender.

The question caught her off guard and she answered without thinking.

"Just three but one is... Well it's an unusual case."

Orient could see she regretted saying as much as she had. He waited, but she avoided his eyes. Having failed at diplomacy, he took the direct route.

"Look, you asked me to dinner for some reason. Most likely it has to do with your *unusual* case. You've known me forever. What's the problem?"

"The problem is I know you'll say no."

As the bartender neared Orient lifted two fingers. Once again Sybelle had outflanked him. Now if he refused, it was his fault.

"Okay, say no to exactly what?"

"I need you to...." she leaned closer and lowered her voice, "...I need you to perform an exorcism.'

Orient's sculpted features hardened and he shook his head. "No way. If your client needs help you should consult a priest. We discussed this befo..."

"Owen, she's not a client, she's my niece."

He blinked.

"Well, actually she's my niece's daughter. But it's the same thing."

Orient didn't answer. He was wondering how he could avoid getting involved.

"I should have called you right away."

"Right away, when?"

She sighed and watched the bartender deposit their drinks. "Savana has been in a coma for almost two months."

"Isn't that a medical problem?"

"They've run every test but the results came back negative. Except for the fact that she's lost consciousness, Savana is perfectly healthy."

"Why did her mother call you?"

Sybelle took a long sip of cognac. "The ring."

Orient waited.

"Savana came home wearing a ring she found in a junk store. An hour later she fell into a coma. When the tests came back negative, she thought the problem might be psychic rather than physical. You see, we can't get the damned ring off her finger and believe me darling I've tried."

"And you think an exorcism with do the trick. Like spiritual olive oil."

"I knew you'd be like this. You are so annoyingly stubborn." She drained her glass and set it down emphatically. "It's not about the damned ring it's about Savana. She's barely fourteen."

Orient lifted his hands in surrender. "Of course I'll help. Look, tomorrow morning when you're a bit more sober..."

"I'm sober now."

"Okay tonight," he checked his watch, "it's almost nine thirty now. At eleven tonight you make a connection with Savana and I'll check it out."

"And then...?"

"If there's something there we'll get rid of it."

Aware he'd been totally out played Orient left his drink untouched and paid the tab.

+ + +

She cornered me nicely, Orient noted as he watched the clock pass ten thirty. He pushed aside his misgivings. There was no room for emotion or opinion where he was going.

He was at his desk, preparing for his interview and it didn't look promising. His spotty resume showed a history of working in various emergency rooms, then quitting for long periods and showing up somewhere else. That he had spent that time compiling a visual record of the technique given to him by the Master Ku two lifetimes ago, while on a spiritual quest to Tibet meant nothing. In fact it was a liability. Any mention of his research with telepathy was a sure deal breaker. .

At ten fifty he left his work, went into the living room, lit a candle and sat in an easy chair. He intended to make contact with Sybelle. Not direct telepathic contact but something akin to orbiting Mars or Saturn to obtain data... a fly by.

Fortunately it wasn't a manned flight. The moment they connected, he was blown back, like positive magnets repelling each other. .

Surprised, he cleared his mind and reset. This time he moved carefully. He took his time, waiting until he was locked into a tight breathing pattern before reaching out for Sybelle. When they connected he pushed, and felt the alien current give way, tearing like fabric and he tumbled into an environment seething with hostility. Instantly he realized he hadn't broken through.... *he'd been lured.*

He severed the link, scrambling like a spectral mouse to escape.

As he blindly shrank back to safety something pursued him. He could sense, rather than see, the entity clawing at his concentration. For a splintered moment it loomed up, dark, feline, *pitiless...* before it vanished.

Carefully, like a scuba diver avoiding the bends, he emerged from the depths of consciousness to the relative safety of his apartment.

Long minutes passed, his measured breathing the only sound in the room. Distant car horns and sirens wove through the thick silence like needles. Dimly he noticed the candle had gone out.

+ + +

That was definitely serious, Orient thought as he called Sybelle.

"Diagnosis correct—The energy around your niece is malignant. When do you want to operate?"

"I'll call you right back. And thank you darling. I knew I could count on you."

It was then Orient noticed the message light flashing. Reluctantly, he pressed the button.

"Hello, Owen, it's Henry. I've just received word of an extraordinary Egyptian piece, an amulet of some sort. The dealer claims it's first dynasty, possibly older. His name is Peter Taegris, and he's showing it tomorrow at his shop. The address is 868 Myrtle Avenue in Brooklyn, right off the bridge. I can't go, I have an important client all day, but I told him you'd be there. Taegris says he's selling it immediately, so I strongly advise you to hurry over. At the very least it's worth taking a look."

Orient heaved a long sigh. A few hours ago all he had to worry about was a crucial work interview. Now was dealing with an exorcism he didn't want to perform and an ancient artifact he couldn't afford.

On the other hand he had a strong affinity for Egyptian objects, especially early period. Henry Applegate was an antiquities expert who shared his interest and often suggested items for purchase. Actually, Henry might be able to help him sell off his own collection, Orient speculated.

The phone rang. "We can't do anything tomorrow," Sybelle said briskly, "I just spoke to Savana's mother. It's her day off and she wants to spend it with Savana at home. And I don't want to mention the exorcism until it's over. Trust me I have my reasons. So we'll have to do it the day after tomorrow. Is that alright?"

It was the day of his interview. Orient paused. "How about later in the afternoon?"

"Perfect. We have to wait until her day nurse goes home anyway."

"I suppose now I can go see this Egyptian amulet my friend Henry is so excited about."

"Henry? Do I know him?"

"Not really. He's an art and antiquities dealer."

"What about this amulet thing?"

"He's very keen on the piece and asked me to look at it. It's at some shop in Brooklyn."

"How fun. Let me tag along. You know how I adore Egyptian art."

Before he could object she said, "I'll drive. What time shall I pick you up?"

The next day Sybelle called twice to change their schedule. Finally she arrived in front of his apartment building behind the wheel of a red Mustang. "I just bought it," she announced, "this will be the longest drive she's taken so far."

"The color is definitely you."

She glanced at him. "You know someone with your... background could do very well with a *few select clients*."

Orient smiled. He'd heard it before, and she was probably right. But fundamentally it would be wrong—for him and for his work. "Thanks, but I'm hoping to get an honest job with a hospital."

"Oh, well then," Sybelle sniffed. She turned up the volume and headed across Central Park to the East River drive. It was a sunny afternoon and the gleaming glass towers of midtown Manhattan formed a magnificent backdrop to the strains of Verdi's opera *Aida* rising from the speakers."

"How did you find this place?" Sybelle inquired as they crossed the bridge and turned onto the local streets, "It's so out of the way, I mean, it is *Brooklyn*."

Her comment was well taken. Myrtle Avenue was near the Brooklyn Navy Yard. After some difficulty they found the shop, which was located in a basement. The top half of the storefront window stood above a cracked concrete sidewalk. It read: *P. Taegris Antique Clocks.*

"What would an Egyptian artifact be doing here?" Sybelle asked.

Good question, Orient thought.

The small, dusty shop was crammed with old-fashioned wall clocks, grandfather clocks, bright neon display clocks, European cuckoo clocks, Bakelite clocks, art-deco shelf clocks, and vintage alarm clocks. A glass shelf at the far end was stacked with pocket watches and wrist watches. There was nothing else. No knick knacks, artifacts, nothing but timepieces.

There was also no clerk in sight. The tinny strains of middle-eastern music could be heard coming from behind a half-closed door in the rear as they moved gingerly through the shop. Sybelle looked at Orient nervously.

"Hello?" Orient called out.

They heard shuffling feet and a bald, overweight man wearing a rumpled white shirt, and round spectacles, peered out from behind the door.

"Yes?" he said. His voice bore the trace of an accent.

"Are you the proprietor?"

"Yes, I am."

"I was told by a friend in the antiquities business you may have an Egyptian amulet for sale. I'm Doctor Owen Orient, and this is my associate Miss Lean."

The man's suspicious squint lifted and he smiled broadly. "Yes. I see. May I ask your friend's name?"

"Henry Applegate."

"Yes. Yes. Of course." He bowed slightly to Sybelle. "I am Peter Taegris. Please, come inside and have a cup of tea while you examine my little treasure."

Sybelle and Orient glanced at each other as the man turned and led the way through the door. Part of the inner room was a workshop, with watch parts and dismantled clocks on a large wooden table. An oversized magnifying glass was mounted on a metal swivel below a strong ceiling light that cast long shadows across the room.

The other side of the room looked like an Arabian salon, with thick leather poufs, and an ornate brass table, on a woven silk rug that covered most of the floor. A silver tea pot and cups were already on the table, as if they'd been expected. Again, Sybelle and Orient exchanged glances.

"Please, please sit," Taegris said, pouring tea into small glass cups with elaborate ceremony.

He was tall and plump, and his face was unlined which gave his broad, stubby features an ageless quality. When he smiled, he displayed perfect white teeth, only his eyes were old. They were dark and piercing, behind silver-rimmed glasses.

The tea was strong, hot, and quite welcome after their intense ordeal on the bridge. As they drank, the proprietor went over to a steel wall safe, opened it, and returned with a framed object wrapped in a plastic bag. With a flourish, Taegris unsealed the bag and handed the object to Orient.

Inside a simple box frame was a triangular swatch of yellowed leather, its long base slightly frayed suggesting it had been cut from a larger piece. Inscribed on the fragment, with impeccable artistry, were three symbols.

In the top corner was the Eye of Horus, well known to every amateur Egyptologist. The one in the center was more obscure, being a six-pointed Star of Solomon, set inside a square. Over each corner of the square was a small circle. Orient recognized it immediately as a powerful occult pentacle.

On the bottom was a black, winged lioness in silhouette, with the breasts and face of a female wearing a royal headdress, her face turned to the viewer. Despite the fragment's age, the drawing was well preserved, outlining the features of a remarkably beautiful, and enigmatic, woman.

"Owen?" Sybelle whispered.

Orient looked up, suddenly aware he had been studying the winged female intently and lost track of time. "Of course, sorry," he said, passing the framed object to Sybelle.

He took a deep breath, focusing his attention. He turned and saw Taegris smiling at him.

"More tea, Doctor?"

Orient shook his head. "It's a most unusual piece. Still, it would be easier to authenticate it if it were on papyrus."

"Before papyrus was perfected, the ancients used leather scrolls, as well as clay tablets, for their important texts," Taegris said, still smiling. "Please to examine it under the magnifier if you like."

They all moved to the work table. Taegris placed the fragment on the table, and adjusted the large magnifying glass over it. Enlarged, it was clear to see the artist's skill, as well as that of the tanner. Although worn and discolored, the leather swatch was still supple and devoid of cracks. Each of the three symbols was meticulously rendered in black ink by the same skillful hand. They were perfectly proportioned and displayed a certain intensity. However, the piece lacked context. Orient's best guess was that it was part of a larger religious or magical text, similar to the Book of the Dead. He knew the center symbol was from the Book of Solomon. Beneath the glass he could make out tiny signs or letters within the star that he recognized. But the lower symbol was both fascinating, and puzzling.

"There's two or three small signs beneath the body," he said, "but they're faded."

"Probably a depiction of the Goddess Bast," Sybelle said sofly. "The cat..."

Taegris rubbed his hands. "Maybe that is correct."

Orient shrugged. "She seems more sphinx than cat. I can't be sure, short of carbon testing the swatch, but this lady might be pre-dynasty, possibly Sumerian."

"*If* it's authentic," Sybelle said.

"I can assure you Madame, the fragment is most authentic," Taegris said hurridly.

"What form of proof do you have?" Orient struggled to maintain some semblance of disinterest in the piece. However the winged black sphinx held his gaze.

"Of course, I have certificates, provenance, whatever you wish."

"And the price?"

He hesitated, his smile fading. "The piece is thirty thousand dollars, firm."

Sybelle arched her brows. "That's a bit steep, for an inscribed patch.'

"True, the piece is expensive..."

"Especially when all one has for authentication is a certificate," she reminded.

The proprietor's stubby features clouded. He clasped his hands, shaking his head as if resigned to being insulted. "Now I must prove this to you,' he said sadly. "Very well, we do this, you leave me ten percent here today, take the piece with you, along with certificates, to anybody you like. Get authentication, then either return piece, or pay remainder, twenty seven thousand dollars. Fair enough?"

"It is fair, "Orient said. "Unfortunately I thought I'd be looking at a smaller, more ordinary remnant of Egyptian culture, so I brought much less than three thousand dollars with me. I'm afraid we have to defer this transaction."

"How much did you bring Owen?"

He glanced at Sybelle She looked determined to acquire the piece, "About twelve hundred or so," he said.

"I can write a check for the rest." She smiled at Taegris. "Would that be acceptable?"

He spread his arms and let them fall in defeat. "For you Madame, it is always acceptable. Please come, I will show you the certificates."

He took them over to a roll-top desk near the worktable and showed them the papers, one certifying the triangular fragment was an authentic example of early Egyptian religious

symbols, as attested to by one Deiter Von Speer, Chairman of
the University of Berlin's School of Archeology. And another,
testifying the piece had come from the private collection of
Rene Grandois, of Paris. Both seemed in order.

The proprietor wrapped the framed object and gave it to
Orient. "It will be an unique addition to your collection."

"You're quite trusting, Mr. Taegris," Sybelle said sweetly,
signing her check. "You haven't even asked me for any ID."

"But, dear madam, your address is on the check," he said,
with a sly wink at Orient.

Chapter 2

When they stepped outside the sun was dropping behind the skyline. It was commuter hour and the trip into Manhattan was tedious, if not grueling.

"I can't really afford the piece," Orient said ruefully, as the Mustang crawled uptown . "I don't know why I agreed to buy the damned thing."

"Nonsense, darling, I can afford it, and if you must you'll sell it at a handsome profit."

"Fine. But since we're stuck in traffic maybe you'll have time to give me more details on your niece's condition."

"It's clear to me now darling. Calling you for dinner was a cry for help. Despite the confused state I was in, I knew you'd recognize the symptoms. And I do apologize for being so bitchy."

Orient smiled slightly. This was the Sybelle of old. She was even looking better. The haggard, worn, look had been smoothed over by her customary aura of vitality. And as always, she took the scenic route to get to the point.

"So how did this all start?" he prodded.

She hesitated. "Some weeks ago my niece came to me with a problem. Her daughter."

"Yes, Savana."

"At first they thought she was ill. She had fallen into a sort of coma. They gave her all sorts of hospital tests."

"You said her mother thought it was connected to some ring."

"Yes, the day Savana came home with the ring she fell into a coma. And the ring won't come off her finger."

"And you tried to rouse her?"

"I tried, but making a telepathic connection was difficult. It left me drained and depressed. I didn't think I would need any sort of psychic protection with her—I mean she's a child."

"Where is she now?"

"She's at her mother's place. I visit at least four or five days a week. After the first time I didn't even know why I was driven to see her as often as I did. Do you know what I mean? There was no schedule. I would be working or out shopping and without warning I would feel compelled to go to her home. Some days I would have to make excuses to her mother. I'm sure she thinks I'm a just a loony aunt."

"What would you do when you visited Savana?"

"Most days I would just sit there, and try to make some kind of contact. But each visit left me with an awful feeling of... imminent evil. It all seemed to center on the ring—as in getting it off her finger."

"Strange." Orient murmered.

"Oh *really*, you think so Owen?" Sybelle said. "The really strange-and horribly sad part is Savana lying there helpless. And we've got to do something."

"Well, of course we're going to help her."

Sybelle heaved a sigh of relief. "Owen you are my rock in a sea of disaster."

While ready to help Orient had reservations. He had the damned job interview the next morning, and he needed to be ready. Still he couldn't leave Sybelle stranded.

+ + +

While they sat stalled on the East River drive Sybelle made two calls to Savana's mother. No answer.

"Well that settles it," she said, "I need a stiff drink ASAP."

They went back to Sybelle's place where she poured two large cognacs, handed one to Orient and fell back on her scarlet sofa.

"To my knight in civilian armor," Sybelle toasted, then drained her snifter.

Orient took a healthy sip and felt the alcohol burn through the tension clamping his muscles. He took a deep breath

"Why don't we take a look at our new treasure?" Sybelle suggested.

"Good idea. Put it on the table, under the lamp."

Sybelle took the framed swatch out of the brown paper shopping bag Taegris had given her. She pulled away the bubble wrap and carefully placed the piece on a side table.

If anything, it seemed even more beautiful in its new setting. As Orient stared at the winged lioness with full, curved breasts and the face of a goddess, something stirred inside him.

"My lord, it's truly magnificent," Sybelle said under her breath.

"May I use your phone?"

"It's over there. What is it darling?"

"I'm going to call Henry Applegate. He'll be able to confirm its origin. He should be curious, after all he's the one who put me on to it... Henry...? Owen Orient. You remember that Egyptian piece? Well I just bought it and hoped you could take a look...."

Orient glanced at Sybelle as he listened. "Dinner at your place? Well that's very kind but I'm with a friend and..."He shrugged and covered the mouthpiece, "Henry invited us to his house for..."

"Tell him we'll be right over, I'm absolutely famished."

Sybelle's idea of promptness was vague at best. It took almost twenty minutes for her to rearrange her hair and makeup. "Cut a girl some slack, darling," she sniffed.

When they arrived, Henry was waiting with hor d'ouvres and champagne.

"So good of you to come on such short notice."

"So good of *you*," Sybelle said grandly, extending her hand. "Sybelle Lean... My what a marvelous place you have, Mr. Applegate."

"All my friends call me Henry... or worse."

Orient could tell by Sybelle's flirtatious laugh that she was interested.

Their host was a tall, distinguished man of perhaps fifty five, slim, with sharply defined features, set off by an aquiline nose reminiscent of a roman bust. His long silver hair matched his grey eyes, which were fixed on the shopping bag in Orient's hand.

"Is that it?

"It's just fabulous," Sybelle said. "Show it to Henry darling."

Orient dutifully handed him the bag,

"First things first," Henry declared, putting it aside. "A drop of champagne to start things off properly."

As they drank and devoured the smoked salmon, flat-bread and cheese, arrayed on the coffee table, Orient could see Henry's eyes darting to the still unopened bag. He also noticed that Sybelle seemed quite taken by their host. "I find your art collection most intriguing, "she trilled, waving her champagne flute grandly. "It's so... *eclectic*, isn't it? From this early Egyptian relief—the falcon Horus isn't it?—to this exquisite Roman glass vase, and of course this lovely Klee."

"Right on all counts,' Henry said. "You have an informed eye, no wonder Owen took you along today."

Sybelle almost choked on her drink. "Well that's certainly one reason. We share an interest in Ancient Egypt."

Henry moved back to the table where he had put the shopping bag. "I know Owen is an avid collector. So when this Taegris fellow called and said he had a piece for immediate sale I thought of him immediately." He looked from Sybelle to Orient. "Well then, shall we?"

Although they had examined it closely a number of times there was an air of expectancy as Henry carefully unwrapped the framed swatch.

"It's truly magnificent," Henry said in a hushed voice. "Sheer artistry."

"Owen thinks the sphinx is Sumerian," Sybelle said quietly.

"Most discerning. If so, the piece must date back six thousand years. But I'd need to examine it. Odd the way it's shaped, a right angle triangle, two smooth edges. From the way the third edge is frayed I'd say it was cut from a larger piece. But I'd have to examine it under a scope. I know a lab in the city that can do carbon dating if you like."

"I like," Sybelle said, glancing at Orient.

"Can we maintain the integrity of the piece?"

"I'll take a slice with my scalpel that's practically transparent."

A stocky woman wearing a black dress and white apron appeared in the doorway. Her broad, flinty features remained expressionless as she waited for Henry to notice her.

"Oh Valka, yes." He clapped Orient on the shoulder and extended his arm to Sybelle.

"Dinner is served. We can discuss it over a bottle of good wine."

Henry was an expert in many forms of ancient art and a connoisseur by inclination. Sybelle flirted with him outrageously and he responded with courtly flattery.

"I find your profession fascinating," Henry said. "I've always been curious about psychic power. Can you enlighten me?"

"Please do call me," Sybelle said. With a flourish she passed her card to him. "I guarantee you'll be more than enlightened."

Painfully aware that he had a major interview in the morning Orient kept one eye on the clock. However, he had to admit that Henry's cook was excellent. She served cous-cous with raisins and nuts, spinach salad with blue cheese, and grilled salmon with spiced mango.

Dessert was vanilla ice cream topped with strawberries.

"Whatever you're paying your cook, it isn't enough," Sybelle declared.

Henry smiled. "Not too loud, she might hear. By the way, how much did Taegris charge you for the piece?"

Sybelle popped a strawberry into her mouth. "Forty thousand dollars."

Orient started to correct her, but Henry cut him off.

"It's probably worth twice that at auction," he said. "I'll be able to tell you more in a few days. If you'll entrust it too me." He added.

"How many days?" Sybelle asked.

"I can return the piece itself tomorrow evening. The carbon dating might take two days. In the meantime I can run off a copy for you both."

Orient shrugged, suddenly ready to go home. "Fair enough. We'll meet tomorrow then."

"First show me a tiny bit of your personal collection," Sybelle cooed, crushing all hope of an early departure.

Later, as Sybelle drove him home, Orient asked her, "Why did you tell him forty thousand?"

"Just good business, darling. After all he is a dealer. And you heard his estimate. I know you don't really want to sell but we do owe Mr Taegris twenty seven thousand dollars. And we stand to make fifty K, if Henry is right."

"You never cease to impress me," Orient said, only half joking.

"And I do find your friend very charming. Perhaps I'll invite him to... Oh hold on, darling, my phone. I think it's Savana's mother."

Sybelle arranged an hour when they could see Savana. Fortunately it was in late afternoon, long after his interview. He hoped he wouldn't be too depressed by then to be of any help. These days just landing an interview took persistence, and luck.

Few were called, and even fewer chosen. And he wanted very much to be back practicing medicine.

Chapter 3

Orient awoke at six a.m. slightly hung over. He focused on his main task later that morning, the interview at St. Luke's Hospital.

It had taken at least three months between sending a resume and actual appointment. He had gone on other interviews but lately there had been no call backs.

After a half-hour of stretching, he went outside for a short run to jump start his metabolism. When he came back, he did some yoga, centered himself, and took a long shower. He put on a CD of ballads by Miles Davis, and spooned a mix of fresh fruit and protein powder, into his blender. As he drank breakfast, Orient scanned the New York Times. His appointment wasn't until ten, but he dressed, and went outside to run an important errand. He stopped at a Catholic church a few blocks away, then joined the early commuters for the long subway ride to St. Luke's Hospital. The A Train didn't stop at the 110th Street station during the day, so he got off at 125th and walked.

It was still early when Orient arrived. It gave him time to get the feel of the place. On the corner was a prominent emergency room. The main building was in the middle of the block, its arched entranceway vaguely reminiscent of an ancient temple. He strolled into the lobby found the name of his interviewer, Dr. H. Wylde, located on the second floor.

He heard the whine of an arriving ambulance. He was aware that even in the lobby there was a constant hum of tension. He found a cafeteria which served the usual toxic hospital coffee before he went upstairs for his interview.

The second floor housed the administration offices. In mid corridor was a desk where he was met by a perky Asian girl. She gave him an inquiring smile. "May I help you?"

"Doctor Owen Orient. I have an appointment with Dr. Wylde."

She picked up the phone, punched a number, and covered the mouthpiece. "Emergency team?" she half-whispered.

"Pardon?"

"You're here to interview for the emergency team?"

"I'm not really sure."

"That's Dr. Wylde's department. She's interviewed twenty so far. You're twenty-one."

Orient tried to keep the news from deflating whatever optimism he'd managed to work up.

"Hello, Doctor, your ten o'clock is here."

The nurse looked up and inclined her head. "Two-eleven, down the hall. Good luck."

As Orient opened the door marked 211, he hefted the attaché case carrying various recommendations, commendations, awards, and a copy of his official resume. It felt light, inadequate.

When he entered, his doubts were swallowed by surprise. Dr. Wylde was a tall, willowy female with deep indigo eyes, and dark hair that curled around classic features. Only her harried expression blurred her beauty. For an uncomfortable moment Orient felt they'd met before.

"Hello, Doctor, I'm Hannah Wylde. Please take a seat. Would you like some water or juice before we start?"

"Thanks, I'm good."

She referred to the Mac on her desk, peering at the screen. "Can you tell me something of your professional history?"

"I graduated from Harvard Medical at eighteen, completed my residency at Johns Hopkins, earned an advanced degree in psychiatry at the University of Vienna, then took a sabbatical before returning to the United States, where I was on staff at New York Presbyterian for three years, specializing in neurological medicine."

Her reaction to the word *sabbatical* was one of passing disapproval.

"I see you were asked to treat the daughter of Vice President Mulnew. But the rest seems to be classified." She turned from the computer screen and looked directly at him. "What was the result of that treatment?"

"The treatment was very successful, but the details are still classified."

"And then you left New York Presbyterian, and the medical profession for four years?"

"I left to pursue independent scientific research, privately funded."

"What sort of research?"

"The nature of human consciousness."

She sat back and regarded him appraisingly. Orient suddenly knew he needed to get the interview back on point.

"When that project was complete I returned to medical practice, at St. Vincent's Hospital., in the emergency room."

Her expression softened. "Indeed, you have a very impressive set of commendations for your work with trauma victims. But then you..."

"...left, it's all there in front of you," Orient said quietly. "Look, that first sabbatical was a valuable part of my education. I barely had a driver's license when I graduated from med school. And as a physician and psychiatrist I felt I needed to get some real world experience before treating patients twice my age. So I grabbed a backpack and went off to study regional medical practices in India and Tibet."

It was partially true. Orient had gone on a pilgrimage to Tibet where he learned the telepathic technique as well as other arcane practices from his Master Ku. Most of the gaps in his medical career had come at the service of teaching telepathic facilities inherent in human consciousness. Others, however, were due to dark occult encounters well beyond scientific explanation.

"My other breaks from formal medicine were in deference to my research which..." he added, "has yielded positive results, in special cases."

For the first time she smiled, and Orient felt a tinge of emotion as her professional mask dissolved. Underneath she was a vulnerable, beautiful woman. "I went to Africa with the Peace Corps after med school," she confided. "My parents weren't very happy."

Orient nodded.

The mask reappeared and the smile vanished. "But when I came back, I joined the staff here and grew with the job. We're very proud of our team here, and we value loyalty."

Orient stiffened at the implication. "Look I know I haven't been more than five years at any of the hospitals listed, but I happen to be a damn good emergency physician, with certified trauma experience. I work hard, honor my contracts and commit one hundred percent. That's what I can bring to your team."

This time her smile was tight. "I'm sure that's true doctor. Your credentials speak for themselves. But we are still interviewing candidates for the position. You will be notified of our decision as soon as the process is complete."

Well, I blew that one, Orient observed ruefully. He left St. Luke's with a leaden sense of defeat. He even questioned if his medical skills were still relevant. In Dr. Wylde's eyes he was a liability, at best an eccentric, at worst a walking malpractice suit. Her parents were probably very happy now that their daughter had become a corporate clone. He wondered what the perfect Dr. Wylde would say if she knew that along with pertinent documents, his attaché case also contained items essential to performing an exorcism.

Still brooding, he ignored his cell phone as he strode downtown to his apartment, and tried to rein in his agitation. Fifteen minutes later he paused, emotions calmed by a walking meditation. A technique he picked up in India during that first trip that Dr. Wylde dismissed so lightly, He checked his phone and saw Sybelle had left a text message: *Dnt frgt 5 pm.*

He took a deep breath and pushed aside the morning's disappointment. It was just eleven a.m. giving him four hours to prepare.

+ + +

Once home, Orient had a light lunch, a meditation session, and a nap. When he awoke, he showered and dressed in fresh clothes. Then he put the things he'd acquired from the church early that morning into a gym bag. He went outside, hoping Sybelle had thought to prepare as well.

When she arrived, he could see she had. She was dressed almost entirely in white, with a touch of pale blue—she was even wearing white gloves.

"Dear Owen, thanks for being prompt. We have a tight window."

He smiled. Sybelle had fully recovered her self assurance, and abundant energy. She had even seemed to have regained some of her weight, smoothing over the haggard lines of a day before.

Sybelle directed the cab to a luxury building on the Upper East Side, They shared little small talk during the drive. Orient hoped the encounter wouldn't be violent.

Savana lived on the tenth floor, in a comfortable apartment with a view of the East River. Sybelle let herself in with a key provided by her mother.

The moment they entered, their physical energy dimmed.

"Until now I never realized how strong the presence is..." she whispered.

Orient hefted the gym bag containing the few weapons he had at his disposal. Like we're about to hunt crocodiles with a feather, he thought grimly. As Sybelle lead the way, the silence inside the apartment gave Orient the impression he was moving underwater.

The door to Savana's room was open.

When Orient entered he saw a teen-aged girl lying motionless on a bed. The room was decorated with the enthusiastic pop images of youth. But the girl on the bed looked older than her years. .

Senses tingling, Orient moved closer. He could feel Sybelle behind him, her energy expanding as she settled into a breathing pattern. He also felt something tugging at his concentration and pulled back, having been lured once before. Carefully, aware of each micro shift in tension, Orient went through a preliminary medical check for pulse and heartbeat. Savana's breathing was regular and with the exception of an odd slackness to her skin which aged her, she was quite lovely. The silver ring was hefty and had designs etched on each side below a glossy artificial pearl. There were a thousand such rings.

He turned to Sybelle. "Let's go find the kitchen."

They returned with two bottles of water, four glasses, and a box of salt.

Moving quickly Orient placed a glass filled with water in each corner of the room. Then he poured salt into his hand, then into each glass, softly intoning words of purification. From his gym bag he took an atomizer containing holy water which he had obtained from a local church that morning, and a large ebony cross that had been specially blessed for such work.

While in the kitchen both he and Sybelle had agreed that Savana was possessed by some form of psychic predator, which would account for her aged appearance, as the entity slowly consumed her youthful vitality.

Orient sprayed a mist of holy water above the bed, and gingerly placed the ebony cross on her unmoving body. Then he braced himself against the coming backlash.

Chapter 4

Nothing happened.

Savana lay motionless. The cross on her chest rose and fell slightly with each shallow breath. The extended quiet seemed to mock their efforts. Sybelle gave Orient a questioning glance.

"Give me your hand," he said, watching Savana.

Hesitantly, Sybelle reached out and took his hand.

"Tighter." He turned, green eyes blazing. "Whatever happens, don't let go, understand?"

She nodded.

Orient took a silver cigarette case from his pocket. An intricate mandala design was etched on the cover. The case had been given to Orient by the Master Ku, as a symbol of his role as a monk of the cities. Orient focused his concentration on the mandala.

"Okay, start breathing and stay with me, we're going to try to merge with Savana's consciousness."

"But..."

His stare cut her off. "She's a potential," he said, "like you were."

Sybelle understood. Eyes closed, she slipped into a deep breathing pattern and felt the familiar brush of energy at the base of her brain. Like colliding universes they circled closer, merging but never touching, until they shared a single whirling center. Its compelling gravity sucked them down, spinning ever faster, blurring all consciousness, and reducing perception to a single vibrating point of light. Senses focused on that distant beacon flashing in the maelstrom, they hurtled nearer at ever increasing speed until it loomed like a gigantic white sun that consumed them whole...

+ + +

The first thing Orient noticed was the warm night air.

The second was the drums.

Their low, steady throb played counterpoint to their unsteady footsteps on the cobblestones.

The drums grew louder as they moved through a darkened alley. He tightened his grip on Sybelle's hand, partially to reassure himself it wasn't some sort of dream. No, her skin was damp and real, the worn stones under their feet were real, as was the sense of urgency that propelled him forward to some unknown destination.

At one point Sybelle pulled him to a stop, chest heaving. "Owen what's happening...?"

"I don't quite know yet."

"Well can we slow down a bit until we do?"

"Sorry, we need to hurry."

"Hurry where?"

"Don't know," Orient said, tugging at her, "but we have to get there."

They kept moving in the direction of the drums. Soon they emerged from the alley onto a large square where drummers, tribal dancers, acrobats and street vendors gathered beneath glowing torches—and Orient knew where they were. He had been to this Marrakech marketplace many years before and it was unchanged. If anything it seemed wilder and more primitive than ever.

However something wasn't quite right. Those men not wearing traditional Moroccan *djelabas*, were dressed in outdated European clothes and fedoras. The women wore long dresses and feathered hats. Even the long Mercedes convertible parked nearby was of vintage stock, complete with running board and back seat windshield. Its dusty olive color was reminiscent of a military officer's vehicle

"Psst... beautiful lady?"

Both of them looked back. Half hidden in the shadows cast by the torches outside, a young man stood at the mouth of the alley. "Come... I have beautiful caftan for you."

Sybelle smiled at the man. "No, thank you."

The man who was in his late teens or early twenties, wore a striped knit cap and tweed vest, over the balloon shaped Berber pants of the region. He grinned, displaying a gold tooth, and nodded at their clasped hands. "Married, yes? I show you valuable jewelry, amber, coral necklace," he persisted. "Everybody in Marrakech knows Mohammed. I get you the best price.'

"Please no, " Sybelle said.

The man's smile didn't waver. "Rug, just for you, a bargain... maybe hashish?"

Abruptly, the drums stopped.

Through the thick quiet, Orient heard loud shouts and turned. Running barefoot through the square was a young girl, headscarf flying behind her, noisily pursued by three men. She darted from side to side, trying to elude, then overturned a fruit stall to block them. As she crossed the square she veered directly toward Orient and Sybelle. .

It was then Orient recognized her.

"Owen look," Sybelle said, jerking at his hand, "it's Savana!"

Orient tightened his grip. "Careful, don't break the connection."

"Savana darling, it's me!" Sybelle cried. But the girl didn't stop, bolting past them into the alley. Sybelle tried to follow but was pushed back by the lead pursuer, a tall blond man with a zigzag scar, wearing black boots and riding trousers. As Orient grabbed Sybelle in a protective embrace, he was roughly jostled aside by the second man in pursuit.

"*Dumkopf...*" He gestured at the man close behind him. "*..Shnell!*"

As they raced down the alley Orient instinctively ran after them, Sybelle in tow. But the tunneled alleys in the deserted *souk* were a labyrinth of shuttered shops and darkened houses. Minutes later the only footsteps they heard were their own.

Orient paused, listening hard. All he could hear was the low, steady beat of the drums in the square. .

"Oh dear, did we lose her?"

Before he could answer he saw a shadowy figure ahead.

"Psst... this way. It is me, Mohammed."

Moving closer he recognized the young man who'd accosted them earlier.

"Beautiful lady... rich sir... you wish to find girl?"

"Quick, man, where is she?" Orient said.

"How much?"

Orient pulled out his wallet. "It's empty."

"Someone must have picked your pocket," Sybelle sniffed, eyeing the merchant.

"Hardly likely he'd take the cash then put the wallet back. Point is, we need something of value. Here..." Orient reached down and slipped Sybelle's gold watch off her wrist.

"Owen that belonged to my grandmother," she squealed.

He ignored her and handed the watch to the merchant. "Will this cover your fee?"

Mohammed's grin widened. "For this, I take you myself."

They followed him deeper into the tunneled maze, which during the day became a bustling market, with everything from donkeys, to sheep, sharing the narrow streets. Somewhere along the way they left the market behind, and entered a seedy residential area.

The drums sounded far away.

Sybelle gave Orient an anxious glance, but he continued to follow their guide. Still admiring the new trinket on his wrist, the guide led them to inside a darkened building and down an ancient stone stairway. A foul smelling canal ran beneath the building.

"Where are we, the river Styx?" Sybelle hissed, as they negotiated the uneven walkway along the canal. Their footsteps echoed against the stone walls.

"All kidding aside, Owen, I'm frightened."

"Have faith, pilgrim, we can't abandon Savana now."

"Hurry," their guide whispered. "This way."

He led them to a narrow curved stairway and paused. "At the top of these steps you will find what you seek." The man said, backing away. "Behind the curtain..."

"Owen, he's running off!"

Orient him watched him disappear behind the stairs. "Never mind him, I see a light up ahead. Come on."

A yellow glow leaked from the side of a heavy, woven curtain. Orient came up the stairs slowly, careful of his footing. When they neared, he heard the muted sound of voices chanting. Their rhythms were deliberate, rising in pitch.

Orient reached out and nudged the curtain aside.

The large, high-ceilinged chamber was lit by a pair of massive carved candelabras on each side of a black marble altar. The man with the zigzag scar stood on one end, knife raised above an unconscious female stretched beneath him. It was Savana. Orient could see the ring on her finger. But it was somehow different. Not as he remembered.

The blond man now wore a purple robe. He had one hand on a large book that was on the altar, beside Savana's head. The other two men stood behind him, arms crossed over their chests.

The blond man continued to chant, as he lifted the knife.

"Owen...!"

Orient moved an instant before she spoke. He dove to deflect the man's arm, and saw the knife miss Savana, slashing the large book on the altar instead. He also saw the two uniformed men rushing at him. He stumbled as he turned and grabbed Savana's limp wrist for balance. By accident he pulled the ring from her finger. As it rolled across the floor something hit him hard. Desperately he tried to maintain his hold on Sybelle but another blow sent him to the floor. He felt his fingers slip and squeezed, trying to retain contact. Suddenly Orient's grip failed and the room began to spin, as if their clasped hands had held gravity in place. The spinning accelerated to a blurred vortex, sucking him down at incredible speed until...

A silent explosion propelled him into darkness.

+ + +

Orient opened his eyes.

He was lying on the floor, limbs heavy and reactions slow. It took long minutes before he was able to recall what he was doing there. He turned his head and saw Sybelle.

She lay still, eyes closed. He lifted his head. Savana was sprawled on the bed, arms flung back. Her eyes were open. Orient felt a flood of emotion. She looked so young, so vulnerable.

Groggily, he rolled over, and one body part at a time, got to his feet.

Savana moaned softly.

The sound energized his drained faculties. He took a deep breath and moved closer to the bed. As gently as possible he moved her frail body back onto the bed, and propped her head on a pillow.

"*Yeeeowww...!*" Savana bolted straight up, face mad-eyed and twisted as she raked her nails across Orient's cheek. Then she fell back unconscious.

He felt warm blood trickle down his skin and mopped it with a corner of the blanket.

He noticed something tucked inside the jumbled blanket. It was a jagged piece of black wood. Then he saw the other piece.

The ebony cross he had placed on Savana's chest had been snapped in two

He noticed something else. The glasses of salt water he had set in each corner of the room were shattered. All of them, spilling their contents across the carpet. Shards of wet, broken glass glinted in the afternoon light.

"Owen?"

Sybelle was struggling to her feet. Orient extended his hand and pulled her up.

"Are you okay?"

"I think so, darling. But where *were* we? Was it Cairo or Casablanca?"

"Close, it was Marrakech. Can you help me with Savana? She's coming around."

"Oh thank God. What happened anyway, why are you bleeding?"

"Savana—just a reflex. I'm going to give her a quick physical. Then I want you to talk her back to full consciousness."

"But Owen, how can..."

"Savana knows you, trusts you. Right now, she can't distinguish reality from the hell she just went through. If I try to bring her out, a stranger, she'll only retreat."

Orient's examination was fast but thorough. There were no broken bones, and aside from a bruise on her wrist, she seemed healthy. He moved aside and let Sybelle take over.

She sat at the edge of the bed. "Savana?" she whispered. "Savana darling it's me. Can you hear me?"

A low groan dribbled from Savana's parted lips.

"Savana? Can you hear me darling? I'm right here beside you."

Slowly, the girl turned towards the voice. Her half closed eyes widened when she saw Sybelle.

"Aunt Sibbie," she said, voice barely audible, "Aunt Sibbie, I had such a bad dream. You were in it... I think..."

"Don't worry darling, you're all right now."

"Aunt Sibbie?"

"Yes dear?"

"I'm hungry..."

Sybelle flashed a smile of relief at Orient. "Of course dear, how about soup and toast?"

Savana nodded, and learned back on her pillow.

"Stay close to her while I prepare a tray," Sybelle whispered. She went into the bathroom and came back with a glass of water. "She needs to hydrate. Get her to drink it if you can."

Orient nodded. As he waited for her to return from the kitchen, he surveyed the room. The broken glass and spilled water looked worse that it was. A good vacuum cleaner would take care of it.

The large ebony cross was another story. Hand carved and blessed by a Cardinal, it had survived at least two past exorcisms. He wondered who could have generated that kind of power-and why.

Savana had dozed off. Orient bent closer to adjust her blanket and remembered something. To be sure, he checked each of her hands. .

The ring was no longer on her finger.

Orient looked around the bed then, recalling her position, arms dangling off the bed, he began to look around the carpet. Methodically, he moved in ever widening circles until he was stepping around bits of broken glass. Finally he found it. The ring was far from the bed, as if it had been hurled across the room. He knelt to pick it up.

"Exactly what the hell are you doing?"

Orient lifted his head. A tall woman with violet eyes that radiated primal rage stood in the doorway.

Dr. Hanna Wylde—the woman who had interviewed him earlier that day....

Chapter 5

"**W**here's my daughter?" Hannah demanded. Before Orient could respond, her expression went from rage to recognition. "Oh my God, it's you. "

She stepped closer, ferocity twisting her rigid features, "If you've hurt her, I'll kill you myself..."

"Hannah!"

Sybelle hurried into the room, holding a tray. "Please darling. Don't you remember? We set a time when I could see Savana. Owen here, is my dear friend and... *consultant* in these matters."

Hannah's indignation collided with embarrassment. "Oh God, I'm so sorry Doctor... I..."

Orient smiled. "I understand. You may feel better if you go see Savana. She's regained consciousness."

"And she's *hungry*," Sybelle added emphatically. "That's always a good sign."

Savana was still weak but her mother's embrace went a long way to dispelling the haggard look that had aged her. She actually regained her youthful aura within the hour, especially after her second bowl of soup.

Hannah held her daughter in her arms, rocking her gently as they talked in low voices. Now that she and Sybelle were together, Orient could see a family resemblance.

Certainly, Hannah shared her aunt's inner strength.

"Mommy?"

"What is it, dear?"

"Where's Jillian?"

Hannah gave Sybelle a helpless glance. "Jillian's been hiding while you've been sick." she said softly. "She'll come out when you feel better."

When Savana fell asleep, they retired to the kitchen. Sybelle prepared sandwiches, Hannah opened a bottle of wine, and poured three glasses. "First thing Savana wants to know is where her cat is," she said, with a tinge of bewilderment. "Funny thing is the cat has literally been hiding in the outside closet all this time, and has hardly eaten anything. Isn't that odd?"

As if on cue, an emaciated, black Siamese cat, crept into the kitchen, and began drinking water from a yellow bowl. "Well, there she is, the poor thing." Hannah got up and spooned some food into an adjoining bowl. "Come on, Jillian, Savana's better now.'

"Animals are acutely sensitive, and are often afflicted by sympathetic ailments from their human keepers." Orient said, forgetting where he was.

Hannah reminded him. "Was that part of your private research, Doctor?"

"There are parallels," he said evenly. "But for what it's worth, I believe the techniques we've developed," he nodded at Sybelle, "helped revive your daughter."

"Well perhaps you can help me understand. Aunt Sybelle knows how confused I've been about this. Ever since she bought that ring..."

Orient started to say he'd found the ring, but Sybelle interrupted.

"I almost became... *afflicted* as well," she said, refilling her glass. "Owen recognized the symptoms."

Hannah rejoined them at the kitchen table. "The mess in Savana's room... what did you do exactly?"

"I'm sorry darling..." Sybelle said, glancing at Orient.

This time he took over. "We protect our trade secrets in the same way Coca Cola and Google protect theirs," he said quietly.

"In our case, there's a tendency to dismiss our work as eccentric, at best."

"And can you reveal the nature of your research?"

Hannah said it with a smile but there was no mistaking the challenge.

Orient met her eyes. "The nature of my research is human telepathy, the facility which allows certain individuals to communicate on an ultra sensory level."

"And how did this enable you to get Savana out of her coma?"

"Sybelle and I linked up telepathically, and manage to dislodge, and hopefully dispel, whatever malignant force had Savanah." He shrugged and picked up his glass. "It's quite difficult to discuss that in detail, considering our circumstances."

Sybelle perked up. "What circumstances ?" She looked from Orient to Hannah. "Is there something I should know?"

"What Doctor Orient means is that I interviewed him this morning, for a spot on our emergency team at the hospital."

"How marvelous, Owen is a wonderful healer," Sybelle gushed, "he'd be perfect."

In the silence Orient could hear the cat purring.

"I have no doubt he is. I'm also deeply grateful to you both."

"So..."

Orient cut in. "Dr. Wylde is speaking as a professional. I understand that."

"Please call me tomorrow morning," Hannah said, obviously grateful to be off the hook.

Orient smiled, also relieved. "Take two aspirin and call me in the morning. First thing we learned in med school."

"But you still haven't told me why there's broken glass all over Savana's room."

As carefully as possible, Orient explained the glasses had been placed in each corner of the room as a barrier to malignant forces. When Hannah realized these forces had shattered four water glasses, and a heavy wood cross, her attitude shifted from skepticism to apprehension.

"I've heard of such cases. TV is full of paranormal documentaries, but I never really believed... especially here, in New York, to my own daughter."

Watching Hannah over the rim of his glass, Orient again had the nagging feeling he had seen her somewhere else.

+ + +

During the cab ride home, Sybelle leaned against Orient's shoulder, part in exhaustion, and part in sympathy. "I'll be furious if she doesn't hire you," she sniffed.

"You can't really blame her," Orient said. "Very few doctors accept the reality of telepathy, much less the occult. In her eyes, I probably seem like a quack witch doctor."

"I'm not so sure of that," she said playfully, "I saw the way she looked at you."

When he didn't reply, she added, "Anyway she did see the evidence, all that broken glass, and the cross..."

Orient smiled. "You had to be there."

"Well there's something else I know she won't understand. I hardly understand it myself."

"Which is?"

"My watch, my grandmother's gold watch. The one you gave to the guide back there in Marrakech."

"Yes?"

Sybelle lifted her wrist. "It's gone..."

"I'll buy you a new watch."

"Really darling, that's hardly the point. Savana is conscious and well, *that* should mean something to he mother."

Orient wished he could muster up as much confidence. That night, he sat up smoking a hand wrapped cigarette and contemplating the mandala on his silver case. He was certain their contact with Savana had taken them back in time. The military limousine looked vaguely like a Nazi vehicle and the men hunting Savana had spoken German. But there was something else about the encounter that kept eluding him.

Later, his fitful sleep was haunted by fragmented dreams.

He awoke early and went through his morning meditation with renewed focus, trying to cleanse the residue of the past night's encounter. Refreshed, he took an easy two mile jog before preparing breakfast. He was reading the Times when his phone rang. Orient checked his clock. It was just seven minutes before nine.

"It's Dr. Wylde," she said, voice taut, "if you recall I asked you to call me in the morning."

"I thought I'd wait until working hours."

"Our trauma unit is twenty four seven."

By that logic he should have called shortly after midnight, Orient thought but he just said, "Of course."

"The reason for my call is, after considering the evidence and your obvious expertise, I'm going to recommend you be put on staff at our emergency trauma unit. However before I do I need another interview. Can you come in this afternoon?"

"Absolutely, what time?"

"How about one o'clock? We can do it over lunch."

"After hanging up, Orient sat for long minutes. Although he was elated, he could tell Hannah Wylde still had reservations. It would be up to him to break them down. He struggled to suppress the rush of enthusiasm flooding his thoughts as he prepared to meet her at the hospital.

He arrived ten minutes early, having gotten a hint of Dr. Wylde's sense of time. He wondered if she ever slept.

Hannah emerged from the elevator two minutes early, and seemed surprised to see him waiting. "Let's go to the cafeteria before all the good tables are gone,' she said briskly.

She led the way to a corner table, far from the entrance, and the food line. They both stacked their trays with salad, tea, and yogurt. Hannah added a chicken sandwich, explaining she saved the other half for later in the day, when things became hectic.

"It's a combination of having to trim our evening staff, and the fact that we get more victims in the evening."

Orient nodded, waiting for her to reach the point. He didn't wait long.

"But after what I saw last night, and what you did for Savana, I'm both impressed and curious. Do you practice magic, Doctor?"

"You mean like a Satanist?"

"Or Wicca."

"Actually I'm a Tibetan Buddhist. However I have researched a wide spectrum of religions," he said mildly. He looked at her and smiled. "Aren't you violating my civil rights with this?"

"Not when it involves my daughter."

"Fair enough. How is Savana today?"

"Sitting up, walking. She showered for a half hour."

Hannah's lavender eyes softened. "Okay, you're not a Satanist, but you are a telepath."

"That is confidential. But I can tell you this, my research with telepathy, links with research in the neuroplasticity of the human brain—which can be of enormous help to victims of spine and neck trauma. A lot of it involves mirror neurons, as well as entangled electrons."

She sat back and tapped her fingers reflectively. "So what's your professional opinion? Is Savana past this, or is she still susceptible?"

"I think she's reasonably safe, so long as you keep this away from her." He dug into his pocket and extracted the ring.

"Ah yes, of course. We couldn't get the damned thing off. She came home with it one day and that's when the nightmare started."

He gave her the ring and they both examined it. The ring was dark silver, with a crude X carved on each side. The top appeared to be a white pearl, possibly fake.

"Cheap thing, it even has a crack in it," Hannah said, pointing out a hairline fault in the pearl. She slipped the ring into the pocket of her smock. "I'll keep it here, where it can't do any harm. "

She took a deep breath and checked her watch. "So, suppose I show you around. If my recommendation is ratified by the other two members of the hospital committee. We'll need you to be ready in four to five weeks. Are your certifications up to date?"

Orient nodded, trying to restrain a grin. "Yes."

"Fine, then pending approval by the committee, you may consider yourself part of our emergency team. I'll save the welcomes for the real thing. Ready for the grand tour?"

Orient felt like a kid. The facilities at St. Luke's were cutting edge, and the staff went about their work with crisp efficiency. It was like arriving at Yankee Stadium after years in the minors. He was also quite taken by Dr. Wylde, an accomplished, intelligent, beautiful woman. But he would have to keep things strictly professional.

Afterwards while walking alone on Central Park West, Orient's cell phone chimed.

"Owen, it's Henry."

"Henry, I was going to call..."

"The item you bought is quite extraordinary. I also have a preliminary lab report."

"Oh? Tell me."

"I'm expecting a client right now. Can you come over for cocktails, say sixi-sh?"

"Good, see you then."

The call reminded Orient he owed Taegris, twenty seven thousand dollars. Now that he had a job it didn't seem so extravagant. Although it is, Orient thought but he decided to reserve judgment until he spoke with Henry. The art dealer was one of the world's foremost experts in Assyrian and Egyptian art. While Orient was extremely curious to know what Henry had found out about the leather fragment, it paled beside the fact of his new position at St. Luke's hospital.

Still, if the piece proved extraordinary, as Henry claimed, it would be a valuable asset. Until now the small collection of ancient artifacts had been one of his major investments. But now he had a chance to do something more important—healing the sick.

As he walked home Orient decided to cool his enthusiasm until he had been officially approved. A lot could happen between now and then, he observed, quickening his pace.

Chapter 6

The man with the zigzag scar kept his eyes on the mirror as he slowly curled a seventy pound dumbbell with his left hand, watching his bicep coil to a peak, before slowly, very slowly, lowering it to the floor. His ice blue gaze didn't waver as he slowly and deliberately brought the right arm up. After completing fifteen repetitions with each arm, he took a thirty second break, marking the time with the titanium Rolex on his corded wrist.

He sat ramrod straight on the padded exercise bench, and lifted the dumbbells away from his torso, held the seventy pound weights in midair for five seconds, then lowered them to his side. He repeated the movement fifteen times, rested thirty seconds, and began again. His eyes never left the mirror.

Methodically, he worked out his body from top to bottom: neck, chest, shoulders, abs, hips, and legs. Then he stretched, finishing his routine by standing on his hands, and circling the edge of the floor upside down.

When he was finished he took a steam and a hot shower, pausing to examine his body in the mirror. He was tall, about six feet three inches with lean, rippling muscles cabled under white skin. His deep set eyes glinted like diamond tipped knives beneath his cropped, blond hair. The scar ran from the corner of his right eye, to the lobe of his right ear, like a pink ski trail on a smooth white slope. He liked to take care of his skin, carefully working his special cream into his face and neck, while his pores were still open.

His daily ritual complete, he dressed in a black shirt and suit, and a dark red, ancient madder tie. He took a black Fendi briefcase from the locker, and checked his reflection one last time. A thin smile tilted the symmetry of his features. Tonight was going to be special. After his project was finished he intended to celebrate his birthday.

He left the Chelsea Pier Gym and walked a few blocks to Pastis, a French bistro in what used to be the meat packing district, now gentrified with designer boutiques and expensive restaurants. At least Pastis was authentic, he thought, following the host outdoors. At this hour, after lunch and before five, he could depend on finding a table.

He lingered over his salade niçoise and white wine, relaxing after his strenuous workout.

He always pushed it on his birthday. But this was significant: Tonight he would possess two of the most important pieces in the puzzle. Only one more would be left.

He flexed his fingers automatically, eager to get on with it. Not yet, he told himself, all at the proper time.

He ordered a cappuccino, and smoked a cigarette, idly scanning the street. It was still early so he read the newspapers, checking all the gossip columns. Celebrities fascinated him. Unfortunately his calling forced him to maintain a low profile. For the time being, he reminded, for the hour was soon at hand.

And he was the chosen instrument, a keystone of the new era.

At precisely four he paid the bill, left a generous tip, and proceeded uptown

The cab deposited him two blocks away. He walked to his appointment, preferring caution to convenience. No sense exposing himself to being identified by some mongrel cabdriver he thought, walking briskly to the apartment house. He knew the doorman would be elsewhere, all that had been arranged by Valka.

He went directly to the rickety, old elevator and pressed the button marked 5. When the doors opened he strode to the end of the hall and rang the buzzer.

Henry Applegate opened the door. Although smiling, he betrayed a hint of apprehension. But the man with the zigzag scar was used to that.

"Oh, Hans, it's you, I was expecting Valka, my housekeeper."

"So pleased to see you too," Hans said, brushing past him. "Really, Henry, are you always this cordial? You should be delighted. I've come to conclude our little... arrangement. You do have it of course."

"Of course," Henry said hastily. He shut the door and locked it. "It's right here in my office. Can I offer you some wine?"

Hans ignored him, pretending to examine all the paintings and artifacts in the apartment. "What an interesting place you have here. All this decadent art. You are such a naughty boy."

"I am a dealer after all," Henry said. He nervously ran his hand through his hair.

"Yes, yes, and you have been of great service to our quest," Hans smiled, revealing sharp canine teeth, "which is why I came personally to reward you."

He took a large FedEx envelope from his briefcase and placed it on the desk

Henry tore it open. The packet was stuffed with hundred dollar bills.

"Five hundred thousand," Hans said, "final payment."

"I'll get your... artifact from my safe," Henry said, his confidence suddenly revived. "I'm certain you'll be impressed with my efforts." He shot an annoyed glance towards the kitchen area. "My housekeeper seems to have vanished. Please make yourself comfortable, I'll open a bottle of wine to celebrate."

Hans lifted his hands. "Don't trouble yourself. I'm anxious to examine this piece I've purchased at such an exorbitant fee."

"One million is hardly exorbitant these days," Henry said with a patrician wave of his hand.

"It is for merchandise of... uncertain provenance," Hans reminded.

Henry stiffened. "You can decide when you see it."

"I'm certain I'll be more than satisfied."

Taking the envelope with him, Henry went to a flat, wall safe, thinly concealed by a Paul Klee painting. Sliding the painting aside, Henry began twirling the combination lock beneath. He pulled the steel door open, put the envelope inside, and lifted out a cloth bundle.

"It was not easy to arrange this," Henry said, carrying the bundle in both hands, "there were expenses."

"Certainly, certainly," Hans agreed, hardly listening. His attention was completely focused on the bundle in Henry's hands. "Put it down here, "he swept some papers aside, "on the desk."

Carefully, Hans unwrapped the bundle. Inside, nestled starkly against a scarlet, velvet square, was an iron spearhead, rough-hewn and black with age, banded by a gold sleeve.

It felt surprisingly heavy, as he hefted it, still cloaked in velvet. For all that it was a common weapon the spear carried the ominous authority of an iron crown.

"At last," Hans said softly. He looked at Henry. "And you swear this is the authentic relic?"

Despite his certainty Henry shrank under the Hans' sharp gaze. "Absolutely. We had a replica crafted by an expert metallurgist in Pakistan. He's also an armorer, makes guns and swords for the local tribesman."

"Taliban?"

"In my experience tribesman are only loyal to their tribe. They protect their interests, be it drugs or power."

"And this," he held the spearhead closer to the light, "you smuggled this out?"

"It was easier getting this here—than replacing the replica in the Shatzkammer."

"But it's such an old museum," Hans smirked, "with such primitive security."

"Yes, true, but I had a man on the inside, just to be sure."

"Very wise, "Hans said, turning the spear over to study the symbols inscribed on the gold sleeve.

"I wasn't able to get a translation," Henry said from his safe.

"Oh don't close it," Hans said mildly.

"Beg your pardon?"

"The safe. Don't close it just yet. There's something else I'm curious to see. Peter mentioned it to me. Sounds fascinating."

Henry silently cursed Peter as he complied with Hans' request. He didn't object for two reasons. For one, Hans was a valued, cash client. For another, he was a bit intimidated by the blond man, with what seemed to be a dueling scar.

He tore open the envelope he'd prepared for Owen Orient, and left it in the safe with the receipt from the lab. The test results were something else that made him nervous, he observed, as he reluctantly handed over the plastic case containing the triangular fragment.

"May I?" Without waiting for an answer Hans took the fragment from the case and held it in his palm. "It's exquisite," he said, "the second side."

Henry gingerly retrieved the fragment. "Second side?"

"Of the pyramid."

Hans waited until the fragment was safely in the case before he moved. He knew three ways to kill a man instantly with his hands, six with a blade. His fingers clamped Henry's neck, under the jaw, while the other hand smothered his mouth and nose.

For a moment their gaze locked. Henry's bulging grey eyes rolled madly, unable to speak or breathe. Hans regarded him with bemused detachment, ice blue eyes blank and pitiless. The art dealer was unconscious within ninety seconds.

Hans half-dragged him away from the open door and placed him face down on the rug. He knelt beside the inert body, and drew a long, ornate dagger from a sheath at the small of his back. With one swift, precise stroke, he drove the blade in the slot between neck and skull.

Perfect, he thought, watching the blood slowly seep from the wound. *A matador could not have achieved a better kill.*

He leaned back as he gripped the ebony handle, anticipating a sudden gush of blood when the blade was removed.

Two things happened that he didn't anticipate.

When he jerked the dagger from Henry's lifeless neck, it slipped from his fingers and slid behind the couch.

At the same time he heard the faint rattle and hum of the elevator starting up.

Hans glanced at the spearhead on the desk, then at the door. He didn't have time to look for the damned dagger. The most important thing was the spear. It must be protected at all cost. The fragment was a bonus. Not quite luck—it was fated—but a bonus nonetheless.

Quickly and quietly he wrapped the spear, put it in his briefcase, then searched the rug until he found the case where Henry dropped it. That too, went into his briefcase.

Aware of the rising sound of the elevator he turned to go, then, as an afterthought he sprang to the safe and snatched the envelope with Henry's fee. He wasn't about to leave his best dagger *and* the money. That would be excessive.

The elevator had nearly reached the top floor as Hans left through the service door and moved directly to the exit stairs as instructed by Valka.

Outside he felt a rush of exultation. Finally, after all the time, blood, and anguish, the Spear of Destiny was his alone.

And with it, the missing section of the most powerful text on the planet.

He took a deep breath as he strode purposefully uptown. Energy rippled across his skin and he suddenly felt hungry. Fortunately, he'd made a reservation at Elio's for dinner. He decided to break his strict abstinence from alcohol and order champagne. After all, it was nearly his birthday.

At midnight he would be one hundred years old.

Chapter 7

For the rest of the afternoon, Orient worked at home. He paid some bills, then called Sybelle, but she was unavailable. He turned his attention to digitizing part of his research onto CDs. While recording the variant forms of demonic exorcism, practiced by diverse cultures, it occurred to him that Savana might recover faster if she was away from the toxic residue left by her predator. However he realized that after the grueling weeks Savana spent in a coma, Hannah probably wanted her to keep her daughter near.

When he had finished his computer work, Orient walked across the park to Henry's apartment building on Seventy-First Street off Lexington. The doorman wasn't in the lobby but Orient needed no directions to Henry's flat. He took the old elevator to the fifth floor and walked to the door at the end of the hall.

There was no answer when he rang the buzzer. Orient checked his watch. It was six fourteen. He buzzed again. When no one came, he called Henry on his cell phone. He could hear Henry's ring tone, Beethoven's Fifth, through the door.

Tentatively he twisted the knob, and pushed. The door was unlocked.

The dense stillness alerted him when he stepped inside.

"Henry? It's Owen. Are you there?"

Slowly, he walked into the inner room. He went past the dining room where they'd had dinner the previous night. No sign of Henry.

He punched Henry's number again, and followed the sound of Beethoven's wintery notes. They led to a large office lined with books and paintings. Papers were strewn across the floor, the desk was in disarray, and the thick steel door of a wall safe stood open.

Henry's mobile phone was on the desk. Orient shut his phone and the ring tone stopped. In the heavy quiet his breathing seemed loud. He stepped closer to the safe and peered inside. Someone had rummaged through the contents. A few gold and silver coins, Mayan figurines, and a small, milk blue vase, were still inside. A manila envelope on the floor caught Orient's eye. Printed on the face with a felt tip pen, was his name, *Owen*. Even more ominous was the fact that it had been torn open. Sticking half out of the empty envelope was a receipt, from Caldwell Laboratories on Seventeenth Street.

Orient checked the envelope again, then put it in his pocket, along with the receipt.

Then he spotted something.

Two feet clad in crocodile loafers, jutted at an improbable angle, past the corner of a brown leather sofa. As he neared he saw the blood pooled on the Persian carpet, and took a deep breath, before moving closer. He knew what he was about to find.

Henry lay face down beside the sofa, his shirt collar soaked with blood from a single stab wound at the base of his skull. Orient knelt to check for vital signs. There were none, but his skin was warm, suggesting the killer could be nearby.

As quietly as possible, Orient searched the other rooms. When he came to the kitchen he noticed there was a service door which was partially open. The door led to a back hall, and an exit stairway.

Orient paused, then hurried to the exit and down five flights to the service alley next to the building. The alley led to the street. He looked both ways as if expecting to see someone fleeing, and realized he didn't know who he was looking for.

A few blocks away he found a working street phone and called 911 anonymously, with the details of Henry's murder.

When he hung up he took the torn envelope from his pocket. Whoever killed Henry wanted what was inside. He stared at his name, printed on the face.

And whoever killed Henry, was obviously interested in him.

+ + +

"Oh my Lord. *Henry?* But *how?* I'm in shock."

Orient shared Sybelle's emotions. He had known Henry Applegate for four years, but in that time he'd developed a deep respect for the art dealer's erudition. He had a vast knowledge of ancient art, and informed taste. A rare combination in today's fast, flashy— and disposable—society. He also knew Henry to be a man of his word. And he felt a gnawing guilt at leaving the scene of his murder

"What else could you do?" Sybelle said, when he told her how he had found Henry's body. "If you hadn't left, you'd probably be sitting in a jail cell right now."

"Not necessarily. If I had anything that could be of help, I'd contact the police."

"You said something had been taken from the envelope."

"That's right."

"What do you suppose it was?"

"My guess is the fragment we brought him."

The memory made Sybelle catch her breath. "Oh my, he was so special," she sighed, "poor man, why would anyone kill him?"

"Perhaps for the fragment."

Her eyes narrowed. "Do you think?"

Orient recited the facts. "There were gold coins, and other valuables left behind, and the envelope with my name had been torn open."

"We don't know that the fragment was inside."

"True enough," Orient said, comforted by the word 'we'. "However I can't just ignore this. Then there's the money I owe Taegris. I can't very well return the fragment now."

"That is a problem." Sybelle brightened, "Why don't we just go to the police, show them the Xerox copy, dear Henry made for us, and ask if it was found among his effects? I'm sure Mr. Taegris will attest to our ownership."

Orient nodded. "I do have the receipts, and certifications." He remembered the receipt he'd found, left in the envelope.

"Let me refresh your drink darling, this must have been a terrible ordeal."

Orient didn't answer, trying to separate his emotions from his thoughts. He'd gone directly to Sybelle with the news and was still trying to recover his balance.

"There's really no question," he said, when she returned with the cognac, "I'm going to tell the police what I know, plain and simple."

"That's admirable darling, but at least sleep on it. If you like I'll go with you. And if you have any brains at all, you'll call Andy."

Orient shrugged. Ex-senator Andy Jacobs was his lawyer, and an old family friend. He knew Sybelle was right. Without counsel a good deed could easily get him entangled in the system, and jeopardize his imminent new position at the hospital.

"I'll sleep on it," he promised, waving off a second drink.

But he knew it would be a long time before he slept

In the morning, Orient gathered the papers Mr. Taegris had given him, as well as the lab receipt and envelope, and put them in a briefcase. He went about his preparations methodically, still slightly numbed by the events of the past few days. The more he thought about them, the more he felt they were somehow connected. Just a coincidence, he kept telling himself. However he knew there was no such thing as coincidence. Whether directly, or peripherally, every action in the universe was linked.

He called the number for Caldwell Laboratories, but the female on the other end informed him they did not divulge information over the phone. He would have to go down in person, with his receipt.

Orient decided to go downtown to the seventeenth street address, before contacting the police. He also left a message for Andy Jacobs.

He took the subway to Union Square, and walked west along the sunless streets, hemmed in on either side by grimy loft buildings. Caldwell Laboratories was on the second floor of just such a building. Orient rode up in a freight elevator that opened onto a glossy white lobby. A blonde receptionist, also dressed in white, sat behind a curved white counter.

Her long red fingernails were sharp contrast to the antiseptic décor. Her smile too, was wide and vivid. She sat up when he approached.

"Can I help you?" she said, eyes flicking back to the computer. Orient followed her eyes to the screen, and recognized the Facebook format.

Orient put the receipt on her desk. "I'm here for the results on this item."

"Just a minute." Avoiding eye contact, the receptionist took the receipt, and went through a door behind her. She came back shortly. "Dr. Namoud, would like to see you."

She ushered him into a large concrete area, partitioned by open cubicles. Orient could see electronic testing equipment in some of them, banks of computers in others. All the employees were dressed in white smocks.

Dr. Namoud was a short, dark man, with carefully combed hair and a shy, courteous manner. He seemed nervous when he greeted Orient, and showed him into a nearby office. He sat across the desk from Orient and folded his hands.

"I expected to hear from Mr. Applegate."

"Henry and I are associates. The item being tested belongs to me."

"I see. And what sort of item is it?"

"I have a color copy," Orient said, opening his briefcase.

Dr. Namoud, peered at the image for a few moments, stroking his chin thoughtfully.

"We thought it may be pre-Egyptian," Orient explained, "so Henry sent a slice to be carbon dated. Is there a problem?"

"Not at all sir," Namoud said, with what seemed to be relief. "In fact this answers some questions we had when we received our preliminary results."

"So you know the age of the piece?"

"According to our tests, this item is from sixty five hundred, to seven thousand years old."

"You said you had questions."

Namoud handed the color copy back to Orient.

"The slice Mr. Applegate sent us... is human skin."

+ + +

Orient walked back to Union Square and found a place to sit. What was most strange about the lab's finding was not so much the age of the piece, although seven thousand years would make it extraordinary. And using mummified skin for talismans was not uncommon in ancient cultures. What was truly remarkable about the piece was its *pliability*. It showed no sign of the stiff, dry parchment quality of mummified skin.

However, the revelation changed everything.

He tried to reach Sybelle, without success. He found Taegris' number among the papers in his briefcase, and called. He recognized the distinctive accent immediately.

"Yes, please?"

"Mr. Taegris, this is Doctor Orient."

"Of course, sir. I trust you authenticated your little purchase."

"Yes I did, and I'd like to discuss it, if you have time."

"Time? That is amusing, Doctor, considering I specialize in clocks. Of course I have time, please come join me for tea."

Orient didn't leave the square for a few minutes. When he did he crossed the street and wet into a café. Over coffee, Orient continued to sift through the events that preceded Henry's murder. If not for the torn envelope, with his name,

Orient would probably have chalked it up to a simple robbery gone wrong. Now he had to consider the possibility that he might be next on the list.

He needed to find out who else might have known about the fragment. Or who might have known he'd given it to Henry. After all, it was Applegate who told him the piece was available from Taegris. Not accustomed to caffeine, his system began revving faster than he found comfortable. During the cab ride to Brooklyn, Orient focused on containing his excess energy. All he needed from Taegris was more information on his relationship with Henry, and of course, some sort of financial arrangement. He wanted to discuss it with Sybelle, but she still wasn't taking his call.

The cab dropped him nearby, and he walked to the basement shop. He could see a light inside the dusty window as he went down the concrete stairs to the entrance.

As soon as he opened the door and walked inside the gloomy space crammed with clocks, Orient felt it. Ticking sounds pecked at the dense quiet as he took two tentative steps toward the workshop in the rear.

"Hello? Mr. Taegris?"

The silence was ominous. Orient considered backing out and going home. Instinct drove him forward.

"Hello?" he called, a bit louder.

His voice seemed to echo as he approached the rear area. He saw the ornate brass table, set with a tea service. The lamp above the large work table was on but nobody was there. Orient bent to touch the silver teapot. It was still hot.

"Mr. Taeg—" As he stood he saw something beside the low couch. A sliver of light reflected in a dark, oily pool that stained the silk rug. Reluctantly, he moved closer.

With each step he paused, and weighed turning back, but knew he couldn't.

Taegris lay face down on the floor, his white shirt collar soaked with blood from the wound at the base of his skull.

Same wound that killed Henry, Orient thought, bending closer. A tapping sound froze his limbs. Crouching, he edged to the door, and looked down the cramped aisle to the entrance.

A uniformed policeman stood at the store window, peering inside.

Orient glanced around the workshop and spotted a rear door. The problem was he'd have to cross the doorway, in clear view of anyone inside the shop. And the police were about to enter.

The first officer waited for his backup to arrive before slowly opening the door.

Body tensed and eyes fixed on the door, Orient stood poised between surrender and flight.

Chapter 8

The man with the zigzag scar was quite pleased with himself.

He had completed his mission, eliminated two key witnesses, and safely dispatched a trusted associate back to the Architect, bearing the fragment. The Spear he would deliver personally. Until then he had the distinct pleasure of possessing it completely.

He had also made sure the psychic meddler would be implicated in Peter's murder. A simple 911 call and the police should already have him in custody, Hans gloated. There was nothing to tie him to the unpleasant events of the past few days.

Strangely, he could feel the power of The Spear, galvanizing his being, even without benefit of ceremony. Merely its possession endowed him with its profound power.

The spear that pierced the side of Jesus Christ while He hung on the cross, had belonged to a succession of mighty conquerors from the emperors Constantine and Justinian, to King Charlemagne, Fredrick Barbarossa, and finally Adolf Hitler himself.

His fuehrer had been the last man to possess The Spear of Destiny, Hans mused, idly caressing the gold sleeve with his finger. After the fall it had been relegated to a museum. And not a very good one at that, he noted wryly.

Still, there was one piece of the triangle not yet in place.

The ring.

He rewrapped the Spear, slipped it into a padded envelope, and reluctantly taped the envelope to the bottom of a bureau drawer. It wasn't the most secure hiding place but it would have to do, for the two or three hours he'd be busy. He had a custom leather belt pack that held his tools, including a small power drill. The pack fit tightly around his waist and was barely perceptible beneath his blue baseball jacket, embroidered with the logo *Soho Art Movers*. To complete the illusion he wore a baseball cap

The final item was his spare field dagger. Not his favorite, but at least it had a previous kill, Hans thought, securing it in the sheath at the small of his back. Then he locked the door behind him and went out for a long walk, one that would take him to the residence of the presumptuous Miss Lean.

If she was away, so much the better, Hans thought, focused on the hunt. If not, he would make her death as painless as possible—perhaps even bloodless. He discounted the notion immediately. His blade craved blood and so did he.

+ + +

The brass plate above the buzzer read: Sybelle Lean, Psychic Consultant.

Hans rang the bell and waited for a response. Getting none, he deftly picked the two locks securing the door. He strolled through the deserted rooms, methodically opening drawers, boxes, looking behind books. He took a long time in the master bedroom, going through jewelry boxes and clothing drawers, as well as the large closet. He didn't overlook the bathrooms, then went back downstairs to the office. There was no safe and the drawers contained the usual clutter. A small room behind the office was devoted to an antiquities collection. Hans studied the pieces with admiration. He was tempted to take one or two of the better Egyptian figures, especially a small cat carved from Lapis Lazuli.

He replaced the piece and moved on.

He was a knight, not a thief.

Because of the many rooms, including a salon where the woman obviously held her readings, it took longer to search the townhouse. Having found nothing, he started to leave through the door behind the kitchen. But just as he opened it, a stocky woman, cheeks flushed with the exertion of carrying two shopping bags, backed inside. She seemed only mildly surprised to see him.

"Hello," Hans said, "I'm the mover. I'm waiting for the truck."

"Are you sure? Miss Lean didn't mention she was moving."

"No? We'll just be moving one expensive piece of furniture. The Japanese sideboard," he added, having noticed it earlier.

"Oh, yes, that monstrosity," the woman said cheerfully, setting the bags on the table, "can I get you some tea?"

"No thanks, I was just going out to check on the truck."

The woman turned and waved, but Hans noticed her smile stiffen when she saw the scar.

With some regret, he paused and returned the smile.

"Know what? Maybe I will have some tea after all."

+ + +

Later, as a cab took him to the West Side, Hans still regretted having to kill her.

It was unavoidable, he told himself, she could identify him. The scar was like having a damned tattoo on his face, he brooded. But he would never have it removed. He had earned it in hand to hand combat

The woman was collateral damage in the new war of the apocalypse. Her death was swift and painless. Unlike the punishment he intended for those who had the arrogance to dabble with powers they could barely comprehend. Such as the gentleman he intended to visit.

Owen Orient lived on the second floor of a two-story building. Fortunately the tenant below was out, sparing him a repeat of the earlier unpleasantness. And fortunately for Orient, he too was not home. Hopefully, he's safe in his new jail cell, Hans thought, moving through the cluttered rooms. He wasn't as careful as he had been in Miss Lean's townhouse, tossing papers aside, toppling stacks of CDs, rummaging through drawers in a haphazard manner intended to disrupt, as well as find the ring.

Orient had done enough disrupting, Hans fumed, now it was his turn. His blood still up from the killing an hour earlier, his anger flared when he thought of the trouble the meddling fool had already caused. Sybelle Lean had been under his complete control, and through her, the ring. He had been *so close.* Enraged he threw a stack of books and papers against the wall, then kicked the computer to the floor.

Hans took his time, on the off chance Orient might come home. His killing would erase the final obstacle to the Grand Design. But in the end, the thorough search found nothing.

He took a cab back to the safe house, which was a two room flat that belonged to one of his followers. There were many such places around the world. And he had the key to them all.

Without bothering to remove his jacket or hat, he went directly to the bureau where he had hidden the Spear. He unwrapped it, and set it on the table, under a lamp. Framed by its dark red velvet cloak, the spearhead exuded regal power.

Eyes fixed on his prize, he removed his hat and jacket, as well as his tool pack, letting them all drop to the carpet.

Then he pulled up a chair, located his magnifying glass, and examined the object closely. The phone rang, but he didn't look up, completely absorbed in his task.

He studied the tiny symbols etched along the side of the gold sleeve. Rune study was required of all SS officers, however he was unable to interpret these signs. He did notice that the gold sleeve covered a silver one beneath it. And then there was the nail used in the crucifixion, which had been imbedded in the base, flanked by two brass crosses.

Within minutes he could feel a surge of exhilaration pulsing through his blood. He left the table and returned with a large, leather bound book. It was his personal grimoire, a hand-written,and illustrated volume containing alchemical formulas and magical spells. Very few of the entries were his. Most had been inscribed by practitioners long before him. But he could channel the links to the deep past.

Hans drew back the rug, revealing a large white circle, inscribed with symbols at four points. It was intended to protect him from the backlash of manipulating occult energy.

Actually it was pure natural energy which binds the universe, but he was tapping it using occult techniques, rather than those of modern science. Both were valid, Hans observed, opening his grimoire. Before starting he fetched his ceremonial Thule dagger, etched with the symbol of a black sun, and placed it beside the Spear of Destiny. When all was in place, he began reciting his incantations, invoking the forces of Apocalypse.

Within minutes the air inside the room began to swirl, and he felt the hairs on his arms and neck bristle with static electricity.

The table began to vibrate, building until a bright lance of ball lightning arced between the Spear and his dagger.

He gave himself completely and was swept into the center of time, where he saw everything at the same moment, and understood it all belonged to him...

Hans fell back, dripping sweat. He shut his Grimoire, carefully wrapped the Spear, and put them both away. The dagger he slipped into the sheath at the small of his back. It tingled warmly against his spine.

He replaced the rug and thought about going to bed, but he knew he wouldn't sleep. His body was still humming with excess energy after his little experiment. And he was hungry. Not only for food, but for action. Yes, he decided, changing his shirt to something fresh and festive, he needed action, movement, *challenge*. He needed to release the raw power seething in his belly.

For a while he toured Greenwich Village, searching for a suitable subject. But the Village was crowded with weight-lifters, and health obsessed executives, too much testosterone for a test run. He moved further east, then south. Once a ghetto, then a haven for artists, the Lower East Side had been transformed by affluent yuppies, and real estate developers, into the East Village. However the were still vestiges of the older, ethnic neighborhoods. Second Avenue abounded with street life, but as he headed further south to Canal, it became more subdued.

He liked it that way, fewer witnesses, less chance of a good Samaritan interfering with his little sport. This was the area where the mongrel races had gathered at the turn of the century for their assault on the new world, Hans thought, stoking himself up. Now he would show them what the Grand Design held for their kind. Crossing Canal Street, he saw a young couple walking ahead of him. The male wore a leather jacket studded with the peace symbol. The female's long, scraggly hair was dyed red, with blonde streaks. Both were pierced: a nose ring for the female, an eyebrow ring for the male. Typical degenerate spawn of a decadent culture, Hans fumed.

They were perfect.

He followed them for half a block. They made the mistake of turning onto Walker Street, which had nothing but converted industrial loft buildings. A bar's neon sign at the far end of the block offered the nearest sanctuary.

Hans waited until they were uncomfortably aware of his presence behind them, savoring their rising apprehension. The boy glanced back, eyes growing wide with disbelief when he saw the dagger.

"Hey..."

"Hello there." Han's playfully slashed the peace sign on the boy's back.

"...What the fuck?"

His question was punctuated by a high-pitched shriek, as Hans' hand flicked out, and snatched the ring from the boy's brow. As his fingers clamped the boy's throat, he felt the warm blood swelling against the jugular, and resisted an urge to set it free. Instead he dropped the boy to the concrete.

It was over so quickly, that the girl hardly knew what was happening until the boy was on the ground, and she saw Hans kneeling on his chest, dagger against his skull.

She screamed, and swatted the back of his head with her bag.

Hans laughed, and stood up.

"Brave little whore," he said before he broke her nose with a snake-fast blow of his open palm.

It's completely under control, Hans told himself, walking away. He hadn't killed the boy, merely left him with a souvenir. Meanwhile the encounter had left him drenched with exhilaration. He was invincible... and insatiable for this new fountain of power.

Before he had sheathed his dagger, two men appeared from the shadows, diagonally across the street. One of them was walking a pit bull. They were both young, pumped up, and unafraid.

Hans couldn't believe his luck.

"Whoa, what's up?" The one with the dog came at him in a slow trot.

"Back off, asshole." Hans warned.

"Barry, he's got a knife!" The other man yelled.

Too late.

The other man lunged and dropped the dog's leash. Growling, the pit bull bounded straight for Hans.

His galvanized senses were operating at warp speed. The beast seemed to attack in slow motion, jaws yawning for the area between his belt and thigh. His dagger caught the beast in mid leap. For an instant the pit bull was suspended high in the air, until Hans' free hand shot up to support his grip on the dagger's handle, and he swung the frantically yowling dog , back at its master.

Ranting and sobbing, both men knelt to comfort the wounded beast as Hans strode away victorious, his ceremonial dagger blooded in battle.

"Tally ho," he called over his shoulder.

Tally ho? Perhaps he was getting a tad giddy, Hans conceded. Best he get home.

Hours later, drained of adrenaline, his exhilaration colliding with depression, he sat sleepless in the dark, brooding over his failure to acquire the ring. Twice he had let it slip away, first in Marrakech, then in Paris, three decades later. It had taken another twenty years to acquire the occult skills to locate it here in New York.

Shuffling through his thoughts, Hans realized he had let anger cloud his reason. He'd been going about his quest the wrong way.

The girl Savana was now protected against further attack, courtesy of her bitch aunt. But the evidence he'd planted, would effectively remove Doctor Orient, from his path.

The person he needed to target was Hannah Wylde, the girl's mother.

Chapter 9

Orient stood frozen, one eye on the exit across the floor, the other on the two uniformed policemen at the entrance of the basement shop. If he moved across the doorway, he'd certainly be seen or heard. The tiny shop didn't afford much cover—and he was running out of time.

As he watched the lead officer step inside, Orient tensed his muscles, ready to bolt.

Without warning, a cacophony of chimes, bells, gongs, whistles, chirps, and cuckoos, flooded the cramped space. All the clocks in the shop were marking the hour. At the sudden eruption of noise both officers stepped back.

Orient didn't hesitate. He leaped across the doorway to the exit, and pushed it open, the metallic scrape muffled by the symphony of synchronized clocks.

Outside, the quiet amplified his heaving breath. He looked around, and saw he was in a courtyard of sorts. His only way out was over a concrete fence.

He clambered over the barrier, and dropped into another courtyard, which fortunately had an alley to the street.

Orient slowed to a walk, avoiding undue attention from the few passers by. Her saw the revolving lights of a police car and headed the other way. As he searched for a cab, he realized it was the second time that day he had fled a murder scene.

+ + +

Owen please come ASAP, Need help!

Orient groaned when he read Sybelle's text message, body drained by shock, guilt and fear. He wanted to crawl into bed and sleep for two days. Instead he directed the cab to Sybelle's townhouse.

When he arrived, Orient saw the crime scene tape across the door and the squad car outside. He stayed in the cab and called Sybelle.

"I'm outside," he said, when she answered,

"I'll let you in." Her voice sounded as weary as he felt.

He waited until she opened the door before leaving the cab. No sense inviting undue scrutiny, he told himself, the situation threatened severe backlash. Bystanders were certain to get hurt. All they could do was contain the damage.

"What happened?" he asked, as soon as he entered. He knew it would be bad, but he wasn't prepared for the answer.

"Someone broke in and... oh God, it's Lena, my house keeper... she's dead. They say she has a broken neck."

Orient wrapped her in his arms. "They killed her too," he whispered, almost to himself, "this is way out of control."

"What do you mean?"

"Peter Taegris. I found him dead in his shop, less than an hour ago."

"What? Oh, that poor man. Owen I'm frightened, three people murdered... Who's doing this? What do they want?"

"The ring. We obviously underestimated its value. Or it's power."

"Where is it now?"

"I gave it to Hannah. She put it away somewhere."

"I need to sit down and talk about what to do, darling. It's getting beyond me."

"Alright, but first tell me what happened here."

"When I came home the front door was unlocked, some-one had been going through the rooms. Then I went into the kitchen and... Owen it was terrible. Lena was on the floor. I called 911, the ambulance came but there was nothing they... the doctor said her neck was broken and called the police. They took her away barely a half hour ago. But they've been questioning me, as if I had something to do with it. They wouldn't let me call, so finally I texted."

As they moved from the entrance hall to the living room Orient saw a man in a rumpled designer suit talking to a uniformed officer. The man in the suit looked up, nodded at them and continued his conversation with the officer.

Sybelle led the way to her study, which was still in a state of disorder, with scattered papers on the floor, and open desk drawers. She ignored the mess, went straight to the sideboard, and poured them both a large brandy.

Orient didn't object. He sat back in a leather chair and let the alcohol burn away the tension and fear twisting his muscles.

They didn't speak, both of them trying to recover their balance.

"We've got to warn Hannah," he said finally.

"Who do you think is doing this?"

"I don't know, but it's connected to that incident we shared, back in time, in Marrakech. Some sort of ritual was being performed, remember?"

"Yes, yes, the German man, with the scar," Sybelle said, "I remember. But that was a psychic vision. What about the here and now? Poor Lena had nothing to do with any of this. Oh my God, dear Lena, I can't believe it."

"Am I interrupting here?"

The man in the brown suit smiled at Orient. "I'm Detective Wagner." He extended his card.

Orient took it. "Doctor Owen Orient, I'm a close friend."

"May I get you a drink Detective?" Sybelle asked quietly

Detective Wagner was a short, barrel-chested man, with thick dark hair, light brown eyes and a broad, insincere smile. "Thanks, but I'm still on duty. So, uh, Doctor, how did you hear about this tragic event?"

"I received a text message from Sybelle, in fact," Orient pulled out his cell phone, "it's still on there."

Wagner stared at the small screen with what seemed to be disappointment. His smile settled into what was a habitual scowl. "So do you have any idea who would want to break in here?"

"It wasn't a robbery as far as I can gather," Sybelle offered.

"So maybe the killer was looking for you, and found your housekeeper instead. She must have come through the back and surprised the intruder."

"I'm sure I don't know who could be stalking me Detective. I was hoping you could tell me that." She said sweetly.

Wagner sighed. "We contacted the family. They'll make an ID at the morgue. We've dusted for prints. If you remember anything, please contact me. My e-mail address is on the card, as well as my phone."

He turned to leave then paused. "Oh, Doctor, one more thing."

Orient's senses shifted into full alert. He knew the detective was about to pounce.

"I noticed the time on that text message. You got here in a hurry."

"I happened to be in a taxi when Sybelle contacted me."

"Oh right, of course." He smiled. "You don't happen to have the receipt do you?"

Orient furrowed his brow. "I can't recall getting a receipt," he said, "sorry."

"No problem," Wagner said, his smile fixed, "I'll show myself out, Ms. Lean."

They watched him leave in silence. Sybelle refreshed her drink, Orient declined, still working on his. Carefully, still sorting out the facts, he told Sybelle of his narrow escape from the police. "It was as if someone sent them, knowing I'd be there."

Sybelle shivered. "I should get in touch with Hannah, but I wouldn't know what to say. She can be quite stubborn,"

"I've noticed," Orient said drily.

Sybelle took a thoughtful sip of her brandy, "I suppose it has to be done."

She put aside her snifter, and went to the phone. "Hello, Hannah? it's your Aunt Sybelle. Please call me when you get this."

She came back and picked up her drink. "There now, that's all done."

"Actually it's not. She's in real danger, and so is Savana,"

"What do you propose we do?"

Orient checked his watch. "Let's get something to eat, and check back with Hannah in an hour or so."

"Good idea, darling, I'm starved. And I know a fabulous Chinese restaurant that delivers."

Sybelle was quite correct about the quality of the food. However the sense of death, hovering over them, prevented Orient from enjoying it.

Thankfully, the phone rang a few minutes after the hour. "Hannah, thank God you called. Look dear this is serious. Is Savana at home? No? Good, we need to talk. Is it alright if Owen and I come round to your flat?"

Orient perked up. He assumed Sybelle would discuss it privately with her niece. But as he knew, assumption was the mother of all mistakes. And in this case it would probably cost him a job he needed.

Still, there was no other way. Sybelle's home had been invaded, three people were dead, obviously this person was a psychotic—and obsessed. If he fixed on Hannah it could be tragic.

To his surprise, the possibility stirred primal emotions. He didn't want this to spill over to Hannah any more than it had. Perhaps he should have kept the ring, Orient thought, with a pang of guilt.

"Owen?"

He looked up.

"I need to gather some things before we go."

During the cab ride he thought about how to convince Hannah that the threat to her was real. "I'm going to depend on you," he told Sybelle, "I'm not sure she trusts me."

Sybelle waved a dismissive hand. "Truthfully, until this happened she's always considered me the kooky aunt. But she's got to believe us after what happened to Savana."

+ + +

It wasn't that simple.

"I know your housekeeper's death is traumatic," Hannah said quietly, after hearing Sybelle's compressed version of events, "however it is a giant stretch of logic to connect that to me somehow."

"At least let me take the ring," Orient said.

Hannah looked at him oddly. "Yes of course. Come by and pick it up tomorrow." She made it sound like he was picking up his severance check.

"Look, both Sybelle and myself are aware how bizarre this must sound to you, it certainly does to me. But someone really did break into Sybelle's home. Someone really did kill Lena and my friend Henry Applegate. And he is... relentless."

"Are you trying to frighten me, Doctor?"

Her gaze was both challenging and curious. It made Orient uncomfortable. He found himself drawn to her, but knew better. He met her stare. "I know I'm frightened. You saw what happened to your daughter. Do you really think it's all a coincidence?"

She shrugged. "I don't think that moving myself, and my daughter, to some undisclosed location is any solution. *If* it's necessary at all."

Sybelle sighed. "I told you she's stubborn."

Orient weighed the situation. If they kept trying to persuade Hannah, she would only become more resistant. "Okay, you've heard the facts," he said mildly. "You proceed as you see fit. But please allow me one simple precaution. May I have your mobile?"

Orient programmed his number and returned the phone.

"Now I'm on there. Call me any time if you need help."

This time Hannah's smile was condescending. "I'm usually the one people call for help."

Orient lifted his hands in surrender. "I meant no disrespect."

"Hannah darling, will you do your crazy aunt one teeny favor? After all you did call *me* for help."

Hannah flushed slightly. An attractive feature, Orient noted quietly.

"Yes, I did call you for help. And you certainly did come through for me. Savana seems to be recovering nicely. So, my dear, crazy, aunt, I'll do whatever you ask," she paused, "short of moving away."

"I took these from home," Sybelle said, rummaging through her big red bag. She pulled out two crosses, one large the other small. The smaller cross was black, wrapped with a red ribbon. A white feather was tucked inside the ribbon. The large cross was also black, and had a silver Star of Solomon at the juncture point.

"The small one is for you. It's a very powerful protective amulet. I suggest you keep that in your pocket at all times. The other one is for Savana's room, just in case."

"Just in case of what?"

Sybelle glanced at Orient. "Oh you know, a *relapse.*"

Hannah's voice took on a tense, harried tone. "If I have this ring everyone wants, why would Savana be involved again?" She put the large cross on a side table, near the piano.

"We don't know why this is happening," Orient said, "but it is. Whoever is doing it is ruthless. And I'm afraid you're in the firing line. So after we leave, I hope you screen any visitors carefully." He forced a smile. "And don't hesitate to call."

"I won't be calling you anytime soon," she said curtly. Her voice softened a bit. "At least I hope it won't come to that. Look, Doctor, Aunt Sybelle, I do appreciate your concern but I've had a long day at the hospital. Savana's due back soon and..."

As if on cue they heard the rattle of a key in the lock and Savana entered.

"Oh, hi, Aunt Sybelle!" the girl said cheerfully. She had lost the haggard, aged look Orient had seen during his previous visit, and looked like a healthy, teen-aged girl. She bent to pick up the Siamese cat that had come over to greet her, rubbing against her ankle. "Hello, Jillian, did you miss me?" she cooed.

She looked at Orient questioningly.

Hannah moved to her side, and put a reassuring arm around her shoulder. "You may not remember Doctor Orient, but he helped cure you when you were sick."

When Savanna smiled, Orient saw the resemblance between mother and daughter.

They shared the same classic features, hazy violet eyes, and a certain graceful reticence.

"Thank you Doctor," Savana said, extending her hand.

As Orient reached out to take it, the cat bounded from Savana's shoulder to his arm, dropped soundlessly to the floor and stalked away, tail raised.

"Jillian you silly girl,' Savana scolded. She turned to Hannah. "I've got a make-up test tomorrow."

"Nice meeting you, Doctor," Savana said, as she kissed Sybelle goodnight.

"We should be going as well," Orient said, after she was gone.

"Please darling think about what we told you," Sybelle implored. If only for Savana's safety."

Hanna embraced her. "Believe me, that is *all* a mother thinks about."

Chapter 10

Finally alone, Hannah Wylde poured herself a glass of chardonnay, and grazed for leftovers in the refrigerator. Of course, pickings were slim since she hadn't cooked a proper meal in two days. Not mom of the year, she thought ruefully. Thank heavens Savana had inherited her independent streak. In her own defense, between working a ten hour day at the hospital, and trying to keep up with a teen daughter, she was exhausted.

It could be worse, she thought, sitting at the piano and idly running her fingers on the keys. She could still be working the night shift on the trauma unit. At least her administrative duties gave her structured time and a home life, however limited.

She checked her reflection in the mirror. Her dark hair brushed her shoulders and probably needed a cut. Despite the long hours and stress, she maintained a youthful look.

And her figure was quite trim, thank you.

She thought about this doctor friend of Sybelle's that she had recommended for the position. There was something about him that stirred her emotions. It wasn't his looks, although he was quite handsome in an intense, bohemian kind of way. And the emotions weren't always positive—or welcome.

Hannah was almost sorry she had approved his CV and sent it to committee.

Realistically, there were at least five weeks before it became official, so she could always reconsider her decision.

However, she had to admit, Doctor Orient had succeeded in getting Savana out of coma, where her high-tech medical staff had failed. He had an enviable education, an impeccable work record, and... he was good-looking.

Now you're thinking like a schoolgirl, Hannah chided. Orient and her aunt were overreacting to the point of hysteria. She drained her glass, placed on the bench beside her, and pressed a key as if to punctuate her annoyance. The note seemed to linger in the quiet. Intrigued by the tone she softly began to play. There was little chance of disturbing Savana who was probably wearing earphones and listening to hip-hop on her iPod, while she was studying.

Despite her daughter's multi-tasking and the melodic piano, the apartment seemed oddly empty. The music seemed to resonate, as if in a large, echoing cavern. She stopped, went to refill her glass, then checked the door lock on her way back to the piano.

It always relaxed her to play. Better than alcohol, far better than drugs, music channeled pure inspiration—especially Chopin.

At one point she had considered a career as a pianist, but put her fingers to better use as a surgeon. Hannah was proud of her professional skills, but they came at great personal cost. Her marriage had ended badly, and her husband had run off to Europe, leaving her with Savana, and two years of residency to contend with. She had muddled through somehow, learning to survive on three hours sleep, cold pizza, and bad coffee.

As she played, the sound seemed to reverberate loudly, and the room became too warm.

Abruptly, Hannah stood, went to the window and opened it.

Even the street below seemed silent.

For a moment she had the feeling someone was standing behind her. A chill breeze brushed her arms and the hairs on her neck stood up. She turned but no one was there. She refilled her glass and returned to the piano, but as she continued to play the air became oppressive. Wrapped up in the music she tried to ignore it. A trickle of sweat ran down her arm, then another. She had difficulty breathing and moved to go back to the open window.

It was then she realized she was unable to stop playing.

She watched her fingers move over the keys as if they were someone else's hands, and heard the music ballooning louder. The sound continued to echo, seemingly vibrating inside the walls.

Frightened, she tried to stop playing but her fingers flew across the keys in a maniacal parody of a sonata. Desperately Hannah jerked one hand back and grabbed for the large black cross on the table nearby. .

As soon as she touched it, the booming echoes stopped. A moment later, the wine glass on the bench beside her shattered.

Stifling a scream Hannah grabbed the cross and hurried to Savana's room. Sybelle had told her to put the cross there, why didn't she do it? Her thoughts froze when she saw Jillian.

The Siamese cat was a hissing ball of fury, blocking her path. She bared small, sharp teeth, her fur standing straight up as if electrified.

"Get away!" Hannah shouted, hearing the panic in her voice. "Jillian, back!"

The cat lunged at her, claws raking her calves. The pain seared away her confusion and she swung the cross hard. The moment it made contact with the cat's paw, the cross cracked in two. She felt the power course from hand to heart, and staggered back

Fear jerked through her limbs and she picked up a nearby chair to use as a shield, but the cat easily leaped on top of it. Screaming, Hannah hurled the chair across the room.

Before it crashed to the floor the cat was bounding towards her, claws bristling and fangs set in a death grin.

Frantically Hannah dug into her pocket and clutched the small, red-ribboned cross Sybelle had given her. She brandished it at the attacking feline like a torch, waving it back and forth. To her surprise the cat stopped short and arched its back, yowling in pain. Hannah stifled her fear and moved forward, jabbing at the cat as if the tiny cross was a sword. The cat jumped back and coiled into a frenzied ball, spitting and mewling.

Suddenly it sprang straight for her throat, its high pitched yowl slicing through Hannah's belly like cold steel. She screamed and clutched the tiny cross with both hands, holding it in front of her face, gaze fixed on the beast's burning yellow eyes,

She stumbled back but the cat had already leaped past her shoulder and was crouched on the carpet. Dimly, she realized the tiny cross created some sort of protective shield that the cat was unable to penetrate.

She carefully took a few steps to the side, angling for the door to Savana's room, but the cat ran in front of her and stood between her and the door, poised to attack. When she paused, the cat scrambled forward, claws raking at her ankles. Instinctively, Hannah staggered back and the cat pounced, leaping at her neck.

This time she felt the beast's steamy body brush her skin. As if stung she scurried back near the window. The cool breeze blowing in through the open window refreshed her senses, and she focused on the rabid beast stalking her intently.

The cat was padding back and forth in a half circle, yellow eyes blazing with primal rage.

Think, Hannah told herself, this damned little horror won't let up anytime soon. She glanced at the door to her daughter's room, praying it stayed closed. If Savana walked into this...

Before she could finish the thought, the cat circled closer and Hannah knew the creature was gathering itself for another strike. A desperate idea came to her.

Tiny cross gripped tight in both hands, she shuffled back a few inches, until she felt the air at her back.

With a high, wailing screech the cat leaped. Hannah ducked and swung, rather than jabbed, at the attacking beast, turning the cross like a divining rod. A pulse of magnetic energy seemed to connect and repel. The cat swerved in mid-air and tumbled wildly past her shoulder.

Except this time there was no place to land.

Unable to stop its momentum, the cat hurtled through the open window, all four of its paws clawing at open air.

Still aiming the cross at the creature, Hannah watched it hover, and for a crazed moment thought it might turn and leap back at her.

Instead it dropped, falling ten stories in slow, spinning motion, puffed tail extended like a rudder, until it smacked the top of a parked Mercedes, cracking the sun roof with a sound that reached Hannah clearly.

Lungs heaving, and hair damp with sweat, she stared down at the inert, flattened outline of her pet Siamese cat, on a web of splintered glass. She saw a couple cautiously approach the car, then look up at her window.

Hannah stepped away, anxious to check on Savana. She hurried to Savana's bedroom door.

When she touched the knob, the metal felt hot.

Suddenly fearful, she clenched the tiny cross and opened the door. Savana was lying on top of the bed, still in street clothes. As Hannah came closer, Savana sat straight up, as if yanked by an overhead wire.

She rolled her eyes and glared at her mother. Then she spoke, voice deep and guttural, and words spitting like gravel.

"Poor fools," her voice rumbled, *"do you dare cast dice with destiny?"*

Sheer panic pushed Hannah from the room. She staggered around blindly for a few moments until she found her phone. Fingers trembling, she punched Doctor Orient's number.

+ + +

Had she looked outside her window, Hannah would have seen four people, standing on the sidewalk below. They were peering at the lifeless body of a Siamese cat that had fallen from the high-rise behind them, and landed on top of a black Mercedes, severely damaging the sun roof.

And like them, Hannah would have been shocked to see the cat twitch, stretch, and slowly get to her feet.

After pausing for another exploratory stretch, the creature yawned, her teeth bared in a hungry smile, then hopped down to the car's hood. From there she bounded into the street and sauntered away, tail raised high to a stunned audience...

Chapter 11

Federal Agent Moe Klein had an acid stomach and an intermittent flutter in the area of his heart. A large man, he moved his body in parts, paunch leading the way and long legs shambling behind. His droopy, hangdog expression lulled people into thinking he was slow witted but he had a bear trap brain, crammed with information on everything from quantum physics to pasta recipes.

Problem these days wasn't storage, it was retrieval, he sighed, lifting his badge as he shuffled past the uniforms guarding the crime scene. He kept moving until he reached the study, and saw the brown crocodile loafers hooked around the sofa.

After you tail a suspect for a while you get to know him, Klein reflected sadly, staring down at Henry Applegate's splayed body. He had been browsing nearby the day Applegate purchased the shoes he died in. Klein recalled the expression of childish delight on Applegate's patrician features, as he counted out the hundred dollar bills for the salesgirl.

Poor bastard, Moe thought dourly. Suddenly he felt very tired

"Thanks for getting here so fast."

Klein turned and saw Homicide Detective Wagner, smiling at him. He didn't smile back.

"I knew the way," he said, "our victim here was a key suspect. Anybody find a weapon?"

"Behind the couch," Wagner said with a trace of pride. "Perp must have lost it somehow. It's some kind of fancy knife. Could even belong to the deceased. He collected all kinds of junk. You ever see such a pile of dusty old crap?"

Moe was aware that the fossils, figurines and paintings weren't for everybody. He happened to be an amateur archeologist, and liked to paint watercolors on weekends.

However he kept his opinions to himself. He wasn't crazy about Wagner, but didn't want his personal feelings to get in the way of this case.

"You have a forensic report?"

"Looks like a professional hit. Single stab wound at the base of his skull."

"You make anybody for this?"

"Lady down the hall thinks she saw a young blond guy enter the apartment. Probably the boyfriend."

"Applegate wasn't gay."

Wagner gave him a shrewd glance.

"How exactly would you know that?"

"I know his girlfriend. He visits her twice a week. Like clockwork."

"He'll be late this week. What else do you know?"

"You got a time of death?"

"Why is the Bureau so interested in Applegate?"

"Smuggled art works. Where's the murder weapon?"

"You mean like fake art?"

"Sometimes. Mainly it's about *real* art that's been stolen, or isn't supposed to be here. Most countries have laws prohibiting any export of ancient art, fossils, whatever. That's where the money comes in."

Wagner nodded.

"Where's the murder weapon?" Klein repeated patiently.

"It's bagged up over here, on the table."

Klein moved slowly, trying not to appear too anxious, but he had a hunch about this case. He'd been tailing Applegate for almost two months and his associates were quite strange.

And among the frequent visitors to this apartment, he recalled a young blond man.

Moe made a mental note to check his field reports, as Weber handed him a storage baggie containing the dagger.

It was heavier than it looked, with an engraved steel blade. Blood stains made the engraved words difficult to read, especially through the plastic, but Klein knew what it said. He also recognized the silver eagle and swastika on the black handle. That and the SS runes at the top told him it originally belonged to someone in Hitler's elite Nazi death squad.

"So what do think?" Wagner said.

"This murder weapon is definitely a collector's item. World War Two, official Nazi SS dagger."

"Nazi? Jesus, you think some skinhead on steroids did this?"

Klein gave him the plastic baggie. "Not really. Perp knew what he was doing. It's hard to kill a man with one stroke of the knife. If you check under the lower cross guards you'll find some serial numbers punched in there. They belong to the original owner, probably long dead."

Wagner stared at the baggie, then at Klein. "Jesus, cross guards...? Tell me Sherlock, you know what it says on the blade too?"

"*Meine Ehre Heist Treue,*" Klein said in bad German, "my honor is loyalty."

Wagner looked impressed.

"Maybe you can tell *me* something now," Klein said. "How were you able to contact me so quickly on this homicide? I thought nobody local knew I was working on Applegate."

"Funny thing, as soon as Applegate's name hit the computer, an FBI flag comes up, telling us to alert you immediately."

Great, Moe thought, now I have some asshole big brother in Virginia, looking over my shoulder. To Wagner he said, "Computers, how did we get along without them?"

The detective shrugged. "So maybe we can have a drink and you can fill me in on some background. I'll give you the forensics and evidence results when they come back."

Moe knew Wagner had to turn over that information anyway, but he needed to go over the details very carefully. Especially while they were fresh in Wagner's mind. With Applegate's untimely death, he'd lost a key link in his case.

"Good idea, but I'll stick to coffee."

"Sure, Jewish cops don't drink, right?" Wagner threw an arm around Klein's shoulder.

It felt like a collar.

Moe hadn't been entirely candid. He used to drink a lot. Especially after Paula left. But these days he liked to lay off the booze. Except for tonight. After his coffee, he decided to order a Jameson. He looked up and saw Wagner regarding him with an odd expression.

"Okay, Federal Agent Klein, how about it?"

"How about what?"

"You know something about this guy you're not sharing."

Klein sighed. Despite the expensive suit, Wagner still looked like a low rent cop on the pad, and he didn't trust him.

"Here's what I know," he said finally, "the guy is—was—a big time art dealer. We're talking multi-million dollar deals, lots of them underground. So we were building a tax case, hoping to get Applegate to open up about his European assets."

"European assets?" Wagner sucked his tooth.

"Yeah, his sources; clients, contacts, everything. So tell me Walter," calling Wagner by his first name. "When did you find out Applegate was murdered?"

Wagner seemed startled by his crisp, procedural approach.

"We got an anonymous 911 call."

"What time?"

"Early, between five and six p.m., why?"

"Don't know why... yet. Did you question the doorman?"

"Of course."

"And?"

"Nothing."

Klein drummed his fingers on the table. "So why would somebody murder Applegate, then call it in?"

"Crime of passion?"

"I don't think so. Maybe somebody else found the body, then called 911." Klein drained his scotch.

"Why not a crime of passion?" Wagner persisted.

"Too clean. Lovers tend to be messy. This was one thrust and goodbye Henry. Like you said, Walter, it's a professional hit."

Wagner beamed at the recognition. "You think he was killed for one of those million-dollar pieces of art?"

"Maybe." Klein considered another drink, and decided to pass. "Makes sense, professional job, quick kill... in and out. The safe was open I noticed, did you take an inventory?"

"I'll send it along with the forensics report."

"Don't bother, I'll drop by your precinct tomorrow."

"Yeah, good. Uh tell me, how did you know so much about the knife?"

"I'm a bit of an expert on Nazi artifacts, including their gold bullion. I also know something about art, archeology and collectibles like coins and stamps. That's why the Bureau assigned me to the case."

And without Applegate I'll be collecting dust behind a desk if I don't come up with something, Moe thought, uncomfortably aware that his progress was being monitored.

"Serious? So you think that shit in that apartment is worth something?"

Moe wanted to tell him that the Paul Klee painting alone would buy the entire building but he knew Wagner would get greedy and fuck things up. And at the moment he needed everything nice and neat, no charges of contaminating a crime scene.

"Not enough to kill him for," he said

That seemed to satisfy Wagner. Still, Moe made a note to revisit the apartment before going to the precinct for his paperwork.

"Anybody get a copy of the 911?"

"Copy?"

"You know, a recording of the call."

"Why?"

"Always helps to listen to it. You get a sense of the caller."

"Yeah, sure," Wagner said, looking at the bottom of his glass.

"Another round?" Without waiting for an answer Klein signaled the bartender and pushed a twenty across the wood. He didn't want another himself, but he needed to hear that tape.

"Okay then," he said, when the drinks arrived, "I'll make sure to mention your cooperation in my report."

"You do that," Wagner said. To a veteran cop it was as much a threat, as an endorsement.

Moe downed half his whiskey, and left a tip.

"Well thanks for your help Detective, I'm much obliged. I'll come to the precinct about three, that okay?"

"Three?"

"You know, to pick up the evidence package, inventory, oh yeah, and don't forget that 911 call."

"Fucking Feds..." Wagner muttered under his breath as Klein walked away.

Moe heard him but he just kept shuffling out the door. He knew how Wagner felt. To must city cops, federal agents came across as arrogant and self-serving. And mostly they were right.

He also knew how the system worked, and at the moment he happened to be on somebody's radar. It could be temporary, or it might be part of an ongoing tail.

Most likely temporary, Moe decided. His methods were so unorthodox, and his niche so eccentric, that he would have been cited long ago, if not fired. No, he speculated, this had everything to do with the Applegate case.

At any rate it was too late to worry about. Moe resolved to get up early and visit an old friend at the downtown office. The Bureau maintained a number of safe houses in Manhattan, and he'd been occupying a one bedroom on the upper eastside for six months.

Occupying was his own term as he didn't really consider it living.

Still he'd managed to bring the small kitchen up to standard, and he kept the place clean and neat. No empty six-packs or pizza boxes. For him, it was *al dente* pasta with sausage, a fresh salad, and a nice bottle of red wine.

He made himself a sandwich from some left over chicken and looked around. Once he cracked this case he planned to retire. He had something saved, with his pensions, enough to fulfill his dream of living in Italy. Until then he had to endure an environment void of art. The only color on the drab, beige walls, was a poster by Marc Chagall he'd found at a street fair.

Moe was aware that until today he had envied Henry Applegate. He envied his daily proximity to fine paintings, rare artifacts; things exquisitely unattainable to Moe. It wasn't really the money, or the connoisseur lifestyle... Moe paused. As he recalled Applegate had domestic help. He moved to the phone stand and scribbled some notes on the pad:

> *blond man,*
>
> *maid?*
>
> *check apt a.m.*
>
> *call Jake.*

Then he went to bed.

He awoke before six and prepared breakfast. It was always the same: fresh ground Kona coffee, scrambled egg whites, sesame bagel, Irish butter. He read the Times and the Post while he ate. Afterwards he took a brisk walk along the East

River Drive, topping it off with pull ups and dips in a local playground. When he returned to his apartment, he downed some fresh orange juice, showered, dressed, and strapped on his holster.

He didn't use a heavy gun, unlike many of his fellow agents. He preferred something light, and dependable At the moment he carried a Ruger LCP which weighed ten ounces fully loaded. His colleagues made great fun of his choice, calling it "momma's little helper", but Moe's chronically stiff back was grateful for any small favors.

Walking to the subway he thought about the items on his list. Applegate's apartment was on the way downtown, and at this early hour it would be empty. He could conduct his own sweep of the place without interference from nosy cops.

The doorman let him into the apartment reluctantly, hovering in the doorway as if to make sure Klein didn't steal something. Probably has his eye on this stuff himself, Moe thought, waving him away.

The doorman remained. "I'm supposed to make sure nobody disturbs anything." He said sourly.

"You see this?" Klein held his ID in front of the man's face.

"Yeah, I see it."

"What does it say?"

"Morris..."

"No, not my name."

"Uh, Federal Bureau of Investigation?"

"Bingo. Which means your work here is finished."

Moe shut the door in his face and began strolling through the deserted flat. He pulled out a note book and began itemizing the better art objects and paintings, for future reference. He doubted if New York Homicide had a clue about Mayan figurines, West African tribal sculpture, drawings by Larry Rivers, lithos by David Prentice, or photographs by Cartier Bresson and Denis Hopper. Not to mention the painting by Klee.

He also examined the strewn papers, still on the floor, and the contents of the safe. There, overlooked, on a bottom shelf, lay a Xerox copy of a drawing. A business card was attached by a paper clip.

The renderings were exquisitely done, although he doubted it was the same hand. He could see the female Sphinx was early dynasty, or earlier. Moe recognized the six-pointed star of Solomon but despite his familiarity with Hebrew, was unable to interpret the signs inscribed within. He was fairly certain The Eye of Horus dated from the third dynasty, judging from the thick black ink and graceful line.

He peered at the card. It was lavender with black script that read: *Sybelle Lean, Psychic Consultant.* Beneath that was a phone number.

Klein put the card in his pocket. Then he found a manila envelope and slipped the Xerox inside. He carefully wrote the time, date, and Applegate's address on the envelope, although he doubted it would be needed as evidence.

After doing another slow tour of the apartment, Moe went downstairs to talk to the doorman. He made a big show of writing down the man's name.

"Chester Delmar, that right? And you were on duty yesterday when Mr Applegate was killed?"

Chester was a big man, with prominent ears, a bent nose and an unhappy expression on his lantern-jawed face.

"I don't know when Mr Applegate uh, expired."

"Between four and seven p.m. yesterday, were you on duty then?"

"Yes, sir."

"Did you see anyone go up to his apartment?"

"No, sir."

Klein wasn't buying the 'sir' crap but he let it pass.

"Is there another entrance?"

"No, sir, oh yeah... there's the service entrance, in the alley over to the right. But the door locks from the inside."

"Did all of Applegate's visitors check with you?"

"Everybody who comes in the building has to call upstairs first."

"What about Mr Applegate's maid."

"Who?"

"His maid, didn't he have domestic help?"

"Yeah, his cook I think."

"Do you know her name?"

Chester looked uncomfortable in his oversized blue great-coat with brass buttons. Beads of sweat glistened on his neck. "Maybe it's Valka, something like that."

"Valka, you're sure of that?" He wrote it down, beneath Chester's name.

"Yeah, sure, Valka."

"You ever speak to her?"

"She comes here five days a week."

"What can you tell me about her?"

"Nothing much sir. She has an accent, Russian or German maybe."

A woman came to the door carrying two shopping bags, and Chester rushed to help her, obviously anxious to be off the hook

Klein decided to come back. He made a note to check Applegate's tax forms for his cook's name and address.

"See you again, Chester,' he said amiably.

The doorman didn't look overjoyed at the news.

As Moe walked to Lexington Avenue, he stopped at a bakery for jelly donuts, before taking the downtown subway to City Hall. While on the train he pulled out his BlackBerry and checked the reports he had e-mailed back to the director. As usual there were no replies. However in the reports he did find three occasions when he had observed a blond man visit Henry Applegate. Twice he had visited Henry's flat, and once they had met for coffee.

Moe made a note to talk to Applegate's neighbors when he went back. Maybe they knew something about the cook.

On his way to the building that housed the New York offices of the FBI, he picked up two containers of French press coffee. Getting past the lobby was like going on an international flight. It took him ten full minutes to get through the detectors, gather his belongings, re-holster his weapon, and board the elevator to the seventh floor. Actually, it should be named Sam Jacobi's floor, Klein mused, watching the numbers above the door light up. Jake had managed to rule his department unchallenged, for twenty years. The biggest reason being, he was the best at his job.

The other reason being, Jake was a master at working the system, Moe observed, let's not forget that. His only Achilles heel was his love of food. The little guy could eat more than two big men.

When he entered Jake's office, he was officially in cyberspace. Sam sat before a bank of screens on a swiveling armchair, his army of techies manning the keyboards, an urban Captain Kirk, going where no FBI agent had gone before. Short and balding, with owlish features that were shadowed by a perpetually unshaven stubble, Sam Jacobi greeted Moe with his patented devilish smile. "So my old friend, you finally decided to visit the brave new world."

"More like the brave new planet," Moe grunted, looking around at the banks of computers and screens. "You still drink coffee?"

"Not from here."

"I brought some from Earth. Along with some old-school jelly doughnuts."

Jake came around his command module to inspect the bag. "You must want something Big Moe. Better tell me what it is before I give in to temptation."

"Somebody on high is tracking me." He explained how Applegate's murder flagged him to New York Homicide. "So as soon as my suspect shows on the data base, my name pops up."

Jake thoughtfully chewed his doughnut. "So your Department Head is tracking your case, nothing new."

"Thornhill always let me do my job without interference," Moe said with a trace of indignation. "We have an agreement. It might be somebody higher."

"Thornhill? You mean Fred Thornhill?"

"Yeah, what about him?"

"Jesus, where have you been? Thornhill was kicked upstairs a month ago. Alfred Caldwell is your new boss. He's planning to consolidate some departments."

Moe gave him a hangdog grin.

"Guess I've been obsessed with this case of mine. Probably should check in more often." He sipped his coffee. "So how would I know if Caldwell is flagging everybody, or just me?"

"Good question. Let's ask Maybelline." He moved back to his console and consulted the screen. "Okay, the bad news is, it isn't everybody."

"What's the good news?"

There's another agent being tracked, Phil Jensen."

"What department?"

"International currency, counterfeit currency, look, it makes sense. Most of the budget is going to Homeland Security and anti-terrorist units these days. *But...*" Jake waggled a finger at Moe, "if they were really zeroing in on you for some reason, you wouldn't know about it. Nobody would be contacting you about a dead suspect. This is actually technology at its best."

Moe gestured with his half-eaten doughnut. "Caldwell probably figures since we're both international he can consolidate us."

"You know what your problem is?" Jake said, his mouth full. "You don't spend enough money. Hence your department is like a third world country. They figure you're not important."

"I've cracked more high profile art thefts than..."

"Not the point Moe."

"What is the point?"

"The system is the point. You've got a budget, use it." He turned back to the screen.

"Let's see, you don't drive a car here, you stay at two star hotels when you travel, expenses are minimal..."

"I thought that was supposed to be a good thing."

"You don't have to go *over* your budget, just make sure you use *most* of it. That way the next year it gets bumped up." Jake flashed a wicked smile. "And so do you."

Moe sighed. "You are indeed a wise motherfucker Jake."

"Just another shmuck, trying to make his way to the top of this wicked world. Do yourself a favor, order a new office computer, and a laptop for when you travel, fly business, and for shit's sake, stay at some decent hotels."

"Sound advice. I'll do it."

"Good. So unless you brought more doughnuts, is there anything else I can help you with?"

Moe dug into his pocket for the lavender business card. "Maybe you can run this name while we're here."

Jake squinted at the card. "Psychic consultant, who is this, your new girlfriend?"

"Found her name at the murder scene. Probably nothing."

"We'll know in less than thirty seconds," Jake murmered, "Sybelle Lean, this is your life..."

He studied the screen. "Pretty tame stuff. Does very well as a psychic reader for the rich and stupid. Does Tarot cards, crystals, the whole meghila. Pulls in enough to maintain a town house with a 10021 area code. You want her tax records?"

"Not really," Moe said, feeling guilty about wasting Jake's time. "Any associates of interest?"

"Mnnn... Well, well..."

"Whatcha got?"

"Miss Lean is mentioned in some classified CIA reports."

"The CIA was investigating her?"

"Not her, the associate. Doctor Owen Orient."

"Doctor?"

"Yeah, seems he cured Vice President Mulnew's daughter back in the day. Since then the CIA has been keeping tabs on him. Mnnn, this guy's been busy, got into some trouble in Jamaica, involved with some dicey characters in New York, Miami... Rome, Tangier... They finally shut down ongoing surveillance after the lead agent, Westlake, was removed following complaints of illegal procedure by senator Andy Jacobs." He turned to Moe. "Be careful, this guy must have some juice."

Moe shrugged. "My job's hanging by a thread and my top suspect is dead. Right now, Sybelle Lean and her doctor pal are all I've got."

Chapter 12

When Orient opened his apartment door and saw the place had been burglarized, he felt a numbing sense of helplessness. Sorting through the debris, he was relieved that his discs, while in disarray, were still functional. He could replace the computer, and with a bit of work, salvage the hard drive on the old one.

He was still trying to assess the damage when Hannah called.

"Owen, please come," she said breathlessly, "Savana... Oh god..." her voice trailed off, then drifted back. "Please come now."

Orient understood she was in shock. "I'll be right there. Put on something warm."

He stopped long enough to gather some things, then ran outside and hailed a cab.

Not knowing the nature of the emergency, Orient had also taken his doctor's bag. On the way he called Sybelle.

"I'm right behind you darling," Sybelle told him. "I sensed a disturbance and called Hannah a few minutes ago."

As the cab rolled east Orient went into a breathing pattern, focusing his resources for whatever would be required. For he had no doubt, that all of them were in mortal combat with a ferocious enemy with powerful occult skills. But he wondered if he was up to the challenge.

He pushed thought aside and opened his senses to the Light. A few minutes, or an eternity later, the cab stopped in front of Hannah's apartment building. Orient emerged reasonably refreshed, if not completely confident.

The woman who opened the door was a shadow of the well-groomed self-assured surgeon Orient had left not more than two hours before. Dark circles haunted her eyes and her hair seemed matted. When she let him in Orient noticed the stains on her clothing and the broken glass on the floor. She was weaving as if drunk.

"What happened? Was someone here?"

She shook her head sadly and sank down on the nearest chair. "I know it sounds crazy but my cat... my cat Jillian, *attacked* me. And then Savana... I don't know, she's asleep now but after the horrible cat... Savana seemed possessed by something... she spoke in a strange, scary voice. Owen I'm going out of my mind here. What the hell is happening to us?"

She was rubbing her arms as if chilled and Orient saw she hadn't put on something warm.

"Look, first let's get you taken care of. Do you have a sweater or jacket you can wear? You're suffering mild shock."

Hannah looked down at herself, and her professional instincts took over. "Yes, of course, I of all people should know better."

"Perhaps a bit of brandy too," Orient suggested, watching her go to the closet and wriggle into a long sweater.

"There's brandy on the sideboard," Hannah said.

Orient poured two glasses and gave one to her.

"Tell me everything, from the time we left." Orient said gently. "Take it minute by minute."

Almost in disbelief at her experience, Hannah went over the entire sequence of events. She had a doctor's keen recollection of detail and Orient was able to reconstruct the dynamics of the attack.

"For some reason the cat seemed afraid of this... cross Sybelle gave me." She took it out of her pocket, but didn't offer it to him. Instead she clutched it in her hand, as if afraid to let go. And when I went in to see if Savana was all right, she sat up and literally growled at me."

"Did she say anything you could understand?"

"Oh yes, let me see... she said, 'poor fools, do you dare cast dice with destiny'. I don't think I'll ever forget it... that voice..." She drained her brandy and shivered.

"Is it alright if I look in on Savana now?" Orient asked quietly. He lifted his black bag.

"Simple house call, I promise."

She managed a tired smile. "Of course, Doctor"

Actually, Savana looked much better than her mother. She had regained some weight and she seemed like a normal, untroubled teenaged girl. Except for a low, whispered moaning while she slept.

Orient opened his bag and began with a stethoscope. Without disturbing her he took her heart rate and pulse, and checked her breathing carefully. He felt Hannah come up behind him.

"Could I borrow that item for a moment," he said quietly.

She handed him the tiny black cross, with its ribbon and white feather. When Orient took it, he could sense the cross had taken a long journey to arrive in Hannah's hand when it did. Very carefully he moved the cross closer to Hannah.

The girl didn't stir, but her moaning stopped. Orient placed the cross directly on the sheet covering her chest. Savana's only reaction was a deep sigh.

Orient returned the cross to Hannah. "She seems okay, but the only way to make sure is to wake her."

"Do you think this might be a... a relapse?"

"Probably not. You were the primary target of a psychic predator," Orient explained. "However, because you had Sybelle's protective amulet in your pocket, you were able to break free. Like lightning, occult energy will jump to the object of least resistance, human or animal, in this case, your cat. When you fought off a second attack, the energy jumped again to Savana. But by then it was considerably weaker."

Hannah nodded, her expression blank with exhaustion. "Perhaps we should let her sleep."

The intercom announced Sybelle's arrival.

"Where is she?" Sybelle said, as she came bustling into the living room. "Are you alright Hannah darling? Did something happen to Savana?"

"She's inside with Owen..." Hannah said, but Sybelle was already moving to the bedroom.

"Owen, is Savana alright? I rushed over...'

Savana's eyes fluttered open. "Aunt Sibbie? Are we having a party?"

"Yes, dear," Hannah said, sitting on the bed beside her "Your Aunt Sybelle and Doctor Orient came over, and they just wanted to make sure you're alright."

"Oh, I'm just fine, mom," she yawned, "just kind of tired."

"Sorry, dear," Sybelle said in a stage whisper. "Your Aunt was concerned. You go back to sleep. Sweet dreams," she added.

"Oh, Mom, I had such weird dreams. You were in them. You had a sword. It was on fire..." Her voice trailed off.

Hannah gave her a hug. "You get back to sleep. We can talk in the morning.'

"You just sit here, darling," Sybelle said, when they were back in the living room. "I'll clean up the mess. We don't want to alarm Savana when she wakes up. And while I take care of that, you can tell me just what happened here."

Hannah and Orient told her about the attack and its aftermath, leaving Sybelle both appalled, and elated. "I had a premonition about that amulet I gave you. It was blessed by a Vatican Cardinal, *and* a jungle shaman."

"Thank god. It was the only thing that protected me from that... beast."

Sybelle swept some glass fragments into a dustpan, then paused for a healthy sip of brandy. "Where is Jillian now?"

Hannah shivered at the recollection. "She came at me. I held up the cross and she flew past me out the window and fell ten stories onto somebody's sunroof. "

"Really?" Sybelle moved to the open window and peered down. "Well darling, it appears they really do have nine lives."

Orient moved beside her. The Mercedes parked on the street below, did indeed have a shattered sunroof. But there was no sign of a cat, dead or alive.

+ + +

They talked for more than an hour. Hannah, no longer a skeptic, was wary but curious about the various forms of psychic energy that could be activated.

"If I hadn't experienced playing piano against my will, I could have easily shrugged off Jillian's attack as simple rabies," she said.

"Amulets don't cure rabies." Sybelle said loftily. "By the way, what happed to the big cross I gave you?"

"It cracked into pieces when the cat touched it. That's when I grabbed this one."

"That you thought to do that, and the fact that it worked, tells me something," Orient said evenly.

"And what might that be, Doctor?" she asked playfully.

"You may be a potential."

Hannah drew back. 'Look I don't think...'"

"It's not about thinking, it's about who you are." Orient paused, not wishing to press too hard. It wasn't uncommon for potentials to feel some anxiety in the presence of a telepath, due to a marked increase in electromagnetic energy generated by the brain. Like static on a radio.

"Most humans have some sort of psychic facility," he explained quietly, "however we are not encouraged to develop it. Some places it's against the law. In that sense it has a parallel to human sexuality." Orient immediately wished he'd omitted the last part, but Hannah seemed to understand. She was listening with full attention

"It's precisely because you have a strong ultranormal facility, what I call a 'potential' in my work, that you were able to fuse with Sybelle's amulet, if only for a few moments, and repel that attack." He paused. "Which was quite real."

She nodded, and sighed. "How do I explain Jillian's disappearance to Savana?"

"That's a problem only a mom can solve," Orient said. He glanced at Sybelle. "We should be going."

"Yes. Well the apartment seems nice and neat again," Sybelle said cheerfully. She lowered her voice. "Unless she remembers something, Savana needn't know what happened tonight."

"Let's meet at the hospital for lunch," Orient suggested. "I can pick up the ring, and perhaps we can come up with a plan."

"Plan? You think this may happen again?" Hannah searched his eyes as if trying to find the answer there.

Orient remained impassive, but he couldn't conceal the concern in his voice. "We... all of us here have already been touched by this malignant force. Three people are dead, and my own apartment was ransacked."

Sybelle clapped a jeweled hand over her mouth. "Owen, you too?"

"They were looking for the ring. Whoever is doing this has resources." He turned to Hannah and tried to muster a reassuring smile. "Which is why we need a plan," he said softly.

Hannah hugged herself and nodded.

Later, while cleaning up the debris in his bedroom, Orient realized that once he had the ring, he would be the prey.

And the predator would soon return.

Chapter 13

Hans was in a foul mood.

He had been ordered, ordered mind you, to stand down until this fool Orient was eliminated, or in police custody as planned. Hans took "eliminated" as the operative word.

After all, there was little to tie him to any of these killings. He had been absolutely precise about that. However his little blood sport of the past evening was ill advised. He had been drunk with the majestic power of the Spear.

He had sought to baptize his Thule dagger, instead he risked exposure. On awakening he had a massive hangover to amplify his regret. The adventure had been reckless, and even worse, needless.

When he opened his computer he saw the Soho run-in was all over the internet. Someone had even tried to video him, but all they got was his departing shadow on the poorly lit street. However there were lots of pictures of the poor, wounded pit bull, Hans noted ruefully. And of course, a few shots of the boy whose face he'd decorated with the lightning rune of the SS. If he hadn't stabbed the dog, no one would have taken notice of the incident. .

Still, it had been stupid. And he had paid dearly. He would no longer have sole possession of the Spear. A stinging rebuke to his authority. He'd been given forty eight hours to deliver the Spear, 'properly secured' to the District Leader. Who was beneath him in rank. He answered only the Architect.

Properly secured, Hans fumed at the wording. As if he was a child. He knew he was being punished for his rash behavior. The Architect had made that clear. They did not comprehend the awesome well of power revealed by the Spear of Destiny,

Hans reflected. And before he turned it over the District Leader, he intended to drink deeply from that well.

Unlike his previous experiment, it wasn't undertaken lightly. He went on an immediate fast, and prepared his quarters with meticulous attention to detail. First he cleaned the room, including the protective circle he'd been using. Whatever energy it provided had been exhausted. Then he secured the room, to confine, if not control, the power generated by the Spear.

He drew a new, more intricate circle, frequently consulting his grimoire, and taking pains to make sure the dimensions were precise. It took hours, and during that time he concentrated on the object of his destruction.

Cut off the head and the body dies, Hans observed. Before his mission here was complete he would decapitate this interloper, who would prevent him from possessing the Seal.

For the next sixteen hours he applied himself to his task. He placed glasses of salt water in each corner of the room, and before performing the rite, bathed in aromatic herbs and oils. Then he lit five candles, one at each point of the pentagram within the large circle, and began.

Naked, he placed the Spear in the center of the circle, and knelt above it, straddling it between his legs. He started chanting the ancient formulas of transformation, and lifted his arms gathering what the Chinese masters called *Chi*, the natural energy around all humans, which can be harnessed using a combination of flowing motion and concentration.

The air inside the room became stifling, sweat poured down his chest and arms.

In the shadowed candlelight he looked like a ghostly temple dancer, his white skin glistening as the heat inside the room began to rise.

Hans had left a window open, to drain off any excess power, but he soon became aware his precautions were futile against the tidal surges drawn up by his incantations. At a certain point he also became aware that to pause, to hesitate too long, or to stop, would bring these surges crashing down on himself. He was obligated to maintain the flow of movement and rhythmic chant, under threat of a sudden, abysmal destruction... of self and soul.

Rather than bend to fear, Hans exulted in the challenge, the primal struggle of all life in the universe. He would be its master.

Opening his grimoire he recited the forbidden words of the alchemist Agrippa, for the transmutation of life from death, and felt the electric flux pulse through his loins, and he became erect. He repeated the formula, and saw the Spear's steel blade glowing red with heat, an instant before a burning white light appeared before him.

Using the Spear as leverage, he swerved the massed energy away from the light-into the dark, orgasmic, vortex of chaos...

+ + +

When Hans awoke he was lying naked in the circle, the Spear beside him. Gingerly, he picked up the Spear and took it into the next room. He felt completely refreshed and confident now. He had been filled with the dark power, like a inserting a clip in a pistol. Using bubble wrap he carefully 'secured' the Spear and put it in a briefcase. Then he went inside to take a shower and dress.

He took his time, using as much of his deadline as he could without seeming unreliable. The District Leader would be annoyed, Hans thought with amusement, always a stickler for tiny details. He would deal with that tiny problem immediately.

Finally he was ready to deliver the Spear as ordered. What no one could know was that he had absorbed its essence. It would always belong to him.

The rest was a rote exercise in false humility.

He offered it up as a test, truly a monk now. Hans carried the briefcase to the subway and took the A train to City Hall. From there he took a cab across the Brooklyn Bridge.

Valka was waiting impatiently. A balding, sleek looking man with beady, bird like eyes was sitting beside her in an easy chair.

Hans kept his face impassive but inwardly he gloated over her barely repressed annoyance. The best part was she could do, or say, nothing. He had delivered the Spear on schedule.

And Valka could shove it.

She had put up her graying hair in a bun, like the German *hausfrau* she was. Valka was a stolid, peasant type, once much admired by the early National Socialists. But in today's vision of the Grand Design, she was a throwback. Her dark, BB eyes glared at him from deep inside her wide, square boned face. Hans made a note to investigate Valka's background more deeply. He was certain there was a Jew in her closet.

"Is everything in order?" Valka said, her voice a threatening rasp.

"Of course," he responded loftily. He looked at the other man in the room. "Why is he here?"

"That's Dieter we..."

"I did *not* ask his name, I asked, why is he here?"

Valka's glare wavered. She tilted her head and he left the room.

"Again," he said with feigned patience, "why is that man here?"

"He will accompany me to the Homeland." She said. "Do you have it?"

Hans gave her the briefcase. "Please examine it and certify it was delivered in good condition."

He waited while she went through the steps of unwrapping and rewrapping the precious object, then gave her a notepad and pen. "Just write the word certified, the date and your name. That should be sufficient for our Architect."

How easy it had been to turn the tables on Valka, Hans gloated, watching her dutifully sign.

Now she understood she was merely a cog in the wheel.

And he was driving the chariot.

Chapter 14

At six a.m. Orient had already been meditating for an hour. He had gone back to the schedule he maintained in the sacred Himalayan valley where Ku had taught him the secret of the Serene Knowledge. Then he had been young with few needs, but over time he had come to require certain temporal comforts.

However, as of this day he renounced all material indulgence. He was at war with an unseen enemy who would attack again, if given any specific link.

The ring would certainly provide that, he noted ruefully. Like the GPS imbedded in a cell phone, the predator would track him, so long as he had the ring.

After his meditations Orient went out for a run. Most of New York was still preparing for their daily assault on the walls of commerce, as he jogged through the park. He stopped off in a playground to do some pull ups and dips, before continuing back home.

He had breakfast, then started putting his possessions in boxes, labeling them as he went.

At ten he called Andy Jacobs.

"Senator I need a sit down,' Orient said.

"Sounds serious."

"It is."

"When?"

"Is four thirty too late?"

"P.J. Clarke's." He hung up.

The senator never did waste words, Orient thought with a smile. Perhaps that's where he'd learned it. In a way he felt secure having Andy at his back, but in cold truth no one could protect him from the gnawing evil prowling at the edge of his senses.

At eleven thirty he arrived at St. Luke's Hospital for his meeting with Hannah. While he wouldn't admit it, he'd been looking forward to seeing her again.

Even the obvious strain didn't diminish Hannah's natural radiance. She was ending a phone call and motioned for him to sit down.

"Alright," she said with a note of finality when she hung up the phone. She gave Orient a conspiratorial smile. "One of our most annoying vendors. You'll get to meet him when you start slaving here. I sent your paperwork upstairs,' she added.

Orient smiled. "So you finally decided I'm not too crazy after all."

"I still don't understand it."

"Very few people do, or even want to."

"I may be one of those people."

"Problem is, your daughter is highly gifted, as are you to a lesser degree."

"A lesser degree?"

Orient shrugged. "Enough to give you trouble. Certainly your Aunt Sybelle is one of the most talented psychics I've ever met. Obviously it runs in the family."

"I've been running all day," she sighed, "let's have lunch."

For the first time Orient felt at ease with Hannah. They chatted about medicine, politics, and art. He was charmed by her love of music, and she by his passion for film.

"How many times have you seen *The Godfather*?" she teased.

"How many times have you listened to Mozart?"

She grimaced as if wounded. "Got me there, Doctor, I must admit.'

Orient liked hearing her call him doctor. He was elated to know she trusted him enough to approve his application. Unfortunately the forces they were dealing with could destroy all that before it began.

"Penny for your thoughts."

"What? Oh sorry, I was thinking about... the ring."

She seemed disappointed. "Yes of course, we can go get it now if..."

"It can wait if you can,' he said.

She checked her watch. "I've got time, and it's nice to talk about something besides hospital work." Hannah took a deep breath. "I need to spend more time with Savana, but I don't know how to arrange it."

"Do you have vacation time due?"

"At least two months worth. I haven't been able to get away for years."

"You mean you haven't been able to let go," he said gently. "This place won't collapse without you, but your daughter might."

She looked at him appraisingly. "How can I argue with that?"

"Actually, considering what's already happened, it would be extremely wise if the two of you went somewhere for a couple of weeks."

"You think we're still in danger?"

Orient nodded. "Sorry about the danger part," he said, "but it seems you and Savana deserve some quality time together."

"It's going to take at least two days to make arrangements."

"Better start right away."

She smiled, and stood up. "Alright, you've convinced me. Let's go get you that damned ring and I'll make a few calls."

"Do you know where you're going?"

"My sister has a summer place on Fire Island. Savana loves it there."

Hannah took Orient to a locker room near her office. The ring was inside her locker, wrapped in a paper napkin.

"What will you do with it?"

"I'm going to take it to a jewelry expert I know."

"But it's just a cheap thing."

Orient put the ring in his pocket. "Somebody thinks it's worth killing for."

+ + +

Beppo Medicino was a proud man. He had studied his craft in studios from Florence to Venice and at sweltering crucibles in the Middle East, where the old ways of metallurgy were still employed. He even spent time at the gold fields in the land called Nubia by the ancient Egyptians.

Beppo was obsessed by exquisite jewelry. Eschewing diamonds as trite, Beppo preferred to work with carved lapis, emeralds, and rubies. But most of all Beppo loved gold. He could identify thirty two distinct types of the precious metal, including point of origin.

Beppo considered himself a modern day Bernini, and his work attested to it.

However the rest of the world had yet to discover this. Partially because Beppo would rarely consent to sell his most favored pieces. And he favored them all.

Orient always enjoyed visiting Beppo's studio. The loft was crammed with sculpted objects, abstract designer jewelry, small figures and shapes, signet rings, bracelets: all fashioned from gold. While he admired the works, Orient had never attempted to buy any of them, which endeared him to Beppo.

"Well, well, look what the dog dragged in," Beppo greeted, arms spread. "I can't believe you took so long to come visit this poor, broken down jeweler."

Orient smiled. In his yellow silk scarf, purple cashmere sweater, twill trousers, and handmade Italian boots, the Beppo looked far from broken down. His shock of white hair was set off by a deep tan that he maintained by frequent trips to St. Thomas and St. Barts, which he liked to call his 'religious retreats'.

"I dropped by to get your professional opinion." Orient said.

Beppo sighed, his round face forlorn. "I should have known. Nobody comes to see me socially anymore.'

Orient lifted his hands. "It's a matter of respect maestro. Who else in New York has the expertise. Tiffany? Harry Winston? Mario Buccellatti?"

Beppo covered his ears. "Don't even mention the names of these philistines in my house. These aren't jewelers, they're clerks. Experts? Please. They couldn't tell a Miriam Haskell bracelet from a hula hoop."

He gave Orient an exasperated smile and took his arm. "Owen, my dear friend, whatever brings you down here, it's good to see you again. Come inside. I'll make espresso."

Orient accepted gratefully. It gave him time to browse Beppo's latest work. He noticed some of it was influenced by early Egyptian tomb art.

"Think of Nefertiti on mushrooms," Beppo explained, bringing over a tray. "So, tell me, are you still doing medical research?"

"Yes, but I may be a practicing physician soon."

"Good. All my doctors are good for are pills. I never die and I never get well." He waved his hand grandly. "I am the last of a kind. There's no one willing to sacrifice for their art anymore. Used to be you shouldn't sell out—now everybody wants to cash in."

Orient sipped Beppo's espresso which was excellent. He knew better than to interrupt. Beppo would get to the point in his own time.

"These corporate people talk about putting me on the internet, web sites, PayPal, somebody looks at a picture, pushes a button, buys my art without even a handshake, or me looking this person in the eye and realizing, maybe I shouldn't sell him my work."

He leaned closer and peered at Orient with intense brown eyes. "Maybe this person is not Beppo worthy." He slapped his knee for emphasis. "Oh no, all these people think about is money, money. So I stay offline. You want to buy my work, you come here, look close at what I do, and I look close at you. When you buy a piece of art, it's like a marriage."

Orient said nothing, but he did know Beppo's pieces commanded a hefty dowry.

Beppo sat back and drained his coffee. "So my friend, what is this professional opinion you wish from me?"

Orient took the crudely wrapped ring from his pocket, and gave it to Beppo.

He examined it briefly, tarnished silver with a thin pearl top, and handed it back. "My professional opinion, throw it in the garbage.'

"I wish I could but it's important." Orient pointed at the cracked surface. "Is it possible there's something underneath?'

"We find out in a minute.'

 Beppo went to a nearby workbench and turned on the overhead light. He took a few moments to select the correct tool, then gently pried the cracked white pearl apart. "You may be right. I think there's something there, but I have to destroy this. Whoever put this piece of crap here should be deported to Antarctica."

"Whatever you have to do. I trust you implicitly."

"Now let's see..." Beppo muttered as he removed the surface of the ring. "... yes it's pearl but so cheap... Ah-hah look at this, oh my, I need my magnifier."

The white-haired jeweler crouched over the object, blocking Orient's view, but he could follow Beppo's progress verbally. "Hmnn, nice work there, but you don't fool Beppo, yes I see now what you did here. Very tricky stuff, good craftsman, but you know what? Now we lift the curtain eh?"

He turned to Orient. "Here comes the delicate part. Somebody who knew what they were doing, put a thin layer of silver over the ring, which is gold underneath. How much gold? we're gonna find out, okay?"

"It's your call, Beppo."

"Good, because I'm into this now. It's a challenge. Miscalculate and we could deface the whole thing. Ready?"

Orient wasn't sure, but he nodded.

"Fine, now I need my gloves, my goggles, and my little eraser."

Orient watched him don a pair of thin rubber gloves, adjust a pair of round goggles over his eyes, then take the top off what appeared to be a large, felt-tipped pen. But the oversized tip held no ink. Instead Beppo dipped the tip into a jar of bluish liquid he had brought to the workbench from his refrigerator. Then he started to gently brush the wet tip across the silver surface of the ring.

Very soon Orient saw the dull glow of gold appear on the side of the ring. He also saw a symbol which had been obscured by the silver X. It was a six pointed star formed by two triangles, that had been precisely cut into the soft metal. In the center of the star was a tiny black stone.

The work went slowly, and Beppo paused for an espresso break. One side of the ring, and part of the other had been completely cleaned of its silver coat.

"It's a special acid I'm using, only works on silver. I got it diluted way down and look," he held up the frayed remnants of the pen tip. "I need another eraser already. Lucky I got three dozen."

Orient watched his friend at work, silently admiring Beppo's fierce concentration on his task. Another hour passed before both sides of the ring were cleaned. The symbols on each side were identical. A six pointed star with a tiny black stone in the center.

It took longer to clear off the top. Every ten minutes Beppo would dip the ring into a bowl of water, which Orient provided from the kitchen area. After each use, he would refill the bowl with fresh water.

"Acid is acid, even if it's dilute," Beppo explained, "we're taking the renaissance route."

When the silver layer was finally removed, Orient saw that carved in the gold surface was an eight pointed star, enclosed within a circle.

"You know what I think this is?" Beppo said, examining the tiny black stones through a jeweler's loupe. "I think it's the Seal of Solomon." He turned and looked at Orient. "I mean I think it's the real thing."

"What makes you think so?"

"The metal itself. This is pure Nubian gold like you can't find for five thousand years and believe me I tried hard. You know what? I bet it comes from King Solomon's lost mines."

"The symbols are definitely those of the Seal," Orient said, but without solid evidence..."

Beppo lifted his hand. "Then we got the little stones. They're special. Black diamonds. But not from here. These little black gems are *meteorites*. A small percentage of meteors contain crystals, called pallasites. Very rare. In the gem world they're known as peridots. Even rarer, sometimes the pressure and heat of entry, makes them diamond-hard, they're called 'detonation diamonds' in the trade.

"You're sure they're pallasites?"

Beppo handed Orient the ring, and his jeweler's loupe. Through the high magnification glass Orient saw that each of the stones each had a similar snaky cracked line, as thin as a gossamer web hair, running through it.

"Those lines are a sure indicator of a pallasite. But these boys are much harder than usual, they'll cut glass, like a diamond." To illustrate he took a small hand mirror and ran the side of the ring along the glass, leaving a definite cut mark.

"Okay, we know the ring is made of very old, very pure gold, the stones on the side are likely from a meteorite, and the craftsmanship is perfect," Orient said. "That doesn't prove it's the authentic Seal of Solomon. Alchemists have been seeking the Seal for thousands of years."

"And they never found it." Beppo said, "Why? Because it was encased in crap. Doesn't it tell you something—that some ancient metallurgist spent the better part of a year, working the silver to disguise the gold? This wasn't amateur hour. This guy was a master. Do it wrong and the ring is gone."

"You would make a great lawyer. But workmanship doesn't necessarily prove authenticity. I do believe it belonged to a practitioner of the occult. And that it is very old."

"This is why you are a scientist and I am an artist. I work on *intuition*."

Orient had never mentioned the nature of his scientific research, so he kept quiet. Beppo was entitled to his ego.

"You've been a great help Beppo, how can I repay you?"

The jeweler didn't hesitate. "Let me make a wax cast of the ring. So I can create a beautiful copy."

Orient was surprised the request.

"It won't take that long to make the cast. I can give the ring back to you in a few days."

"That works. But do me one more favor."

"Just ask."

"Make a copy for me as well. I'll pay for the gold.'

"On the house. I'm going to do a classic lost wax casting. With real bee's wax."

Orient checked his cell phone and remembered his appointment with Andy Jacobs.

"I'm due uptown. I'll be back tomorrow afternoon."

Beppo beamed, showing straight white teeth against his tan. "Next time, we'll have lunch, I'll make *penne arrabiati.*"

+ + +

Andy Jacobs was waiting in the back room of P.J. Clarke's, when Orient arrived.

"Let's get goin', Owen," the ex-senator brayed, employing the persistent bit of wit he had employed since Orient was a boy.

Lately it had stopped bothering Orient. Perhaps age had something to do with it, he reflected, both his and that of the Senator, whose blunt vitality belied his eighty plus years. Andy's mane of white hair and bullfrog scowl gave him the manner of a hanging judge, but Orient knew him to be a highly honorable and just man. He had been Orient's mentor since the death of his parents in a jungle plane crash many years past. .

"Sorry I'm late, I was all the way downtown."

"I don't suppose you're having a burger," Andy said, studying the limited menu.

"Too early. The spinach salad is always good."

Andy ordered a cheeseburger, Orient the salad, and when the waiter left Andy leaned closer.

"I take it you have a problem to discuss."

Orient hesitated. "Well I have good news and bad news."

"Let's hear it all.'

Orient began by telling Andy about his interview with Hannah and his tentative acceptance.

"Well Owen, I couldn't be happier for you. Man should be working at his chosen profession. You're a healer. Not too many of those." He paused and fixed Orient with his mournful gaze. "Now let's hear the bad news.'

Explaining the events of the past few days without revealing too much of the occult details proved difficult. However Andy Jacobs did know the general nature of his research, which he called 'E.S.P', so he was able to understand that the murders Orient described were occult related. He seemed especially distressed that Sybelle's home had been invaded and her assistant killed. "It could have been Sybelle," he declared between bites of his burger, washed down by a draft beer. "Much as I disapprove of her, I've always liked the woman personally."

Orient shrugged. "Right now we have a stalker problem, but I'm betting that we'll have a police problem pretty soon. I'm connected to three homicides."

"Only circumstantially," Andy said firmly, "they have no hard evidence."

"Yes, but a homicide investigation wouldn't sit too well with the directors of St. Luke's Hospital."

"True enough Owen. " He drummed his stubby fingers on the checkered tablecloth.

"My advice would be to take a vacation until things settle. You did say the board over there will take at least three, four weeks to decide. And if I know committees, they'll take even more."

Orient considered it. He could use a week out of New York. The thought of Sybelle left alone gave him pause. No doubt she'd scream bloody hell if she got the idea he was staying in the city for her sake. But he intended to stick around anyway.

"You thinking about Sybelle?" Andy drawled.

Orient smiled. "You must be psychic, Senator.'

"I just know you. And you're not the kind to leave a friend behind. In this case, nobility could backfire."

"Always does, that's why it's noble."

Andy snorted. "Tell me how I can help."

"Well I could use a place to store all my research files, and some computer equipment, in case I do decide to take a vacation."

"Bring it to my New York office. I've got a spare room"

"Other than that, I'll try to keep a low profile."

"I'll have my sources check these homicides from my end," Andy said, snatching the check. "I hope you have a good dinner tonight. You missed a fine burger."

+ + +

Andy was prophetic. Sybelle called and asked him to join her at Odeon. Orient always enjoyed the unpretentious, Parisian look of the place, and the lively characters around the bar.

"I needed to meet someplace upbeat," Sybelle said, after they'd ordered. "I went to poor Lena's funeral this morning."

It was then realized that Sybelle's choice of black for the occasion had nothing to do with fashion.

"I'm sorry," he said, "I know she was with you a long time."

"Seven years, we got to be friends..." She choked back a sob.

The drinks arrived and Sybelle raised her glass. "To Lena Modena. One of the finest ladies I've ever met."

Orient sipped his wine. Neither of them mentioned the cause of Lena's death, but it hovered like black wings over his thoughts.

"Hannah told me you convinced her to take a vacation." Sybelle said after a few moments. "How did you do it? She's a bit of a workaholic."

"I didn't convince her, Savana did. Hannah realized she needed time with her daughter."

"She's taking her sister Nan's place out on Fire Island."

"I had a talk with Andy today. He thinks I could use some time away."

Sybelle beamed. "I've just had a brilliant idea. Why don't you and I go to Fire Island?"

"I think we'd be intruding..."

"No, darling, not to Nan's place. They're in the Pines. My place is in Cherry Grove."

"Your place?"

"Well, yes, dear. I love it out there. Especially late in the season when there's few people around."

Orient hesitated. It did make sense. He could get away and keep an eye on Sybelle at the same time.

"Are you in or not, darling?"

Orient nodded. "All in. When do you want to leave?"

"Let's have dinner first, I'm starved."

Orient was grateful for the gift that had just dropped in his lap, but he couldn't help wondering about the downside. He was wary of fate these days.

Abruptly, a silent fist smacked the table, spilling water, alcohol and appetizers everywhere. They both stared in stunned silence at the debris.

Sybelle's plump red lips formed a silent O. After a moment she looked at Orient wide-eyed.

"What in hell was *that*, darling?"

A waiter rushed over. "Is everything okay over here?"

"Yes, I think so," Sybelle said, dabbing a napkin on her wet dress. "Was it some sort of earthquake?"

The waiter stared at her in disbelief. "I don't believe so ma'm. Uh, see, everyone else seems alright."

Orient looked around. True enough, the other diners were staring at them curiously from neatly set tables. Reflexively he checked his watch, it read 9:02. He also went receptive, senses dowsing for signs of hypernormal residue. He found them, lingering like noxious fumes after an explosion. But the actual impact had occurred some distance away.

Sybelle waited until the busboy reset the table, then leaned closer to Orient.

"Tell me darling, I sense you're probing. Are we being attacked?"

"Not really," Orient took a deep breath and drew back. "What we felt was an aftershock."

"Aftershock? You mean like a nuclear bomb?"

"Almost exactly like a nuclear bomb. Someone generated ritual energy, and sent it back against itself, like charged atoms in collision."

"But why us, why here?"

"Nothing personal this time. We just happen to be in the loop. The energy follows paths of least resistance. Paths created by past attacks."

Just then their dinner arrived. Sybelle had ordered grilled salmon and a Cesar salad,

Orient had opted for a salad Nicoise, but he broke his fast and joined Sybelle with a glass of white wine.

"I think I lost my appetite," Sybelle said in hushed tones.

Orient smiled. "I have faith you'll find the inner resources."

"I hope you're not going to make fun of me out at Fire Island," She pouted.

Since being freed of her psychic predator, Sybelle had regained weight. Her chubby features glowed pink beneath her frizzy red hair and her dark eye shadow framed clear green eyes.

Orient lifted his glass. "What really matters is that you're healthy."

Sybelle sipped her wine then stared thoughtfully into her glass. "Owen that aftershock was extremely powerful. Do you have any idea what we're dealing with?"

"No," he said softly, "but I'm afraid that sooner or later, I'll find out."

Chapter 15

Moe Klein had an acid stomach from the donuts he'd eaten at Jake's office.

He took the subway uptown to sixty eighth and walked to the nineteenth precinct on sixty seventh between Lexington and Third Avenue. The five story building looked like a schoolhouse with its red brick and blue window frames.

Even with his FBI credentials, security was tight, and when he surrendered his Ruger LCP, he could tell the police guard was amused.

Fuck him, Moe thought moving to the stairway. Macho asshole thinks firepower trumps good investigative work. Then he wonders why he's still in uniform. Fuming all the way, he took the stairs to the third floor.

Except for a few computers, Homicide Division wasn't very impressive. Detective Wagner's office was a large cubicle, and his desk was loaded with the usual stacks of files. Although Moe had called ahead, Wagner wasn't in.

Moe went over to a snack dispenser and put in a dollar for a Coca -ola. When he pushed the button nothing came out. In frustration he went for a ginger ale instead. Anything to settle his stomach.

He was considering a second trip to the snack machine when Wagner appeared, his blue shirt sweat stained, and his pin-striped suit trousers wrinkled. Only his brown, carefully combed hair stayed firmly in place.

"You're here," he said by way of greeting.

"Like I promised an hour ago."

Wagner ignored the attempt at humor. "I've got the Appelegate file you requested," he said, checking the various piles on his desk. Finally he located the file, and tossed it to Moe.

"What about the recording?"

"What recording?"

"You know, the 911 call."

Wagner let out an exasperated sigh. "That's gonna take some humping."

Moe hesitated, mind sifting his options. He could pull rank, which would only make Wagner more obstinate and uncooperative. Or he could use his noodle.

"Jesus, you must have a shit load of cases," Moe said, waving his hand at the cluttered desk. "How many guys do you have helping you?"

"You're looking at him," Wagner said, his beleaguered tone telling Moe he'd struck a nerve.

"No shit? Just you on this murder?"

"Not just this one. I caught another stiff. Second in two days, can you believe it?"

"Shooter?"

"No. Perp broke her neck."

Moe shook his head. "Man, how do you handle it? You need a vacation."

Wagner opened his desk drawer, revealing a bottle. "Here's my vacation. Care for a snort?"

It was early for Moe, and his stomach was still acting up, but he smiled.

"Why not?"

Wagner eyed the open door then poured a shot into a paper cup which he passed to Moe.

"Don't let the bastards grind you down," Moe toasted.

"Amen." Wagner said mournfully.

Moe sipped his drink. It was vodka. When it hit his stomach he shivered.

Wagner, noticing, said, "Nice."

"No orange juice?"

"Ruins the flavor."

Moe went for the closer. "Who would've thought it'd be illegal to smoke in a police station?"

Wagner half laughed, half snorted in agreement. "Shit. You're not as bad as most FBI guys. Act like they're appointed by Jesus on high."

"That certainly wouldn't apply in my case."

Wagner missed the joke. He drained his cup and tossed it into the wastebasket at his feet. There were other cups in the basket.

"There's a fifty-fifty chance they're shutting down my department," Moe said.

"Sorry about that. Good thing about murder, there's always a market. But they're cutting budgets everywhere. Right now I've got two hot homicides and no partner."

Moe nodded. "Any suspects on the new one?"

"Zero. Except for the broad who owns the place. She's a weird type."

"Weird how?"

"She some kind of psychic. Could be the killing was a cult thing."

"Oh yeah? What's the woman's name. Maybe she's got a bunco sheet."

"Good idea, hadn't thought of that. Thanks Klein," he opened the file on his desk.

"Yeah, Sybelle Lean, that's some name ain't it?"

"Ain't it though," Moe said , crumpling his cup and dropping it in the basket. "Look I've got to get back to my office. Thanks for pulling the Applegate file for me. If you get a chance I'd appreciate a copy of that 911 recording."

"Sure, try to have it for you in the morning," Wagner said affably

Moe left the building in a hurry. He stopped at a luncheonette on Lexington Avenue and ate a bowl of rice pudding to calm his stomach. Then he took the subway downtown. Along the way he called Jake.

"Jesus, I don't hear from you for six months, now you're all over me like a cheap suit," Jake said, when he answered.

"If it wasn't for cheap suits I'd be naked. Can I come over? I've got something."

"I hope it's something better than donuts this time.'

Moe detoured at Astor Place. He left the subway and walked east to the Second Avenue Deli. He picked up two pastrami sandwiches on rye with mustard and pickles, and two bottles of Doctor Brown's black cherry soda. For himself he bought a bottle of celery tonic. This case is going to destroy my digestion, he thought morosely, hailing a cab.

+ + +

"Pastrami," Jake said suspiciously, "my favorite. This must be a doozy."

"How about the cream soda?"

"Get ye behind me Satan. I'll take a soda but no deal until I know more."

"I need to hack into NYPD homicide.'

"Why not CIA headquarters while we're at it?"

Moe unwrapped the sandwich revealing the pickle. "Come on, NYPD is minor league shit. You remember the lady I asked you to check out."

Jake nodded, sipping his cream soda. "She was a professional psychic as I recall.'

"Her housekeeper was found dead in her town house. Broken neck."

"If you know this, why do you need me?"

"I need to check all homicides in the city area, in the past seven days. Especially stabbings and broken necks."

"The outer boroughs too?"

Moe waved at the array of equipment and assistants behind them. "With this kind of firepower, how long could it take?

Look we can discount crimes of passion, perps already in custody, even the shooters for now. I got a hunch on this one."

"You think it's a stabber?"

"I think it's a pro. Single thrust to the back of the skull. Broken neck... who the hell knows? That's why I need you to check it out."

"Seven days, eh?"

"No more, no less."

Jake sighed. "I'll let you know after I check out this sandwich."

Fortunately he ate half of Moe's as well, sparing the agent a digestive flare. He sat in amazement as Jake devoured the pastrami, pickles and soda without any problem. "You know for a guy your size you can really pack it in."

Jake flashed him an impish grin. "It's my Russian heritage. We're driven to excess."

It was fascinating to watch Jake go about his work, fingers flying over the keyboard. "As it happens the FBI has courtesy access," he muttered, "but we're gonna crash the upstairs bedroom. C'mon Maybelline, show us what you're made of baby."

Without much difficulty, Jake accessed the Applegate File, as well as that of Lena Modena. He put them on separate screens, side by side.

"So let's see, what else do we have in town this week?" Jake said, keeping up a running commentary, as if announcing a ballgame. "Multiple stabbing domestic, domestic shooting, family life in Queens is dangerous, ah, there's a hit, Brooklyn, homicide, single puncture wound, base of the skull."

"Lemme see that," Moe said,

Jake brought up the file on a third screen. "Peter Taegris," originally from Greece, naturalized in sixty-seven, antique dealer, killed Friday night, few hours after Applegate, single knife wound...."

"Antiques, eh? Can you find out if there's any connection to Applegate?"

"Cross reference evidence... that will take time. Well look at this, here's one for you... Some wacko in Soho attacked a young couple, carved an S into the boy's face, broke the girl's nose, then stabbed a pit bull belonging to a passer by. What a freak. Somebody even posted a video on You Tube. I love this shit, let's take a look.'

Moe wanted to tell his friend to stay on point, but he knew he was merely a guest in Jake's world. They watched the shadowed, jumpy video that showed a tall, light haired man walking towards the camera, knife in hand, yelling aggressively. There were two people on the sidewalk behind him. Abruptly a pit bull came into view and attacked the man, who stabbed the dog then heaved the yelping beast aside with relative ease, before he turned and marched quickly away. The clip was less than forty seconds in length.

Jake whistled between his teeth. "Ain't that a bitch. Wouldn't want to meet him on a lonely street."

"Can you run that again?"

Why not?" Jake glanced at him. "Question is why? You got something?"

"Not really sure until I... can you stop it there?"

"There?"

"Back a bit, back, right... there."

It was a shot of the man approaching. His face was obscured but Moe could see the knife. had a long blade. There was something familiar about its shape.

"Can you blow up the knife?"

"Yeah, why?"

"The blade isn't like most daggers. Could be like the one they found behind Applegate's couch."

"I'll print it out for you.'"

As the printer whirred into action Jake idly scanned the man's face, and blew it up. But the pixels broke down before he could get better than a blur.

"What is that on his face?"

Jake moved the cursor. "Here?"

"Yeah. Is that a scar or something?"

"Can't really tell. Pixels were blurred to start with."

"Can you print it out anyway?"

"Why not, it's your pastrami which, I might add, is fast running out."

"Hey, you're the guy who wanted to bring up You Tube. What I really need is to find out is if there's any connection between this Sybelle Lean and her friend the doctor, to these murders. Especially Applegate, and this antique dealer in Brooklyn.

"Is that all?" Jake pensively drummed his fingers on the keyboard. "It'll take time to set up."

"I'll owe you one."

"If you're around that long."

"What does that mean?"

"Make nice with your department head. Bring him pastrami."

"Is that a warning?"

"It's good advice my friend. Don't worry, I'll run both files through the grinder, see if we make a sausage. Call me tomorrow."

+ + +

Moe went to his small office in an anonymous building further downtown that housed the bureau's lesser operatives. He sat at his aging computer and wrote a five-page report on the case he was working on.

He stressed the homicides, but had to skirt around more esoteric details involving the art. He also submitted a request for a new iPhone and a MacBook Pro laptop.

A smart guy gives advice —a genius takes it, Moe thought, pressing *send*.

Chapter 16

D r. Hannah Wylde felt like a young girl again. Actually she wasn't exactly old, she observed, still on the right side of forty. But working hospital hours had a tendency to age one prematurely. And for the first time in years she was taking a real vacation, with her daughter.

Taking a long, deep breath of fresh salt air, she looked out at the curving white sand beach in front of Nan's house. She had envied her sister growing up and now she knew why. While she'd been working her ass off in surgery, Nan had made a killing in entertainment law. At the moment her sister was in Hollywood making yet another million, which left the Fire Island house free. Hannah made a mental note to buy Nan a gift.

The sun was dipping into the ocean, and the distant clouds were layered in shades of pink and gold, above the wind flecked water. Savana came outside to join her on the deck.

"It's so gorgeous out here," she said in hushed tones, taking Hannah's arm.

"Yeah," Hannah murmured, grateful for the moment. It had been a long time since they'd been this close.

"You know I've been thinking, Mom."

"About what?"

"Maybe I should become a lawyer, like Aunt Nan."

"What made you change your mind about marine biology?"

"Well she gets to meet movie actors and rock stars. Right now, she's working on a deal with Mika."

"Who's Mika?"

Savanna giggled, and poked her rib. "He's only one of the biggest selling pop stars in the world."

"Oh, well I guess that makes me the dumbest doctor in the world. How do you know Aunt Nan is working with him anyway?"

"We tweet."

Hannah rolled her eyes. "Of course, I should've guessed."

"I'm getting up early to go running tomorrow, wanna come?"

"I think I'm going to be sleeping in, on my first vacation day in a century. But I'll be on the beach after a late breakfast. We can go swimming if it's not too cold."

"Sounds like a plan."

Hannah heard a ring tone, sounding tinny against the rushing waves.

She expected Savana to pull her Android phone from the pocket of her short, cut off jeans. Instead she reached inside her belt and took out a small cell phone. She turned away from her mother briefly, laughing confidentially about something.

"How many phones do you need these days?" she said, when Savanna hung up.

"Oh, the Android is for tweeting, Facebook, e-mail, downloads, all that stuff. And the Blackphone is just for personal calls and texts. Very few of my friends have the number."

"Well I certainly don't," Hannah said, with mock severity.

"I'll just call your cell and it will record my number. Easy."

"Doesn't look like there's much room in those shorts for two phones," Hannah commented, when Savana finished the call and put away her Blackphone. She regretted saying it immediately. Lighten up, Hannah told herself, you sound like a cranky mom.

"There's a pocket inside these jeans that's just big enough for this little guy," Savana assured, "now I'm biphonal."

They both laughed and Hannah felt better.

They stood outside together until the sun had set, and a chill breeze blew in from the ocean. As darkness fell, the two of them prepared dinner. Later, while Hannah had coffee in the living room, Savana read a book by the light of an old fashioned gas lamp. There were a many such lamps in the house, and well as candles, since the island experienced frequent black outs.

"I miss Jillian."

Hannah looked up from her magazine.

"What did you say baby?'

"I can't believe Jillian would run away. I miss her."

"I'm sorry, dear." Hannah smiled, but the memory of that terrifying night frayed her sense of well being. For the rest of the night the fear rippled through her thoughts like a tattered flag in a cold wind. .

+ + +

As hoped, Hannah enjoyed the luxury of sleeping late, and awoke to the soothing sound of distant waves. The morning mists were burning off and sunlight glinted on the dewy grass around the wooden stairway leading to the beach. Savana was standing at the water's edge, staring at the horizon.

Savana's face brightened when she saw her mother approaching. "Good morning. Isn't it glorious?"

"Absolutely. Have you had breakfast.?"

"Juice and toast, but I *am* getting hungry."

"Good because I'm famished. Come on I'll race you to the stairs."

There were few people on Fire Island during the week and except for a man walking his dog the beach was deserted. They arrived at the stairs out of breath and laughing, and padded barefoot along the wooden planks that formed a walkway between houses. Many of the shops were closed early in the week but there was a café that served breakfast.

Hannah ignored her dietary rules and ordered a short stack, eggs and bacon. Savana had the same and the two of them sat chatting like schoolgirls on an outing.

"Sybelle's friend is handsome isn't he?" Savana said, studying the weathered Black Crowes poster above Hannah's head.

"Which friend is that?"

"Come on mom, you know, the doctor who helped me. Doctor Orient."

"Oh, him, well I suppose he's not bad looking. I hadn't noticed."

"Well, I noticed you looking at him."

Hannah wrinkled her nose. "Listen young lady, what you notice and what's really going on, are not always the same. Did you know he might be coming to work as part of the emergency team?"

"No. But I think it's a neat idea. He's a good doctor."

"How so?"

"I don't know, he has a way of knowing how you feel. I can't explain it."

"Well intuition is part of being a good physician. Only we call it making a calculated choice."

"Calculated risk you mean," Savana teased.

"Just for that you're going swimming with me."

"Mom, you know I don't like cold water."

"It'll wake you up. But not right after this big breakfast. We'll go back to the house and relax."

Savana finally consented to go into the ocean with her. While the water was cold, their bodies adjusted in a few minutes and they splashed in the waves like happy porpoises.

Later they lay on their towels, warming in the sun. Hannah had never felt so close to her daughter.

By the third day on the island, Hannah had nearly shed the tension of the past few months. After breakfast at the café, which had become a daily ritual, they walked back over the salt dried planks to Nan's house. As they approached they heard the phone ringing. Savana ran to answer but by the time she arrived the caller had hung up.

Later that afternoon, she and Savana took a walk along the wet, spongy sand at the ocean's edge. Fire Island was loosely divided into communities with names like Fair Harbor, Saltaire, Seaview, the Pines where they were staying, and an area called Cherry Grove that had a number of colorful restaurants and cafes.

They were nearly there when Hannah spotted an odd couple strolling toward them. The woman was stocky and wore a black, one piece swimsuit that set off her red espadrille sandals, which laced halfway to her pink knees. Large dark glasses obscured most of her face but her frizzy red hair was familiar-as was the lean, lanky man walking beside her, dressed in tan bathing shorts. He was dark, and his longish hair had a distinctive white streak. Even at a distance she could see the intense green eyes inside the sculpted contours of his face.

It was Doctor Orient and her Aunt Sybelle.

"What brings *you* out here?" Hannah said, somewhat surprised.

"I invited Owen to spend a week at my place," Sybelle said. "I called earlier."

"You both look as if Fire Island agrees with you." Orient said.

"We should have come out here sooner." Hannah glanced at Savana who took her hand.

"Well perhaps we can all meet for dinner," Sybelle said, "Owen insists on taking me for forced marches in the afternoon."

"Dinner sounds like fun," Savana said, before Hannah could object, "we've been hermits these last few days.'

"Good, then it's settled. Come over to my place at six. You can't miss it. It's the last house on the beach boardwalk. And it's *red*. Just ask anybody for the *Smith* place."

Savana was beaming for the rest of the afternoon, looking forward to their dinner party.

Hannah pretended she was delighted by the prospect, and in truth she always enjoyed her flamboyant aunt's hospitality. But she really wasn't anxious to spend social time with Doctor Orient. She was only too aware of the attraction, and knew it could complicate her life immensely.

+ + +

Orient felt a bit uncomfortable about dinner. However as Sybelle's houseguest he could hardly object. He knew the root of his discomfort, and that he was reacting like a schoolboy going to the prom. Still, he hadn't had feelings for a woman in quite some time. And Hannah was a very special woman.

Shaking off his thoughts he ran across the sand and splashed into the foaming ocean, diving into the cold shock of an oncoming wave. After a long swim, he ran along the beach to a deserted stretch, and sat at the edge of the restless water. He gazed out at the horizon and emptied his mind of thought, taking long, deep breaths of fresh salt air. As his senses expanded he became aware of a persistent tingle at the base of his brain, like a distant alarm. He looked up and saw gulls circling overhead.

Orient got to his feet and ran back to the red house at the end of the beach, trying to clear the static clinging to his thoughts

The ladies arrived at sunset. Hannah wore a simple black sleeveless dress, with a dark blue silk shawl that highlighted her smoky violet eyes. Savana was more casually attired in a plaid shirt over cut-off jeans.

"Wonderful, we're all here," Sybelle said, "let's go out on the deck, I've made mimosas!"

They sat outside and watched the sun's fiery dive into the steely water, the sky turning deep purple streaked with yellow.

"What a wonderful house Aunt Sibbie," Savana said.

"Thank you darling. It's actually built on the site of Jeramiah Smith's mansion."

"Who's that?"

"Mr. Smith happened to be a murderous scoundrel dear. He made his fortune luring ships to their doom, then killing the crew. He built the first house here in Cherry Grove. Right on these very grounds."

"Was it red?"

"No dear, that was your Aunt Sibbie's idea. Isn't it brilliant?"

Orient and Hannah smiled at each other, as if sharing a secret joke. They both knew Sybelle's flamboyant ways. Then they looked away in mild embarrassment.

"How long have you had this place?" Orient said, trying to steer things into neutral ground. He couldn't help noticing Hannah's long smooth arms, and softly glowing skin... or the graceful line of her neck.

"I bought it some twenty years ago," Sybelle was saying, "well ahead of this insane real estate curve."

"It all started when they phased out rent control," Hannah said, "my nurses can hardly afford to live in the city. Finally I convinced the board to buy a couple of places further uptown, renovate them, and offer our staffers reasonably priced apartments."

Orient was happy to see Hannah had a strong social conscience. Very few doctors or surgeons cared about staff problems. They usually left all that to the human resources office. However he just nursed his mimosa and tried to stay in the background, content to listen to the melodic drift of female conversation.

Sybelle got to her feet, waving her glass at her guests. "Is everyone hungry? I know I am." The sun had fallen and darkness was closing in. They could see house lights strung like dim lanterns along the beachfront as they went inside the spacious living area.

The house was octagonal in shape with the entire top floor given over as a dining and recreational room, with a free

standing kitchen on one side, and two banks of window couch-
es on the other. A low, well stocked bookcase adorned with indoor plants, and a wide Moroccan rug separated the two areas.
All eight sides of the octagon had large windows that afforded
views of both sea and land. On the floor below were the guest
rooms.

Sybelle lit the old-fashioned kerosene lamps placed around
the big room, and asked Orient to help her set up a folding
table, and chairs. She kept the electric light over the stove and
kitchen counter, as she moved back and forth preparing dinner.

"Savana, darling, why don't you choose some nice dinner
music from those CD's over there," she said, pouring herself a
white wine from an open bottle on the counter. "I hope everyone likes fish. It's absolutely fresh. Owen I made a special salad
just for you."

"Doctor, are you a vegan or something?" Savana said, from
the CD player.

Orient smiled. "Please call me Owen," he said, suddenly the object of everyone's attention. "Yes, I am a vegan... or
something. I did eat fish occasionally, but I'm back on the good
foot."

On that, the sound of Strawberry Fields by the Beatles
floated across the room.

"I picked something retro," Savana said.

"Doctor, you must know there are some amino acids we
can only acquire from fish or meat," Hannah said, with a note
of challenge in her voice.

Orient met her eyes. "We may acquire them, but do we
*re*quire them?" he asked quietly.

"Most nutritionists..."

"...mostly disagree. As far back as recorded time we know
every tribe, every cult, every warrior, had their own ideas
concerning diet. The ancient Egyptian high priests were vegans. The Hebrews had strict dietary laws. Swahili tribesmen in

Africa drink a mixture of cow's blood and urine. Ultimately it comes down to what works for your particular engine. "

"Well put darling," Sybelle said. She proudly lifted a serving plate, bearing a large, crispy fish. "But tonight this family tribe is having sea bass, spiced with ginger and sweetened with honey."

Hannah leaned closer to Orient and lowered her voice. "You won't object if I devour Sybelle's sea bass. She's a superb cook."

He caught a faint trace of perfume. "Vegans get bad press," he confided, "I never picket at the dinner table."

She laughed, and Savana looked at her mother curiously as they sat down to dinner.

"And for you, darling, my own special avocado, tomato, arugula salad, topped with grilled tofu and my secret sesame barbecue sauce," Sybelle announced, coming back with a large salad bowl."

"Mnnn, smells good," Savana said, "I may become a vegan myself."

"No need for that, dear, I made plenty." She struck a match and lit the candles on the table. "Let's bow our heads and give thanks. And everybody please dig in."

Sybelle was in rare form that night. She wore a floor length red dress with blue flowers and the sun had given her plump cheeks a rosy sheen. She entertained them with gossip and anecdotes until abruptly, the music shut off, as did the kitchen lights.

Chapter 17

The man with the zig zag scar knew people were staring at him.

Secretly pleased, he strolled along the beach, his expression impassive. Both women and men admired the tall, muscular figure whose white skin seemed impervious to the rays of the sun, He might have been an ancient Greek statue carved of veined marble.

With the stress on ancient, Hans noted smugly. He had the physique of a thirty year old athlete, but he had been born a century before.

However, today he had more important concerns than common vanity. He had come to Fire Island to finish the game with Doctor Orient and his fat friend, the psychic.

Americans are naïve and stupid, Hans observed, scanning the crowded beach for a glimpse of a plump female with curly red hair. It had been no trouble tracking Sybelle Lean. The woman had announced she was departing for Cherry Grove on her Facebook page.

Now it was merely a question of finding just where she was. No doubt her doctor friend wouldn't be far behind. Hans walked from Cherry Grove to the Pines and back. He could only reconnoiter once. He was too noticeable for a second tour.

After a long swim he left the beach and followed the boardwalk to the dock where his boat was anchored. *Valkyrie* belonged to the Long Island cell controlled by Valka.

The single crewman on board was enjoying a beer on deck when Hans arrived. He stiffened and set the bottle down.

Hans nodded. "Carry on, Alex. "

The young man relaxed, obviously relieved. He was about twenty seven, an experienced sailor with sun bleached hair, blue eyes and a casual, informal demeanor.

"Bring me one of those," Hans called over his shoulder, "I'm going below to change."

The beer was waiting on the table, when Hans emerged from his shower. Alex is a competent young man, he mused, as he took a long pull of cold brew. But he might have a problem which was yet to be revealed. He'd noticed that Alex seemed to spend a bit too much time staring at the gay boys who populated the Grove.

No matter, Hans thought, draining the bottle, either way it would make little difference. After he had dressed Hans grabbed his shoulder bag and went up on deck, where Alex was comfortably sipping a fresh beer. The crewman got up as Hans came outside. "As you were, Alex," he said with a paternal smile. "I want you to stay aboard ship while I'm gone. Do you understand?"

"Aye, sir," Alex said, "stay aboard. How long will you be away?"

The question annoyed him and the pale fire in his eyes caused Alex to shrink back an inch. "I really can't say. Could be an hour, could be four. However long it is, you will remain on board and have the boat ready to cast off."

"Aye, aye," Alex said, but Hans was already moving down the gangway. The young sailor watched Hans for a long time before he vanished from view. Only then did he settle back in the deck chair, and pull out his cell phone.

The sun was starting its descent and the boarded pathways were crowded with colorfully dressed gay men, and a smattering of women in designer outfits. It was cocktail hour and most of the residents were on their decks, or gathering at the few local restaurants that served alcohol. Hans found a place with a small bar and ordered a beer. He left a large tip to encourage the bartender's cooperation.

"I've been looking for my friend's place all day," he said when the bartender brought him a second beer. "You happen to know a lady called Sybelle Lean, kind of plump, red hair...?" The bartender was a muscular man in a red tank top. His smooth, tanned face, and long, well cut black hair, spoke of expensive grooming. "Hmnn, actually I do know the lady you're speaking of." He leaned close to Hans and looked into his eyes seductively. Whatever he saw made him draw back a notch. He picked up a glass and held it up to the light. "But I'm not sure where she lives. I'll ask around. Drop by in a couple of hours."

Making a mental note to correct the bartender's attitude when he had more time, Hans continued along the boarded walkway until he spotted a sundries shop and bought a pair of sunglasses.

He had better luck at the next place he stopped. The waiter was a flamboyant youth wearing several earrings, a pierced eyebrow, eye shadow and rouged lips. Unlike the bartender, this one didn't seem to pick up any strange vibes, being too busy preening. Hans was satisfied the new sunglasses veiled his contempt.

"Oh, *her*, she's fabulous," the boy said, voice high above the Lady Gaga track playing in the background. "And she has the most *incredible* house. It's this octagonal red thing, over at the end of the beach? You can't miss it."

Hans nodded and left a nice tip, suppressing the urge to break his pretty jaw. It wouldn't do to bring undue attention. He'd learned that only too well. But as he strode toward the beach he felt the power of the Spear burning inside him, and knew its power would be unleashed that night.

The sunset sky was streaked with gold and Hans knew that all over the beach, affluent gay men and lesbians were gathering on their decks for cocktails—and most likely the intrusive sow, Sybelle Lean, and her consort were doing the same. From his shoulder bag he took a pair of small, but powerful binoculars made for birdwatchers. He pretended to scan the sea then turned his lenses to the red house.

It was more than he could wish for. They were all there, the girl, her mother, Orient, and the annoying palm reader. There, making small talk, while he circled for the kill.

Actually he needed Hannah Wylde, and her daughter. He could dispense with the other two. However the logistics were complicated. He couldn't take two hostages back to the boat. And killing the other two would be difficult. With Applegate and the others he had the advantage of surprise. While he might be able to get one, the other posed a problem. He almost wished he had brought a pistol along, although he knew it would create more problems. His dagger was swift and silent.

All he needed was a chance to get close.

A chill was coming off the water and he marched back to the walkway. He ambled about until he found the street entrance to the red house. There was a fence that would be easily traversed, a tiled patio with only one light, but the first floor of the house had a number of separate doors, guest rooms no doubt.

That might be a problem, Hans speculated, moving back to the more commercial area. It was Wednesday, which meant the decadent weekend crowd wasn't around to clog the gears. During the week Cherry Grove became nearly deserted after dinner.

It also meant he had time for a burger and coffee. His quarry wouldn't be going anywhere for a while.

After a spare meal, augmented by a salad and fries, Hans ambled back to the beach. Here and there the local talent eyed him seductively however his days of gay bashing were behind him. He had bigger game in mind.

Although it was dark, Hans could make out a few writhing couples on the shadowed dunes. He ignored them and moved closer to the red house. He could see activity on the second floor.

Abruptly, the lights on the island went out, throwing him into total darkness.

How propitious, Hans thought, waiting for his eyesight to adjust. He could see the dim glow of kerosene lamps in the houses along the beach. Hans waited, surveying the red house. Since the light on the tiled patio was now out, he decided to enter from the street side. But before he started back to the walkway, Hans saw two figures emerge from the beach side of the house, a man and a woman.

Knowing he wouldn't be recognized, Hans moved within striking distance.

Strolling directly towards him were Dr. Hannah Wylde and Owen Orient.

Chapter 18

Hannah was enjoying herself thoroughly at dinner. She was also beginning to feel better about Doctor Orient. He was courteous without being stuffy, knowledge-able without being pompous, witty without being malicious and strong without being a macho asshole. Savanna also seemed to have taken to him, listening attentively when he spoke, which was seldom. As usual, Sybelle was on center stage and she made the most of it.

Then the lights went out.

"Don't worry, black outs are a weekly occurrence around here," Sybelle announced cheerfully, "Wreaks hell on the refrigerators and then we have to lug supplies back from the mainland."

"The candles and kerosene lamps are actually quite nice," Hannah ventured.

Orient nodded, his chiseled features outlined sharply in the candlelight.

"How are we going to get home in the dark?" Savana said, a note of panic straining her voice.

Hannah picked up on her daughter's fear immediately. Despite her daughter's seeming resumption of normal life, she knew the effect of the past weeks had left Savana a bit skittish. Even as a child she had been afraid of the dark. Hannah would have to rock her to sleep in her arms.

"We'll be alright," Hannah assured, "I'm certain Aunt Sybelle can lend us a flashlight.'

"No," Savana said flatly.

Orient smiled at her. "The power outage is probably tempo-rary," he said calmly. "Let's wait it out and see what happens."

"Do we have enough candles?" Savana asked, her expression like a little girl kept after school.

Sybelle stood and patted Savana reassuringly. "Well, this shouldn't prevent us from having dessert. Coffee, anyone?"

But after key lime pie, coffee, and another cognac, the lights still hadn't returned.

"Problem is, I'm expecting an important call at my sister's place," Hannah said, "I didn't trust the cell phone connections out here."

Sybelle rolled her eyes. "Are you kidding? This is tweet central. If cell phones were blocked, people would be swimming back to Long Island."

Hannah could see that Savana looked intimidated by the prospect of a long walk on a dark, deserted beach. For that matter so am I, Hannah thought, putting an arm around her daughter.

"I have an extra guest room," Sybelle said brightly. "Savana can sleep here and Owen can take the flashlight and escort you home."

Savana was visibly relieved by the suggestion. In a way, Hannah liked the idea. It would give her a chance to complete her assessment of her new Trauma Team member. But she knew she was rationalizing. She felt a definite attraction to the lean, soft spoken physician with eyes as green and deep as the sea. Listen at me, she thought, trying to keep her expression neutral, I sound like a schoolgirl's diary.

Sybelle turned. "Is that alright with you, Owen?"

"Sounds like a plan."

"But you guys don't have to leave right away," Savana said, no longer distressed.

Hannah looked at Orient. "That depends on Owen.'

Orient's lips curled into a curious smile. It occurred to Hannah it was the first time she'd used his given name, and she felt her skin flush. Thankfully it was too dark for anyone to notice.

"We can start any time you say," he said casually.

They lingered a few more minutes, Hannah starting to wish the power would return.

But it stayed dark, and after a few more minutes searching for a flashlight, they were standing on the deck, waving their goodbyes.

"Be careful, you two," Sybelle called from the doorway. "Come Savana, let's play Scrabble."

They took the stairs to the beach, Orient lighting the steps. He switched the flashlight off when the reached the edge of the water. They both took off their shoes and headed for the neighboring community, the Pines, a little over a mile away. Neither of them said much as they walked, and shortly, her eyes adjusted to the dark and she was able to see that the area was largely deserted, except for a couple sitting on the sand ahead, and a tall man walking toward the water. As they continued past the couple, she saw them kiss.

"Good night for stargazing," Orient said, his eyes on the cloudless sky.

The crescent moon was a curved silver blade surrounded by glittering gems. Their sharp light glinted off the lapping waves as they walked.

Orient pointed upward. "That's Mars over there. Actually does look red. There's Saturn, and Jupiter is very bright...'

"Are you an astronomer as well?" Hannah asked, with mock disbelief.

Orient smiled sheepishly and nodded. "An amateur, really. But I am fascinated with this universe of ours."

At that moment he seemed like a little boy. Impulsively Hannah moved closer and kissed him. She was almost as startled as he was. "I'm sorry if, I just wanted to thank you..." she said awkwardly, stumbling over her words in embarrassment.

"And I want to thank you," he said, returning the kiss. His lips lingered on hers for what seemed to be a long time, dispersing her discomfort, her fears, everything except the electric warmth of his embrace.

Orient gently pulled away and looked at her. "This...'

Before he could say more he stiffened, and gasped softly.

+ + +

Exultation pounding through labored lungs, Hans loped across the darkened beach, his lifeless prize draped over his shoulder. He could count on at least an hour start before anyone would look for him. Probably should have killed the bitch, Hans speculated, but he needed her alive to set the trap.

His diagonal route across the sand took him close to the wooden walkway that led to the dock. He paused to deposit his human baggage against the beach stairs, then went up to assess the traffic. There was very little. However, he was still one landing away from the dock.

After scanning the path ahead for stray lovers Hans heaved his limp human bundle over his shoulder, and trudged on. The body was heavier than he thought, or... he was getting older. He barely suppressed a laugh.

Everything had conspired to help him accomplish his mission, right down to the power outage, Hans mused smugly, now within sight of the dock, and the lights of the *Valkyrie*. He paused, scoped the area, hefted his burden, and marched to the gangway as if delivering a sack of potatoes.

As soon as he boarded he knew something wasn't right. He set the body on the padded seats along the stern.

"Alex?"

There was a scuttling sound below. Moments later a thin young man wearing an unbuttoned shirt, emerged from below, zipping the fly on his designer jeans.

"Oh hi," the young man said, averting his eyes. "I'm Ricky."

Cold fury stiffened Hans' spine as Alex climbed on deck. Alex too, avoided Hans' withering glare.

"Start the engine," he said, voice low and calm.

Alex quickly ducked back inside.

"Who's that?" Ricky mumbled, staring at the blanket wrapped body.

"Oh, it's nothing." Hans said genially, coming closer. "My friend had too much to drink. Look there, Ricky, can you see?" The young man gaped drunkenly at the place he pointed out. "I..."

It was instant.

Hans caught him as he fell, the dagger still lodged in the base of his skull. He tugged the blade free, and dumped the body over the side at the same time Alex started the engine, covering the splash. Then he quickly cast off, and signaled Alex to get underway. Just then the dock lights came back on.

Hans went below, his expression wreathed with benign disappointment.

"I believe I told you to stay aboard."

Alex concentrated on steering the boat between the other vessels anchored off Fire Island.

"I did stay aboard," he said evenly. "I called a pal to join me for a beer."

Hans shook his head. "I don't like strangers on my boat."

Alex half turned. "I thought Valka..." when he saw the icy wrath in Hans' eyes, his voice faltered

"Just keep a steady course," Hans said quietly. He had disposed of matters so efficiently Alex was hardly aware of the surprise package on deck. The fool was too mired in his own guilt to notice. But he needed Alex for the moment. The best thing was to keep him at the wheel—and in the dark—as long as possible.

The trip to the mainland was uneventful. The power on Long Island was still on, and the strings of lights along the shore were sharp contrast to Fire Island's shadowy waters. He would have to take care he wasn't seen, when he transferred his package from the boat to the Mercedes.

By the time they reached the dock where the *Valkyrie* was to be moored, Hans had formed a crude plan.

"I'll secure the boat," he told Alex. "Bring the car around and open the trunk. Here are the keys."

Alex moved off the boat quickly, but he couldn't help but see the human bundle still resting on the deck seat. However he was sufficiently cowed by his own sins that he wordlessly hurried off to complete his task.

Hans anchored the craft, and made sure his trophy was well covered, before he effortlessly lifted the motionless body over one shoulder and moved down the short gangplank to meet the approaching Mercedes.

After depositing the body in the trunk, Hans got into the passenger's seat and gave Alex the address of his safe house in Brooklyn.

They said very little for the first half hour. Finally Alex spoke. "I hope you didn't misunderstand about Ricky. He's an old friend."

He won't be getting older, Hans thought. "Of course," he said.

"I'd appreciate it if you didn't mention this to Valka. You know how she can be."

She can be vicious towards gays, Hans thought. But he nodded, his expression thick with macho camaraderie. "Believe me," he assured solemnly. "Valka won't know anything about what happened tonight."

It was nearly midnight when they reached the safe house. Hans went up and unlocked the outer door, then returned to fetch his trophy from the trunk. With minimum effort he lifted the lifeless body over his shoulder and carried it up to his second floor apartment. There, he carefully placed the body on the rug that concealed his occult pentacle.

Then he turned off the light, locked the door, and went back downstairs to where Alex waited in the Mercedes.

"Well that's finally done," Hans said with forced affability, "I'm ready for a drink. How about you?"

Alex seemed relieved. "Yeah, that would be cool."

Hans directed him to a dive called Gangway, in what was formerly Hell's Kitchen, but had been renamed Clinton, for gentrifying purposes. The bar catered to gays, which put Alex at ease. By his second drink he was confiding in Hans.

"Valka's such a stickler for discipline," he said, words slightly slurred. "Know what I'm saying?"

Hans nodded solemnly.

"I like taking care of the boat and I'm good at it."

"Of course.'

"Can I ask you a question?"

"Who was that we brought from Cherry Grove?"

Hans shrugged. "A candidate."

"Candidate? For what?"

"Elevation."

Alex blinked, blue eyes blurred with tequila. "Really? You mean like the next level?"

Hans smiled benignly. "I mean that exactly, the next level."

"So can you tell me anything about it?"

Hans looked around. The relative quiet was punctuated by the raucous laughter, the juke box, and loud voices fishing for attention. He motioned Alex closer.

"Not here." He inclined his head toward the door behind the bar, leading to the men's room.

Alex looked around and nodded.

If Alex was a spy he'd last about thirty seconds, Hans thought.

"I'll go first," he said.

He found an empty stall and waited for Alex to arrive, amusing himself by reading the crude rhymes and bawdy epigrams scrawled on the walls. He was perfectly calm, and certain of what needed to be done.

When Alex entered the men's room he checked his reflection then looked for Hans, who smiled and held the door open. Once he was inside the stall Hans locked the door, and kissed him on the lips. Alex was surprised but pleased. "I never thought..."

They were last three words he spoke before Hans snapped his neck.

He left Alex sitting on the toilet, leaning against the wall. Just another drunk passed out, Hans thought, pleased with himself.

There was no place for degenerates in the Grand Design.

Chapter 19

The shrill image skidding across the base of his brain, jerked Orient's head aside. Alarmed by the intensity of the distress call, he pulled away from Hannah.

"Sybelle's in trouble." He began trotting back to the red house.

Hannah struggled to keep up. "What's happening?"

"Don't know."

Although aware she was falling behind Orient increased his pace across the damp sand. He sprinted the last forty yards, splashing through the surf to come around to the gated patio.

The gate was open and Orient could see light as he bounded up the stairs. When he dashed inside he saw a small table and vase were overturned. Then he saw Sybelle.

She was lying on one side her hands, ankles and mouth bound with duct tape. One side of her face was a swollen bruise. Orient found a knife in the kitchen and freed her ankles and hands, then gripped the end of the tape covering her mouth and yanked.

"Owwwdamn! Owen he took Savana! Find him, he can't be far."

"Who took her?"

The blond man with the scar—from Marrakech."

Orient knew who she meant, but had a moment of doubt. "Are you alright?"

"Damn it Owen, go after him."

Hannah burst in breathlessly. "What happened?"

"Take care of her," Orient said, rushing outside.

He took the beach exit and started trotting along the side of Sybelle's house, scanning ahead with his flashlight. Which route would he take if he was dragging, or carrying someone?

160   *Frank Lauria*

Obviously he'd want to avoid the walkway, so the darkened beach made sense. There weren't many places to go unnoticed, especially when the lights returned. So he had to be taking her to a house in the area, or... a boat?'

As Orient angled toward the dock, his flashlight caught a bright glint. Bending to pick it up he saw it was a smartphone. He put it in his pocket and continued toward the dock.

The lights abruptly came back on when he reached the walkway, illuminating the dock ahead. The area was deserted but Orient saw the wake of a departing boat. He ran but the boat was already clear and moving fast. From the end of the dock he made out the name painted on the stern: *Valkyrie*.

He stood there for a moment, watching the boat's lights. He had no idea if Savana was on it, or still on the island. He began searching the dock area for anything that might have been dropped or discarded, then beamed his flashlight over the water.

The first thing he saw was a plume of blood, dark and oily, spreading over the surface.

Floating just below it, arms spread in surrender, was a human body.

+ + +

The local police responded to Orient's 911 call.

He pressed them to enlist the Coast Guard but by the time they mobilized, the *Valkyrie* was out of range.

His discovery of the murder victim gave weight to the theory that Savana was on the departing boat. The blood was fresh as was the corpse, dead less than a half hour.

Sybelle was sedated, but Hannah was still up, long after it was clear there was nothing more they could do.

She sat with her arms crossed, rocking back and forth. "I'll give him all the money I have, no questions asked.

"We haven't found a ransom note yet," one of the policemen said. "Maybe he'll call."

"I don't think he wants money," Orient said, after the policeman had gone. He reached out to touch her shoulder but she shrank back.

"Then exactly what is it that *you people* want?"

Surprised by her sudden vehemence Orient stood silent.

"Hannah please," Sybelle said, from the doorway. "Owen is doing all he can do. It's not his fault. If anything it's mine."

"I'm sorry," Hannah said, getting up to embrace her. "I didn't mean it that way. But there's so much I don't understand. I never should have left Savana." She glanced at Orient and he realized she felt guilty about their flirtation on the beach.

Sybelle moved over to the pantry, "Owen our island policemen aren't qualified to handle this. Isn't there *anything* we can do?"

Orient checked the time. He had never awakened Andy Jacobs before, but this seemed appropriate. "Hello Andy, sorry but it's an emergency. Sybelle's niece has been kidnapped from Fire Island and there's been a murder. Local police are good but we need the FBI."

"I'll alert the Bureau Chief in New York," Andy said, "are you alright?"

"I believe the girl was taken aboard a small vessel named the *Valkyrie,* no more than two hours ago." He gave him Sybelle's address and phone number.

"I'm on it, Owen."

The phone went dead. Orient would never get used to the ex-senator's abruptness but. Andy was also known for his ability to set wheels in motion. In fact, within the hour two Federal agents appeared at Sybelle's front door.

Both wore dark suits, one was heavy the other thin. The beefy agent was called Albert Huff, the slim one introduced himself as Hector Chavez. They were well trained, efficient, and immediately contacted the Coast Guard and had them search the Long Island side of the bay.

"I found this smartphone on the beach when I went after Savana," Orient told them. "I think it belongs to her."

"Let me see it," Hannah said, voice tight. She examined it, then handed it to Huff.

"Yes, its hers."

"Why didn't you give this to the cops who arrived?" Huff asked.

Orient shrugged. "They would have put it in a baggie and taken it back to the station house. But the truth is I forgot I picked it up."

"Can you show me where you found it?"

Orient picked up his flashlight. "Let's go."

The first yellow tendrils of dawn were creeping at the edge of the dark sky as Orient led Agent Huff along the approximate route he'd taken in pursuit of the kidnapper.

"I had an idea he might be heading for the dock," Orient said, flashlight dowsing back and forth.

"Can you point out where you and Dr. Wylde were walking when the attack occurred?"

Huff was smiling but his eyes were hard, and Orient realized he and Hannah were being questioned separately, to see if their stories matched.

"Of course, we just followed the surf line, perhaps a hundred yards further, before we turned around."

"I see. And you ran back to the house?"

"Yes."

"Why?"

"What?"

"Why did you run?"

"I received a distress call from Sybelle."

"On your cell phone?"

"No. We have sort of a mental link. What you might call it a hunch."

"I see. A mental link."

"Look, Agent Huff, before you make me a suspect perhaps we can search the dock area where I found the body."

Huff looked away. "We have a team scouring the area, Doctor. And we know it was you who called Senator Jacobs. We're just trying to find a motive here. You say there's been no ransom demand?"

"No."

"Any idea who would want to..."

"We believe it's the same stalker who burglarized Sybelle's house in New York and murdered her cook."

"Murder? You mean this kidnapper murdered two people?"

"No. I'm saying that someone murdered Sybelle's cook during a burglary. That's why we came out here—to recover from the trauma."

"Do you think there's some connection?"

Orient watched the darkness crack like an eggshell and the red dawn slide across the sky. "There must be a connection, but I don't know what it is."

Back at the house Orient saw his assessment had been correct as he watched Huff and Sanchez compare notes. Sybelle and Hannah sat listlessly on the couch, their sleepless faces shadowed by exhaustion and anxiety.

Sybelle looked up, hand half-raised as if asking teacher a question. "There is something you might want to consider. I believe the man you're looking for is a tall, blond man with a scar over one eye."

"Thought you said you really didn't see your attacker."

Sybelle touched the swollen purple bruise on one side of her face. "I didn't get a good look, no. But I'm sure the man I described did this."

Orient held his breath, wondering if Sybelle was going to recount their voyage to the past, which would only complicate the investigation—and compromise their credibility.

"How would you know this Miss Lean?" Sanchez said politely.

Sybelle drew herself up. "Well, I *am* a professional psychic."
The agents looked at each other.

Sanchez smiled and nodded. "I'll contact our outside team
to make inquiries. Tall, blond, scar over one eye you say?"

"Yes. May we go to bed now Agent Sanchez? My head if
splitting and I'm sure everyone is exhausted."

"Of course. But we must ask you not to leave the premises.
In case the kidnapper tries to make contact."

"The guest rooms are downstairs." Sybelle said, rising unsteadily to her feet. Orient moved to help her.

Sybelle waved him off. "Come Hannah I'll show you to
your room."

Orient trailed reluctantly behind them, his fear for Savana
amplified by a sense of complete helplessness.

+ + +

He slept fitfully for a few hours. When he awoke it was still
early morning. He went upstairs and found that three crime
technicians were conferring with Huff and Sanchez.

"We put a tap on the phone," Sanchez told him. "If any
ransom demand comes in we have it covered. Oh yeah," he
added, "we checked around and sure enough, there was a tall
blond man with a scar asking about Miss Lean's residence.'

"Just him, no one else?"

"Seems that way. We also ID'd the victim. His name was
Ricky Potts, twenty four year old working as a waiter in a
restaurant out here. The night he was killed he told someone
he was meeting a friend on a boat. Everything seems to check
out." Sanchez scratched his head. "Still can't believe how Miss
Lean could give us the perp's description like that."

Orient shrugged. He could see Sybelle standing on the
deck, talking to Hannah. She was wearing a pink, terrycloth
robe, sunglasses, and a wide-brimmed hat that partially concealed the swollen bruise on one side of her face. He excused

himself and went outside. As soon as he arrived Hannah stiffened and edged away. Orient pretended not to notice.

"They're ready if the kidnapper calls,' he said.

"He's not going to call," Hannah said, over her shoulder. "This isn't about money."

"I'm sure Savana is still all right darling," Sybelle said, "I can feel it."

Orient realized that there was nothing he could do, or say, that would be of any use. He went back inside and poured a cup of coffee. It was black and bitter, like his outlook. He knew what he needed was some time for meditation but for now the coffee would have to do. From the kitchen he watched as Hannah came inside and spoke to Agent Huff who smiled and nodded. She went back onto the deck and walked to the stairs, trailed by Sybelle.

Huff hurried outside. "Uh, where are you going?"

"My niece is going back to her house and I thought I'd walk with her. Is that all right?"

"I'm afraid not, Miss Lean. We need you to stay here."

"Stay here? But *why?*" Sybelle demanded.

Orient had moved closer to the deck and saw that the other people in the room were listening. Especially Sanchez. The slim, hawk faced agent seemed poised to give chase.

Hannah continued on alone as Sybelle stormed back inside, her injury overshadowed by her indignation. "Can you people tell me why in hell I should be a prisoner in my own house?"

Orient looked at Sanchez. "What's the problem?"

Sanchez smiled. "We received word earlier this morning to hold Miss Lean here. And you, Doctor," he added, as if delivering a party invitation.

"And me?"

The smile faded. "Some one wants to talk to you."

Chapter 20

Moe Klein was wary of boats.

His already sensitive stomach reacted badly to choppy water, which led him to seriously consider ordering a seaplane. In the end he took the ferry and was rewarded with a smooth crossing.

This case had him excited.

He reviewed the growing file with morbid fascination.

It started with the Applegate murder. From there it expanded like a lethal virus. Taegris, this kid Potts; all three victims killed by a single knife strike to the base of the skull, weapon of choice being a Nazi SS dagger. Then there was the housekeeper, broken neck, in every instance, a clean, professional kill. Now a kidnapping/murder with Miss Sybelle Lean and Doctor Orient standing in the middle of it all.

If nothing else it gave him a chance to question the pair without a warrant.

The only downside was the presence of Huff and Sanchez. Actually he liked Hector Sanchez but Huff was a plodding company man who was more interested in arresting people than getting the facts. Justice was an academic concept to Huff —and too many others he knew in the Bureau. Still, he knew a lot more good, tough, hardworking agents, Moe told himself. So don't let the Huff's grind you down.

It was late in the season, so there weren't many vacationers on the ferry. As the boat neared Fire Island, Moe took a deep breath of fresh, salt air. It reminded him of how long he'd been cooped up at work. He also realized he was overdressed in his navy suit and maroon tie. It was Indian summer and the afternoon was warm.

Walking along the dock Moe saw that the denizens of Cherry Grove were extremely colorful and casual. It reminded him of the Florida Keys. He had flown down last year on a case involving stolen Picassos, and the residents seemed from an alien planet. He needed subtitles when they spoke.

At least here on Fire Island they talk New York English, Moe thought, draping his suit jacket over his arm. Even so his shirt was damp as he neared Sybelle Lean's red beach house. Ever fastidious, he went into at a souvenir shop, and bought a towel. Then he stopped in a café for a latte and toweled dry in the cramped rest room.

Refreshed, he arrived at the octagonal house ready to piece together why all these people were being killed.

Huff, Sanchez and their tech team were conferring on the deck. Two others seated on the couch: a tall, lanky male who Moe took to be Doctor Orient, and a full-figured woman sporting a nasty bruise who was obviously Sybelle Lean. Ignoring the couple on the couch, he shuffled outside to join his fellow agents.

"Morris Klein," he said, flashing his badge, "I got an alert on the homicide."

Huff grinned. "Museum Moe. Are you still carrying that toy gun?"

Moe ignored him but he wondered if people called him that behind his back He looked at Sanchez. "The killer's m.o. fits our profile. Single stab wound to the base of the skull, is that right?"

Sanchez nodded. "Haven't found the weapon."

Moe dropped his jacket on a nearby chair and folded his arms. "So what *did* you find?"

+ + +

After his short briefing on the deck Moe came back into the living area, discreetly followed by Sanchez. At his request Huff remained outside.

The couple on the couch looked tired but they sat up as he approached. Moe did his best to give them a reassuring smile, but from the look on their faces, he failed.

"I'm Agent Klein,' he said, handing each of them his card. The man managed a smile. "I'm Doctor Owen Orient and this is Sybelle Lean. As you can see, she's been through a lot."

Moe got the message. He didn't intend to squeeze too hard but these two had a lot to answer for. "Yes, of course. Now, exactly what was your relationship to Henry Applegate?"

As intended the question took them by surprise. "I had dealings with him as a collector," Orient said finally "Sybelle and I had dinner with him the night before he was found murdered."

"And Peter Taegris?"

"Why are you asking us these questions?" Sybelle demanded. "A young girl has been kidnapped."

"And a young man was murdered. In exactly the same manner as Mr Applegate and Mr Taegris," Moe said patiently. "Not only that but we found an uncashed check from you, made out to Mr Taegris."

He watched them carefully for a reaction.

Orient met his gaze. "I went to his shop to purchase an Egyptian amulet, a fragment really. Sybelle went with me. I didn't have enough money so Sybelle wrote him a check Why he didn't cash it I don't know. From there I called Henry to take a look at the piece. He invited us to dinner."

"Can you describe this er... fragment.'

"I can do better. I have a copy at home."

Moe nodded. This case was becoming more interesting by the second. "General description," he pressed, "I'm an amateur Egyptologist." He didn't mention he'd already seen the copy.

"It was triangular, perhaps four inches on each side, with an Eye of Horus, which I'm sure you're familiar with, as well as a Pentacle of Solomon—and an early period black sphinx with a female head."

"Well I'm certainly looking forward to seeing your copy. I'll check and see if this fragment is among Mr. Applegate's effects."

Orient's expression remained impassive. Moe sensed he was holding something back. He was obviously trying to protect Sybelle Lean, but it wouldn't be that easy.

"Then of course the tragic death at your home."

Orient started to speak but Sybelle put a restraining hand on his shoulder.

"Yes it was a tragedy," she said quietly. "Lena Modena had become family."

"I understand."

"We came out to Fire Island to escape these horrible events, but it seems we couldn't. Now poor Savana..." Sybelle's low voice cracked.

Moe waited uncomfortably. He could see the emotions were genuine. But the doubts continued to nudge his intuition. "Do you have any idea who could be stalking you—or why?"

Sybelle shrugged. "Of course my work attracts a certain *fringe* element".

"Your work? You mean as a psychic?"

"Yes, I..."

Before she could say more, Hannah appeared on the deck. She said something excitedly to Huff, and handed him a mobile phone. The burly agent examined it, then escorted her inside. He gave the device to Sanchez.

"Take a look at this."

Sanchez squinted at the screen. Klein took the phone from his hand. It was a text message.

Hlpme!

"I just got this," Hannah said breathlessly. A layer of perspiration glistened on her skin. "Savana has a second phone. I had forgotten..."

"Give me the number," Klein said. "GPS can pinpoint her location."

The first person he called was Jake.

"This won't take long," he responded cheerfully, "by the way you've got another broken neck victim. They found him in the men's room of a Clinton gay bar."

"Thanks Jake, but one thing at a time. Right now, this girl's alive."

"I'm on it like butter on toast."

Who the hell is this guy? Moe thought. He's a one man swat team.

"I'm making sandwiches, is that all right?" Sybelle called.

Everyone heartily endorsed the idea, especially Klein who hadn't eaten since early breakfast. He saw Orient leave the couch and join her in the kitchen. Hannah sat stiffly, hands clasped, as if in prayer. He watched the pair in the kitchen to see if they were conferring, but they went about preparing a snack with quiet efficiency. He also noticed that when they served the food, Hannah seemed to avoid Orient.

The call came while Moe was wolfing down a ham and cheese sandwich.

"The phone is somewhere in Brooklyn. It's moving, makes it hard to locate exactly."

"Stay with it. When you have an approximate location, seal off the area. "

"Jesus, Moe, they should bump you up to field general."

The phone went dead. Then he heard the beep announcing a text message. He looked at his phone but the screen was blank.

"That's my phone," Hannah said.

He checked the Blackberry in his other hand. Sure enough there was a message.

Nice try

"What does it mean?" Hannah demanded.

Moe handed her the device and waited for Jake's call. He knew what it meant. The kidnapper had found the girl's phone, and any hope of locating them would be soon floating down a Brooklyn sewer.

+ + +

Hans discovered the girl had a cell phone by chance.

He had parked the Mercedes and walked about the block a few minutes, pretending to smoke a cigarette, while he made sure the area was deserted.

After unlocking the front door of the small building where his safe house was located, he went back to the car. Some feet away, he popped the trunk and was amazed to see a terrified face lit by a cell phone.

Without hesitation he slipped his dagger free and pressed the tip just below her left eye. "Phone," he said.

Almost fumbling it, she handed it to him with wooden fingers.

"Try anything like that again..." To emphasize his meaning, he sliced her earlobe with the blade. Then he snatched the blanket and tossed it at her. "Wrap yourself in this. You look like a whore."

Shivering, the girl did as she was told.

"Upstairs, quickly," he hissed.

As they walked he sent a text to the previous number, then dismantled the phone. Once inside the apartment, he led her to the bathroom and locked her inside. He returned with a pair of old khaki trousers and a man's shirt. "Put these on now," he said, then shut the door and waited. A few minutes later he opened the door. The shorts and tank top were covered by more modest dress.

He was a knight, not a barbarian, Hans noted as he took the handcuffs from his pocket. He cuffed one of the girl's wrists to a pipe next to the toilet. With his foot he pushed some magazines within her reach. Then he locked her inside.

For now the girl has everything she needs: water, a clean bathroom, some diversion, he told himself, hurrying outside

He had smashed the phone's chip but today's technology was devilishly clever.

He drove for a half hour before stopping at a dark corner. One by one, he dropped the broken chip and the other components into a sewer grating. He still proceeded cautiously until he was out of the area, respectful of satellite surveillance, especially after his little fiasco on YouTube. Still, what he had accomplished would erase any error, and enable him to seize the final link of the triangle.

Ever the good commander he went to a cyber cafe and sent a coded message to the Architect. The reply was terse; a telephone number, also in code. With a trace of annoyance he went outside to make the call. He would have to get rid of yet another cell phone tonight.

The Architect answered on the first ring.

"Yes, Hans. This plan of yours has risks."

"It is only logical. We need the ring, we need her, and we need to remove the impediment. Yes, there are always risks in any great undertaking."

"This means we shut down our operation in the city."

"Now that we have the Spear what does it matter?"

"True, and we have you to thank my dear Hans. I received it yesterday."

"Then you know."

There was a pregnant pause.

"Yes."

"We are at the gateway of the Grand Design. We must dare anything."

"So long as you leave no trail."

"All they will find are questions."

"Do it."

The phone went dead.

Hans didn't bother dismantling this phone he just tossed it in a dumpster. He had more at home, all disposable.

On his way back he stopped at a grocery store and bought bread, cheese, cereal, milk, bananas, orange juice, a gossip magazine, and chocolate donuts. He wanted his prize Judas Goat fatted for her appearance.

After providing his guest with her basic provisions, Hans took time to clean, and oil his ceremonial dagger. He wasn't in any particular hurry. By now all phones would be bugged, including the Lean woman and Doctor Orient.

So he had to do it the old fashioned way.

Up close and personal.

Chapter 21

Orient returned to New York exhausted.

His apartment was still in disarray from the burglary, adding to the sense of chaos ripping through his life. He took a deep breath and clutched the remnants of his concentration.

It was important he reconnect. He took off his clothes and stuffed them in a laundry bag. Then he lay on the carpet and began stretching and breathing deeply in a rhythmic pattern. Anxiety, fear, and travel had stiffened his muscles. It took long minutes before they responded. The same held for his breathing. At first the patterns were shallow but gradually the rhythms deepened and his consciousness billowed like a sail finding wind.

He drifted above the chaos into a strong current that restored his balance.

Even here he could sense the gathering hostility in the wake of his thoughts, as he sorted through the events that had brought him here—alone and hunted. For as long as he held the ring, he was the prey. And he had underestimated the ferocity of the predator.

The ring was his only weapon. In a moment of clarity he understood Savana's ransom would be the Seal of Solomon.

And his own life.

+ + +

Emerging from his meditative state Orient took a long shower and put on fresh clothes. He dressed for battle: black jeans, black turtle neck, athletic shoes. Then he called Beppo.

"Owen—where the hell you been hiding? I called you."

Orient realized he'd neglected to check his messages. There were six.

"Sorry, Beppo. I had to leave suddenly. Is that offer of *Penne Arrabiati* still good?"

It took Beppo a moment to realize what Orient was saying.

"Of course my friend."

"What time is dinner?"

"If you're hungry. I start cooking right away. I have all the ingredients."

"See you then," Orient said, grateful for Beppo's suspicious nature. He'd picked up on the need to be discreet over the phone. Before he left the house he checked his messages. Three were from Beppo, two were hangups, one was from an administrator at St Luke's Hospital, asking for some information.

On the subway downtown to Beppo's loft, Orient reminded himself that as far as the FBI was concerned they were still suspect, if not actual suspects. On Fire Island, they had been asked, most politely for blood, saliva and hair samples before Klein cleared them to leave. The lead agent seemed slightly different than the other law officers he'd been encountering all week—more compassionate and definitely smarter. Orient had no doubt his phones were being tapped.

Which made him wonder, how exactly would Savana's abductor contact him?

The odors inside Beppo's loft were both sweet and spicy and Orient could see pots simmering on the huge stove in the kitchen area.

"Look, it's the prodigal son" Beppo greeted, "did you meet a new girlfriend or something?"

"Something like that."

"You look like you could use some good Italian wine. Come."

Beppo had prepared appetizers of mozzarella and tomatoes drizzled with olive oil and basil, as well as an olive and garlic paste served on seeded wafers. "Somebody listening when you called?" he asked casually.

Orient nodded. "Somebody will always be listening for a while."

"It's our brave new world," Beppo sighed and poured the wine. "Let's drink a toast to the good old days when you could hide."

Orient was hungry and devoured the pasta with surprising gusto. *Penne arrabiati,* translated to 'angry penne' but Beppo balanced the heat with cool herbs like mint, and the result was worthy of a culinary world cup.

"Just simple stuff I have around the place," Beppo said, waving off Orient's compliments. "So, did you tell me everything about this ring?"

"How do you mean?"

"I mean I just set up my 'lost wax' casting equipment, everything going along perfect, then *kaboom* it's like an earthquake hits the place. Lucky my sculptures are mostly gold because they all fell down."

"What about the cast?"

"I had to start all over again."

Then it came to him. "Did this happen Tuesday, a few minutes after nine?"

"Yes, yes, exactly. Why? How did you know?"

Orient shrugged. "Something similar happened to me at dinner. Shook the entire table."

"So you think it's because of the ring?"

"Yes. It definitely has... unusual properties."

"Unusual? You should be a lawyer. It was positively *freaky.* I couldn't wait to get this ring back to you."

"But you cast two copies anyway?"

"Of course," Beppo said proudly, "no true artist is afraid of the unknown." He gulped his wine. "So—you want to see or not?"

+ + +

"Perfect," Orient said as he examined each of the three rings Beppo had waiting on his worktable. Even under a large magnifier they were identical.

"I used the oldest, most pure gold in my collection. I even had to melt down an ancient necklace."

"How do you distinguish the real one?"

Beppo gave him the jeweler's loupe. "Take a look. I couldn't replace the black pallasite, so I used obsidian. But only a pallasite has the tell-tale thread."

It was true, under the powerful glass Orient could see the metallic line, as faint as a gossamer strand. He tried the Seal of Solomon on his own finger and found it fit perfectly.

"Maybe you should wear the copy, like my society ladies do, and keep the real one in your safety box."

Orient nodded and made the switch, putting the Seal in a zippered pocket. The copy felt to be the exact weight as the original.

Beppo read his reaction. "I made sure to the microgram they're the same."

"You did a magnificent job, *un cappolavoro*, as they say in Rome."

The tanned goldsmith flashed a brilliant white smile. "Of course, I am Beppo."

"I still feel I should pay..."

Beppo stopped him with a lofty wave. "It is I who is grateful my friend. For a change this project was worthy of my talent." Abruptly, his expression darkened. "But we both know the ring is no toy. I *felt* this power in here," he patted his belly. "And believe me I got respect. Look,"

He pointed to a gold cross on the worktable. "I keep it handy just in case."

A pistol against a charging rhino, Orient observed as the cab sped uptown. The ring's power was born millenniums before the crucifixion. But even a relative layman like Beppo could sense the Seal of Solomon's awesome potential.

+ + +

Orient's musings came to a crashing stop when he saw the white envelope beneath his door. He knew what it was before he bent to pick it up. A cloying panic stilled his breath as he opened it and read the message inside. Crudely taped, a series of cut up words from the newspaper delivered the terse ultimatum.

she for ring

Cloisters Wednesday 11 pm

Alone or she die

For a moment Orient considered calling Agent Klein. But he knew this was about him as well as the ring. There would be no way the kidnapper would allow him to walk away with Savana. The man needed Savana, he needed the ring, and he needed to kill.

Even the choice of leaving a note was an ominous message which said: 'I know where you live, and have access to your door any time I damn please.'

Orient took a hand wrapped cigarette from his silver case and sat behind his desk.

"Om, aing, chring, cling, char-muda, yei, vijay," he whispered, intoning the ancient Brahmin mantra for the consecration of Bhang. As he smoked he stared at the Mandala on the case, which signified his role as a monk of the cities, and his place in the hierarchy. At the moment his place seemed low indeed. He had to try to ransom Savana, despite the knowledge that he was enabling his own execution.

He put on a Lightning Hopkins CD and changed into shorts and a sweatshirt. Then he took the authentic Seal of

Solomon from his jacket pocket and slipped it on his finger. After securing the copy, he stretched out on the floor and entered a state of deep concentration, slowly extending the orbit of his senses. The spare guitar lines helped tune them to a high pitch, as his consciousness wrapped around the gold ring on his finger, probing its inner core. Its deep metallic vibration pulsed against his flesh with a strange, urgent rhythm that merged with his heartbeat... and then he saw him...

A tall, angular male with pale skin, and a zigzag scar above one eye, was moving through the shadows. There was a full moon overhead and he could see its gleaming reflection on the silver blade, as the scarred man lifted a dagger and drove it into the neck of a man dressed in black. When the victim fell his face lifted to the moonlight.

A cold shock broke Orient's contact.

He was the murdered man.

For long minutes he sat huddled on the floor, trying to control his surging emotions. Despite the terrifying vision, he had emerged with more than when he entered. He now understood the power of the ring.

And what he must do.

Chapter 22

Moe Klein felt he was closing in for the kill. He knew Orient and Lean were withholding evidence so he decided to put a tail on the good doctor. At the same time he had Jake correlating forensics in the multiple murders. He had also started sending progress memos to the new director, and was rewarded with the hardware he had requisitioned.

No doubt the kidnapper would contact either Sybelle Lean or Orient. His gut told him it would be Orient. It also whispered this wasn't about money.

The worst part of a stakeout was the lousy food one ended up consuming during the long hours sitting in a car or standing in some dark alley. Tonight it was a tuna on rye, a Dr. Browns cream soda, and a Grande Starbucks coffee. Why can't they just call it a large, Moe brooded, watching the entrance of Orient's apartment building.

He had seen Orient enter the building earlier, returning from an unknown location. Unfortunately, by the time Moe was in position, Orient had already gone out. Since coming back, he had remained in his apartment.

Probably for the night, Moe speculated, sipping cold coffee. He had brokered a deal with Detective Wagner, offering to cut him in on the case in return for manpower to maintain twenty four hour surveillance. Wagner was practically salivating for the chance, and Moe figured whatever was going down, would happen within the next seventy two hours.

His replacement, Detective Mancuso, showed up ten minutes late, with a pizza box and a shopping bag full of pretzels, chips, beer, and a bottle of milk.

"No coffee?"

Mancuso, a dark, slender man despite his diet, shrugged. "I can't sleep anyway."

Moe reluctantly abandoned his post. "Call me if he leaves."

Sleep eluded him as well, that night. Mainly he wasn't that secure about Wagner's boys. They were all graduates of the same prehistoric academy and this stakeout was crucial.

Daylight brought Moe some relief. Mancuso called to report no activity, and his own bureau colleague, Agent Sanchez took the next watch. This way he'd get a proper briefing when he took over the night shift.

He awoke late, ate a bowl of oatmeal and soymilk which seemed to soothe his stomach, and took a cab to his office. Taking care to get a receipt, he called Jake as soon as he arrived.

"Moe, haven't you ever heard of Skype?"

"What is that, a new energy drink?"

"Alright, get over here, bring the new laptop, I'll give you a tutorial."

"What's this gonna cost me?"

"Not that much, maybe some nice sable, whitefish, nova, onions, cream cheese, a few bagels, we can nuke the bagels here."

When Moe arrived Jake was waiting with trays, paper plates and plastic forks.

"You're getting real formal. What's the occasion?"

Jake flashed a devilish grin. "Five interconnected murders and a kidnapping. Congratulations, you've landed a career making case."

"Couldn't have done it without you Jake."

"I know that's why I'm now officially part of your team." He proudly produced a memo. "What do you say? If you think I'm crowding you..."

Moe lifted his hands in mock surrender. "Who said anything? I'm grateful you've got my back. If it wasn't for you and Maybelline," he gestured at Jake's computer bank, "I'd be still working on Applegate's murder. Which reminds me..."

"What?" Jake spread cream cheese over an onion bagel. "Originally I was tailing Applegate for a completely different reason. Word had come down that a very important art piece was about to be stolen from a museum in Austria. Apparently a wealthy collector commissioned the theft. When Applegate was killed, the trail went sideways, but I've been thinking: Nazi SS dagger, Austria, could be some connection. What do you think?"

Jake chewed thoughtfully then gave an elaborate shrug. "What's to think? I'll run it by Maybelline and see what she comes up with. Any more details?"

Moe shook his head. "All I ever got was a possible theft from a museum in Austria which was connected to Applegate. Now he's dead so is the case."

"Nazi SS dagger?"

"Murder weapon in Applegate's murder. Killer left it behind. But the other two had similar wounds, single stroke, base of the skull. It's all in the files."

"Anything not in there?"

Moe told him about his interview with Doctor Orient and Sybelle Lean, and his impressions. "They're not telling me everything I know that, but the woman is uncanny. She gave us an accurate ID from a psychic reading. White male with a scar over one eye."

"You mean like that dog slasher on You Tube?"

"Maybe, all I know for sure is that those two are holding back."

Jake applied a slab of cream cheese to another bagel, then added onion and nova. "I'll look into all this. Meanwhile let's get you started on some basic skills common to most ten year olds."

When Moe left Jake's empire he had a Skype account, knew how to text, and could send e-mails and photos from his Blackberry. He also had low grade heartburn.

His next stop was Wagner's precinct. Moe wasn't ready to share information on the kidnapping so he let Wagner believe he was still working on the Applegate murder and Orient could be a material witness. Being anxious to close two cases at once, Wagner scrounged up a rookie for the detail.

The rookie was useless, Moe thought as he walked from the subway to the 19th Precinct. More importantly, Wagner had finally found a copy of the 911 call.

On Lexington Avenue Moe stopped at a coffee shop and ordered a rice pudding. It was an effort to protect his stomach from the vodka Wagner would offer him. It had become a minor ritual with the homicide detective.

Politics and crime make strange bedfellows, Moe reflected, heading for the precinct house. He heaved his bulk up three flights of stairs to Wagner's cubicle, where the detective sat waiting, behind a desk stacked with files.

Wagner greeted him with a big-toothed grin. "You look like you could use a snort."

"All those stairs."

"We got an elevator." Wagner filled a paper cup with vodka and handed it to him.

Moe drank with a flourish. "Hits the spot."

Despite the rice pudding, the vodka burned its way through his esophagus, before igniting an inner glow that he would pay for later. Moe decided to enjoy it.

"So you think this Doctor Orient knows something?" Wagner said, watching him carefully. "Could he be in on it?"

"Not likely. But you never know." Moe leaned closer. "The Lean dame gave us a description of the perp using her psychic power."

Wagner sat back. "No shit? Serious?" He grabbed a pen. "What she say?"

"Tall white male, scar over one eye..."

"Motherfucker."

"What?"

Wagner tossed his pen aside. "We got the same ID of some psycho who attacked three people downtown, about a week ago."

Klein tried to look surprised. He still hadn't told Wagner about the kidnapping. Sybelle Lean's vision had been verified by a few people on Fire Island.

"What's this puke's problem?" Wagner said, refilling his cup. "Serial killer?"

"Definitely seems to like his work "

Wagner moved to pour another vodka, but Moe waved him off. "I'm pulling graveyard shift tonight," he confided. "Oh, by the way, did you get the 911 call for me?"

"Right here on a new CD," Wagner said proudly. He shuffled through a thick file and found the disc. "This is the call reporting the Applegate murder."

"Great. I can run this through our voice scanner," Moe said.

It was bullshit. He just wanted to hear the caller's voice, and hopefully pick up some hint of what transpired that night. It was his own little way of being psychic, Moe observed as he walked back to his apartment. Another fact he'd kept from Wagner was his address. Next thing you know the burly detective would be dropping by for a few belts.

When he reached home, Moe put the CD in his player. The first time he heard the male voice calling in Henry Applegate's murder, he knew.

That deep, cultivated tone belonged to Doctor Owen Orient.

+ + +

By the time Moe left for his stake out, he had culled enough evidence to ask for a subpoena to monitor his every move. He intended to nail Orient within twenty four hours. Meanwhile they were watching him twenty four seven.

He arrived twenty minutes early. Moe had worked out a system. To minimize the possibility of detection, each man on the stake out team came in his own car. Only the parking space remained the same.

Sanchez pulled out, waited for Klein to park, then backed up, and leaned toward the open passenger window. "He's been inside all day. Nobody in or out. One call to Sybelle Lean about doing yoga."

As Sanchez pulled away, Klein mulled over his report. The yoga thing could be a code.

He was still thinking about it when he spotted Orient walking out of his apartment building. Moe's first instinct was to call Sanchez back but a radio cab pulled up in front of Orient and he got inside.

Still fumbling for his phone, Moe followed the cab as it headed uptown. He caught a break when the cab stopped at a smoke shop on 86th street.

Moe punched Sanchez's number. It went into voice mail. Sanchez had turned off his phone. Frustrated he watched Orient go into the store.

The smoke shop was typical of many across the country. Besides cigarettes, it sold drug paraphernalia, Heavy Metal T Shirts, motorcycle jackets, studded leather jewelry, whips, chains, handcuffs, lewd bumper stickers, skull flags: the usual crap so symbolic of a culture in decline.

What Orient was doing there was another question. He didn't seem the type.

Even more curious, when Orient emerged he was attired in a black motorcycle jacket, and a black wool watch cap. He looks like he's on his way to an old fashioned rumble, Moe thought, watching the radio cab pull away and head further uptown.

Two to one he was going to ransom the girl.

Sanchez finally responded when Moe was somewhere near Washington Heights.

"Jesus, I'm sorry," he said without conviction, "I stopped to eat when my shift ended. Where are you?"

"On the Henry Hudson going north. Our boy is on the move. I'll need back-up."

"I'm rolling now. Phone's open."

"Use the lights and siren, you'll make better time.'

Moe tried to keep his distance but traffic was heavy, forcing him to stay close to the radio cab. On the other hand the heavy traffic slowed things down, giving Sanchez a chance to catch up.

The radio cab turned off at the Fort Tyron Park exit. Klein redialed Sanchez.

"Take the first exit after the Washington Bridge. Kill the siren and lights when you get there."

He followed at a distance, and saw the cab circle back north and finally stop in front of an area familiar to him. He punched the phone. "Looks like our boy is going to the Cloisters."

"Where?"

"Use your GPS." Moe said impatiently, watching Orient leave the cab. He shut the phone, quietly opened his door, and followed on foot.

Taking care to stay in the shadows, he moved slowly, barely able to make out the black clad figure ahead. He saw a low light and edged closer. It took a few seconds to recognize his surroundings. He was standing in front of the entrance to the Cloisters.

Moe had visited this New York landmark a few times, always impressed by the graceful medieval archways, the stained glass windows, the views of the Hudson River and the Palisades beyond, the verdant gardens, and the massive art collection housed inside the beautiful reproductions of five French monasteries.

However, at the moment the Cloisters were shut tight. And Orient had disappeared.

Chapter 23

Since finding the note under his door, Orient had concentrated on focusing his strength. His weapons were meager: for the past few weeks he'd been honing rusty skills in the martial art of QiGong. Once a red belt, now he was barely qualified for yellow.

However he had the ring.

Since the vision of his own death, Orient had not removed the ring from his finger, as he gathered his resources.

Along with the breathing and stretching of QiGong, were certain herbs used to increase vitality, or decrease anxiety. Orient had many of them, stored in mason jars for years. He prepared an infusion, boiling the foul smelling herbs for over an hour then letting the mass steep for another hour, before pouring off the dank liquid.

He stored the herbal elixir in the refrigerator then settled down for a few hours rest. But his fitful sleep was stalked by a shadowy black feline, prowling the edge of his dreams. Although he never quite saw it, he knew it was out there, he sensed its bestial hunger... and only the fire kept it at bay...

When Orient awoke his skin was slick with perspiration. He checked his watch. It was four a.m., barely three hours sleep.

As Orient prepared breakfast, his mind went back to the dark creature of his dreams. It had been out there waiting, waiting for him to fall asleep, to weaken, ready to pounce. He realized it had been frustrated by the power of the ring—the fire.

Orient went about carefully structuring his day for the coming exchange. He couldn't afford to fail, for Savana's sake. He began with the deep, deliberate, stretching and breathing of QiGong, amplifying his *chi* to its maximum. Forty minutes later, he felt ready to test its power. He selected an object on his desk and *pushed* with an upraised palm, stopping a yard short of his target.

A large mug filled with pens toppled, spilling its contents.

Confident he had achieved control of the *chi* energy orbiting his body, Orient concentrated on fusing his physical powers, to those within the Seal of Solomon. He lost track of time as the energy expanded, morphing into a small, pulsing universe with the ring at its center, irradiating his being with strength he's never known.

When he carefully disconnected and eased back, his senses tingled like ultrasensitive antennae, and his body felt in perfect balance.

Overconfidence was a luxury he couldn't afford, Orient observed. His adversary was a dedicated killer and he had no doubt tonight's meeting was a trap. There would be no victory. The best he could hope for was a stand-off. The objective was to free Savana.

At about noon he took a long nap. He slept well this time, and awoke refreshed. The dark, cloying predator haunting his dreams had been dispersed.

The first thing he did was call Sybelle. Both of them knew their phones were being tapped so he kept the conversation short, and the message oblique.

"Owen, are you alright?"

"I'm fine. I just wanted to remind you to practice your Yoga today."

"My yo...? Oh of course darling, you know I practice every day."

"Good. I'll be home if you need anything."

Orient hung up knowing she'd understood. He had called to ask her to link her psychic energy with his, to buttress his defense against an experienced adept. Savana's abductor had proven his facility with the occult arts.

He went back to the mat and began the breathing patterns that expanded his consciousness until it merged with Sybelle's waiting presence. Once their link was secure, he recharged his connection to the ring, forming an orbit with palpable gravity.

Orient emerged an hour later. He knew Sybelle would maintain their link as long as necessary, and for the first time he felt prepared.

Psychically perhaps, but not quite physically, Orient noted, recalling the man's skill with a knife. He wouldn't have a weapon but body armor might be a good idea. He googled a nearby store that carried the items he needed, Then he called a cab service and ordered a pick-up.

When the hour neared, Orient tried to remove the gold ring from his finger, but it was difficult. It seemed to have formed a painless bond with his flesh. However he found that by focusing on the ring, its grip receded, allowing him to slip it off his finger.

Without the ring Orient felt his new found strength receding as well. But he couldn't take the chance of it falling into the killer's hands. He put the replica on his finger and secured the Seal of Solomon in the watch pocket of his trousers. Having it close to his body was a secondary source of power.

He was ready when the cab arrived, and directed the driver to a store on 86th street that sold what he needed. He purchased a heavy leather motorcycle jacket, a thick turtleneck sweatshirt, a black watch cap, and a studded leather neck collar—what the clerk referred to as a 'dog collar'. He put the leather collar underneath the turtle neck, so the metal studs were not so conspicuous. As he left the store, he glimpsed his reflection and was startled by his menacing image.

With each mile Orient felt that intensity building. He had drunk the herbal infusion before leaving the apartment and renewed vitality was coursing through his system. He felt alert, aware... and apprehensive.

The cab reached the Cloisters about ten forty five. Orient hoped the extra time would be enough to become acclimated to his surroundings. He had visited the lovely monastery gardens before and was vaguely familiar with the place, but at night, shut down, the Cloisters could have been the dark side of the moon.

As Orient edged around the perimeter he heard his cell beep. It was a text message:

south side

gate open

So much for the element of surprise, Orient observed ruefully. Now the abductor would know exactly where he'd be coming. He moved slowly through the shadows, waiting for his eyes to adjust to the darkness. He saw a half open gate and circled around it. There was no sound, no movement.

Rather than use the gate, Orient looked for a less predictable, entry point. The Cloister's was a museum, housing a huge collection of valuable tapestries and artifacts. He expected to encounter guards, alarms, high security. Instead the area was deserted.

Keeping the gate in sight, Orient continued along the shadows. He saw a wall low enough to reach and on impulse, pulled himself over and dropped down into the garden on the other side. He stood stock still, listening.

A rustling sound drew his attention and he half turned.

The blow was silent, swift, and steel hard.

Despite the collar the dagger pierced the studded leather to the skin. He felt a hot slice of pain and stumbled forward, brain ringing from the jarring shock. Dimly, he realized what was happening. He also realized his attacker was incredibly strong.

As Orient fell to the ground he felt something jerk his neck back. A muffled curse signaled he had a window. He rolled aside and scrambled to regain his feet. A moving darkness crossed the corner of his vision and he pushed blindly.

An electric bolt seared his palm, and he leaped back, bouncing off a thick tree. Pressing his back against the tree he braced for another attack, straining to see through the shadows. In that instant he breathed deeply, inhaling the damp, rich air of the gardens, and felt his senses clear. A coppery scent filled his nostrils. He glanced down and saw his fingers were slick with blood.

Orient heard him before he loomed up beside the tree, one hand reaching for his throat, the other lifting a knife. Again, the studded collar protected him, preventing his attacker from getting a solid grip. Orient slipped aside and dug his open hand into the man's ribs. He heard a surprised grunt, and the man stepped back.

"The girl," Orient said, his voice a heavy rasp. "We had a deal."

The man smiled. "I thought we'd renegotiate.'

Still smiling he struck, long knife lashing out like a whip.

This time Orient was balanced. He snapped another open-handed blow that stopped six inches short of his attacker.

The man exhaled sharply and staggered back. "QiGong... very good."

"The ring for the girl." Orient said breathlessly, trying to control the adrenalin singing through his body.

The man lifted his head and began tracing slow circles with the knife. "The ring is mine, the girl is mine," he said flatly. "Now you are mine."

Orient saw the scar and the maniacal glaze in his pale eyes, and realized—*knew*—that he had been the interloper in Marrakech seventy years ago. In that microsecond the man moved.

Stunned by the speed of the attack, Orient was unable to avoid the blade. He turned, and felt a jolt of pain bite into his shoulder. He half fell, good arm flailing wildly, anticipating a fatal wound.

A beam of light drilled through the darkness.

194   *Frank Lauria*

"Hold it! Right there..."

Orient looked up. A uniformed security guard was advancing toward them, an automatic pistol, pressed against his flashlight.

"Put the knife down," the guard said, shuffling closer.

The attackers' eyes gleamed like those of a blue-eyed tiger. Slowly, almost mockingly, he placed the knife on the ground.

"Now step back, and turn around," the guard ordered.

When the man turned, he lowered his flashlight and produced a set of handcuffs. "Stay where you are," he told Orient, who was still on the ground. .

"Both hands behind your back," the guard said..

Slowly, the man complied.

For a moment the guard juggled cuffs, flashlight and weapon.

In that blurred second the attacker whirled and was behind the guard, one arm around his neck. The guard's eyes bulged in surprise as he brought his pistol up Orient heard a sharp crack. The guard's eyes dulled and his body sagged.

The attacker let his body fall to the ground and picked up the flashlight. He located his knife then looked for the pistol. Desperately, Orient focused, and pushed.

As the attacker bent to pick it up, the pistol skittered away.

The bobbing flashlight abruptly turned on him. Through the blinding light Orient caught the sharp glint of steel and lifted his arms.

A vice-like grip squeezed his wrist. "You won't need the ring."

Suddenly Orient realized the man intended to cut off his finger. When he jerked his hand back an agonizing pain shot through his arm.

"Freeze!"

At the command, the attacker spun and hurled the flashlight directly at the voice. Then he melted into the shadows without a sound.

Heart pounding and arm throbbing, Orient got to his feet.
His savior had picked up the flashlight and was beaming it
at him.

"Owen Orient?"

Orient blinked.

It was Agent Klein.

"You're under arrest for murder."

"You think I did this?" Orient gestured at the fallen guard
The flashlight swung around. "What the fuck?"

Instinctively Klein bent to aid the guard.

Orient took a step back and ducked behind a thick growth.
He scooped up some pebbled earth and threw it behind the
crouching Agent. Klein lumbered off in the direction of the
sound, sweeping the area with his flashlight.

Edging quietly through the unfamiliar gardens Orient had
two problems. His right arm was pulsing with agony. And he
had no idea how to get out. He glimpsed the light and heard
Klein beating through the bushes. In a matter of minutes back-
up would arrive, and he'd be trapped.

Orient listened to Klein thrashing about in the garden. His
flashlight chopped through the darkness like an axe as he came
closer. Unable to move in any direction, Orient held his breath,
listening to his pursuer approaching, now only a few feet away.

Abruptly the flashlight beam stayed fixed on one place, and
Klein stopped moving. In the quiet Orient heard the cough of a
motorcycle starting up. Klein heard the same thing and lurched
off in the direction of the sound.

After a few moments Orient followed him. He was surprised to find he was slightly unsteady on his feet. Using Klein's
flashlight to mark his position, he made his way through the unfamiliar maze of shadows as the motorcycle's cough became a
throaty rumble. He saw Klein break into an ungainly trot, then
bustle through an open gate.

When Orient reached the gate he paused, partially to make
sure Klein wasn't there, and partially because he was suddenly

exhausted. Adrenaline depletion and blood loss were pounding at his temples like tympani drums. He knew he had to find some refuge where he could bind his wounds.

There was some light outside the gate and he could see Klein still trotting after the departing motorcycle. As quickly as he physically could, he scurried across an open parking area to a shadowed dumpster. He crouched behind the steel container, and tried to remove his jacket. The pain almost made him cry out.

The wail of a police siren convinced him to keep moving. He peered around the corner of the container and saw an unmarked car pull up about sixty yards away. Klein ran over to the car and got in. Tires screeching, the vehicle took off after the motorcycle.

Orient started walking in the opposite direction. As he neared Riverside Drive he spotted a gypsy cab and frantically waved it down with his good arm. He gave the driver Sybelle's address and slumped against the back seat.

A flash of pain jabbed him awake, The cab driver was standing over him.

"Come on, get out. You got blood all over the car. I ain't gettin' involved. Call 911."

Swaying, Orient watched him drive off. Slowly he sank to the ground. With his last reserve of energy he focused, and reached out for Sybelle. He felt as if he was melting, like a snowman in the desert, dissolving part by part: arms, chest, legs —until finally his consciousness liquefied, and flowed into the pounding blackness...

Chapter 24

Sybelle was restless.

She managed to maintain contact with Owen but she wasn't as advanced as her mentor. And she knew he was in great danger. A toxic vibration pervaded her consciousness. She took a few deep, rhythmic breaths to calm herself. It was important she remained steady.

Once contact had been secured, she went into the kitchen to fix a cup of tea. As she went about her preparations she could feel the link at the base of her brain. At the same time she couldn't help thinking about poor Lena. She'd been murdered in this very kitchen. And now Savana was in the hands of her killer.

Sybelle was certain Orient had gone to find her. Thank heavens he had stepped in when he did, she thought. Who knows what might have happened to all of them.

Still jumpy, Sybelle took her tea into the den and put on a CD of Maria Callas singing Aida. Halfway through the duet she felt a familiar tug at her senses. He pulse rate elevated and an image flashed up in her consciousness: a street sign, 95th at Riverside.

Sybelle knew what the message meant, and was highly aware of its urgency. As she was putting on her coat, the doorbell rang. Inpatient to leave, she answered without using the intercom.

Hannah stood there. .

She looked terrible: hair unkempt, face drawn.

"Help me, Sybelle," she blurted when the door opened, "I haven't been able to work, I can't sleep..."

Sybelle embraced her. "Perhaps you'd better come with me."

Hannah pulled back. "Where?"

"Please trust me darling. I just got a message from Owen."

Hannah tried to say more but Sybelle put a finger to her lips. "It's an emergency. Let's go."

They hailed a cab and sat silently holding hands as the vehicle headed uptown. Sybelle's heart was still beating rapidly and she wondered if she should have brought Hannah with her. Of course she had no choice, Sybelle noted, as Hannah rested her head against her shoulder, emotionally exhausted. Anyway Savana was her daughter and she deserved to be kept in the loop, even though she was a civilian, so to speak.

When the cab arrived at 95th street Sybelle became confused. Owen wasn't there.

Could she have misinterpreted the image, the intent behind it? She anguished over the possibilities as they stepped out onto the darkened sidewalk. Before she could ask the driver to wait, he roared off. Probably to look for more festive clients, she speculated grimly.

Hannah stared at her. In the short time since her arrival at the house, she seemed to have recovered her balance. "Well, we're here. What now?"

"I'm not sure dear. Give me a moment."

During the ride uptown Sybelle had maintained a shaky link with Owen. She intensified her concentration, and probed the silence.

Nothing.

"Wait here," she said softly, walking closer to a shadowy area between buildings. She heard a hissing sound and moved closer. There was a narrow alley lined with garbage cans, and as she stepped closer Sybelle heard a man's voice.

Then she remembered something. There was a tiny flashlight on her keychain. She snapped it on and followed its glow into the alley.

She saw a plank protruding from behind a garbage can, but as she moved closer realized it was a leg. A guttural curse broke the quiet, and the metallic glint of a knife caught the dim light. Instinctively, Sybelle kicked the garbage can over and scuttled away.

A man stood up, his hair disheveled and his eyes gleaming wildly. He had been kneeling over a body. The body was matted with blood.

"Help!" Sybelle shouted, running awkwardly back to the sidewalk

The man blinked, took a step toward Sybelle, then bolted in the other direction.

Sybelle hurried to the body, which lay very still on the ground.

"You okay?" Hannah yelled, bursting into the alley.

When Sybelle's light brushed the man's face, her emotions imploded.

Owen lay sprawled in a pool of blood, skin chalk white and lips blue.

Hannah appeared at her side. "Are *you* alright?"

She saw Orient, and knelt beside him, her fingers probing his jugular vein. After a few moments she looked up at Sybelle.

"I can't find a pulse."

+ + +

"...lost a lot of blood."

Orient was dimly aware of being rolled along a white corridor, nose and mouth covered by a plastic mask. When he woke up again, he was in a hospital room, body attached to various tubes and wires.

It took him a while before he recognized Hannah. She was dressed in scrubs, her hair under a cap, face damp, mask down around her neck.

He managed a grin. "Tough day at the office?"

Hannah smiled. "You kept us pretty busy. How do you feel?"

"Numb, mostly. I'm still piecing together how I got here."

"Sybelle told me where you went, but I'm not sure why."

"Savana's kidnapper contacted me. He wanted to ransom Savanna for the ring."

Hannah's smile sagged, "Is she alright, Owen?"

"I think so. She wasn't there. The kidnapped tried to kill me and take the ring."

"Everyone seems to want that damned ring. Sybelle stopped some derelict from trying to cut it off your finger."

He looked down and saw his hand was bandaged to the wrist. Even the replica carries karma, Orient observed, fatigue stealing over his awareness. The realization that he was a fugitive, stirred him awake.

"Sybelle's been waiting to see you," Hannah said.

Orient gathered his strength. "Good. I need to talk to you both. Did you register me as a patient?"

"Not yet. I called the ambulance directly. They arrived within minutes, thank God. You've been here less than two hours."

"You might want to register me as a John Doe for now. I'll explain when Sybelle gets here."

"Darling, what happened?" Sybelle exclaimed when she came inside. "What were you doing on Riverside?"

Calmly, Orient told them of being contacted by text, and lured into a trap. "I half expected that," Orient said wryly. "What I didn't expect was Agent Klein."

"Why was he there?"

"He did save my life —but he was there to arrest me for murder."

Both women were silent.

"But why you Owen?" Sybelle said finally.

"I don't know. But I do know this kidnapper wants the ring and will contact me again. If we ever hope to bring Savanna home, I have to stay free."

Hannah nodded. "So that's why you want me to register you as a John Doe."

"Yes."

"But, Owen, you need to recover. Where will you go? They'll be watching my place."

His head sank back on the pillow. "I haven't figured that out yet. But I'll need some cash. I won't have access to my bank accounts, or credit cards."

"Perhaps I can help." Hannah said.

Sybelle shook her head. "They might be watching you too."

"St. Luke's maintains a few low cost apartments for staff. One of them happens to be vacant, and technically you are staff. It's furnished. I can have you over there in a few hours."

"You know this may have serious repercussions."

Hannah's violet eyes looked into his. "My daughter has been kidnapped by a killer. What's more serious than that? We've got to get her back."

Orient nodded, but he wondered if he was up to the task. His wounds would heal but he had already failed. Then again, so had his adversary, Orient noted, if without conviction.

+ + +

Hannah proved to be an extremely efficient administrator and in less than three hours had Orient out the door and in a cab, headed for his new address. He was still a bit unsteady from the hospital drugs and fell into bed as soon as he entered the small walk-up, on 112th street.

He was sleeping when Sybelle arrived. She had two shopping bags full of food and an envelope fat with cash.

"There's ten thousand to start with. Let me know if you need more. I also brought some nice hot chicken broth. Best thing when you're sick. I know you're vegan darling, but it's just *broth*. Anyway it's stuffed with vegetables, so eat it."

"Thank you... for everything.'

"Please, darling, I'm the one who got you into this.'

"If you recall, I'm the one who took you to see the fragment. Either way it seems inevitable.'

Sybelle started unpacking groceries and bustling about the kitchen. "Strange isn't it, I mean all these disparate elements being somehow interconnected."

"Over time," Orient added.

"Yes, true. What do you suppose *that* means Owen? Are we part of some cosmic tragedy?"

"I don't know," Orient said, "but I'm going to try to find out."

"But Owen, how?"

"As soon as I heal, I'm flying to Marrakech."

Chapter 25

Moe Klein was angry at himself.

He'd botched the arrest, let two suspects escape and had nothing to show but a poor dead security guard. At least the homicide was out of Wagner's jurisdiction, Moe reflected morosely.

He moved around the kitchen stiffly like an athlete after a tough game. The guard's name was Stanley Wicks, and he lived in New Jersey. Moe had made the trip to Union City to pay his respects to Stanley's wife. He knew he couldn't have prevented the murder but he felt somehow responsible. Stanly died instantly, his neck broken by a professional.

Moe was sure Orient wasn't his professional killer. But the mysterious doctor knew a lot more than he was telling. Orient was at the scene of at least three murders he noted, embedding bits of garlic into the salmon before consigning it to the grill.

What was he doing inside the Cloisters long after closing anyway? Moe asked himself. It was highly doubtful he went there to kill the guard. He methodically chopped a Bermuda onion and added it to his Romaine and heirloom tomato salad. Then he carefully laced the fragrant mix with extra virgin olive oil and a drop of balsamic vinegar.

The only thing that made sense was that Orient went there to ransom the girl. But from who —and for how much? If he was so goddamned anxious to bring the girl home, why wouldn't he cooperate with the bureau? Moe fumed. He set two plates, and two glasses on the kitchen table.

After opening a bottle of Coppola Chardonnay he set it down to breathe. Moe liked his white wines at room temperature, just like his reds. He checked the fish, then poured himself a glass. In between sips of wine he kept his eye on the salmon.

The doorbell sounded at precisely seven. That was another thing about Jake, besides his computer skills and appetite. He was always punctual.

Moe buzzed him in, left the door open and continued monitoring the salmon which was near done. "Come in and have some wine," he called as he heard Jake on the stairs, "I'm almost finished here. "There's some cheese and olives on the table. Nothing fancy."

"Smells pretty fancy to me. Nice hovel you have here, Is it the best they could give you, or did you fuck up?" Jake's impish grin erased any hint of malice. He lifted the shopping bag he was carrying. "I brought cognac and cigars—for dessert." Jake was a wealth of bureaucratic gossip. He had a handle on who was moving up, who was in disfavor and who commanded the biggest budget. He especially liked to rank the ten most wanted agents in the bureau.

"Right now you're at eleven," he confided, helping himself to more salmon. "A case this big gives you *memo power*. You've become an economy unto yourself. Which reminds me..." He nibbled at the salmon thoughtfully.

"What?" Moe said, marveling at how Jake's short, thin frame absorbed all that food. He had devoured the appetizers and drank half a bottle of wine before dinner.

"I brought a list of tech stuff we'll need. Some of it for you," he added, beaming at Moe "I need to bring you up to speed."

Moe smiled, in spite of himself. "Always working the room."

"Of course. So, tell me what happened the other night."

"I let my suspect escape."

"Before that. Give me details please."

As he retold the events leading up to finding Orient in the cloisters, he began to feel better. "Climbing that wall was a bitch. I heard something that sounded like a struggleand there he was," Moe said, "then there he wasn't. It was dark, bushes, plants. I heard a motorcycle, ran after it but he got away."

He started to refill his wine glass but Jake stopped him. "Time for some fine cognac, and a good cigar."

Moe found two snifters and served the apple pie he'd been warming.

"So when you followed this doctor," Jake said, between mouthfuls, "you said he stopped at this punk store. Did you find out what he bought?"

Moe stiffened. "What kind of question is that? Of course I found out."

"My apologies if I inferred otherwise. So...?"

"So, what?"

Jake deftly slipped the last of the apple pie onto his fork. "So what did he buy?"

"A black leather motorcycle jacket, a black watch cap, and a studded leather collar.

The clerk said it's called a 'dog collar'."

"Aha!" Jake said, chewing thoughtfully. "So what do we get from that? First option: He's gay and went to the Cloisters to meet a friend, maybe even the guard." When Moe didn't react he went on. "Second option: He's a serial killer and got dressed up for the kill."

Moe shrugged. "Could be, but I don't think so."

Jake passed the snifter under his nose and inhaled. "Third option: He was on his way to meet a man known for his knife work and was wearing protection."

"That's my guess too." Moe lifted his glass. "Thanks for coming over, I was feeling lousy."

"You cook, I'm here, except we've got to talk about putting in for better digs. You need a two bedroom, at least."

"This place is fine, really, Jake."

"...with a decent kitchen."

That got Moe's attention. His cooking area was cramped, even by New York standards.

"You think?"

Jake gave him a sly grin. "I'll start working on it."

Moe's elation was temporary. He slipped back into brooding. "I don't even know who the fuck was on that motorcycle I chased. Meanwhile I've got a kidnapped girl, an escaped suspect, and a serial killer on the loose."

"So you don't think this doctor is involved."

"Oh he's involved all right, I just don't know how deep."

Jake carefully lit his cigar. "Maybe it's time to put more pressure on his lady friend, the psychic."

Moe sipped his drink. Its hot breath warmed his throat and stomach. "Good cognac."

"Try the cigar."

"Cuban?"

Jake looked shocked. "Please Moe, we're federal agents."

"Could be right about the Lean woman. She knows plenty she's not telling."

"What can you lose?"

Moe lit his cigar. "So where's this list of yours?"

+ + +

The next morning he was at his office early. He sent a progress memo upstairs, along with a request for additional computer equipment and an expense allotment for Agent Sanchez.

Jake was right, the bigger the budget, the better he was treated. He was also right about Orient's pal. It was time to turn up the heat.

At nine a.m. Moe was at the door of Sybelle Lean's townhouse.

She seemed mildly surprised to see him but not flustered. "Agent Klein. Oh dear, did something happen?" she said, with a hint of apprehension.

Moe tried to look intimidating. "I was hoping to find Doctor Orient."

"Well, he's certainly not here. But you're welcome to look. Would you like some coffee? I was just having breakfast."

As Moe followed her inside he had to stop himself from wiping his feet. Miss Lean certainly had a way about her, he observed. Out on Fire Island he had learned that the full-figured psychic was flamboyant but far from stupid.

"Why would you come here looking for Owen?" she asked, moving easily around the kitchen. "Please sit down. Here's coffee, there's milk and sugar on the table. I'm about to toast a bran muffin, would you like one?"

"Yes, thank you. I came here because Doctor Orient is not at home."

"Did you try calling?"

"Ms. Lean I think you should know that last night I tried to arrest Doctor Orient."

Sybelle turned. "Tried to arrest him —whatever for?"

"The murder of Peter Taegris."

"You can't be serious."

"Then there's the charge of withholding evidence," Moe said slowly, watching her reaction. If the veiled threat hit home it didn't register. Sybelle took the muffins from the toaster and brought them to the table. "There's Irish butter in that dish."

"Coffee's delicious."

Sybelle sat across from him. "Accusing Owen of murder is preposterous. Do you have any evidence?"

For a moment Moe felt he was the one being grilled. "Actually I do," he said.

"May I ask what?"

Moe carefully buttered the warm muffin.

"I *am* Savana's aunt. She was taken from *me* remember? And if you're wasting time investigating the most honorable man I know—you'd better have something more than suspicions."

"I have the results of a DNA test that links Doctor Orient to Savana Wylde's disappearance."

"But that's absurd. Why on earth would Owen harm her?"

"You never know. But DNA doesn't lie."

Moe took a bite of the muffin which was delicious. But his attention was on Sybelle Lean. She seemed distracted.

"Where would you get Owen's DNA?"

"On Fire Island, at your place. We collected samples, remember? From you as well."

Sybelle's green eyes flashed with indignation. "Oh yes. Another example of our police state. Investigate the victims."

Moe lifted his hand in surrender. "Just covering all bases."

"I still don't understand what sort of DNA evidence could possibly link Owen to Savana."

"We found a blanket belonging to Savana with Doctor Orient's blood on it."

"A *blanket* with…" Sybelle sat up. "Of *course*, well I can tell you why Owen's blood got…"

She looked at him with a helpless expression. "Actually I can't tell you."

Why not, Ms. Lean?"

"Because you would never believe me."

Moe sipped his coffee. "Try me."

Hesitantly, Sybelle told him how she'd recruited Owen Orient when Savana was in a coma. And how he had recognized the symptoms and performed an exorcism.

Open mouthed, Moe listened, half fascinated, half wary. "So the girl scratched his face?"

"Yes, she was quite out of control. "

"Doctor Orient exorcized her and she came out of a coma…?"

"Absolutely, yes. I was there."

"This is great coffee." Moe said, trying to process what he'd just heard. A medical doctor who practiced exorcisms, that alone was worth investigating.

"Would you like another cup?"

"If you don't mind."

"Not at all."

"This may sound strange, but I have a tendency to believe your story."

Sybelle poured the coffee. "Oh? Why is that?"

"My specialty is primitive art and archeological artifacts. Digging around I've encountered a fair amount of unexplained phenomena."

She gave him a dazzling smile. "Then you will stop trying to arrest poor Owen?"

"I'm afraid we need to talk to him."

The smile froze. "We?'

"This is a criminal matter. I have a federal warrant."

Sybelle stiffened and folded her arms. "And I suppose you have one for me."

"Not at all. But I do appreciate your clarifying a few things."

"I happen to know something about the law. I did invite you, so you may look around if you wish. But then I must insist you leave."

Again Moe raised his hands. "Please, I did not come here to arrest you, or search your house. I do thank you for your hospitality and frankness. But before I leave I would like to ask you one question."

Sybelle pouted. "Fine, ask away..."

"Did you know if Mr Henry Applegate collected any Nazi memorabilia?"

"Nazi... well I only knew Henry for less than forty eight hours, but there is one thing..."

"Yes?"

"But again, you probably won't believe it."

"I'll listen. That I promise."

Without divulging any secrets Sybelle told him about the Nazi presence in the "vision" she had shared with Orient,

As he listened, something occurred to Klein. "Is Savana's mother involved in this, er.... psychic group?"

"Not at all. In fact, until Savana became afflicted, she didn't believe in any of it. Still doesn't in a way. There's no cult here, if that's what you're inferring."

"But you believe Savana's kidnapping, and these murders, are connected to some pyschic..." he searched for a word. "... magician?"

"We prefer 'practitioner', magician has such coarse connotations, it suggests trickery."

Moe nodded. He had a healthy respect for cultural and spiritual beliefs and was mildly superstitious himself, but this was getting into another realm. "Do you know where Doctor Orient is now?" He said, trying to bring the conversation back on point.

"I can call him and ask." Sybelle said sweetly.

"Please do."

With a flourish Sybelle produced a mobile phone and pecked at it with one long red nail. She pressed the speaker button and Moe heard the phone ringing, then Orient's voice asking the caller to leave a number. "Hello dear it's me. Please call me back."

"There," she said, putting the phone on the table, "anything else I can help you with?"

Cute, Moe thought. He considered bringing her in as a material witness. Instead he smiled, and pushed himself to his feet. "No, I think you've been quite forthcoming. And the coffee was great, as was your gracious hospitality."

"Well, I must say you are a gentleman, Agent Klein."

"Thank you. Here's my card. Call me if you have any questions."

Her green eyes fixed on his, and Moe felt the intensity behind her words. "I have no questions —only profound fear for my young niece."

Chapter 26

Hannah dropped in on Orient every evening after work. Although his wounds were comparatively superficial they restricted arm movement, and he needed to recover from blood loss. However, after two days, Orient became anxious to move.

"I don't have time for rehab," he told Hannah. "And the longer I stay here the deeper you're involved. Harboring a fugitive could look bad on your resume."

Hannah gave him a tired smile. "I'm afraid I haven't been doing a great job at the hospital. I'm so sick with worry."

"I'm certain Savana is okay," Orient said gently. "Look, I'm leaving here tomorrow but I'd like you to do something for me."

"Of course, Owen, what?"

He gave her his mobile phone. "I should have thought of this earlier. The kidnapper sent me a text message. Give this phone to Sybelle and have her deliver it to Agent Klein. Perhaps they can trace the source."

"Why don't I deliver it to the FBI directly?"

"Told you. I don't want you compromised."

She kissed him lightly, and nodded. "I'll take it to Sybelle right away."

After she was gone, Orient took a shower and prepared to leave. All he had were the clothes he was wearing the night he was attacked. He took the subway to Bloomingdale's and bought a basic wardrobe, which he put into a new carry-on bag, and a knapsack. He left the store wearing a brown tweed jacket, jeans, and sneakers, giving him what he hoped was a low key, professorial look.

Then he found a travel agency catering mainly to Latin clients and booked a round trip ticket to Paris the next evening.

"I'm going to need your passport," the agent told him

"I'll bring it in the morning,' Orient said, wondering if the FBI would be waiting at the airport gate.

The next day he went to his safety deposit box and retrieved his passport without incident. That night he was on a non-stop jet to Paris. Again, he didn't seem to be on any watch list. Stay alert, Orient thought, it's just a matter of time until you are. He pushed his knapsack under the seat ahead and settled into the cramped space allotted coach passengers.

+ + +

Charles de Gaulle airport housed a sprawling mix of architectural visions. Some of them, like the bent pyramid in Egypt, were added to replace flaws in former designs. Others aspired to overshadow their rivals. However, none of the three massive terminals sought to ease the traveler's burden. The complex was a glossy hodge-podge of competing functions but few services.

Once past customs, Orient made his way to the Air Maroc ticket desk and purchased a round-trip seat on a jet to Marrakech that departed three hours later. When he landed in Morocco, he had been on the road for twenty hours, and his battle-sore body was feeling the strain.

The airport terminal was small and the customs inspector was polite, but suspicious.

For a moment, he thought he was on some Interpol watch list, but after a brief, surly scrutiny the inspector stamped his passport and waved him through.

Not even the cheap gasoline burned by the local vehicles could stain the clear desert air outside the terminal. Located at the edge of the Sahara, Marrakech was an urban sprawl of squat concrete dwellings, pastel villas, and sand colored minarets with Djemma el-Fna the ancient market square, at its epicenter.

Rather than wait for the local bus, Orient haggled briefly with a taxi driver who drove him to the Omar Khayyam,
a modest hotel on Rue Tetouan. The lobby was decorated in
dramatic Moroccan fashion, with low brass tables, thick black
and red drapes, red leather poufs, and a large, brightly colored
Berber tribal rug, glistening with sequins. The hotel clerk sport-
ed a red fez, and the boy who took his bag wore ballooning
Berber pants and pointed yellow slippers. In contrast Orient's
room looked like an American Super Eight motel, including
the shrink wrapped toilet. The window overlooked a cramped
garden and even at a distance Orient could hear the dull throb
of drums in the marketplace.

Exhausted, he barely was able remove his clothes before he
fell asleep.

At dawn Orient awoke hungry. It was too early for a hotel
breakfast so he decided to stroll to the *souk*.

The wide avenues were relatively deserted. The only traffic
was the occasional donkey bearing baskets of goods bound for
the marketplace. Here an there were men sleeping inside their
hooded *djelabas* in the alcoves of modern office buildings. As
he walked along Avenue Mohammed V, named for the king revered as a saint, the office buildings and stucco villas gave way
to luxury hotels. The traffic swelled a bit as people streamed
towards the square. Two men passed on bicycles, a boy drove a
trio of sheep, followed by a woman on a donkey. Behind them
a pair of veiled women with tattooed hands, strode in perfect
step, large bundles balanced on their heads.

The early morning sun had begun to disperse the desert chill, and when he passed through the walls of the fabled
square there were already signs of activity. Orient spotted an
orange vendor nearby and bartered a price for two glasses of
fresh juice. Other vendors were setting up for business and he
found a tiny stall with a single chair and folding table where
he stopped for a bowl of yogurt and honey. At another stall
he bought some bananas, eating one as he wandered about the

ever more populated marketplace. The straight lines of tiny
stalls formed lanes and in between, arrayed on carpets or straw
mats, were the performers: acrobats, dancers, musicians, jug-
glers, magicians and story tellers. Sharing the stage were various
healers, herbalists and tarot card readers

At the moment most of them were involved with their
preparations. Orient paused to watch some young acrobats going through their morning stretches which were not too different from his own. A few feet away a fortune teller was carefully
placing a worn deck of Tarot cards on a milk box covered with
a black silk cloth, its bangles glinting in the sun.

Many in the square looked as if they had just crossed the
Sahara by caravan, with their blue wash turbans and piercing
kohl-lined eyes peering above black face masks. A good number
had curved knives dangling at their waist.

The crackling sound of an amplified voice singing the
morning prayer, floated across the square from the minaret
outside the walls. Orient took refuge on the roof terrace of the
Argana Café at the edge of the square. From his table on an
outside terrace he drank hot tea and watched the crowd pour
into the souk, as the melodic prayer faded into the murmur of
activity. Somewhere a drum began to beat, and another joined
in.

Djemma el-Fna, can be loosely translated as "mosque of
the dead." At one time it was used as a place of execution, later
as a gathering area which grew into a marketplace and performance area.

Fascinated, Orient watched the rich tapestry of humanity weaving through the square: black Africans in tribal robes,
fierce Berbers, Arabs, desert Tuaregs, English tourists, all
flowed beneath him, forming circles around various stalls and
street performers. With the exception of the surrounding hotels
and young Moroccans on cell phones, the souk had changed
little since the time of his visit two decades before—or even
the time of his vision, seventy years in the past.

As he left the café and entered the flow of people, Orient became aware of various smells. The scent of spices, of grilling meat, of mint, of myrrh incense and of kif, all mingled with the musky human odors of the market. He opened his inner senses, dowsing for connections he knew were there.

Turning a corner around some food stalls he found himself in a section dominated by fortune tellers, amulet writers and snake charmers, all sitting in chairs, or squatting on mats, their backs to the sun. The amulet writers and Tarot readers used black umbrellas to shield their clients from prying eyes.

The atonal notes of a *ghaita*, a Moroccan folk oboe, drifted above the murmuring drums, like desert bagpipes. A vivid streak of color drew Orient's attention. A large cobra was rising from a wooden box, its flared neck marked with a yellow-edged red diamond. The snake arched higher, weaving from side to side, as if seeking someone in the crowd. Abruptly it stood stock still, hooded blank eyes fixed on Orient.

For a long moment they remained locked on each other, the cobra, mimicking his slightest move. If he edged aside, the cobra edged with him. When he turned so did the deadly snake.

At least so it seemed. A few in the tightly bunched crowd were starting to notice. Orient felt a strange, primal pulse at the base of his brain, connecting him to the reptile.

The atonal pipes broke the link, lifting to a peak, and the reptile moved closer to its master. As the drums intensified, the cobra began to weave back and forth, in a deadly dance, still staring at Orient.

Orient shuffled nearer and saw the musician was a dark, wiry man, dressed in a short, white robe that reached to the knees of his white pants. He was crouched beside the open, wood box, a number of smaller snakes coiled beside his bare ankles as he played.

The man kept glancing at Orient, then at the cobra.

When the music rose to a fever pitch the snake charmer got to his feet and approached the cobra. He began to slowly sway in rhythm with the poisonous reptile's movements. Abruptly he stopped playing. The distant drums sounded louder in the silence as the white-robed snake charmer bent close to the nervous, stiff-bodied cobra, its huge neck inflated for a lethal strike... and kissed it.

The crowd's applause jostled Orient's fascination with the serpent. The audience dropped coins and bills into the basket as they dispersed. The snake charmer carefully coaxed the cobra back into the box, before he gathered the other reptiles, swiftly putting them in straw baskets.

Then he scooped up the money dropped into the clay bowl. Orient started to add a bill to the small pile but the wiry performer lifted his arm.

"For a brother, the show is free."

Taken aback, Orient managed a smile. "We are all brothers," he said.

The man wagged his finger. "Only a few understand." He inclined his head toward the wooden box housing the cobra. "She recognized you."

Orient didn't know what to say.

"I am Ganwi." The man took a theatrical bow. "Will you take tea?"

Without waiting for an answer he led Orient to a nearby stall where a crude café was set up, with a large teapot boiling on a charcoal grill. Orient followed hesitantly, not at all certain he wanted to sit chatting with the snake charmer when he could be pursuing his mission. However he could use a tea break and Ganwi might be helpful in locating the people he was looking for.

"My name is Owen," he said, when they were seated across from each other at a wooden picnic table. "I am looking for a guide, a man named Muhammed."

Ganwi laughed and swept his hand over the crowded square. "There are two thousand guides named Mohammed in the Djemma el-Fna my friend. But tell me, you are not surprised to meet a queen cobra?"

"Many people here have met her before me."

"But none as closely as you. You have touched the soul of the serpent. I felt it myself."

Orient sipped the fragrant mint tea, aware that the market abounded with con-men and tricksters. There were probably many tourists attracted to the cobra. Perhaps its vibrant yellow and red markings had a hypnotic effect, he speculated. It was part of the show.

Ganwi snapped his fingers and a young boy ran to his side. He said something in a language Orient didn't understand.

"I was talking Berber. You know Arabic?"

"*Shwea*," Orient said, meaning he knew a little bit. He was being modest.

Ganwi smiled. Orient studied the wiry performer as he drank his tea. He was between thirty or forty, and his large head seemed slightly out of proportion to his small frame, His movements were fluid and quick, and his grey eyes glinted brightly. His white shirt and trousers were immaculate, despite performing in the dusty marketplace.

Within minutes the boy returned with a large black umbrella. Ganwi opened it and motioned Orient to his side. "Imshee," he said, shooing the boy who lingered curiously.

Veiled from outside view, save for the proprietor who was busy putting glasses in a tea caddy for delivery, Ganwi rolled up his sleeve.

On his forearm was a tattoo of an eight pointed star. In the center square was the word, *AGLA*. Orient recognized the image. It was the same sacred symbol etched on the gold ring in his pocket: the Seal of Solomon. On both sides, were coiled cobras.

Ganwi leaned closer. "All snake handlers and scorpion eaters in Morocco... We all belong to the Isawi Brotherhood." He paused to touch his forehead reverently. "Sidi Muhhammad bin Isa is our saint. Since fifteenth century." He pointed to the tattoo.

"You know this sign, you understand the serpent. You are brother to the Isawi."

Orient bowed his head, touched by the recognition. "I am honored by your generosity."

Ganwi rolled down his sleeve. He folded the umbrella, and tossed it to the boy, who was waiting nearby. He turned and beamed at Orient. "It was known we would have a visitor. Tell me what you seek."

Orient didn't ask how. He knew the square was bristling with magic of all types... love potions, crystal readers, Sufi mystics.

"I'm looking for another man. He had a shop inside the souk." He pointed to the entrance of a structure at the edge of the square which led to a maze of indoor tunnels.

"The man, you know his name?"

Orient would never forget.

Many years before this shopkeeper in an obscure souk, had used his enormous power as an occult adept to aid Orient in another vital quest.

"His name is Ahmehmet, he is an antique dealer."

Ganwi sat back, nodding thoughtfully. He turned and said something to the boy, who ran off in the direction of the indoor souk. Then he sighed, and took a small red pouch from one pocket of his long shirt, and from the other drew a snake-skin case. Inside the case were two sections of a carved wood pipe. Ganwi put the sections together then carefully fitted a small clay bowl on one end of the long pipe stem.

Slowly, as if performing a ritual, he filled the bowl with bright green *kif.* "Sans tabac," he said. Meaning it didn't contain the traditional black tobacco.

Ganwi lit a match and carefully passed the flame over the bowl as he inhaled, then passed the pipe to Orient.

"Om, aing, chring, cling, char-muda, yei, vijay," Orient murmured, invoking the ancient Brahmin mantra for the consecration of bhang. Tentatively he drew on the pipe, found the smoke smooth and sweet, and drew deeper. He handed the pipe back to Ganwi and felt his skin cool despite the heat of the noon sun. The tensions wrapped around his thoughts eased a few notches, and he felt his limbs relax.

Ganwi nodded approval and passed the pipe again.

The strains of music that collided in the marketplace: the classical Arabic strings and techno pop on various radios—the live guitars, *ouds*, drums and oboes—all separated and reformed into a soothing harmony. The shuffling passers by were distinct one from another, even as they continued to merge and move on.

As they sat sipping their tea, Orient sensed the connection between himself and his new brother. He watched a trio of scowling western tourists, all three trying to avoid contact with the parade of humanity flowing around them like water past rocks. The female winced every time someone brushed against her, which was often.

Gamwi caught his eye and they both laughed. Still chuckling Orient watched Ganwi's young assistant come running through the crowd, and whisper in his ear.

"Very good," Ganwi said. He smiled at Orient. "Aza, will take you to Ahmehmet's shop." He reached into his pocket and produced a small pouch on a crude leather string. "This is to protect you—and also what is most valuable to you. I pray for your safe passage my brother."

Ganwi solemnly gave him the pouch and they embraced. Orient turned and followed the boy, still wondering what Ganwi meant by his parting remarks.

Chapter 27

There were fewer tourists inside the tunnels.
The souk was walled with corrugated metal and
dusty rays of sunlight filtered through slotted roofs.
Small shops selling everything from jewelry to spices lined both
sides of the bustling maze.

A constant stream of people shared the narrow passages
with bicycles, carts and livestock, as they had been doing for
five hundred years. Leading the way, Aza moved through the
crowd easily, but Orient found it difficult to keep him in sight,
as he dodged masked Berber women on cell phones, blue robed
Tuaregs wearing Nikes, and the occasional burro. The alleys
converged and split off in various directions, and Orient hurried closer, having momentarily lost all sense of direction.

Then he saw Aza waiting at an alley crossroad. The boy
waved and moved on. For a moment Orient hesitated, the place
had a dreamlike quality, as if he had been there before. A moment later the dream cleared.

He had been here, many years ago, while on a similar quest
to save a life in peril. Back then he had failed, Orient noted
grimly, trying to suppress his growing excitement at seeing
his old friend and mentor. It did little to control his surge of
emotion.

Even before Aza stopped in front of the brightly beaded
curtains, Orient recognized the antique shop where he had first
encountered Ahmehmet, the master occultist. He quickened his
step and ducked inside.

It was as he remembered, all of it. The thick rugs, the
gilded cash register, the vase of lush flowers, the ornate pillows,
the shelves displaying Berber jewelry studded with red coral, antique silver coins, ancient Roman glasses, and various oddities,

the light from old fashioned oil lamps, the carved wood desk beside the entrance to the inner room... it was all the same.

Except for the man sitting behind the desk.

He was perhaps thirty years old, with smooth features and large black eyes that seemed to take in everything. Although youthful, there was a certain gravitas in his demeanor as he rose to greet Orient. "Welcome back," he said, "it has been many years."

Orient smiled through his momentary confusion. The young man seemed to know him.

"Time runs faster than the clock can follow," he replied.

"You have journeyed long to reach us."

The words resonated like chimes in his mind. It was the traditional greeting known only to the initiates of the Serene Knowledge. Orient paused, not certain.

"The journey is like the flow of water," he said finally, using the formal reply.

"And water finds the thirsty man."

The young man got up beaming. "It is good to see you again, Doctor."

Orient paused, uncertain of how to react.

The young man saw his hesitation and turned to Aza who stood near the beaded entrance, watching wide-eyed. "Go back to the market and tell Ganwi all is well."

He watched the boy depart then turned expectantly.

"The journey is strewn with illusions," Orient said softly.

"Then the journey will take long to complete." The young man extended his hand.

"The journey will complete itself in time," he said, finally convinced. As Orient took his hand, a small shock of recognition cleared his memory. "Yousef, you've grown since we last met."

Yousef laughed. "That will happen in twenty years. Come inside, and have tea."

When they last met Yousef had been an eleven year old apprentice. Now he was a self assured adult. Orient noticed the talismans inked on his hands, Kaballistic symbols from the Secret Books of Moses.

Those same symbols were embroidered on the thick drapes in the inner room, where a silver tea service and cups, stood ready on a low wood table, beside thick pillows. Orient remembered this room, and all that he had learned here from Ahnehmet. He sat on one of the pillows and accepted a cup of tea.

"And how is the master?"

The moment he asked, Orient knew the answer. Yousef's smile faded, and his sorrow was palpable in the lamp-lit room. "It has been two years now, since Ahmehmet departed on his appointed journey. Without him, I still feel like the apprentice you knew."

Orient nodded. Although he had known the master briefly, he felt a deep sense of loss.

"My prayers go with him, and with you." He took a sip of the strong black tea. "However it's clear you have risen above an apprentice."

"Ahmehmet taught me well," Yousef said, with a hint of pride. "But few men, ever reach his level of enlightenment." He looked at Orient. "He often spoke of your strong powers."

Orient shrugged, and said nothing.

"If you can tell me what you sought from Ahmehmet," Yousef said slowly, "perhaps I can be of some help."

"I'm trying to locate a guide named Mohammed."

"Do you know this man?"

"I met him seventy years ago—in a vision."

Yousef thoughtfully regarded his cup. "This man might be dead."

"Then I will have failed in my quest."

"To find this Mohammed?"

"To find a young girl who's in extreme danger."

"Did you speak to Ganwi of this man?"

"Yes, he said there were many Mohammads in Djemma el-Fna."

"That is true, but not many would be so old."

"He was very young when I met him. So he's probably near ninety."

"Believe it or not, many Mohammeds live to be ninety—and more—in Morocco, simple food, good air, no alcohol, much walking..."

"Many wives?" Orient suggested, with a wry smile.

Yousef raised his hands. "That will age one most quickly," he said laughing. Then he grew serious. "Do you have anything that can connect you to this man, some object perhaps?"

"No," Orient said regretfully. Then he remembered. The ring on Savana's finger, was the one used in the ceremony he'd interrupted many years before. And Mohammed had led them there.

He reached into his watch pocket and pulled out the gold Seal of Solomon.

Yousef's eyes widened. "May I... see it?"

He took a small magnifying glass from his pocket and examined the ring closely.

"It is the true Seal," Yousef said, voice hushed. He handed it back. "But you should keep it in a more... respectful place."

"I understand. Will this do?" He showed him the small pouch he had just received from Ganwi. .

"It is very good," Yousef said after a brief study. "These are rare herbs and powdered roots inside. You can conceal the ring under those."

He was right. The ring disappeared beneath the dried herbs inside the pouch.

"Allow me to knot it around your neck."

When it was done the simple leather pouch hung out of sight under his shirt.

"This is similar to the medicine bags worn many tribes and clans around the world," Yousef explained. "The one you wear is the ancient amulet of the Isawi Brotherhood."

He half bowed and left the room. He returned holding a blue ceramic bowl filled with water. He set the bowl on the table between them. Then he lit a candle and placed it beside the bowl.

"So Doctor, if you wish—let's try to locate this old man Mohammed."

+ + +

It took only a few minutes for Orient to enter a state of deep concentration. Opening his senses, he became aware of Yousef's vibrational orbit. As their psychic energies merged, his gaze was drawn to the blue bowl. The candle flame sent reflections dancing across the water. His focus narrowed as he watched, sharpening his sight. The reflections became a slow spinning mosaic of color until... the churning fragments congealed into an image....

...A dusty taxi waiting in the market.

Orient saw a slender old man emerge from the driver's side. He wore Berber balloon pants and a black vest. Despite the man's advanced age Orient recognized him immediately.

His concentration wavered, and he sat back.

When he looked up, he saw Yousef waiting expectantly.

"Mohammed. I think he's a..."

"...Taxi driver." Yousef said. "Yes, I saw him as well." He stood up and moved to the beaded entrance to his shop.

Orient watched him gesture to a couple of young boys, and say something. The children ran off. Yousef returned, and poured them both a fresh cup of tea.

"This Mohammed is well known. His taxi has occupied the same spot in the souk for years. My messengers will find him and bring him here."

Orient nodded, grateful for the favor. He hadn't slept much since leaving New York and he was in an early stage of exhaustion.

Yousef was curious about the ring, and Orient gave him a brief account of its journey.

"You think the Seal had something to do with the girl's possession?"

"The ring was an instrument, not the cause. We managed to repel the negative influence."

"But it remains waiting beyond the Light, like a predator, waiting."

"Yes." Orient admitted, depressed by the thought.

They were interrupted when Aza came through the beaded curtain in the front room, with what appeared to be a Scandinavian couple.

Yousef rose and went to greet them. Orient sat in the small, candlelit back room while the couple browsed the shop. He noticed it was young Aza who attempted the hard sell, while Yousef was more host than salesman.

Aza unrolled a long, Berber rug, woven in tribal patterns of red and black. The female tourist, very young, was obviously smitten with the rug, The male, equally young, seemed more interested on an antique Arabic dagger, its curved scabbard studded with turquoise.

After haggling briefly, Yousef sold the dagger to the male, who seemed pleased with his purchase. When they left the shop Aza turned to Yousef.

"Why did you sell him the knife for such a low price? We would have made more profit if we sold them the carpet."

Yousef smiled. "Tell me, my young businessman, what did you see?"

The boy seemed confused.

"The couple," Yousef urged, "did you notice anything about them?"

"She wanted to buy the rug," Aza ventured.

"True, very good. Anything else?"

Aza shrugged. "She was maybe not happy when he bought the dagger."

"Excellent. Then you should know what will happen next."

"I don't understand, Master," the boy said after a few moments.

"Perhaps you only saw what you wished. The young couple is newly married. The girl sees the carpet in their new home. The young husband sees a trophy of his adventure. What he doesn't see is his new wife."

"I still don't understand. They did not buy the carpet, and your price for the dagger was too low."

"Yes. But this evening the new wife will be distant. Perhaps she will have a headache. The new husband will be lonely that night. In the morning it will come to him. He bought the dagger at such a good price that surely he can bargain a good price for the carpet. He will make his new wife happy again. And tomorrow we will sell him the carpet."

Looking dubious, the boy nodded.

Yousef laughed and clapped his hands. "Go now, and find some new clients."

As Aza left, an old man ducked through the beaded curtains.

"Master Yousef, do you need a taxi?"

Orient rose and moved to the outer room. The man was old, with deep creases in his face, and thin neck, but he carried himself with the alertness of a younger man. When he saw Orient, he narrowed his eyes as if trying to recall something. .

Yousef gestured to Orient. "Is this the man you seek?"

Orient looked. The man wore a knit cap, Berber pants and a vest, much like the clothes he wore in the past vision. Then he noticed the gold watch on the man's wrist. Sybelle's watch, the one he'd traded.

He smiled at the man. "You are Mohammed?"

"Yes. Do you know me?"

"The question is, do you remember me?"

Mohammed peered at Orient. "Perhaps, you seem familiar but..."

"Many years ago, when you were a guide, you took me to a place underground. There were German soldiers, a strange ceremony..."

"Allah bless me, I do remember!" Mohammed exclaimed suddenly. "How could I forget? My life changed that very night."

He turned to Yousef and smiled. It was then Orient saw the gold tooth.

"We saw the girl running from the soldiers. You ran after her but you didn't know the streets. I was able to follow. Then I came and led you to her."

"For a price."

"A man must live. Anyway the price you paid was worthless." He lifted his arm and pointed. "A watch that refuses to tell time."

"But tell me, how was your life changed?"

"There was great confusion that night You stopped the man with the knife from killing the girl. Everything went dark. I heard shouts, gunfire. I hid myself behind a stairway and when I came out, it was quiet. As I made my way through the shadows, I saw a gleam of light on the floor. It reflected the full moon shining through a broken window— a ring of pure gold."

He paused and extended his arms. "I sold the ring to a rich German. With the money I bought my first taxi, and have prospered—because of you my friend."

"Who was this rich German?" Orient said. "Do you remember his name?"

The old man nodded. "Von Speer, he is still alive. He resides here in Marrakech. I can drive you to his house if you wish."

Orient knew the name from certification papers given him by the late Peter Taegris. Deiter Von Speer had been chairman of the University of Berlin's School of Archeology, But he too would have to be an old man by now.

Mohammed answered his question as he drove Orient to Von Speer's house. "This man Von Speer was a little older than me. But like you, he never seems to age."

It would be difficult to explain to Mohammed why he hadn't gotten older, Orient thought. Still, the comment about Von Speer was curious.

+ + +

The elderly guide was a careful driver, weaving slowly through the chaotic foot traffic.

"You still have the ladies watch I gave you..." Orient asked.

"Yes, yes, but it will not work. It is stopped."

"Then why do you still wear it?"

"As a token of that night when I became rich. But the watch is worthless."

"In that case I will buy it back from you. Is this enough?"

Mohammed reached over his shoulder and took the bills.

"It's more than enough."

He pulled over, took the slim gold watch from his wrist, and handed it to Orient.

Orient looked at it. "I thought you said it doesn't work."

Mohammed's eyes went wide when he took the watch. "But how is it possible. I took this to the finest watchmaker in Marrakech and still it would not tell time."

Time.

Orient knew it was why the watch hadn't functioned. They had traveled back in time, creating an anomaly that froze the piece in a parallel reality. Contact with its departure point, revived the dormant works.

"You promised me one thing," Mohammed said, handing the watch back.

"Yes?"

The elderly taxi man fixed Orient with his dark eyes. "Tell me the secret of your youth."

Orient hesitated. Trying to explain was too complicated, even if Mohammed believed him. Finally he said, "Eat no meat, drink much water, walk seven kilometers each day, and trust in Allah."

Mohammed squinted, as if trying to discern the truth. Then he turned and started the engine.

"Alright, I will do this. But when my new son is confirmed I must eat lamb."

Orient shook his head and smiled. Mohammed needed no advice on eternal youth.

"Voilà, we are here."

He peered out the car window at a walled villa, made of burnt orange stucco. All the window shutters were closed and there was no one at the gate.

Mohammed left the car and rang the bell. A dark woman with blue facial tattoos appeared behind the gate. They exchanged a few words and the elderly driver returned.

"She say Von Speer went to his house in Pass France."

"Pass, France? Is she sure?"

"She's a Berber woman from the mountains—maybe she's sure."

"Maybe *Paris,* France?"

"Maybe."

Orient took that as a yes.

"But she said he won't be back this year."

His brief bubble of enthusiasm deflated. He'd tracked Von Speer to the edge of the Sahara, only to find he was gone. Possibly to Paris. He took a deep breath and tried to stave off a wave of depression. He was exhausted, hurt, hungry and had a low grade headache.

"Please take me to the Omar Khayyam hotel on..."

"Rue Tetouan, yes I know it. Good you take a rest. Feel better tomorrow."

When Mohammed dropped Orient off, he gave him explicit directions to his taxi stand for future reference. "I'll see you tomorrow, old friend," Orient said. But he wasn't sure if he would make it.

+ + +

The first thing Orient did when he returned to his room was to get under a long shower. Afterwards he checked his watch and saw it was too early for dinner. The last time he'd eaten was at dawn in the market, and his blood sugar had hit bottom. He dried his hair with a towel, and dressed, preparing to scour the neighborhood for a grocery store or café, when the phone rang.

"The boy is here with your meal," the desk clerk said.

"Who is here?"

"The boy, Aza, is here with your meal."

"Of course, please send him up," Orient said, somewhat confused.

When he opened the door, Aza stood holding a tray, covered with a white cotton cloth

"Ganwi sent this food for you." The boy said. Without ceremony, he stepped past Orient and deposited the tray on a low table near the bed.

Orient pulled back the cloth. On the tray was a plate of *cous-cous* with vegetables, two containers of yogurt, a small jar of honey, bread, cheese, figs, and a bowl of milk.

"You must place the milk next to your bed," Aza told him.

When Orient looked puzzled he added, "Ganwi said it will protect you."

Orient smiled. "Of course," he said. But he was still puzzled.

He tried to give the boy some money, but Aza shyly refused. "It is my honor, Doctor," he said.

"Your teacher should be proud of you."

Aza beamed. "Ganwi and Yousef, both my teachers. Someday I will learn to be a doctor like you."

"Please give Ganwi my thanks." He said, as the boy politely backed out of the room.

Ravenous, Orient ate all the food on the tray. He placed the bowl of milk next to his bed as requested by Ganwi, but after sifting through his memory, he could not find a link to the offering.

Although spent, he felt restless. He had a sense that some-one or something was watching him. He went to the window and peered down at the garden. Except for a couple strolling below with drinks in their hands, there was nothing.

Jet lag, he told himself, you've been pushing it. A dull ache in his shoulder and arm reminded him that his knife wounds were far from healed. He took off his shoes and stretched out on the bed for a moment.

An instant later he was wandering toward the hazy light, to-ward the distant voices drifting above. Everything was luminous grey, before it began to clear,

A dank, silent forest surrounded him. Effortlessly he moved across the damp grass. His skin, too, felt cold and damp and he sought warmth. Instead it became colder. He paused and raised his head to see where he might find his way out, when an icy fear dropped over him. It was very heavy, like a glacier crushing his lungs. In panic he lunged blindly, thrashing his arms...

A hot slash of pain jerked him awake. His arm was burning. The lights were on and a dark, repellant shape was on his chest, staring with small, red-rimmed eyes, its bloody teeth bared in anticipation.

Shouting, Orient blindly swatted the creature aside. But something stabbed his toe with rabid fury. When he saw the creatures attacking him, his shouts became a low battle growl.

He drew his feet under him and pressed his back against the wall.

Seven or eight large hairy rats half-circled the bed. At least four looked to be over a foot long.

Chapter 28

The rat that had bitten his toe crouched at the far corner of the mattress, mouth wet with fresh blood. The one he'd smacked off his chest sat crouched on the other corner.

At first Orient thought the bowl of milk had attracted them, but then he saw the creatures avoided that area.

Was that Ganwi's idea of protection?

For a wild second he glanced around for a weapon but there was nothing but a telephone and a copy of the Koran on the night table. On the other side was a large painted ashtray.

Instinctively he shouted, freezing the creatures, and grabbed for the ashtray. It was made of glazed clay, smooth and light. Too light for a club. Orient tapped the ashtray against the wall. It cracked into three sharp pieces. He grabbed two of them, a crude knife in each hand.

It didn't faze the rats. He could feel the momentum building.

Orient got his feet under him and started to stand, but before he found his balance, both creatures on the bed attacked at once, knocking him back down against the wall. He hit one with his fist, but the other bit deep into his hand. The blazing agony forced a savage rasp from his throat as he punched the creature with the clay blade. The glazed point drew blood then broke.

Incredibly, the rat seemed to know this. It arched its back and bared its sharp teeth in a mocking grin, a harmless red streak on one side of its fat, pink belly.

Suddenly a third rat leaped onto the bed. As he stared at the three creatures poised to strike, he realized the second wave on the floor would attack while he was trying to ward the first, here on the bed.

Breathlessly he clutched his useless blade. The other still had a point, but was small. It would deter momentarily, not defeat. Flaming tongues of pain licked at his forearm, hand and foot. Oily red blood was spreading over his fingers, its scent exciting the rats.

On his knees, facing the creatures, he again tried to get his feet under him, succeeding only in throwing him slightly off balance.

In that frozen nanosecond Orient knew they would all attack him this time—eight sets of fetid teeth drooling saliva and blood, digging into his flesh, tearing him apart piece by piece. He looked at the door. He could run the gauntlet. They'd be nipping at him all the way. Still better than being slowly devoured where he was.

As he was about to make his move two of the rats leaped for his wounded foot. Before he could slash them off, they had both bitten him badly. Desperately, he heaved himself erect ready to race for the door.

He almost collapsed when the agonizing bolt, shocked his foot. Steadying himself against the wall, he tried to kick at the nearest creature. With whip-like speed it eluded the kick and bit his ankle. Roaring in pain and frustration he grabbed the rat's neck and flung it away.

Through the confusion Orient realized in a few moments the creatures would come in force, gnawing at his exposed wounds until he could no longer fend them off.

He readied himself, blood galloping through his temples. Then he lunged.

On contact with the floor white-hot agony speared his bloody foot, and he fell. Helpless he curled into a cat-like ball on his back, ready to claw and kick at the filthy creatures coming to feast on his flesh.

His eyes locked on the largest of the rats. The creature had had leaped off the mattress after him and now its eyes glittered with feverish triumph as it advanced, dodging his feeble thrusts, its hungry army fanning out behind.

Orient saw it first.

Emerging from beneath the bed like a swift stream of black water.

The liquid body lifted from the carpet and flared, framing a yellow-edged red diamond above blank, crescent eyes. It was over six feet long, and its pointed tongue darted restlessly.

The hair on the lead rat's back bristled with static electricity. Abruptly, without turning, it leaped away.

Too late.

The cobra struck, catching its prey in mid air. The large rat jerked spastically as the serpent injected its lethal venom into its pinkish belly. The cobra swayed from side to side, the twitching rat still impaled on its fangs, as if displaying a trophy.

Its fellow creatures scurried back, but remained out of striking distance, watching their leader's stiff-limbed death throes. But instead of swallowing its prey, the cobra deposited the rat on the floor and slithered to the bowl of milk Orient had placed there.

A cold film of sweat soaked through Orient's shirt as the cobra drank the milk in the bowl. It was then he understood.

With difficulty, he rolled to his knees and saw the rest of the rats were still there. He stared numbly as the creatures warily moved closer to their fallen comrade. And then, to his horrified amazement, the rats begin to drag the dead leader across the floor.

Slowly, inch by inch, they pulled the body all the way to a half open closet, and disappeared inside.

When Orient turned, the cobra was gone.

So was the milk.

He stumbled to the phone and called for a taxi.

+ + +

The young doctor who dressed Orient's wounds strongly suggested rabies injections.

Normally, Orient would have prescribed the same treatment, but he knew his injuries required a healer with more ancient skills.

Still not fully recovered from his earlier battles in New York, Orient limped out of the French Hospital, the fresh gashes on his foot, hand and arm, smoldering like embers under the bandages. The large rat had attacked the same arm slashed by the blond man in the Cloisters. And despite expert treatment by the emergency ward physician, it felt as if it had been seared in boiling oil.

It was well before midnight and Orient could hear the drums becoming louder as his cab approached Djemma el-Fna. He made his way toward the sound, avoiding contact with the tourists and vendors crowding the torch lit square. In the flickering half-light of kerosene lamps, candles and small torches, the shadows exaggerated the exotic faces and costumes standing in knots around the tribal dancers, street magicians, acrobats and drummers practicing their arts. He found Ganwi in midst of a performance, his high pitched pipes coaxing his serpents to dance. Until the drumbeats intensified—and the Queen Cobra made her appearance scales shimmering like black silk as she swayed up from her wooden nest, tongue flicking nervously.

The reptile slithered along the edge of the gathered audience driving them back a few paces. Orient stood motionless as the reptile paused in front of him, flat eyes fixed on his, before circling back to where Ganwi was waiting to conclude his performance.

Afterwards Ganwi came to him.

"My brother what's wrong, are you ill?"

Voice hoarse from exhaustion, Orient tersely told him about the encounter in his hotel room. "Many thanks for your protection."

Ganwi shrugged, glancing around the square as if looking for spies. "Both Yousef and myself saw the dark creature stalking you. And it waits for you still... Come, we will heal your wounds."

He took Orient back to Yousef's shop inside the tunneled souk. They made Orient comfortable while Aza went for an herbalist.

When Orient told Yousef the source of his wounds, the shopkeeper's face clouded. "Your enemy is master of beasts, perhaps part beast. Ganwi's protection is strong. But away from here you will need more."

"I have this," Orient said, touching the leather pouch.

"Always wear the ring when you are alone," Yousef told him, "it will gather strength and help heal your wounds. But these... *bites* are quite serious. Most certainly they will become infected. We must cleanse them immediately."

Orient nodded and lay back on his pillow "At least the knife wounds weren't infectious."

Yousef sighed "For a good man you seem to have... how do you say it, *pissed off* too many people.".

Aza returned with a large-breasted Berber woman, with traditional facial tattoos which included a distinctive star pattern on her forehead that resembled a faceted jewel.

When she smiled at Orient her skin crinkled like webs around her eyes and mouth, revealing her advanced age. After a brief conversation with Ganwi in the Berber language, she examined the wounds and silently went to work.

The healer carried an array of bottled liquids and creams in a wool shoulder bag. She set to work mixing some of them in bowls provided by Yousef. As she worked she muttered under her breath.

Orient had a working knowledge of many languages, but only those born to the tribe could understand Berber—it being an oral tongue, largely unwritten. It might have been a prayer, or an old woman's complaint at being hauled out to treat a stranger.

At the same time his wounds began to smolder, and he felt the onset of fever.

He was aware of the old woman looming over him, uttering incomprehensible sounds in a deep rhythmic voice. He felt a damp cloth cool his foot and a soothing cream douse the fire that seared his shoulder.

Sometime after that he slipped into a deep, secure sleep.

Chapter 29

The night jet to Paris was half full, and Orient was able to stretch out his long legs.

The old Berber healer had left a jar of cream, with instructions to apply it to his wounds every time he changed bandages. Happily, both his foot and shoulder remained functional.

He had awakened mid-morning in the back of Yousef's shop to find himself free of fever or pain. He had spent most of the day wandering about the primitive marketplace, bubbling with ancient magic, primitive healing and ageless customs. And twelve hours later, he was flying at thirty thousand feet, inside the belly of a cyber-age machine, completely guided by computers

We have our parallel universes right here on this tiny planet, Orient noted, using his phone to confirm a hotel reservation in Paris.

Orient arrived at three a.m. and left his room at ten, feeling reasonably refreshed, and remarkably recuperated from his losing battles. He had recovered free range of motion in his shoulder and his foot gave no hint of injury as he walked the wet Parisian streets.

He had found three D. Von Speers in the phone book, all in different parts of the city.

However it was raining and traffic was snarled, so he found it easier to walk. From time to time, when the rain became too heavy, he sought refuge in a café. Over coffee and croissants he watched the Parisians scurry about their daily errands, and wondered how his life had taken such a strange trajectory. Speaking of parallel universes, he thought, idly leafing through a French newspaper.

He started to turn a page then stopped, his eye drawn to a small box in the corner of the Arts section. There was a photograph of a Ming Vase. Beneath it read:

Dietrich Von Speer
Antiquities & Fine Arts
Since 1929
277 Rue Setrapi
Paris 345277 01

Orient stared at the advertisement for a moment then checked his phone for the exact location.

Rue Setrapi was a twenty minute walk from the café. Unfortunately the rains peaked ten minutes after he left. From a street vendor he bought an outrageously expensive umbrella, which did little for his wet shoes.

He arrived at the address, soaked from the knees down and in need of a dry bistro.

Von Speer's gallery was located in a large, expensive, apartment building, a few blocks from Rue St Germaine. A uniformed concierge sat in a booth, at the entrance to a courtyard.

Orient told him he was there to see Von Speer, the art dealer. The concierge, a thin, elderly man with a dyed moustache, clucked sympathetically. "Monsieur Von Speer, left four days ago."

For a sinking moment it crossed Orient's mind that he had missed Von Speer in Marrakech. "Do you know where he went?"

The concierge twitched his moustache. "Yes sir, I do."

Orient extracted a bill from his wallet and passed it through the slot in the booth's window.

The concierge smiled. "He is in Salvador Brazil, in Bahia."

"Brazil? Do you have an address?"

"I'm sorry sir he leaves no address when he goes to Brazil."

"He goes often?"

"Every year. It's like a ritual with him."

+ + +

Waiting for the cold rain to subside over coffee and cognac, Orient tried to temper his disappointment by planning a trip to Brazil. He had a return ticket to New York and decided to book the first flight to Rio.

He discovered he would need a visa. It would hold him back at least three days.

Orient decided to call Andy Jacobs.

"Is that you Owen? What the hell are you doing in Paris?"

"Trying to get to Rio. That's why I'm calling. It's imperative I be in Brazil, but I don't have a visa."

Andy snorted. "That was their retaliation for our slapping a visa tax on them. What a bunch of moronic bureaucrats we have on the hill."

Orient listened patiently to the ex-senator's rant on the absurdity of politics. Andy was preaching to the choir.

"I agree Senator, but do you think I can shorten the process? I'm taking the red-eye to New York tonight."

"What's the rush?"

"Urgent business."

"I thought you were going on staff at the hospital."

"That's why it's so urgent," Orient said, trying not to lie to his old friend.

"I'll look into it. Call me when you land."

After ending the call Orient thought about his impending position on St. Luke's trauma unit. He wondered if Hannah was still keen on the idea. The last few times they had contact, she had been distant.

She came to see me every day, Orient reminded, and put herself on the line. Cut the girl some slack. He left the bistro and hailed a cab to the airport. .

During the gloomy flight home, seated amid lighted screens and snoring passengers, Orient continued to brood about his future as a trauma doctor. The interview seemed so long ago.

And Hannah had always been hesitant, both about his joining her staff, and being in her life. It had been a while since a lady stirred his emotions. But he wasn't sure he liked being on the defensive.

Thankfully, when the plane landed at six a.m., New York time, the lines going through customs were light. He'd go directly back to his new apartment, call Andy, and dive into bed.

As he shuffled closer to the customs agent checking bags, he glanced around for any sign of law enforcement. The area was nearly deserted.

When he walked through the doors into the terminal all that changed.

"Owen Orient?"

Orient turned and saw two men, nearly identically dressed in dark suits and tan raincoats. One of them wore sunglasses the other was holding a document.

"FBI," said the sunglasses, "we have a warrant for your arrest."

Chapter 30

The Tombs was aptly named.

The original design for the jail had been taken from an engraving of an Egyptian mausoleum. Basically a holding pen for prisoners awaiting their court date, it was a tower with enough cages to house about four hundred men. Currently, the Tombs held over a thousand offenders. The tower was built above the remaining section of the original facility at 100 Centre Street, and still had two underground tiers.

It was there they put Orient, after he was fingerprinted and booked. His request for a phone call was being processed they told him, taking him down a steel elevator in handcuffs.

The first thing that struck Orient was the noise, a cacophony of human pain and the electric hum of need. Then the smell: sweat, fear and hostility, in a dense mix at close quarters.

And close they were. Once inside the steel door, there were two tiers of cells, one above the other. A series of picnic benches on the ground floor occupied the remaining space outside the cells. The guards led him to a cell in the rear. Six by six, it had a coverless toilet and two bunk beds. The top bunk was occupied by a bearded man with grey, mottled skin.

Orient heard jeering sounds as he entered the cell. He wasn't sure it was directed at him.

"Wild thing!" someone yelled.

The bearded man peered at Orient, who stood uncertainly inside the cell.

The iron lock's solid clank made it certain.

"When that door bangs shut, you know you're inside," the bearded man said, settling back on his bunk.

Orient was carrying a small pillow and a blanket. There were no mattresses on the bunks, only bare, sagging springs.

He tossed the bundle on one end of the bunk and sat down. Outside, the raucous jabber and occasional shrieks continued. Orient wondered when his phone call would be 'processed'.

His cell mate said nothing, and Orient lay back gingerly on the springs, his limbs protesting. The agents had taken away the jar of healing cream given him in Marrakech, and he was worried his bite wounds would become infected down in the damp, airless prison. At this point no one knew where he was. He wasn't even sure the FBI knew.

It's certainly a better situation than Savana's, Orient reminded himself. The thought only increased his frustration. He went into a breathing pattern which calmed his anxiety, but also made him aware of the stale, sweat oiled, air.

"You smoke?"

The voice roused Orient from his brooding.

"No tobacco."

The man above him snuffled. "What, weed? That your beef?"

Orient took a second to sort out the question. "Uh no. That's not the charge."

"So how'd you get jammed up in here?"

"Murder."

There was a long silence. "I'm up on a drug rap. Probably get an ace. Less with time served. "

"Ace?"

"A year. You never been inside before?" It wasn't a question.

"No."

"Well you better get yourself a ten thousand dollar lawyer. With a public defender, you'll get death in a state where there ain't no death penalty."

The man laughed, and lit a cigarette. He carefully blew the smoke out the small, barred window near the top bunk. "Not supposed to smoke. Shit."

He took another puff and carefully stubbed out the cigarette. "Name's Dan."

"Owen."

"You got a day gig?"

Again, it took Orient a moment. "Not lately."

"I hear that. What's your bail?"

"I don't know. I haven't even made a phone call."

Dan sat up. "That ain't right. Must be a federal beef huh?"

"Yes, FBI arrested me."

"That's how they do, the feds. They get you in isolation, so nobody knows where you are. Sweat you, put you in with the general population, so when they finally let you call and give you a coke, maybe cold pizza, you're so grateful you'll flip on your own mama."

Orient made a note to bear it in mind when the time came.

While Dan rambled on about the system, the cell lock abruptly swung open.

"Lock out time," Dan grunted, hopping onto the floor. "They lock us *out* of our cells for an hour, twice a day."

The cell door swung open and Orient walked into the common area, divided by rows of picnic benches.

"Most all tables are spoken for, except for those, "Dan nodded towards two benches being used for deep pushups. "Those boys are too strong. Later dude," he added, fading into the swirl of newly uncaged men.

As Orient wandered along the aisle, he saw what Dan meant. Loose factions ruled various tables. There was a table for chess and card players, a Black Muslim table strewn with pamphlets and copies of the Koran, a Latino table, an all white table, and a few multi ethnic tables marked by their New York neighborhoods.

He made his way to the exercise tables, hoping to stretch out the pain in his arm. No one paid much attention, intent on their precious minutes between benches, stretching pectorals and deltoids, pumping blood through atrophying bodies.

Aware of the constant tension underlying the placid murmur around him, Orient tried to remain unobtrusive, but he was new man at the bench. Everyone was alert to his presence. Some at other tables had turned to stare.

At the last moment he realized deep pushups were probably not the best idea for an injured shoulder. Too late. He straddled the two benches and eased down smoothly, but halfway there his shoulder protested.

Orient went back up, took a deep breath and lowered his torso between the benches. The second time was easier, but as he came up something popped in his shoulder. He rolled to his feet. When he looked down he saw blood seeping through his shirt.

"Sheeeit."

Orient looked up and saw a heavily tattooed man with broad shoulders and small, deep set eyes smirking at him.

"Move your punk ass aside and let a man work out," he said, loud enough for other tables to hear. Orient had never been in jail but he had weathered some serious confrontations over the years, and he recognized his position

He was toast.

Chapter 31

The man blocking his only exit was intent on a fight. He was a short and broad shouldered, with thick legs and big hands attached to long, muscular arms. His tiny, deep set eyes were blank.

"Out of the way, bitch," he sneered, lashing out.

His fist connected with Orient's bloody arm.

The pain galvanized Orient's defenses. He stepped back, arms swooping precious *Chi* energy from the foul air. At the same time he rooted his feet, bringing energy from deep earth to the base of his spine.

"Fuck Bruce Lee!" The man roared, swinging his fist up from the ground with deliberate force.

Before it connected, Orient pushed the gathered *Chi* like a moving wall. His attacker spun as if struck, and tumbled over the low bench behind him.

"Everybody freeze! Right there!"

Two guards pushed their way though the aisle, batons flailing at anyone nearby. Another two guards stood guard at the barred entrance to the cell block. Orient remained where he was, one hand pressed against his bloody arm.

"Fucking Mako jumped you," the guard said, preparing to handcuff the tattooed man who was still on the ground.

Orient suddenly became aware that the entire cell block was silent. He saw his cell mate Dan at a nearby table. He and the men beside him waited for his answer.

"No," Orient said. "It didn't happen that way. I tore my stitches doing pushups. I need to see a medic.'

"What about this animal?" The guard said, backing off a step, baton ready.

"He must have tripped over the bench."

The guard gave him a disgusted look. I thought you'd be different, being a doctor and all."

"When you're in hell, everybody's equal," Orient said, suddenly exhausted and sickened by the rampant hypocrisy that put him inside. "Do I get to see a medic?"

As he was being led away, a few of the prisoners showed their approval with various signs. Dan leaned over when Orient passed.

"You get back, you sit with us, bro."

+ + +

Orient never did return to the underground cell block.

When the nurse checked the computer she saw that the prisoner had been refused his special medication and had yet to be given his phone call, the nurse, who took her calling seriously, let him use her cell phone. Then she re-stitched his wound, and applied the medication to the terrible bites on his foot and arm. Only then did she inform the Duty Sergeant, who informed FBI Agent Morris Klein, who rushed over to the prison clinic an hour later.

By then Orient had called Andy Jacobs.

The aging ex-senator arrived at the same time as Klein, his long white hair shining beneath a black fedora, and blue eyes brimming with indignation.

"What in hell are you trying to pull? Your subpoena expired two days ago. And why is he being held incognito like some terrorist?" He added, before Klein could respond to the first question.

"With all due respect, Senator, Doctor Orient is an evidentiary suspect in one murder, and a material witness in at least two other homicides. Not only that, I'm about to charge him with resisting arrest in connection to another killing at the Cloisters."

Klein leaned against the desk and folded his arms. "Please, sir, take a chair."

Reluctantly, Andy sat down. "You know of course that holding my client without charge and without access to an attorney, *or medication*—weakens anything you have."

"How about DNA evidence, strong enough?"

Andy's indignation barely eased a notch. "Nothing excuses the inhuman, unlawful, treatment of a *suspect* Agent Klein. Not even a proven criminal."

Moe took a deep breath and sat behind the desk. He grabbed a thick folder and held it up. "Senator I've got a serial killer-slash-kidnapper on my hands and Doctor Orient is holding back vital information. Not only that but he's playing detective and obstructing..."

"Knowing Owen, he isn't playing," Andy rumbled, with a hint of amusement. "Maybe he's making you guys look bad. Is that why he was denied medication and treatment?"

Klein tossed the folder onto the desk. "Senator, I had no idea. I trust his medication has been returned."

"It's all been returned.'

"Good." Klein paused. He thought he heard an alarm signal in those last four words. "Uh, what do you mean, it's all been returned?"

The senator's mournful, hound dog expression didn't waver, but there was a mischievous note in his tone. "Judge Jack Martin signed a writ of Habeas Corpus and my bicycle courier delivered it an hour ago. Owen is waiting for me in one of the outpatient cubicles."

Klein was more frustrated than angry. He'd overplayed his hand. He should have questioned Orient right away. But very few suspects had an ex-senator as their lawyer.

"May I see your writ?" He asked mildly.

Andy Jacobs reached into his briefcase and produced the document.

"You know of course I'm going to file for another subpoena, charging Doctor Orient with murder, and resisting arrest. He's graduated from material witness."

"Why don't you tell him yourself? He's waiting to see you."
Klein maintained a poker face. "What's this gambit,
Senator?"

"No gambit. Owen is willing to tell you everything he
knows—*off* the record. I only ask you to bear something in
mind. Some years ago, Doctor Orient enabled the daughter of
the Vice President to walk, after years in a wheel chair. Now
that—is a fact."

"And the methods he used are still classified.' Klein said.

Andy nodded. "You've done due diligence. Yes his methods were unconventional, but the fact remains, they succeeded."

"And?"

"Just keep an open mind."

+ + +

It would have been difficult for Klein to believe Orient if he
hadn't spoken to Sybelle Lean. Both her story and Orient's were
the same. He listened to Orient tell of Savana's demonic possession without prejudice.

He's encountered various phenomena occasionally in the
line of duty. Nothing this heavy of course. But seeing this
blond killer in a vision of the past? He couldn't buy it quite.
And he told Orient as much.

Orient's sculpted features remained impassive but his green
eyes were alert. "I probably would have the same reaction."
He dug a hand in his pocket and produced a gold ladies watch.
"But here's tangible proof."

Not to Klein. But he believed most of it. Especially that
Orient wasn't a murderer.

"Whatever this man intends to do with Savana, it will happen soon," Orient said quietly.

"You think she might be in Brazil?"

"Salvador, Bahia to be exact."

"Still a big, strange country."

"I speak Portuguese."

"Look ,Doctor Orient..."

"Sorry but I have no choice. You're still looking for her here. I have a lead I intend to follow."

"What sort of lead? The word of his concierge?"

"More than that. I have a special... link to Savana."

Klein sighed. "I could stop you, you know."

"I'll keep you informed."

Sure you will, Klein thought.

"Better yet, why don't you come along?"

Klein stared at him. "You sound like you've got a jet waiting outside."

"Almost. The senator has arranged for me to be aboard a diplomatic courier that takes off at midnight for Rio. That's plenty of time for you to make arrangements."

"Why so magnanimous all of a sudden?"

Orient shrugged. "I want to find Savana... and you carry a gun.'

+++

He should only know how small it is, Klein reflected later, dialing Jake for advice.

"Are you serious?" Jake crowed. "Of course you are going. This is brilliant memo material. I see our budget expanding like the universe. But do not leave without seeing me. I have some special equipment you will absolutely need."

Chapter 32

After a few days, Savana's head began to clear.
She knew she had been abducted, she knew she
had been drugged, and she knew she wasn't in New
York. Judging from the weather, and the vegetation, she could
be in Florida, or Hawaii, or some tropical island.

Her fear had subsided, overcome by the sheer monotony
of her captivity. But the prison camp had many fascinating
characteristics. If she had a notepad she would have kept a
diary.

Like Anne Frank, Savana thought, and the fear came rushing back.

She took a deep breath and tried to enjoy the warm, sunny
morning. Her austere cell was comfortable enough. And it featured an open area, like a large patio bounded by a metal fence
and barbed wire. Every morning the door to her patio was
unlocked so she could get some fresh air and exercise.

There were other prisoners in the compound but she only
caught glimpses of them when meals were served. Otherwise
she was alone. Her captor, the tall blond man, never appeared.

However there was no shortage of blond men and women
in the camp. All of them were young and in perfect physical
shape. Some, like the camp guards, wore uniforms. As far as
Savana could tell, the young people passed their days undergoing various physical drills or going to class. Occasionally Savana
would see students walk past, reading what seemed to be textbooks. They never seemed to notice the strange female doing
yoga poses inside her cage

Savana noted that the menial work was done by darker people, possibly Mexican or Asian. They were the ones who served
meals, and did repair work.

One day a monkey climbed onto the wire mesh cage. Using various bits of food, Savana enticed the monkey closer. She dropped a piece of chocolate by mistake and before she could pick it up, the monkey began tearing at the wire mesh to get at the delicacy.

It gave Savana an idea. Over a period of days, she used her precious chocolate ration to trick the monkey into enlarging the hole at the base of her cage. Soon it was big enough for the monkey to crawl inside—but not big enough for Savana to crawl out.

Not yet anyway, she speculated, feeding her new pet a bit of cheese.

She named the monkey Bumpy. It had black fur, a reddish belly, a white moustache, and pointed ears that made it look more like a bat than a monkey. Bumpy loved to play games with Savana, and learned quickly. Especially when motivated by sweet treats. .

One afternoon a trio of blond youths, two boys and a girl, strolled past her prison. One of the boys was taking pictures with an iPhone. He spotted the monkey, who was foraging outside Savana's cage and snapped a photo.

The boy said something to the other two that made them burst out laughing.

The boy bent closer to the monkey for a better shot. Then, still laughing, he straightened up and waved Savana closer.

Savana realized what they'd been laughing about. As far as they're concerned I'm a monkey in a cage, she thought, turning back inside. Then she paused and moved back to the fence where the boy crouched with his camera phone. Perhaps she could play a little joke on them.

Smiling she bent close to the tiny opening in the wire, a piece of chocolate in her hand.

From their hours of play, Bumpy responded to certain vocal commands, much like a dog. Except Bumpy intuitively seemed to know what she wanted.

As the boy crouched near, camera extended, Savana whispered, "Fetch now, Bumpy bring it here, bring it here." She wiggled the chocolate enticingly. "Fetch now, that's it."

Grinning at the small screen, the boy was literally bowled over when Bumpy snatched the iPhone and scurried through the hole in the fence.

"Good boy!" Savana said, taking the phone and giving him his reward.

Outside the boy was yelling in a strange language. Suddenly Savana realized what she had done. Her spur of the moment prank had given her a chance to contact her mom. But from the corner of her eye she could see uniformed guards running toward the boy who was shouting and pointing at her.

Heart pounding, Savana blinked at her picture, still on the screen. There was no time to try a call. Then it came to her. With trembling fingers, she E-mailed the photo to her mother.

She barely had time to press *send* when two guards came bounding through her cell into the open area. One of them grabbed the phone from her hand and pushed her roughly against the cage.

The other guard stepped between them.

He muttered something under his breath and Savana's attacker instantly backed off. The guard turned to Savana, half bowed, and marched away.

When the guards left the prison, the boy tried to retrieve his phone, but they motioned for the trio to come along with them.

Good, Savana thought, I hope they get sent to bed without any supper. She called for Bumpy but he had run away during the excitement. Actually, she was still psyched by the possibility the message had gone through. If these people have iPhones, they must have access to satellites, she reasoned. Her spur of the moment prank had reaped unexpected rewards.

That night, after dinner had been served on a metal tray, and removed, she had a visitor.

It was the man who kidnapped her from Fire Island.

Despite being in the bright sun daily his skin was chalk white. She shrank back when he entered. The man smiled. "Don't be afraid, my dear. Right now you are under my protection. Nothing will harm you."

"I want to go home," Savana blurted.

His diamond blue eyes didn't waver. "Of course, when the time comes. However we have another matter to discuss. I've come to invite you to a community meeting, after lunch tomorrow. I'll escort you myself."

Savana looked at him blankly.

"I want you to observe first hand, the consequences of your rash act."

He turned, and walked slowly out of her tiny cell. He paused at the door.

"One more thing. There will be many people attending this meeting. You might want to clean up a bit. I'll send someone round to help you."

For the first time since her arrival, Savana felt a deep sense of dread.

+ + +

As usual she was awakened by the sounds.

First the distant crowing of roosters, then the shrill cries of the brightly colored birds that nested in the trees bordering the compound. The morning harmony was joined by the lowing of cows, and the shouts of men performing various military functions.

The weather was the same every morning. Cool and damp, quickly followed by hot and humid. That and the brightly feathered birds made Savana think she was in Florida, or some Caribbean island.

But this morning did not proceed as usual.

The woman who brought her breakfast tray kept her eyes averted, as if afraid of something. Then after breakfast she led

Savana to the shower room and provided her with soap, towels, a toothbrush, and various toiletries.

It had been a long time since Savana had a mirror and a hairbrush. After a long shower, the woman gave her a clean white dress and flip flops to wear. Then she locked Savana in her cell.

Savana went outside to let her hair dry in the sun. She put a snack out for Bumpy, but the monkey had run away when the boy who lost his phone started shouting. The way the boy carried on, he sounded scared. Maybe he was afraid of Bumpy she reflected, smiling at the thought.

Her smile faded when she saw her blond captor, striding toward the prison area, flanked by two uniformed youths.He opened her cell door and beckoned her closer.

"I'll be your escort today," he said, voice almost gentle. "We must insure order is maintained."

Savana didn't understand, but followed him outside the prison.

Her first breath of "freedom" was exhilarating.

The two uniformed escorts fell in behind them, so there was no chance to make a run for the fences. For one thing, it would be a long run. The compound was much larger and than she first thought. And then there was the thick jungle vegetation that seemed to surround the huge complex. Even if she somehow made it outside, she wasn't sure she could survive.

As they walked out of the prison area, Savana noticed posted signs that read:

Verboten!

She had picked up enough German on her first trip to Europe to know the sign meant:

Forbidden!

Savana realized why the boy had sounded so scared. He had been trespassing, on a sight seeing trip through the prison.

When they walked around a large wood and brick building that faced the prison, Savana saw the place was even bigger

than her previous assessment. It looked like a small city, with
low, neatly set buildings, stretching as far as she could see in
three directions The building were grouped in quadrants, creating three main avenues, that converged in the square where she
stood.

The square itself was on high ground, giving Savana
a good view of the spectacle before her. And it was
overwhelming.

All the avenues were filled with people, mostly young, mostly blond, dressed in white shorts and shirts. It was then Savana
realized that her captor was also dressed in white—as was she.

The endless lines of people stood quietly but she could feel
the anticipation pulsing through the throng. Their neat white
rows formed a shimmering pattern in the noon sun.

Awed by the sight, Savana felt slightly dizzy.

Her scarred captor took her arm and escorted her to a low
stage on the far side of the square. When they mounted the
stage Savana saw it afforded a view of the entire compound.
The perimeter was marked with guard towers and there uniformed men lined up beside the people in white. Their uniforms were tan with twin red lightning bolts on the sleeves. All
of them were armed.

Over each quadrant flew a large black flag with the same
red lightning bolt logo. Savana sensed the power in the huge
gathering. As if this Aryan horde could roll over any army in
front of it.

What Savana found most ominous, was the silence.

When her captor stepped up to the microphone and lifted
his arms, it was hardly to quiet the crowd. He spoke softly,
calmly, but the echoes came back in disembodied electronic
phrases Savana didn't understand. She knew it was German,
and wondered who these people were, and what they were doing in this strange environment.

She did understand that her abductor was their leader.

He said something in a crisp, command tone.

A tall man wearing a surgical mask and cap mounted the stage, followed by a female similarly garbed in nurse's scrubs. Both masks bore small red lightning bolts.

The nurse carried a medical bag which she rested on a ping pong table at the rear of the stage. There were various bottles and pans already set up on the table, as well as a fuming Styrofoam ice chest on the floor.

As the medical team busied themselves, it occurred to Savana that she might be the patient. Perhaps it was to be punishment for e-mailing the picture. Her heart began pounding against her ribs so loudly she thought it was being picked up by the microphone.

Her booming heart, the shimmering heat, and primal fear, made her faint. She felt a hand on her shoulder. It was her captor. He was holding the mike in his hand, and speaking in a steady voice to the still silent throng

He gently led Savana to a chair at the end of the stage. She sat down gratefully, breath heaving in relief. When she lifted her head she saw the leader was standing beside what seemed to be a square, wooden altar, the size of a small butcher's block. It was covered with a white cloth embroidered with a pyramid symbol and a cross, and stood on one side of the table. There was an empty chair behind the altar. Savana wondered who it was for.

A moment later she knew.

The young man slowly mounting the stage was the boy who had taken her picture, and had his iPhone stolen by Bumpy. His bland features showed no emotion as he approached the altar. The leader whispered something and the boy sat down, limbs rigid. Savana could see he was making an effort to conceal his fear.

The leader spoke, and the boy nodded.

The medical team approached the altar. The woman carried the ice chest, the male, a tray of instruments, which he set on the altar. The male said something to the boy and he placed his arm on the table.

The male doctor looked at the leader who nodded, and said something to the audience.

The doctor sterilized the boy's arm and picked up a shiny steel knife that resembled a small machete. To Savana's horror, the masked doctor swiftly, and expertly, severed the boy's hand, above the wrist.

The boy's eyes rolled back and Savana heard a shivering intake of breath, but he did not utter a sound. Immediately the nurse slipped the bloody hand into a plastic envelope and put it inside the ice chest. At the same time the doctor swiftly knotted a surgical tourniquet around the boy's wrist, staunching the spray of blood. Then he injected the boy with something, and his rigid limbs went limp.

As the leader spoke to the crowd, two uniformed men put the boy on a stretcher and carried him off. The nurse picked up the ice chest and went after them, closely followed by the doctor.

Savana sat frozen, watching them leave. For a moment she thought she might vomit.

The stage was now bare, except for the leader and the blood soaked altar.

She turned and saw that the crowd had thinned considerably, dispersing like white ants in all directions.

The leader beckoned, but her legs felt like rubber beneath her.

"I see you're a bit squeamish my dear," he said, coming closer. He gestured grandly with one hand. "Please rest assured the offending hand will be *reattached*. We are not barbarians. Here we have the most skilled surgeons in the world. There will be ninety percent function recovery. All young George will have left is a scar around his wrist. A bracelet—to remind him that discipline is essential to a highly evolved society."

Highly evolved. The term prodded her numbed brain awake. She was about to ask if he thought kidnapping and mutilation were standards of evolution, but couldn't find the words.

"Who... are you?" was all she could manage.

He regarded her for a moment. "I'm a scientist," he said, with a wry smile, "and I'm a priest."

+ + +

When she returned to her cell, Savana was exhausted. She ignored the waiting food tray and fell onto her cot, struggling to shut out the memory of what she had just seen.

Later, she was awakened by the oppressive heat inside her cell. She wiped her face and arms with a towel and examined her lunch tray. There was chocolate for dessert.

Savana took the candy bar outside. She noisily tore open the foil wrap, knowing the familiar sound would draw Bumpy's full attention. He was totally addicted to chocolate, licking the gooey inside of the package until nothing remained.

As she looked around for him, she noticed something.

A wooden box, near the fence.

Savana went near and kicked at it tentatively. The cover was loose. With her toe, she nudged the cover aside, and bent closer.

A sledge hammer whacked her belly and she dropped to the ground, retching violently.

Bumpy lay dead inside the box, his neck bent at a surreal angle.

Chapter 33

"I'll admit you are something, Doc," Klein said, lifting a glass of cabernet. "I arrest you for murder and twenty-four hours later you've got me on a private jet to Brazil."

Orient gave him a lazy wave. "Pays to have a good lawyer."

The moment he had boarded the Lear, Orient had settled into a leather recliner, strapped in, and dozed off. He had awakened briefly for dinner, and was in the process of going back to sleep.

However, invigorated by the wine, Klein was in a mood to talk. "So you really think this Von Speer can lead us to the girl?"

It was more of a challenge than a question.

Orient shifted erect in his seat. "It's the best we've got right now. I'll know better when we get to Bahia."

"Why then?"

"If Savana is anywhere within a radius of a thousand miles I'll pick up something. She has natural psychic ability, like her aunt. Still undeveloped, but I can get an inkling of her whereabouts."

Inkling. Klein liked that. He didn't bother asking a lot of questions. Orient had told him as much as he ever would about the psychic connection to all this. And as little as possible. Instead Moe concentrated on facts he could deal with.

"How did you know Von Speer was in Marrakech?"

Orient decided to join Klein in a glass of wine. It would be a long flight.

"Actually, I went to find the man who guided us when we first went there. You recall the, er... vision I described?"

Klein did, and he was already sorry he'd asked. He had hoped to guide this expedition onto firmer ground. "Yeah, I remember. So did this guy exist?"

Orient smiled. "You mean, did I find him?"

Klein wiped his mouth with a napkin. "Of course."

"Yes. I managed to track the old guide down, and he took me to Von Speer's home. However Von Speer had flown to Paris. I followed him there, but he had already left for Brazil. His concierge in Paris told me he goes every year."

Orient didn't mention the Seal of Solomon, tucked in the medicine pouch around his neck. He liked Agent Klein and knew he was an honest man. But he also knew all men were flawed in one way or another. His own lifetime of searching had yet to produce a perfect human and he had learned to distrust the authorities.

"Is it possible Von Speer is part of this Nazi connection?"

"He is definitely connected to the Egyptian fragment stolen from Henry. According to the certification papers Deiter Von Speer was Chairman of the Archeology department at the University of Berlin. But that certainly doesn't make him a Nazi."

Klein shrugged. "It does make him old enough. And the murder weapon is an authentic SS dagger." He heaved a deep sigh. "Tell me again about this attack in Morocco. Some animals, dogs... You got infected?"

Orient took a deep breath, followed by a long sip of wine. "I was attacked by rats. And, yeah, the wounds became infected."

Klein peered at him, expression set between sympathy and suspicion.

"Rats? Where—in an alley or something?"

"My hotel room."

"Rats—I don't get it."

Orient met his skeptical stare. "Look, Agent Klein..."

"Call me Moe. The agent thing could be a tip-off. We're supposed to be undercover."

"Look, Moe, the attack was provoked by psychic forces—and it damned near succeeded. Their bites were highly toxic. Luckily I was able to find a healer."

"Healer? Not a doctor?"

"Modern medicine doesn't cover this species of virus."

Klein shook his head and poured himself a healthy measure of Cabernet. His hope of finding firmer ground had ended in a swamp.

Unfortunately for Orient, the dredged memories pelted his attempt to sleep. The wounds on his foot and arm had receded, aided by daily applications of the cream given him in Marrakech. Still, he could feel the waning infection gathering for a death throe. The throb in his foot was like a war drum.

The new stitches in his shoulder still burned, but he was slowly regaining mobility. However his last eighteen hours of incarceration had darkened his outlook.

He felt most afraid for Savana, facing these fiercely rabid forces alone, without any weapon to defend herself.

Problem was, even if they ran down Von Speer, it was still a long shot, Orient brooded. He looked across at Klein, who was dozing.

At least he had stopped asking questions, Orient noted gratefully, tipping the seat back, and pulling the blanket up to his chin.

+ + +

Rio lives up to its reputation as a hedonist's paradise – and one of the most dangerous cities in the world. Sex and death dance daily on its white sand beaches, lush thoroughfares, festering drug alleys, and wide open clubs.

The Lear Jet touched down at a private airport used by diplomatic courier planes, enabling them to dispense with customs and visa formalities. Klein forgot he was carrying a weapon, but it didn't matter. Nobody checked.

As soon as they left the airport the voluptuous pulse of the city was evident. Everywhere Klein looked there were bright colors and nubile ladies swaying to some inner Samba. Even the cemetery, with its grimy rococo tombstones, had a certain gothic flair.

Klein was sweating profusely as the cab took them to Rio's main airport for a domestic flight to Salvador, Bahia. He glanced at Orient who seemed cool and relaxed. But the bastard always looks that way, Klein noted, with a trace of envy. Orient was strange but extremely smart, he conceded. The man was fearless when it came to his ethics. In fact, Moe was grudgingly beginning to like this medical doctor with psychic powers

They had first class reservations, courtesy of the FBI and Klein had no problem with the small Ruger concealed inside his check-in bag. When they landed, a waiting car took them to a hotel on the beach, where they were given a three bedroom apartment suite.

As soon as they arrived Klein set up his laptop and called Jake, via Skype. The sight of Jake's unshaven face and impish grin went a long way to soothe his misgivings over this trip. It had been Jake's encouragement that convinced him.

"Break this case and you're an international star," Jake told him. "But even if you don't, just going to Brazil makes you a player. Think budget."

At the moment it was an hour earlier in New York, which made it eleven p.m.EST and Jake was still at the office. Probably slept there at his master-of-the-universe console, Jake thought.

"Intel on this Von Speer character is skimpy. Found a picture from his days at Berlin U but that was in forty-nine. That's *nineteen* forty nine, so he's changed a bit. Probably put on some weight. I know I have."

"The way you eat I'm surprised you can still walk.'

Jake ignored him. "We do show visas between Paris and Brazil, Von Speer travels on a German passport. As for background—during those all important Nazi years he was teaching archeology. A real academic."

"All books and research no doubt. I don't believe Hitler's boys hired free thinkers back then. Any Brazilian address, listed on those visas?"

"You're in the right city. We have one address from an old visa and it is in Bahia. Google says it's in the old city square. Called the Pelourinho."

"An address, right here? Great work Jake. I owe you a big dinner."

"Make sure to mention me in your memo."

Jake shut down, but the small printer attached to Moe's new laptop began running pages. Two each, he noted, very thoughtful of Jake. He separated the pages into two neat piles.

"Good news," he called over his shoulder, "Jake found Von Speer's address. We can check it out in the morning. How does six a.m. sound?"

All he got in response was dead silence. He looked inside Orient's room and saw he was in bed, already asleep.

Klein shook his head and shuffled to his room. He would make sure to rouse him at six.

+ + +

Orient awoke at five a.m.

He felt renewed by the hours of undisturbed sleep and immediately began his stretching and breathing exercises. The familiar patterns redirected his *chi*, sending the energy flowing along his spine and through his chakras, irrigating his parched, damaged cells.

Showered and refreshed, he checked the refrigerator. Inside were the usual staples including milk, eggs, cheese, and coffee. He left the room and went out in search of a market. When he returned twenty minutes later with a bag full of mangoes, bananas, berries, honey, yogurt, and herbal tea, Klein was at the stove frying eggs. The tempting aroma of coffee greeted him as he dumped his groceries on the table, and set about preparing his own breakfast.

"Nice day out," Orient said. "Want some of this? Fresh fruit, farm yogurt...."

Klein grunted. "What are you, vegetarian?"

"Mostly." Orient peeled and sliced a mango and put the pieces in a bowl of yogurt.

As Klein silently ate his eggs he saw Orient glance at him. "What?"

Orient shrugged. "Nothing. Enjoy your breakfast."

"Doctor told me to lay off the eggs."

"Well your options are limited. That's why I went out."

Moe changed the subject. "When can you be ready to roll?"

"I'm ready now."

"Twenty minutes."

Leaving what was left of his eggs, Moe went inside to take a shower. He had the feeling he'd been somehow shown up by the cool, slender, early rising Doctor Orient.

Orient was fluent in Portuguese, which saved them a tour of the city by the insistent driver. "I show you evereethin', high and low," he said, laughing at his own pun.

"For now, the high part is fine," Orient told him. Salvador was divided into an upper city and a lower city, connected by funiculars, or cable cars, built in the late nineteenth century. In fact the entire city seemed frozen in time. Echoes of a long past colonial era mingled with rhythmic music from a thousand radios in the cramped, crowded streets. The heavy architecture and open markets had a certain frontier energy, as if Portuguese buccaneers, armed with a cutlass and a cross, still roamed the port in search of fortune.

In a sense they still did, Orient reflected as the cab climbed to the upper city.

The lower city was devoted to commerce, the upper city to religion and art. The historic center of the upper city was called the Pelourinho, and the small square teemed with activity.

The cab had to stop at the edge of the square. Despite the driver's blandishments, Orient and Klein went the rest of the way unescorted.

+ + +

Groups of women drew water at the public fountain, while children played in knee deep pools in the broken cobblestones and potholes. Orient noticed that among the jewelry and souvenir shops lining the square, were an inordinate number of casket makers, their intricately carved wares on display.

The address was somewhat confusing, but after much questioning, and discussion by the locals, Orient managed to find their destination.

To his surprise, Von Speer's residence turned out to be— a church....

The convent and church of San Francisco stood at one end of the square and Orient could see it was quite old.

"Probably early eighteenth century," Klein ventured. "Nice example of Portuguese colonial architecture—if you like that sort of thing. Looks like your boy Von Speer gave a phony address."

"We'll see. Let's go inside and ask around."

Walking past the huge doors was another long step back in time. Not so much the overwrought style, but what the structure said about the single-minded faith of the people who built it, so far from their native land. The god they worshipped was one of ego and power.

The interior of the church was dark and massive, with every inch of its walls, pillars, and arches layered with detailed baroque carvings of holy figures. The ceilings were completely covered with ornately framed paintings of saints and angels. Huge gilded archways gleamed in the light of the flickering

candles below, while an agonized Christ hung on a crude wood-
en cross above a golden altar.

Klein waited while Orient looked for someone in charge.
He stood in the shadowed area, staring at the black and white
checkered marble floor. Churches made him uncomfortable. So
did temples, for that matter.

Despite the rich profusion of holy images there was something dark and ominous about the place, he decided. His stomach was getting queasy. Probably the damned eggs. There were
few tourists and fewer worshippers at that hour, and he was
about to step outside, when Orient returned.

"The nun told me the father will be here for ten o'clock
mass. Which gives us a couple of hours downtime."

"I need a Coke and a bathroom," Moe declared, heading for
the door.

Outside, some men were lounging at the base of the large
stone cross facing the church. Klein felt relieved to be freed
of the almost palpable sense of oppression inside the place of
worship.

"What's up with the Coke?" Orient inquired.

"Stomach's acting up. Coke settles it sometimes."

Today was not one of those times. Moe enjoyed the bever-
age itself, which was loaded with more sugar and caffeine that
its American counterpart, but it failed to deliver its soothing
effect.

Finding a bathroom in the ancient neighborhood was also
a problem. After a long search Moe finally found refuge in a
hotel. He came out of the restroom far from relieved. The acid
in his belly had escalated to shooting pains that doubled him
up. He was also sweating heavily.

"I'd better get back to the safe house," Klein said.

Orient took him by the shoulders and sat him down on a
couch. "Hang on a second, let me take your pulse."

"You're going make a diagnosis right here, in the lobby?"

"Yes. My diagnosis is you're sick. Of what, I can only guess—probably me."

Orient noted his elevated pulse, the perspiration soaking through his shirt, and the wincing pains. Klein could have anything from a cold bug to cholera.

"Excuse me. Do you need some help?"

They looked up and saw a tall, dark young man, wearing aviator glasses, leaning closer with and expression of concern.

"If you're sick I can..."

"I'm not sick," Klein said, glaring at him.

The man backed up slightly. "Just trying to help some fellow Yanks."

Klein got to his feet. "I'm fine."

But as soon as they went outside, Klein was bent over by a sudden nausea. He crouched behind the corner of a building, vomiting his breakfast.

"Hey, guys, there is a clinic in the hood."

Orient looked up and saw the young man who'd spoken to them in the hotel lobby. He was in his twenties, with dark skin, and red blond hair in jheri curls. His eyes were hidden behind his glasses but his smile was reassuring.

Orient nodded. "Thanks. Maybe we'd better visit this clinic."

Stomach churning with acid and head pounding, Klein was in no position to object.

"The name's Malik," the man said. "Can you walk? The clinic isn't very far.

"I can walk," Klein growled. He didn't like strangers interfering with an investigation. And this one smelled like a con man.

Actually, he was unsteady on his feet and had to lean on Orient.

Malik led the way up a cobblestoned street, above the square, and through an alley, to a two-story, white-washed building, at one end of a courtyard populated by nursing mothers, small children, and patients in wheelchairs. Inside was an immaculate white waiting room, furnished with chairs, a small table, and a restroom which Klein entered immediately.

He locked the door, sat down on the commode, and passed out.

Chapter 34

A nurse in a white dress was attending to a young mother and her child.

Malik whispered something to the nurse, who pointed to the double doors in the rear. He lifted a hand, indicating Orient should wait and went inside the other room.

Orient nodded and looked around.

A black Christ hung on one wall, nailed to a black cross, face and body streaming bright red blood. The red ribbon tied around the base of the crucifix, alerted him that the object had tribal roots. He knew that much of Salvador's population originated from West Africa. The red ribbon on the black cross paid tribute to the Yoruba god Chango. Odd that it should hang here, in a medical clinic, Orient observed.

Malik returned with a broad shouldered, bearded man wearing a white smock, and a stethoscope around his neck. He looked more like a football linebacker than a physician.

"I'm Dr. Borges," he said brusquely, "where's this patient?"

Put off by his tone, Orient tilted his head. "In there."

"Get him out."

Orient knocked on the restroom door. "Ag... uh Moe, are you alright?"

No answer.

Orient rattled the knob. "Moe, unlock the door."

A few seconds later the door opened. Klein sat slumped against the wall, shivering with cold despite the tropical heat. He was having difficulty breathing.

"You two help him up," The doctor said, "I'll be right back."

As Orient and Malik half carried Moe out of the restroom, Borges appeared with a wheel chair and a blanket.

"Get him inside."

Orient pushed the wheelchair through the double doors. Inside was a small hospital ward, with five beds on each side. Two of the beds were occupied with male patients on IVs, another by a woman with bandages over her face.

"Over here."

Borges directed them to a curtained cubicle which served as an examination room and pharmacy. Orient watched him take Klein's temperature, check his pupils and glands, then tap his chest for congestion. The bearded doctor worked efficiently and quickly.

"He'll have to stay overnight," Borges said, preparing a syringe. "He needs an IV."

"What's the diagnosis, Dr. Borges?"

Borges kept his attention on what he was doing. "In laymen's terms he has an aggravated flu."

"I'm a physician."

He paused and studied Orient with laser gray eyes, as if he could read his academic degrees and practical experience at a glance.

"His symptoms are fever, conjunctivitis, swollen lymph nodes and forced breathing," he said, swabbing Klein's shoulder.

"Could be WNV, West Nile Virus," Orient ventured.

Borges completed the injection. "My conclusion exactly. Malik, help me get him to a bed. We'll set up an IV and monitor his breathing."

Malik seemed to know his way around the clinic and within a few minutes had Klein in one of the beds, hooked up to a drip and resting comfortably.

"It hit rather suddenly," Orient said as Borges made sure he was breathing easily. .

Borges removed his latex gloves. "It's a combination of factors; fatigue, dehydration, bad food— and the wrong mosquito bite. In this case the *culex* species, imported by jet from Africa."

"I noticed your Yoruba cross in the waiting room."

Again Borges gave him an appraising look. "We're a clinic, not a house of worship. But gives these poor people comfort to feel Christ is one of their own. In a way they can understand."

"Lucky thing I was around the hotel," Malik said.

It was Orient's turn for an appraisal. He shared Klein's aversion to the young man, but perhaps he was being unfair. He had been a great help, and obviously was known by Borges and his nurse.

"Fortunate for us. Are you American?"

"I'm an ex-pat, from Detroit. Decided to live where it never gets cold." He removed his aviator glasses, revealing sky blue eyes. "And there's always music in the air."

"And you, Doctor?" Borges said. "Why have you and your friend come to the Pelourinho?"

Orient kept his expression neutral. "We came to visit someone, but turns out the address we have is for the church of San Francisco."

Malik and Borges exchanged a quick glance.

"We were trying to figure out who to talk to when Moe got sick. Which reminds me, perhaps I could take his wallet and ID," Orient said casually. He didn't want Klein's official status revealed.

"Of course," Borges said. He handed Orient a plastic bag. Go through your friend's things and take what you like."

"And I'd like to pay you for..."

Borges lifted his hand. "We take no money here. This clinic is privately funded."

Orient nodded and extended his hand. "I should have introduced myself sooner. I'm Doctor Orient. Thanks for all your help."

Borges hand was strong and rough. However he smiled for the first time. "This is why we exist. To heal our fellow man."

For some reason Orient felt the remark was directed at him. "Of course. When can I visit Morris again?"

Borges shrugged. "Anytime you like."

"I'll come back after I go to the church. Perhaps the priest in charge can tell me where I can find my, er... friend."

"Why don't you let Malik help you? He knows everyone in this neighborhood."

+ + +

Carrying Klein's wallet, badge and passport in a bag, Orient let Malik accompany him to the square. Under the circumstances he could hardly have refused. But he was still wary of this accommodating expatriate.

The square was swarming with tourists armed with camera phones and children selling trinkets. The church too, was packed with sightseers. Malik and Orient worked their way to the altar rail. A nun was behind the rail, cleaning the altar and keeping an eye on the valuable artifacts.

Orient asked her in Portuguese if the priest was still there.

"Bishop Navarro left after mass," she said. "He's very busy."

"How can I reach him, Sister?"

"Come back tomorrow at ten, he'll be saying mass then."

"I know where he lives," Malik said, "let's check it out."

"How do you know that?"

"Everybody knows everybody around here. Not many movies, TVs, or computers to distract you. In the Pelourinho, you've got a choice of music, crime or religion. And *Arch*bishop Navarro," Malik emphasized the title, "is more important that the president, to some people."

His tone implied he didn't share their enthusiasm.

Orient moved to the door. "Let's see if he's receiving visitors.'

The archbishop's home wasn't far from the square. They walked up the main cobblestoned street, past the clinic, to the crest of the hill. Orient saw the house had a view of both the sea below, and the church at the end of the crowded square. He also saw the long line of supplicants at the gate. They were mostly women with small children, and old, infirm men. Their ragged clothing made it clear they were very poor.

A nun stood at the entrance to the gate, making sure the line moved smoothly, and there were no interlopers, such as Orient and Malik.

"I'm sorry, but the archbishop can't see any more people today," she said, sweeping a hand toward the waiting line, "there are so many who need him. And he is only one man."

There was no mistaking the reverence in her tone. Unlike most of the residents of Salvador, she was fair, with tired grey eyes and sun webbed skin. She wore a white kerchief, a grey smock, and white shoes. Other nuns, standing at the door of the house were dressed in similar habits. All wore silver crucifixes around their neck.

"The archbishop decided to turn his villa into a haven for our wretched souls in need," she explained. Please return at eight tomorrow morning, I'll make sure he will see you briefly."

"Thank you Sister, I won't take much of his time," Orient said, trying to mask his frustration.

"Told you," Malik said, "he's an important man around these parts. "Come on, I'll take you to the best lunch in the 'hood."

Reluctantly, Orient let Malik lead the way. He was tired and could use something to eat and drink. He was pleasantly surprised when they arrived. The small restaurant had a garden dining area, and the simple food was fresh and delicious.

"So you think Archbishop Navarro knows this friend of yours?"

Orient sighed. "Probably not. They run in different circles.'

"How is that?"

Orient sipped his strong tea. "The man I'm looking for isn't the saintly type."

"Oh, and you think Navarro is? Saintly, I mean."

Orient looked at him. Malik sat with one arm over the back of his chair, in an aggressive slouch, head cocked to one side. He eyed Orient with a mixture of contempt and compassion as if regarding an errant schoolboy.

"Just an observation. Archbishop Navarro seems to be working to help people. Just like Dr. Borges. I'm impressed by both of them." Orient met Malik's gaze and held it. "The person I'm looking for is more interested in profit. He's an art dealer. Since you say everyone knows everybody, maybe you know him. His name is Von Speer."

"German dude?"

"I think so."

"New one on me."

When the check came Malik pushed it across the table.

"I thought you were taking me to lunch."

Malik grinned. "I said I'd take you to the best lunch in the hood—and I did. The tab is on you."

When they returned to the clinic Klein was still semi-conscious but breathing well. Dr. Borges was not at the clinic however three nurses attended to the patients in the ward. From what Orient could see, they were highly professional, and had had access to modern equipment.

He poked around a bit, then, satisfied Klein was in good hands, decided to take a walk and clear his head.

"Look, Malik," he said, as the young man started to accompany him, "I'd like to do this alone okay? I'll be back in an hour or two."

Mailik lifted his hands. "Hey that's cool. If I don't see you later—thanks for lunch."

Orient left the clinic with a sense of relief. It had been a while since he had been alone, and he needed to recharge his soul, and mind. A taxi took him back to the lower city and dropped him off outside the harbor area.

As he walked he took deep breaths of the heavy tropical air, salted by the breeze coming off the sea. He headed in the general direction of the hotel, looking for a place along the beach where he could sit, and spotted a park bench, in the shade of a palm tree.

Grateful for small favors, he sat down carefully, aware of the lingering stiffness in his foot and shoulder.

For a few minutes he stared at the sun spotted surf, and the children building forts in the sand. Slowly he eased into a meditative breathing pattern, focusing his consciousness.

All of his senses became tuned to the rhythms of his being as they merged with the endless ebb and swell of the sea.

When he finally emerged he checked his watch and saw he'd been in deep meditation for seventeen minutes. Too long, he noted. There were only a few people on the beach now, just a few yards from the busy seawalk. And the three youths lounging nearby gave off predatory vibes.

They lay on the white sand about five yards to his right—watching him.

One of them got up and moved closer to the water. Like the others, he wore shorts, a soccer shirt and sneakers. One of the remaining two stood up and circled behind the tree. Orient realized he was effectively surrounded.

The one on his right got to his feet. Orient did the same, gathering his chi energy. He stepped away from the bench and they closed in. The one coming from the surf side had wide brown shoulders and a silver blade in his fist.

Chapter 35

The boy with the knife was very fast.

He came within striking range and thrust. The point of his knife grazed Orient's shirt. "Money!" he rasped in English. He pointed to the plastic bag in Orient's hand.

Klein's wallet, badge and passport were in the bag. Orient shook his head and reached into his pocket. "Money," he said.

Suddenly the youth behind the bench hit him with something like a small bat. It smacked Orient's wounded shoulder and he hit the ground. He rolled to his feet, gathered his *chi* and pushed. The youth with the bat, stopped short, and stumbled back against the bench.

A steely glint slashed past his face. The blade flashed in the sunlight as the boy circled for a opening. Out of the corner of his eye, Orient saw the third youth coming.

"Back off, motherfucker!"

The shout was punctuated by a pistol shot.

Instantly, the boys scattered and disappeared. Chest pounding, Orient scooped up the plastic bag and looked around for his benefactor.

Malik stepped from behind the tree, the revolver in his hand trailing smoke. He regarded Orient with a knowing grin.

"Lucky thing I decided to keep an eye on you."

That's two lucky things in one day, Orient thought, but there's no such thing as coincidence. "Thanks," he said, "I definitely owe you dinner. "

"What was that thing you did?"

"What thing?"

"You know, you didn't touch that shithead with your hand, but you shoved him back anyway."

Orient nodded. "Martial art called QiGong—all about bio-energy cultivation."

Malik scratched his head. "That's some serious shit. My martial art is Capoeira. I'll trade you lessons sometime."

"So why did you follow me?"

Malik spread his hands. "Like, *helloo,* Doc. Salvador can be a tough town. We got high crime and tourists are number one on the hit list."

"And you decided to be my bodyguard?"

"More like a personal assistant. Face it, Doc, at the very least you need a guide. You tell me what you want and I'll help you get it."

When Malik gestured, Orient noticed the beaded bracelets around one wrist. He started walking back to his hotel.

"Unless you know where Von Speer is, you're not much help."

"Hey, there's lots of other stuff you need."

"Right now I need to take care of some business. Tell you what, I'll meet you at the clinic in three hours. After I see to my friend, I'll take you to dinner. Fair enough?"

Face set, Malik folded his arms. "Fine, be like that. Brush me off like lint. But I'll need cab fare back to the Pelourinho. Oh yeah, plus an ammunition fee. Bullets are expensive."

Orient gave him a hundred dollar bill. "Will this cover your services?"

A slow smile erased his wounded expression. "See you in three hours."

As soon as Orient reached his room, he began to stretch, going through the long neglected patterns of QiGong. He had learned the Martial art during his stay with the Master Ku, in the Tibetan Himalayas. During his years in the city he had let his practice lapse in favor of other, equally useful, skills. But twice now QiGong had helped him avert serious harm. Aware the universe was telling him something, he focused on dusting off some forgotten finer points of the art.

Sensing the chi energy begin to mount Orient took the Seal of Solomon from its pouch and slipped it on his finger. He intensified his concentration and felt the chi building momentum as powerful as a rushing wall of water.

Using the golden ring's powerful gravity, Orient drew the *chi* energy around him like a heavy cloak, both protective and potentially dangerous. Primed and armed, he went outside for a long walk.

The sea walk was crowded with people going home from work, or headed to a café or bar. Many, like him, were just out for a stroll along the white sand beach that bordered the city. Every so often he would spot a group of young toughs trolling for a victim, but they instinctively avoided him. As if they knew he carried a concealed weapon.

The sun set abruptly, due to Salvador's proximity to the equator. Refreshed by his walk, Orient took a cab to the upper city.

Klein was sitting up when Orient arrived at the clinic.

"What happened? I can't understand anybody here," he said, waving his hand around the ward where two nurses attended to six patients.

"Have you seen Dr. Borges?"

"Just these very nice nurses who don't speak English. But I'm telling you doctor, I'm feeling a hell of a lot better."

Orient noticed that his IV had been disconnected. "Let's wait until Dr. Borges shows up. Looks like he knows how to treat this virus you picked up."

"Does he know...?" Klein let the question fade.

Orient shook his head. "I secured your wallet and passport. So while we're waiting for Dr. Borges, is there anything you need?"

"A new body, but I'll settle for some fresh juice."

"Done. Don't go anywhere, I'll be right back."

On his way out Orient ran into Malik.

"Where you headed, Doc?"

"My friend needs fruit juice, and I've been looking for Dr. Borges."

"I'll handle it. Go back inside."

"Who was that?" Klein asked, when Orient returned.

"My new best friend. You remember Malik. He brought us here."

"Where's my fruit juice?"

Orient smiled. Even sick, Klein had the truculence of a snapping turtle. "It's coming. How about some water in the meantime?"

"Deal."

Ten minutes later Malik entered the ward holding a large plastic pitcher, and a box of paper cups. Behind him was Dr. Borges.

Malik stopped at Klein's bedside and ceremoniously poured each of them a large cup of fruit juice. Then he went to the other patients in the ward and did the same for them.

"Good evening Mr Klein, they tell me you think you're well."

Moe glowered at Borges. "I'm feeling much better thank you doctor. Maybe I could get back to my place and recuperate there. Probably what I need now is chicken soup."

Borges smiled, his face taking on an almost cherubic expression beneath the beard. His gray eyes were as clear as a child's, twinkling with amusement. "Well in that case you can leave right now. I'm sure Doctor Orient can assist you home, or wherever you're staying."

Moe glanced at Orient, who shrugged. "Think you're up to it? It might be too soon."

"Course I'm up to it." The burly FBI agent sat up. Slowly, and painfully, he rolled his legs off the bed, and placed his feet firmly on the floor.

"There, that wasn't too hard."

With a grunt he pushed himself to his feet. He stood for a moment, swaying slightly, then took a step.

Orient caught Klein as his knees collapsed under him.

Borges shook his head sadly. "Maybe you'll honor us one more day." He took a glass bottle from his pocket and showed it to him. "However I prepared a special herbal remedy which will speed your recovery."

Klein eyed the bottle suspiciously. "What's in there?"

"A tincture of Amazonian herbs." Borges snapped, his genial demeanor gone. "Drink it, followed by plenty of liquids, and you should be able to walk to the loo by morning. "

Making a face, Klein downed the contents of the bottle.

After a brief physical check, Borges left to tend to his other patients.

"You have to get me out of here," Klein said, under his breath.

"Take it easy. You said yourself you're feeling better. Be patient."

"Yeah, patient. I guess that's where the word for sick people comes from."

"Look, in the morning I'll see the archbishop and try to clear up this Von Speer thing. I'll try to get a line on him."

Malik joined them. "Don't forget, you owe me dinner."

"Watch out for that guy," Klein said, as Orient prepared to leave.

"Actually, he saved me from being mugged and losing your ID."

"You ever hear of a con job? Mugger could be his pal— the old switch."

Orient shrugged. "Get some rest, and remember, lots of liquids." But as he walked outside where Malik was waiting, he couldn't help being wary. Not really a bad thing, he decided. Strange place, strange people, strange days; he'd be wise to keep one eye on Malik, and the other on his own back. He hoped Klein recovered soon. He could use another pair of eyes.

The restaurant Malik chose was situated at the top of a hill. They ate on a terrace, cooled by a breeze coming from the sea.

A tilted crescent moon floated overhead, reclining against a black sky.

"Your pal will be better by tomorrow," Malik assured between bites if grilled river fish. "You sure you don't want some of this? It's fantastic."

"This black bean soup is pretty good too," Orient said, "But I will have a Brazilian beer."

"Good choice. Let me ask you something. What happens if you can't find the Von Speer cat you're looking for?"

Orient didn't want to think of that right now. It would mean Savana being lost for good. And that was unacceptable.

"Keep looking I suppose."

"Brazil is a humongous country. The Amazon jungle is almost as big as the USA."

'Maybe you'll tell me something," Orient said, anxious to change the subject. "Those bracelets you wear—fashion or religion?"

Malik sat back and regarded the thin, beaded bracelets around his wrist. "Both. The blue and white beads are for Lemanja, goddess of the sea, the red and black are for Chango. The other one is fashion."

"Candomble?"

He looked at Orient, blue eyes steady. "No disrespect but Candomble is sort of a country cousin to Macumba, even though hey both come from the Bantu tradition."

"Then you practice Macumba?"

"So do a million other people. We got over sixty thousand churches in Brazil. You happen to know anything about it?"

"It's a form of Voodoo that originated among the Yoruba tribes of West Africa. It's called Obeah in Haiti, Lucumi in Cuba, and Macumba in Brazil. The names refer to three languages from that region."

Malik gave him a grudging nod. "You're a well informed dude. Read a lot?"

Perhaps it was the beer, but Orient rose to the bait. "I've seen my share of ceremonies."

"Great. Then you'll come along with me tonight? See how it's done."

It was a challenge Orient couldn't resist. No doubt this young neophyte expected him to shrink back when confronted by blank eyed dancers in the thrall of powerful Voodoo gods. And maybe he would.

In the end it was his curiosity that tipped the scales.

"Sounds interesting. I'm in."

Later he would have cause to rethink his decision.

Chapter 36

The night remained clear.

After lingering over coffee and brandy, Malik led him down a cobblestoned alley, half lit by the dim illumination coming from the windows and doorways of the shacks lining both sides. The alley was narrow, scarcely wide enough for one person, and the heat quickly became oppressive.

Orient took a deep breath, relaxing his diaphragm. The intensity of the last few weeks had fine tuned skills he hadn't practiced in years—such as controlling his body temperature. Tibetan monks in the high Himalayas were known to meditate outdoors in the coldest weather naked, clad only in a sheet, raising their body heat with a practice known as *Sushumna.*

Here it was the reverse. Bit by bit, he cooled his skin as they made their way to Malik's church. This also helped suppress his anxiety about following a stranger to an unknown destination in the middle of the night. Soon he heard the muffled sound of drums.

The street widened and opened onto a small square. The drums throbbed louder as Orient crossed the deserted streets, and he could hear the sound of human voices singing.

Malik half turned to make sure Orient was still with him then proceeded up a short, cobblestoned street, much wider than the others. At the top of the rise was a simple white building, with a steeple. A white cross stood above the steeple, and someone had tied a large blue ribbon around it.

There was a scattering of people on the street; two or three sitting outside a tiny café, a pair of women dressed in white entering the church, and a young flower girl.

On impulse Orient paused to buy a bouquet of white roses.

Malik eyed him impatiently. "What's up?"

"An offering," Orient said.

"Good move. Maybe you did see a few ceremonies at that... back in the day."

The interior of the church resembled a simple Catholic chapel, with a few exceptions. For one, there were no pews, just a large open area where the worshippers gathered. For another, the large, garishly painted, plaster saints arrayed on either side of the altar were actually Macumba gods and goddesses. All around them were large white candles.

Everyone, male and female, wore white, with many women wearing white turbans or kerchiefs. And everyone was swaying to the steady rolling beat of the drums. Orient noticed that some worshippers, made offerings to the various saints in the form of liquor, or cigars, or food. He moved through the crowd to the plaster effigy of the Virgin Mary, wearing blue robes, and placed the white roses at her feet.

"Very good," Malik whispered, "Lemanja is my favorite saint."

Orient knew the goddess of the sea was very popular, with two major feast days every year in her honor. Her Catholic counterpart was the Virgin Mary. He also sensed that his gesture had eased the tension created by a stranger in their midst.

When he neared the statues, Orient saw the two figures seated in throne-like ebony chairs, in front of the altar. One appeared to be male, the other was a heavy-set female. Orient couldn't be certain because their faces were masked by white lace veils.

The three drummers accelerated their deep, steady beat and the worshippers started to dance. The masked female lit a large cigar and began puffing clouds of smoke.

The male stood up and made his way to a statue of St Geronimo, which represented the god Chango. He picked up a pipe and a bottle and made his way back to the chair with lazy dance steps. He lit the pipe, and like the female, blew large streams of smoke in every direction. Between puffs, he drank from the liquor bottle.

Orient understood that in many cultures tobacco is revered as a sacred herb, due to the belief that tobacco smoke can carry messages between the physical world and spirit world. The liquor the man selected was also important, for each god had a favorite brew. The choice identified the god the veiled priest was courting. Chango was known to be very fond of rum.

Within minutes the ceremony escalated. The drumming intensified, taking on a hypnotic throb that vibrated through Orient's body, and he felt himself responding to its infectious beat.

Some of the worshippers began chanting in Yoruba, while others became more animated, dancing in frenzied circles. It was then Orient saw the girl with the yellow eyes.

She had long gold hair, smooth, tawny skin and supple limbs that seemed to float above the driving beat. Her eyes glittered like yellow diamonds in the candlelight as they focused directly on Orient.

Their eye contact was like a mid-air collision.

She exuded a primal magnetism that drew Orient's full attention. Riveted, he stared as she arched and twisted, bare feet slapping the floor in time to the drums. A film of perspiration oiled her skin and her hair was heavy with moisture in the confines of the hot, crowded room

Sweat trickled down Orient's neck and he realized his concentration had wandered. It had all shifted to the blonde lady in the center of the room.

Abruptly, the veiled priest got up and performed a series of stiff limbed movements. Brandishing his rum bottle overhead like a flag, he made a circle around the floor, speaking in a hollow, guttural voice. Occasionally he would pause, swig some rum, and laugh harshly, before continuing. Finally he sat heavily in his chair, arms and feet splayed like a drunken monarch.

A line of supplicants made their way to his throne, anxious to petition the god Chango, who had 'mounted', or taken possession of the priest's body. This enabled Chango to dispense advice, warnings, and blessings to his congregation. .

Orient noted all this peripherally, his attention still absorbed by the blonde girl dancing closer to him. Sweating freely he watched her move closer.

"Something, isn't he?"

Malik's question jerked him out of his reverie. Orient turned. Malik was intent on the veiled priest, half smiling in admiration.

"You mean the priest, or Chango?'

Malik shrugged. "I mean the Babalocha. Look, he's curing them."

The veiled priest was passing his hands over his supplicants, healing their physical and spiritual ailments. And Orient could see Malik's admiration was well founded. When the worshippers left the priest their faces were ecstatic, and their limbs, no matter how stricken, or aged, seemed to recover their vitality.

Orient glanced back at the blonde dancer.

She was gone.

His eyes scoured every corner of the floor but she had vanished. Oddly disappointed he watched the worshipers whirling and dipping, as the drums grew louder, their tireless beat sucking the air from the room. It took all his discipline to maintain a calm focus through the rising hysteria.

A few of the dancers had also been possessed by the gods, and they moved in jerky spasms, like marionettes, eyes rolling back, uttering incomprehensible sounds. The others gave them room, aware their strings were being pulled from the spirit world—and were capable of explosive aggression

One of them had taken a candle and was waving it in a threatening manner, another was spinning rapidly. The two of them somehow bumped into each other which sent the spinning man against the chair occupied by the veiled priest.

There was a collective intake of breath at this breach of respect. With a roar the high priest rose from his chair and lifted his veil. Red-rimmed eyes blazing with rage he pointed at the offender, ranting in some unknown tongue.

Shocked, Orient gaped at the priest in disbelief.

It was Dr. Borges, his face contorted, spewing curses at the now unconscious dancer.

Chapter 37

Everything in Dr. Hannah Wylde's neatly ordered life had been swept away. Everything.

In the space of two months her family, career, scientific beliefs, and self esteem had disintegrated like tract houses in a tornado. Now she found herself alone and helpless, and for the first time in her adult life without any purpose—except to find Savana and bring her back home. She was estranged from Sybelle, and had crushed a promising relationship with Owen.

At least the mysterious Doctor Orient was actively pursuing her daughter's best interests, Hannah thought ruefully.

Hannah lit a cigarette. Since she left St. Luke's she had picked up the long discarded habit. That and wine, she noted. Lately she had stopped liking herself. If she hadn't been so arrogant, so dismissive of the esoteric skills practiced by her aunt Sybelle and Owen, Savana might be safely home.

Every time Hannah thought of Owen, she felt a pang of guilt. She had acted like a schoolgirl. And there was no way to make it up to him. She ground out her cigarette half-smoked, and called Sybelle. Nobody home, she left a message.

Sybelle was slow to answer of late Hannah observed, with a tinge of regret. At one time Sybelle had been the only mother figure in her life. When she was about seven her real mother had disappeared without a trace. Many suspected foul play but Sybelle had always maintained that her sister was still alive. She had provided a loving home for her niece including her precious piano lessons.

At fourteen Hannah won a scholarship to Georgetown Academy and had gone on to a brilliant medical career. Except her marriage had failed she reminded herself, lighting another cigarette. And in the end she hadn't been able to protect her own daughter.

However through every aspect of her life her aunt had been supportive and forgiving. Nice way to repay her Hannah brooded, by acting like a whining bitch.

Another glass of wine later she sat dissolutely in front of the TV, watching but not seeing whatever was on the screen. It was like sitting underwater. Thick, dark, water.

When she finally surfaced for air, she had lost track of time. Her cigarette had gone out, still tucked between her fingers. The wine glass was half empty and there was some inane pimple commercial on the tube. Three separate products for one zit. Just stop eating fries and chips she thought, switching off the remote.

As she leaned over to drop her cigarette in the ashtray, she noticed something.

A message on her Blackberry.

She opened it with difficulty, No message just a photo. For a long time she was unable to comprehend the image—a slender, tanned girl inside a wire cage, with a monkey crouched nearby. At first she thought it was some sort of joke.

When it finally dawned that it was Savana inside the cage, the blood drained from her belly, leaving her chilled. Afraid she might drop the mobile device, she carefully placed it on the coffee table. Then she took a long breath and went unsteadily to her desk.

After some fumbling she found Agent Klein's card. She punched his number on her land line, unwilling to tamper with the image.

"You've reached Morris Klein's office. I'll be out of town for the next week..."

"Godamnit!" Hannah slammed down the receiver.

For a moment she sat motionless, breath heaving and heart tripping rapidly. Finally she got to her feet, coldly certain of what she intended to do.

+ + +

Hannah stood at Sybelle's door, and leaned on the bell. The cab stood waiting, in case she was out for the evening. Finally Sybelle opened the door a crack and peered over the thick chain.

"What's wrong?" She unlatched the chain and swung the door open. She was wearing a bathrobe. "Darling, come in."

Hannah waved the cab on his way and hurried directly into study. "Look at this," she said over her shoulder. "We've got to do something now."

Mouth open, Sybelle gaped at the photo. "You think Savana sent this to you?"

"Her or her kidnapper." She lit a cigarette.

Sybelle noticed, but said nothing. "My God, the poor child's in a cage like an animal. We need to call Agent Klein."

"I did. The bastard is away."

"Yes. He went to Brazil with Owen."

"Brazil? Why there?"

Sybelle ignored the question. "He must have left an emergency number. I mean he is the FBI."

Hannah felt her cheeks redden. "I... hung up on the message. I felt so..."

"I know how you felt, darling—scared and frustrated. Let me call his number."

"...if this is an emergency call Agent Sam Jacobi." Klein's voice droned.

Sybelle wrote down the number and quickly dialed. "I need to contact Sam Jacobi, regarding the Savana Wylde kidnapping," she said to the voice that answered.

Her eyes widened. "What? You're there so late?"

She quickly told him about receiving the picture then hung up the receiver. "I'll be right back, darling. Just let me change out of my bathrobe."

"What did they say?'

"That was Sam Jacobi who answered," Sybelle told her. "He wants us to bring the phone to his office right away."

+ + +

As their cab cruised downtown, Hannah and Sybelle sat huddled in the rear seat.

"Aunt Sybelle, I'm so ashamed of the way I've been acting toward you..."

"Nonsense, darling. You've been under enormous pressure. And in my opinion you've handled it quite well. I mean, of *course* you're upset, depressed, angry—whatever. You've got *every right* to feel that way. After all, Savana was in *my* care when she was taken."

"Oh no, Sybelle, it never entered my mind to blame you."

"Well, that's a relief. I confess I have been feeling unusually guilty."

Hannah leaned over and hugged her. "You've always been there for me. Even when I was a little brat."

"You were never a brat darling. Always been my pride and joy."

When they arrived at their destination, both women were wiping away tears,

Chapter 38

Orient remained awake for half the night before he finally quelled his raucous fears.

First thing in the morning he would remove Klein from the clinic, Orient decided, right after his visit with Bishop Navarro.

Every instinct told him to take Klein out of there immediately, but he knew it was unrealistic. It might actually harm Klein, he noted with a weary sigh. No, the morning would be soon enough.

He gripped the pouch containing the ring, and focused on creating a protective bubble around Klein, to prevent psychic attack. He did the same for himself. At dawn, when he woke up, he was still holding the pouch.

Orient's routine of stretching, breathing and QiGong did little to ease his stiff shoulder, or disperse the dark cloud hovering over his consciousness. After a breakfast of fresh fruit he showered and went out to find a cab. He wanted to make sure he was early for his appointment with the bishop.

It was overcast, a thin grey blanket waiting for the morning sun to shred it apart. The city didn't look so charming in the dawn haze. The gloom amplified the flaws and cracks in the blue wash houses and grimy white huts. Bahia looked tired without sunlight Orient thought, looking for a cab in the empty streets.

He arrived at Bishop Navarro's gate early, and found a short line of people already waiting. Fortunately the nun he had spoken to the day before recognized him and waved him inside.

"You said you would be brief," she said briskly.

"You have a good memory, Sister," he said, hurrying to keep up as she led him into the house.

It was cool and dark inside. The nun's heels clicked through the silence. Orient saw that all the rooms: dining room, salon, music room, and library, radiated from the center hall. At the far end was a large double door that was partially open. Inside was a relatively modest office equipped with an ancient computer, fax machine, stacks of files, and an antique wall clock. A large ebony crucifix hung above an oversized mahogany desk.

Behind the desk sat a dark haired man with cherubic features, thick eyebrows, and shining black eyes. He looked up when they entered, his gaze both wise and penetrating.

"Good morning," he said mildly, his voice betraying no trace of an accent, "I am Bishop Navarro."

Orient extended his hand. "Doctor Owen Orient."

Navarro's grip was firm. "Oh, yes, the American doctor who's friend became ill." He smiled at Orient's surprised expression. "This is a very small, tight knit community. And I was told he took ill in my church."

"That's true. We came hoping to speak to you about a certain Dieter Von Speer."

"Oh? Why me, Doctor?"

Orient took an envelope from his pocket and extracted a copy of Von Speer's Brazilian visa. "If I'm not mistaken that is the address of your church."

Navarro sat back, eyebrows raised. "You are correct, Doctor." He handed the document back to Orient. . "Please do not misunderstand me. I am acquainted with Mr. Von Speer but I have not seen him in at least a year. However I do know where he resides."

"Thank you, Bishop. This is a big help. Can you give me the address?"

The bishop beamed. "I'll do better than that. I'll drive you there myself. Then we can both straighten out this little mystery. Mr. Von Speer has a villa an hour or so from here."

"That's very kind. But are you sure you can spare time away from..."

He waved his hands and stood up. Orient realized Navarro was somewhat dwarfed by the huge desk. He was almost as tall as Orient, with a barrel chest which he thumped playfully. "We can go on my lunch break. I need some exercise anyway."

Sister Eva knocked. "Forgive my interruption but we have a poor woman outside who's lost her husband and her home." She looked at Orient admonishingly.

Navarro shrugged. "Sister Eva is the real bishop here," he said under his breath, "come back at twelve."

Relieved by the bishop's offer, Orient walked quickly to Dr. Borges' clinic. At least he'd managed to get a real line on Von Speer. Now he needed to pull Agent Klein out of a toxic environment. He cast no judgment on Macumba, Candomble, Lucumi, Obeah, or any of the West African religions. But powerful forces were frequently unleashed by practitioners without sufficient experience or control. And as a civilian, Agent Klein could be wounded in the spiritual crossfire.

He needed Moe healthy, Orient speculated. He'd grown to like the paunchy FBI agent, and more importantly had learned to trust him. Something he couldn't say about Borges.

The cobbled streets of the Pelourinho bustled with life. Little boys in shorts played barefoot soccer between the feet of fruit vendors and early morning shoppers. A lingering haze accentuated the sadness beneath the light samba music that trailed him along the alleys.

Dr. Borges was out when Orient arrived. Escorted by one of the nurses he went into the ward and found Klein sitting up, eating bread and broth.

"I hope you came to get me out of here," Klein said, not looking up from his tray.

"Exactly my intention. Can you walk?"

"I've been to the bathroom a hundred times in the last ninety minutes. I'm ready."

Orient informed the nurse that he was taking Klein home. She shrugged in disapproval, but returned with Klein's clothes.

She gave Orient a plastic bottle filled with a dark greenish liquid. "Dr. Borges said he must take this three times a day until it's finished. It is herbs from the Amazon the doctor brews himself."

"Thank you, Sister. We are grateful for your help." He proffered a bill. "I'd be honored to contribute..."

The nurse held up her hand and smiled. "We do not take donations here. Dr. Borges provides."

The reverence in her gaze made Orient wonder how much sway Borges had over his followers. And where he got the money to keep the small clinic operating.

+ + +

"Jesus, I do feel a hundred percent better just getting out of there," Klein said, as they walked in search of a cab.

Despite his claims of recovery, Klein was still weak and leaned on Orient.

"Maybe we should stop for coffee," Moe wheezed, pausing to gather himself.

"Soon as we get home I'll brew some strong tea. No sense exposing yourself when your immune system is compromised. Tell you what, I'll park you on the corner, you can hold on to the tree—and I'll bring the cab to you."

It was easier finding a cab alone and Orient returned in a few minutes. Klein was still there, talking to someone. Orient's mood darkened when he saw who it was.

"Hello Malik, you're up early."

Malik lifted his aviator glasses in greeting. "Leaving us so soon?"

Orient wasn't up to small talk. "My friend needs familiar surroundings," he said, helping Klein into the cab. "See you around."

When the cab pulled away Orient glimpsed Malik watching them intently. For some reason it made him uncomfortable.

There's no such thing as coincidence, he brooded, as Malik receded from sight.

Chapter 39

"She's here—dammit she's here!" Klein shouted. Orient came in from the kitchen. Agent Klein had set up a mobile office in his bedroom, connecting his phone, laptop, and printer. His eyes never left the screen.

"Jake's been trying to reach us. Your girl—Savana—e-mailed a picture from an iPhone. He traced it to a place about a hundred miles in from the city of Belem, at the mouth of the Amazon River. That's about three hours away."

Orient checked the photograph. It was good to see Savana looked healthy, despite the cage. "Squirrel monkey... indigenous to the Amazon," he murmured, studying the image intently. "We're getting close."

"Close don't pay the rent," Klein growled, "I'm booking two seats on the next flight."

"Negative. You're in no shape for the Amazon jungle. Or even fly on a plane. Right now you need to drink this tea I brewed up—and plan this out. For starters, we're going to need a boat."

Klein took a deep breath and nodded. "Tomorrow morning then—I'll have Jake arrange for help when we arrive."

For the next few hours Orient kept Klein hydrated and fed. With some reluctance he gave the agent some of Dr. Borges tonic and was relieved that it seemed to relax him. Klein was dozing peacefully when Orient left to keep his appointment with Bishop Navarro.

There was still a line of people waiting to see the archbishop, and a nun attended to their needs and questions, "Bishop Navarro must have his lunch now," she told them, "be patient. Food is being sent out to those out here who wish to wait."

Although Orient was sure she'd never seen him before, the nun waved him inside. He walked directly to the bishop's office and found him hunched over his computer. He got up as soon as Orient entered.

"Oh, Doctor, thank the Lord," he boomed cheerfully, "you've come to release me from bondage.'

Orient smiled. "I thought you were doing me a favor."

The prelate clapped him on the shoulder. "Not at all. Any excuse for a few hours respite from the woes of humanity. I haven't left the Pelourinho in weeks. Come, we'll sneak out the rear exit. The sisters will minister to the flock in my absence."

He led Orient through the large kitchen where two cooks stood preparing fragrant pots of food. The cooks paused respectfully as they passed through the rear door to a courtyard, where a red Land Rover was parked.

"I love to drive but seldom get the chance," Navarro said, putting the vehicle in gear.

The road out of town became a crude trail that cut through farmland and fruit groves which eventually gave way to jungle. Navarro kept up a running conversation, pointing out places of interest, greeting those farmers he knew by sight, and asking discreet questions concerning Orient's interest in Von Speer.

"He visits Salvador a few months every year," Navarro said. "I understand he is an art dealer."

"Yes, that's how I know him," Orient said, skirting the truth. "And you?"

"He is a generous contributor to our church. As you have seen there are many of my parishioners in dire need. It is my duty, and joy, to minister to them."

"Must be exhausting, day after day..."

Navarro glanced at him. "I see you understand, Doctor," he said with a rueful smile. "I was an athlete in my young days, but lately I've been feeling tired, burned out I think you say. That's why I jumped at the excuse to get away."

"I'm afraid it's a poor excuse."

"Nonsense, I'm curious find out why Mr. Von Speer listed my church as his residence."

The Land Rover bumped along the dirt road for miles through thick vegetation. Orient occasionally saw monkeys and brightly feathered birds flitting through the branches of low trees. Finally the road reached a fork. One side went deeper into the jungle area, the other to a rise of cleared land, planted with grass, flowers, and magnolia trees. A colonial mansion at the crest of the hill overlooked the tropical vista.

It was a scene from another era. It might have been a plantation in Louisiana, with a horse and carriage waiting near the veranda, Instead there was nothing but a wheelbarrow in evidence as they approached.

"Hello?" Navarro called. "Mr. Von Speer?"

The windows were all shuttered and the doors locked. Orient walked around the side of the house and saw a long row of rusty tin huts. They were more like cells than dwellings, having no doors or windows.

"They are the old slave quarters," Navarro said with a regretful shrug. "This region was built by African labor. Three quarters of the population of Salvador are descended from slaves. Even the word for my church's neighborhood, the Pelourinho, is named after the pillories in the square, where men were bought, sold, and flogged. It is a shameful past."

A short, dark skinned woman came cautiously from one of the cells. She was barefoot, and a red scarf covered her head. When she saw the bishop, she half knelt and crossed herself.

"The *padron* is not here, Holy Father," she said, in a Brazilian dialect Orient only half understood.

"Where is he then, Sister?" Navarro said gently.

The woman stared down at her toes. "Maybe he went to Belem do Para, Holy Father. He did not say. It is not my place to ask."

"And how do you know then?"

She shrugged and crossed her arms. "The others, his driver... It was said."

Navarro gave her a bill. "Thank you, Sister."

The woman knelt and kissed his ring.

"My people are very poor—and worse—ignorant," Navarro explained on the drive back. "But that will change. Already I have petitioned the Vatican for funds to build four schools: two primary, one secondary, one college. All free to the people of Salvador." He winked at Orient. "The real trick will be to get them to attend."

Orient half-listened, his mind racing. Von Speer in Belem... The mouth of the Amazon. Not far from where Savana had been located. He hoped Klein had made the necessary arrangements.

The ring tone on the bishop's phone was a Bach cantata. As Navarro listened his expression clouded. He put the mobile aside and stepped on the accelerator. "I've got to get back immediately," he said tersely.

Orient could see the bishop was quite agitated. His face was set in a fierce scowl, as if about to go into battle.

As it turned out his assessment was accurate.

The usual line at the gates had become a worried knot of people, huddled together a short distance away, as if afraid to get too close. Navarro pulled the Land Rover around the side and slid to a stop in the rear courtyard where Sister Eva waited.

"My black bag is in the back—bring it," the bishop said, following her into the house.

Orient found the old-fashioned doctor's bag and hurried after them. He heard someone shouting down the hall, but as he neared he realized it was more than that. The sounds were guttural, bestial... the roars and squeals of an animal fighting for its life.

And they were coming from a little girl.

Chapter 40

Despite the efforts of the two nuns trying to pin her down, the girl's thrashing threatened to break their tenuous hold. Her voice was coarse and heavy, spewing vile insults from deep inside her heaving body. .

"My bag," Navarro said, never taking his eyes from the girl.

Orient handed it over and backed away, aware that the bishop was about to perform an exorcism on the child. The girl's parents stood huddled in the far corner, both dressed in soiled white clothing.

The nuns and Bishop Navarro went about their work like a skilled surgical team.

As the two women kept the girl's arms and legs from kicking, punching or scratching, the bishop took an ancient missal, a vial of holy water and a large black cross from his bag.

The little girl screamed when Navarro sprinkled the holy water over her body, and began to invoke the names of God and his angels He petitioned them to aid in this battle against the demonic force possessing the child.

"By the power of the Great Adonai, Eloim, Ariel, Jehovah, Tagla... and by all the other holy spirits who will compel thee against thy will..." Navarro intoned in Latin, his words punctuated by the shrill cries and curses of the child struggling to free herself.

He touched the cross to her head. "I command thee by the writ of the Great Living God, by his son and by the Holy Spirit... and I vow that within a quarter hour I shall smite thee with this awesome blasting wand! Amen."

The child seemed to relax her limbs. The bishop placed the cross on her chest and reached into the bag. He extracted a pair of scissors and bent over the girl,

Very carefully Navarro cut the red and black ribbons tied
around her pigtails. The girl fell back on the carpet, eyes bulging
and mouth twisted in a fierce grimace that made her resemble
an old woman.

Still moving deliberately, Navarro gripped the head of the
cross, and held it like the hilt of a sword. He sprinkled holy water over the girl and her limbs began to twitch. Then he placed
the cracked missal on the girl's chest.

"Grant me, O Great God, the power to dispose of them,"
he said, lifting the cross above the girl's head. "By the fearful
and powerful names of the *Clavicle*: Adonai, Eloim, Jehovam,
Tagla, Mathon. Amen!"

Orient understood. The black and red ribbons were the
colors of the god Chango, of the Yoruba hierarchy. Cutting
them off dispersed he connection to the displaced spirit inhab-
iting the child's body. From her white dress and her parents'
white clothing, Orient guessed the girl had been inadvertently
possessed during a ceremony not unlike the one conducted by
Dr. Borges.

But he wasn't prepared for what happened next.

As Navarro invoked the words of dismissal a long black
caterpillar, its wet bristles trailing slime, crawled out of the
little girl's mouth. It slithered with surprising speed across her
tongue and face and dropped onto the carpet.

At that moment Navarro swung the cross down on the
creature's back, crushing it into two sections. Amazingly, both
sections, continued to writhe and crawl.

Over and over again, Navarro pounded the severed pieces
with the heavy cross until the insect was nothing but a loath-
some, jelly-like substance.

Suddenly it was quiet.

Orient heard a heart beating in the silence and realized it
was his own. The little girl was semi-conscious and quite docile.
Her arms and legs were limp and the nuns now turned their
attention to reviving her.

Slowly Navarro put his tools of exorcism back into the black bag. Before he replaced the cross he washed it carefully with a cloth soaked in holy water. He got to his feet and heaved a weary sigh.

, "Sister Eva, please cancel my appointments this afternoon." He turned to the girl's parents who were moving hesitantly to assist their daughter. "She will be fine now. But you must turn away from this barbaric Candomble religion or the demon will possess her again."

The parents nodded and crossed themselves, heads lowered in shame. "Father, I promise we will protect our daughter," the man said haltingly, "please forgive us."

Navarro lifted the consecrated fingers of his right hand. "*Te absolvo,.*" He said softly. "Now see to your little girl."

The man picked the little girl up and carried her outside, closely followed by his wife. The nuns immediately set about scrubbing down the area where the exorcism had taken place.

Navarro looked at Orient and shook his head sadly. "These poor ignorant people practice Candomble, worhip gods from Africa. They bring to these ceremonies children with no defenses against demonic entry. We perform at least thirty exorcisms a year. Very few are children. Most of the adults don't understand the forces they call up."

Orient just nodded. He never revealed his work to strangers, no matter how well intentioned. Actually, he was more interested in science than religion. However, he knew Navarro was quite skilled at handling the forces at his command.

The bishop gave him a shrewd glance. "Most people might have panicked at something like this. But you remained quite calm."

Orient smiled. "As a scientist I was interested in the process, as a doctor I've seen my share of human horror."

"Of course, well then, Doctor, may I offer you a coffee?"

"I'm afraid you've given me too much of your time already. After this, I'm sure you must be exhausted."

"I can't deny it," Navarro said, "I'm looking forward to a long nap."

As Orient passed through the gates the knot of people nearby avoided his eyes.

+ + +

When he reached the lower city Orient sought refuge from the rising heat in a small café shaded by a tattered blue awning. The strong coffee helped revive his flagging energy and he mentally prepared a shopping list for dinner. The incident he'd just witnessed reminded him that they were rushing into the lion's den. Not only was Savana's abductor a serial killer, he was an occult adept. Agent Klein's small pistol was no match.

Especially in the Amazon Jungle, he reflected. Many lifetimes before, when he was just nine years old, his parents had disappeared in the Amazon when their plane went down. So this trip held a certain foreboding for him. Right now premonitions didn't matter, he decided. All focus was on bringing Savana back safely.

Walking back to the apartment he stopped at a beachfront market. Browsing for a fresh fish for Klein, he glimpsed a familiar form.

She was walking across the beach, carrying her sandals in one hand, the other swinging with the effortless sway of her hips. A short red halter and a blue sarong accentuated her flawless torso and long, graceful legs. She moved the way he had seen her dance the night before at the Macumba ceremony.

Her tallow blonde hair was wet from the sea and pulled back, framing her startling gold eyes. They flashed recognition when she saw Orient in the open air market. . She paused and half smiled. Orient took his wrapped fish from the merchant and moved in her direction.

Her smile widened and she waited for him to come near. "I saw you last night," she said simply. "You were staring.'

"You're a lovely dancer." Orient said, without thinking.

Her laugh was as light as crystal. "Oh, I thought perhaps you disapproved."

"Why would you think that?"

She furrowed her brow. "Because you looked so serious."

Orient shrugged. "I always look that way."

"Not now, now you look..." she cocked her head, "yeah you're right, you do look serious."

They both laughed.

She pointed at the package in his hand. "Are you cooking for someone?"

"Yes. My friend has been ill."

"Then your friend is in luck, I'm an herbal healer," she whispered as if divulging a secret.

"What do you recommend for West Nile Virus?"

"Ah, the *Culex* mosquito. I do have a remedy."

They had started walking slowly to the street as if agreed on their destination.

"Really? What's your potion made of?"

"It's a trade secret. But I go to the Amazon and collect the herbs myself."

"You're familiar with the jungle?"

She shaded her eyes against the sun and looked up at him. "Nobody is familiar with the jungle. Even the local tribes have a day to day pact."

"You speak English very well."

"I spent a few years at Tulane studying botany and pharmacology."

Without any apparent sign between them, they both sat at a sidewalk café. She ordered drinks for two.

"So why were you at the ceremony last night—tourist?"

"Something like that. I was invited by a local guide," Orient said, skirting the truth. "And you—are you a worshipper?'

She shrugged. "I'm attracted by the intensity, the drums. I love to dance, it's therapy for me. And yes I'm a believer, if not quite a worshipper. I'm not often around people. My work entails a certain amount of solitude."

As does mine, Orient thought, completely taken by this beautiful young woman.

"You haven't told me what sort of work you do," she teased. "Are you a criminal on the run?"

"A bit more boring than that, I'm an MD on vacation.'

"A doctor, so we're both healers. How long will you be in Bahia?"

"Actually we're leaving tomorrow," Orient said, suddenly reminded of Klein.

"What a shame. I could have shown you the *real* Salvador. Not the usual Pelourinho routine."

"Next time," Orient said, getting set to leave. Just then their drinks arrived.

He hadn't realized how thirsty he was, and gulped down half his glass. "Really good, what's in it?"

A mischievous glint lit up her expression. "It's named after me."

Orient smiled ruefully. He had forgotten to ask her name. "Sorry, didn't mean to be rude..."

She leaned closer. "...but it doesn't seem to be important, does it?""

"It does now."

"Why?" Her voice held a hint of challenge. .

He lifted his glass. "How else can I order this special drink?"

When she laughed Orient felt her delight. She was right— their names weren't important. Their connection was immediate, and primal. Human chemistry at the ignition phase, he thought, but it wasn't the time.

"It's Alvira Charisma," she said shyly, "what's yours?"

"Owen. Owen Orient,"

"Owen..." She made it sound grand. "What a nice name."

"Alvira suits you," he said, "and this wonderful drink."

She smiled, and tapped her glass. "My recipe is mango, melon, acai berry, coconut milk, and..." she touched his hand conspiratorially, "...a dash of overproof *cachaca*."

Her skin felt lush and electric. He took a deep breath. "I've got to get back to my friend..."

"Do you have fifteen minutes? I'll get you the remedy."

"Of course. It's very kind of you." He dropped some bills on the table.

She pushed them back at his. "No charge. This is my neighborhood café. I live not far, want to walk me?"

Orient finished his drink and followed. "Were you born here?"

"I was born in Rio. My father was Italian, my mother Swedish. I went to private school in Rome, and college in America. I lived in New Orleans after I got my masters at Tulane then came here to set up my business, Botanica Bahia. Nearly eighty percent off the world's medicines and pharmaceuticals come from the Amazon. And from Bahia I can ship anywhere in the world. All I need is a laptop."

It wasn't difficult for Orient to imagine this sensuous female as a captain of industry, given her intelligence and a certain, quiet strength.

"Come along then," Alvira said, "we're wasting time."

They walked across the avenue to a side street, shaded from the afternoon sun. Art studios, jewelry stores, fruit stalls, restaurants, pastry shops, and boutiques abounded on both sides of the lane, and everyone seemed to know Alvira. Any hope Orient had of remaining anonymous in Salvador evaporated in the flurry of waves, greetings and curious stares that accompanied them along the way.

"This neighborhood is its own little planet," she said, taking his hand, "I'm at home here."

Orient knew what she meant. Her fingers fused with his, like interlocking parts of an engine. The street curved and opened onto a square dotted with stalls selling neon bright blossoms, luxuriant birds of paradise, and an abundant variety of verdant plants.

"This is the flower district,' Alvira said proudly, "and I live up there."

She pointed to a large terrace on the top floor of a nearby building. It was bursting with vegetation, as if the jungle itself had erupted like a volcano.

The inside of the stone building was cool, with a marble stairway curving up to Alvira's penthouse. The interior of her apartment was as fertile as the flower market below. Vivid abstract paintings and woven mats decorated the walls, and native pottery competed with potted plants and cut flowers for attention. There were views of city rooftops and of the sea through the vegetation that crammed both terraces.

The large kitchen had floor to ceiling shelves, which were stocked with jars of roots, plants and herbs. The living room was furnished comfortably and there was a small office room with a large computer. One side of the office was piled with mailing boxes. An old fashioned balance scale decorated the massive wood kitchen table

Alvira went to the refrigerator and studied the contents, her long legs outlined against the light. She selected a glass bottle and returned to Orient. "Put this tincture in your friend's tea. It will restore his strength."

Her gold eyes searched his face. "Would *you* like some tea?"

"You've already given me a lot on short acquaintance."

"The strange thing is, I feel we know each other somehow. You probably think I'm..."

"I feel the same thing," Orient said.

"Do you believe in past lives?"

"I believe in the present. And I believe in what we're experiencing."

Her lips were cool and moist on his, and her body flowed against him like water. Then she pulled back and grinned sheepishly. "I know, sick friend. I don't want to be the temptress."

Orient smiled, reluctantly letting her lush body slip out of his arms. "I have a feeling we'll meet again."

"Well, now you know the way," she said huskily, her mouth brushing his. Her breath had a sweet scent that lingered in his nostrils like perfume.

"Don't forget my little herbal remedy," she whispered.

Walking back to the main avenue along the beach, Orient realized he'd left the fish in Alvira's apartment. He stopped at a local market and paid double for the same item.

There's a lesson in there somewhere, Orient reflected, flagging a taxi. Perhaps he had dodged a bullet.

But he couldn't stop thinking about her

Chapter 41

"Where the hell have you been?" Klein growled. He had gotten out of bed and was hunched over the laptop on the desk

Orient avoided the question. "Good to see you sitting up Are you hungry? I bought some fish . You can use the protein."

"What about you?"

"Pasta, salad, fruit, yogurt, I'll survive."

Klein squinted at the computer screen. "See? What did I tell you, the man does not eat."

Orient came behind the desk and saw an owlish looking man, with a dark stubble grinning at him. "Say hello to Sam Jacobi," Klein said, "Jake this is him, the vegetarian doctor."

"Hello, Sam."

"Take good care of my friend, Doctor. Moe's not used to places where you can't get bagels."

"Sam is handling everything we need," Klein explained. "It'll be waiting for us at the Hilton in Belem."

"What about our flight?"

"Private courier, leaves at nine a.m."

"One more question, has Sam pinpointed Savana's location?"

"He's got it within seven miles."

"Seven miles is a lot in the Amazon."

"Ain't many cell towers in the Amazon doc," Jake said stiffly, "even Google has trouble zooming in there. Thing is we keep running into an anomaly. Could be a scrambler."

"Do we have a choice?" Klein said. "We find a good guide and wing it."

Orient shrugged. "I'll make some food. So long Sam," he said to the image on the screen, "thanks for your help."

"Thank you. You're going to make our Moe famous."

Grateful he didn't have to account for his absence Orient busied himself in the kitchen. He grilled the fish with garlic, onions, and a splash of white wine.

"For a vegetarian you can cook," Klein congratulated, "this is damn good."

"Glad you recovered your appetite."

"So what did our bishop have to say?"

"He was very concerned. Drove me out to Von Speer's farm."

"And...?"

"Nobody home. The caretaker said he might be in Belem."

Klein nodded thoughtfully. "You know I've been thinking. There's the SS dagger that killed Henry Applegate, and you say you saw Nazi military in your, er... vision."

"Yes, that's true. You think Von Speer...?"

Klein waved a fork at him. "A lot of ex-Nazis escaped to Argentina and Brazil."

"The Amazon jungle is definitely a good place to hide out." Orient heated up the tea pot.

Klein scooped up the last morsel on his plate. "But what do Nazis want with Savana?"

Orient kept his theories to himself. He wanted to avoid any references to magic or telepathy. However he was aware of the occult roots of the Nazis. And he had no doubt Savana's abduction served a ritual purpose.

As he poured the tea he remembered Alvira's tincture and decided to try a few drops as prescribed. Borges remedy had been quite effective but there was little left.

Orient set the cup in front of Klein. "This should make you feel better."

"Another magic potion? Like that clinic?"

"Over eighty percent of our medicines originate in the Amazon," he said, repeating Alvira's words. "Anyway, Doctor

Borges herbal cure seemed to take. You couldn't walk two days ago."

"Alright already, Doc, I'm drinking the tea."

After an initial flurry of energy that inspired Klein to catch up on his progress memos and expenses, Klein went to bed early.

Before going to sleep Orient s invoked the power of the ancient ring around his neck, to protect them on their quest. And while he did has best to set aside the memory of his afternoon encounter, the touch of Alvira's lips lingered in his senses....

+ + +

She was the first thing he thought about in the morning.

It took a concerted effort to focus his consciousness on the task ahead. He stretched, meditated, and energized his chi practicing QiGong. When he finished he was surprised to find Klein up early, and ready to go.

"You were right about that tea, Doc. I slept like a babe and woke up feeling like myself."

"How's that?"

"Stiff and cranky. But at least I can make myself breakfast."

Orient was impressed by Klein's renewed vitality. The FBI agent had lost weight over the past two days. His shuffling pace had picked up and his posture improved. Only the hound dog expression remained unchanged.

On the flight to Belem, Klein was in constant touch with Sam Jacobi via Skype and e-mail. Apparently, Alvira's elixir was effective Orient thought, as was Dr. Borges' remedy. He tried to suppress a ripple of emotion at the memory of his encounter the day before. Remember where you first saw her dancing, Orient reminded, the Macumba ceremony. There could be a connection between Alvira and Borges.

During the short drive from the airport Orient saw that Belem was much different than Salvador. It was wilder, more primitive. He had a sense of being at the edge of civilization. The damp equatorial air was sweltering and looking up at the dingy hotels, through glassless windows, he could see men lying in hammocks. Tattooed street vendors sold knives with carved bone handles and regarded their passing with wary stares, as if they knew the law had arrived.

The city was mainly composed of rows of small houses on nondescript streets with the exception of the wide avenue leading the Hilton hotel. The air conditioning hit them the moment they stepped inside. As promised, the equipment Sam Jacobi had requisitioned was waiting in their suite.

"Two state of the art satellite phones, two GPS trackers, three walkie talkies, and..." Klein paused, "...what the hell is this?"

He lifted a black .45 calibre pistol from the Fed Ex box. There was a note attached. "In this jungle you need something more serious than that Ruger Lite you carry. Love SJ," Klein read aloud.

He shook his head and grinned. "The crazy bastard."

"What about the boat and a guide?"

"I'll Skype him later."

"You're pretty handy with the high tech stuff."

Klein smiled proudly. "Jake plugged me in."

For the next hour they went over the working of their electronic gadgets, especially the GPS which enabled them to track each other, as well as guide them through unexplored territory.

Jake had thoughtfully included two waterproof knapsacks equipped with flashlight, battery pack, waterproof matches, compass, hunting knife, water purification tabs, Swiss Army Knife, packets of dried fruit, protein bars, fish hook and line, insect repellant, first aid kit, and a pack of cigarettes for trade purposes.

Even with the electronic gear, the knapsack was reasonably light, Orient conceded. But two New Yorkers tramping around in the jungle with no fixed destination wouldn't last very long.

"Jake? " Klein said, to the laptop screen. "Any news on a boat?"

The answer came in disjointed phrases. "Negative. Our rep... in Belem... still... looking... I'm on it."

Orient felt restless. He wandered to the window and looked out. There, right in front of him, a few hundred yards across the river, was the jungle—an endless expanse of low green vegetation that was home to the most dangerous creatures on the planet. It was the first time he had traveled to the place where his parents had disappeared.

He turned and saw Klein was still absorbed in his laptop conversation with Jake. He signaled Klein that he was going out. The agent nodded and waved.

"Oh, Doc, something I forgot to ask."

Orient turned. "What's that?"

"That stuff you put in my tea. I think I need a little more."

Orient measured a few drops and mixed it with water. "You've become quite attached to this tincture. Problem is I'm not sure what's in it."

"Yeah, well, the stuff sure works for me."

+ + +

The moment Orient stepped outside a thin layer of sweat oiled his skin. He took a deep breath. The air was heavy with moisture. The trees shading the avenue did little to ward off the deadening heat. The street vendors were all crouched listlessly behind their wares, which consisted of sinister knives and decorative bowls obviously made for tourists.

A slight breeze came off the river as he turned the corner. He headed for what seemed to be a bustling dock area and came upon a crude marketplace jammed with shoppers.

There were shades of tattered straw above the poles and tables displaying various goods from leopard teeth, vials of mercury for gold prospectors, skins of all types, from cat to reptile, monkey skulls, fresh caught fish and newly killed chickens. The food tables were piled with rock salt which was liberally sprinkled, to protect the arrayed flesh from spoiling in the heat. It was the frontier. And a few hundred yards away were the savage lands where man made, and paid for, his own law.

The people too, seemed more at home on the river than the city, most of them barefoot or wearing rubber sandals, shorts and T shirts.

Orient approached a few of the fishermen at the dock about securing a boat and perhaps a guide, but they regarded him with suspicion and suggested he hire a tour boat. Disappointed but undaunted, Orient scanned the area and saw small boats of all types. One of them would undoubtedly be available. The problem was, how soon.

During the flight to Brazil he had tried to sort out the occult aspects of Savana's abduction. If she hadn't been taken for ransom, then it had to be for ritual. His vision, the missing fragment, and the killer's attempt to get the Seal of Solomon, made it a no-brainer. Exactly what the ceremony entailed he didn't know, but he could make an educated guess as to when.

On the flight from Salvador Klein's laptop made it easy to check the astrological—and astronomical—charts. In six days the summer solstice and a lunar eclipse would coincide in a rare celestial event.

The sun's solstice had been a source of power for the ancient Nordic rituals. Orient had no doubt the man with the scar was preparing for the next week's phenomenon.

He also knew the theory had to be put to Klein carefully.

At least they'd have a timeline, if not a specific direction, Orient reflected wandering through the market, looking at the exotic goods for sale. There was raw guarana, the root-like substance with high caffeine content, necklaces made of raw crystals, unidentifiable strips of meat, piles of berries, a variety of machetes, bright rolls of fabric, clay pots, and jars of honey. On impulse Orient bought two serviceable machetes, certain they'd be handier than a Swiss Army Knife in the jungle.

The heat and his recent flight finally caught up to him and he looked around the market for a café where he could sit out of the sun. He saw a number of flower stalls nearby. Just behind them was a storefront that looked like a restaurant.

To his relief it did serve food, coffee and tea made from guarana. But more importantly he could sit in the shade. He ordered the tea, and looked out at the market. The flower stalls reminded him of Alvira. His mouth still resonated from her kiss.

He noticed that the stalls here displayed plants and hanging vines he'd never seen before. There were also long wooden boxes filled with red dirt, sprouting unusual herbs.

The warm tea had an oddly cooling effect. He took a deep breath of humid air salted with sea water from the Atlantic. In a few minutes he felt both relaxed and energized, the effect of strong tea and guarana.

As he prepared to leave he saw a familiar figure silhouetted against a bank of flowers. She turned and saw him, yellow eyes as bright as suns. It was like clouds parting. Smiling with surprise and expectation, he moved toward her.

She ran to meet him, golden hair streaming.

"I knew we'd meet again," She said taking his hand. "Come back inside, I need a drink."

"I highly recommend the guarana tea."

"Good choice."

It was as though they'd been together for years. Still holding his hand she sat close beside him. Her sweet scented breath caressed his ear. "I dreamed I saw you."

Orient found it difficult to stay distant. Her hand felt cool against his, but his blood was racing.

"What are you doing here?" he said.

"I come to this market three times a month for special herbs from the jungle. Sometimes I go upriver myself to collect rare plants."

She cocked her head and looked at him. "Actually it's me who should ask that question. And why did you buy those machetes?"

"I came to find someone who lives in the jungle."

"Then why were you in Salvador?"

"He lives in Salvador too. But when I went to his villa, I was told he's in Belem."

"Who is this person? Perhaps I know him. Everybody in Salvador..."

"...knows everybody else." Orient said. "So I've heard."

"So?"

"What?" Orient was getting lost in their closeness. He hadn't felt this way for a long time.

"His name."

"Oh right. His name is Von Speer. Dieter Von Speer."

"The art collector?"

"You know him?"

"Yes. He comes here every year to buy native artifacts. He has a small compound upriver about seventy miles or so."

"Have you been there?"

"I've passed it. I can draw you a map if you like."

Orient kissed her cheek. "I like very much. This solves one big problem."

The light touch generated static electricity. Their bodies were humming, vibrations in complete harmony.

"Mnn that was very nice Any more problems I can solve?"

"Know where we can rent a boat?"

"Of course. I told you I make my living in the jungle."

The tension fell from Orient's body like a discarded cloak. "You seem to have everything I need."

"You know I do," she said softly, "And you're right, this tea is good."

For a few moments they were silent, both basking in the moment. Activity in the market had slowed, and across the brown river the jungle looked lush.

"Come on," she said, "let's find you a boat.'

"Were we going?"

"I live not far. I have a phone there. And I can make you a detailed map to Mr. Von Speer's little compound. It's actually a trading post."

"You have apartments everywhere."

"This one is more a crash pad for my Amazon visits." She took his hand. "Have you been to the interior before?"

"First time."

"The jungle is cruel. You'll need more than those machetes."

Orient was only half-listening, entranced by Alvira's natural grace. He hadn't realized how much he had wanted to see her again. The offer of a map and a potential boat had dispersed his anxieties concerning the mission. And for the moment, Alvira consumed his reality.

"We're here," she said, unlocking a metal gate that covered the front door. "Lots of thieves in Belem," she explained. They went up two flights to a two room flat with a view of the river and jungle beyond, as well as a section of the market. The small kitchen had a Formica table and two chairs. There was a worn couch and easy chair in the living room, a bed canopied by mosquito netting and little else. A small TV sat atop the refrigerator. The one touch of luxury was a second, larger, refrigerator.

"Told you, just a crash pad,' she said, "I'd offer you something but as you can see..."She opened both refrigerators. They were crammed with jars of herbs and bundles of plants.

"Have a seat at the table while I find my river charts."

Alvira was wearing jean shorts and a simple blue halter that clung to her fluid body as she moved. She returned with a packet of maps and charts. She laid one of the maps, a chart of the river, and a sheet of blank paper side by side on the table.

Patiently she went over the route to Von Speer's compound using the map as a broad guide. She referred to the chart for specific instructions, and gave him a hand drawn map as back-up, with notes on landmarks and tributaries.

Orient found it difficult to concentrate with Alvira bending over him so closely. He could feel her hair against his cheek, the warmth of her bare arms brushing his shoulder. Then too was her low voice against his ear as she plotted the course.

It happened spontaneously.

Their mouths came together in a deep, dizzying kiss that swept everything away except the primal hunger scratching at his senses. She took his hand and pulled him gently to the bedroom but they never made it. Still entwined they fell on the couch. The touch of her naked skin ignited small explosions of pleasure. Her writhing body merged with his in an ecstatic rush, and he felt her nails raking his back. Like collapsing stars their beings compressed to a single pulsing point then erupted, lighting the universe.

They both fell back, legs and arms entangled, drenched in perspiration. She nuzzled his wounded shoulder tenderly and it felt healed. He felt balanced and at peace.

"Mnnn, I feel so good..." she murmered, "...so *right*."

He didn't answer knowing it wasn't necessary.

"What's this you wear around your neck?" she said lazily.

"It's a Moroccan medicine bag, "he told her, hoping she wouldn't ask more about it.

She ran her finger along the stitches in his shoulder. "And these?"

"An accident."

"I have something that will help." She slipped out of his arms and went to one of the refrigerators. Orient followed her long, tawny legs across the floor, her alert, apple breasts glowing in the refrigerator's light.

She returned with a small bottle that contained an oily cream which she rubbed on his stitches.

"This will help it heal fast," she whispered, smooth skin against his.

"Feels better already."

"Let me show you Belem this afternoon. I know a quiet place where we can..."

She knew his answer before he could speak.

"...But I suppose you have to get back to your obligations."

He gave her a regretful smile but her eyes reprimanded him.

He drew her close. "Will you be here for a few days?"

"I have to be back in Bahia tomorrow."

"Then I'll see you there, for sure."

She kissed him. "If you don't forget me in the jungle."

Chapter 42

Orient knew he could never forget Alvira. She was imprinted in his consciousness like a childhood song. He left her apartment reluctantly, carrying his new machetes, the river charts, and the name of the boatman who would meet them at the dock tomorrow at noon.

The sun had dropped when he stepped outside but the heat was relentless. He walked slowly back to the Hilton, savoring the moment, and the memory of Alvira running toward him. A child of nature with no hesitation about expressing her feelings

"Hey, Doc."

It took Orient a moment to realize the call was for him. When he saw the caller , his mood clouded..

"Malik, when did you arrive?"

The young man grinned. "Came yesterday. Stayin' with a friend here. Guess you're at the Hilton."

Orient wondered if Malik had seen him with Alvira. He also wondered if Malik was following him.

"Why Belem? You don't strike me as an explorer type."

Malik laughed. "You got that right doc. I'm a lover, not a fighter. I'm here for the ceremony."

"I thought your church was in Bahia."

"Not exactly Macumba, Doc. This is the church of Santo Daime. It's a special Ayahuasca ceremony for the lunar eclipse. You should check it out."

The lunar eclipse. Orient's brain sifted through the possibilities. "I'm getting an early start in the morning," he said.

But he was curious. Ayauasca was a psychedelic vine which, combined with other herbs produced ecstatic visions. It had been used for centuries by the tribal shamans of the Amazon

"Don't tell me you disapprove, like you do Macumba."

Orient smiled. "I never disapprove of any man's quest for divine illumination."

Malik's posture relaxed. "Yeah well, I see you got some jungle shanks. Need more than machetes in there."

"So I've heard."

"What, you still lookin' for that pal of Navarro's?"

"News travels fast out here."

"The bishop ain't exactly invisible, even though some people wish he was."

"Why?"

"Maybe they know him better than you," Malik said, blue eyes hooded. "Anyway I'll give you a call, see if you change your mind. Ceremony's at nine tonight."

Orient stared incredulously. "You have my phone number too?"

Malik laughed. "Of course not. Your gonna give it to me."

"Even better, give me yours."

"My friend doesn't have a phone."

Orient shrugged. "Then I guess this is goodbye. But I'm still curious."

"Yeah?"

"Why the attitude toward the bishop? I've seen what he does for his people."

Malik leaned closer.

"He would steal the last supper from Christ."

+ + +

"I'm calling you Houdini from now on," Klein greeted, "you have a tendency to disappear."

Orient dumped his packages on the table. "I have a map to Von Speer's place."

"Where the hell did you come up with that? And what's with the swords?"

"They're machetes. We might need them tomorrow."

"Jake still hasn't been able to locate a boat."

"I think we found one. We're meeting him at noon tomorrow."

"You definitely have been busy. How'd you hook up with all this?"

"While I was looking around the local market, I ran into a friend."

"A friend? From New York?"

"Bahia."

"Not that guy Malik."

"Actually I ran into him as well."

"Something about him I don't like."

"He's in town for a special ceremony for the upcoming lunar eclipse."

"I don't get it."

Orient explained his theory. Savana was abducted to take part in a Thulian ritual that would take place on the summer solstice.

"And it happens the lunar eclipse is that same night," Orient said. "You may recall that the members of the Thule Group were occultists who formed the core of Nazi mysticism."

Klein gave him a rueful smile. "Believe me, I recall. In fact we've heard chatter, you know gossip, that there's been a major art theft in Austria and Von Speer's name keeps coming up."

"The Shatzhammer Museum, by any chance?"

"Yes as a matter of fact. Why do you ask?"

"Better tell them to check something known as the Spear of Destiny."

"Problem is nothing is missing."

Orient fingered the duplicate gold ring in his pocket. "Maybe it was replaced with a perfect copy."

Klein snapped his fingers. "Worth a shot. I'll contact Jake. By the way, when is this solstice you're talking about?"

"About five days from now."

Klein nodded and shifted position, leaning closer. His jaw was set and his eyes studied Orient. No longer affable, he had the steely edge of an interrogator

"Tell me about this friend from Bahia."

Orient took a deep breath, aware it would sound eccentric at best. At worst Klein would think he was a romantic fool. When he finished giving Klein the broad details of his encounter with Alvira, he waited for the agent's reaction.

As expected Klein was skeptical. "You first saw this girl at a Macumba ceremony right?"

Orient nodded.

"And Malik took you there?"

"Yes."

"Do you think your friend Alvira might be at this lunar ceremony with Malik?"

It had crossed Orient's mind. "I don't think so. But..."

"...we can't rule it out."

Klein's flat tone made it clear he believed Orient was influenced by his emotions.

"What do you propose—that I go to the Santo Daime church tonight?"

The agent shrugged. "Tomorrow morning we check out this boat. We already have Savana's general location. If her map turns out to be bullshit we take it on our own and use the GPS."

"And if it's some sort of trap?"

Klein snorted. "She had you trapped already."

Orient smiled, but it hit home. "I'll drop by the ceremony and have look."

+ + +

The Santo Daime church was easy to find, but difficult to enter. Finally he had to use his password. "Malik, invited me, he told the glowering giant at the door. "Malik from Bahia."

"Ah, Malik from Bahia," the man repeated, his frown relaxing. "Stay here."

He returned with Malik, who seemed more pleased than surprised by Orient's visit.

"Come in, we're about to start shortly. Will you partake of the sacrament with us?"

"I'm here as an observer, if that's alright."

Malik grinned. "That's fine. But it may get funky."

Orient soon learned what he meant. The participants, perhaps sixty of them, sat at three long tables. A priest sat at the head of the center table. Like most of the congregation he was simply dressed. There was a large carafe at the center of each table, and a glass in front of each participant.

Empty buckets and pails were strategically placed nearby.

After the priest's blessing, everyone filled their glasses and drank the sacred Ayahuasca wine.

The ceremony was simple. The priest would read spiritual passages, and the participants would drink another glass. In this way the priest could guide the visions induced by the Ayahuasca.

However, imbibing the wine had side effects. It also caused some to purge their bodies. By the third glass, at least twenty people had to vomit into the buckets provided. The visions would come later.

Orient decided to quietly slip out. But he was satisfied. He had carefully scanned each of the participants and Alvira wasn't among them.

Chapter 43

Orient woke at dawn and went though his daily routine of meditation and QiGong. But try as he might to stay focused, Alvira kept easing into his thoughts.

Klein was still asleep when he finished. Orient took a quick shower and went down to the hotel dining room for breakfast. As he passed the reception desk he heard a familiar voice.

"Orient... Owen Orient, or perhaps Morris Klein. Of course they're here."

He paused. The humidity had wrung her frizzy red hair into damp strands, her lipstick had dimmed, her mascara smudged, but her attitude was as crisp as ever.

Sybelle Lean was at the front desk, a large pink suitcase by her side. Hannah stood just behind her, looking lovely despite the dark circles around her lavender eyes.

Orient's quick pang of guilt was engulfed by sheer amazement.

"There you are, darling," Sybelle said, "the clerk had trouble finding you."

"What are...?"

"I know, that nice FBI man, Sam Jacobi, warned us not to come, but poor Hannah has been distraught. And when she saw that picture of Savana in a cage... well what else could we do?"

Orient looked at Hannah. She seemed happy to see him but unsure of herself. He gave her a polite embrace.

"You ladies must be hungry and tired," Orient said quickly, "leave your bags at the desk and join me for breakfast. We can talk there."

"Have you located the place where they're holding Savana?" Hannah asked the moment they sat down.

"Close, but we haven't pinpointed it yet. But I've gotten hold of a map, and we're due to hire a boat this noon."

Sybelle's eyes widened. "A boat. You mean you're going into the jungle?"

"Yes—and no you can't go with us." Orient said gently. "But we'll be in touch via satellite smart phones. "

Hannah touched his hand. "You have a map, to where?"

"To the compound of a man who's very much involved. He knows where Savana is, and who's holding her."

Hannah's touch rekindled a memory of their past attraction. Orient knew she was vulnerable at the moment. .

"I... just had to be close to her," Hannah said, half-apologetic.

"Of course."

"What do they want with her?"

The question tore at his tightly held emotions. He looked at Sybelle. "I did run across one interesting fact. In five days the summer solstice *and* a lunar eclipse occur during the same twenty-four hour period."

Sybelle seemed to wilt when she heard the news. Orient sensed she was holding something back. He stared at her.

"Does that mean anything to you?"

Sybelle looked at Hannah, then at him. "I probably should have told you sooner, but I didn't realize it myself until a week ago."

Orient waited.

"The vision we had, in Marrakesh. The girl we thought was Savana. I finally realized who she *really* was."

She took Hannah's hand. "My aunt, your grandmother..."

Klein shuffled into the dining room. "Am I interrupting anything?" he asked warily.

Hannah gave him a cool smile. "My aunt was just recounting some family history."

He nodded and sat down. "I just got an e-mail from Jake that you two were on your way." He scanned the menu. "Probably our last good meal before we get on the boat."

Klein's presence had put a damper on Sybelle's revelation, but Hannah appeared unruffled.

Not Sybelle. During breakfast she broke her silence. "I was telling Hannah a family secret actually."

She nervously stirred her coffee and went on. "I've rarely discussed this with anyone, but my Aunt Helene was a very gifted psychic."

"Yes I've heard that," Hannah said, "but I rejected that part of our family history. And so did mom as I recall."

Sybelle patted her hand. "It's difficult for most people to deal with darling. I had no choice really. I inherited our family's psychic gene. But more to the point— Aunt Helene had a distressing fascination for the dark side."

"What happened to her?"

"She disappeared in Paris during World War Two."

Orient looked up. "And you believe she was the girl we saw in the vision?"

"Obviously not Savana, she hadn't been born. It's the only thing that makes sense. And it explains why someone would go to great pains to abduct Savana. To complete what we interrupted with our family blood."

Hannah's expression didn't change but Orient saw her fists clench.

Sybelle noticed too. "I didn't mean it that way," she said softly. She gave Orient an imploring look.

"We stopped the rite once before," Orient said, "and we know where they're holding her."

Hannah nodded, grateful for the slightest hope.

"Come on," Orient said, "let's get you two some rooms."

Klein looked up from his food, fork in hand. "Hold on, I was thinking. We're leaving this afternoon right? The ladies can

take over our suite..." He grinned at Sybelle "...if they can stand
it."

Sybelle instinctively patted her hair. "How generous, what a
wonderful idea, Agent Klein."

"Please call me Morris."

Hannah stood up. "Owen, could you help me with the lug-
gage? I need to get settled."

"The suite has two bedrooms," Orient said, as they crossed
the lobby. "I can clear out my stuff and you can grab a nap.'

She cocked her head. "Don't you know better than to tell a
lady she looks tired?"

"No I..." To Orient's relief she was teasing. In the elevator
she stood close to him as if waiting for him to speak. But he
didn't know what to say. The spiced scent of Alvira's breath still
lingered in his senses.

"Well, here it is," Orient said, unlocking the door. Aside
from Klein's strewn clothes the suite was reasonably neat.

Hannah took a deep breath, as if she'd just completed a
long run. "I want you to know how grateful I am Owen. I don't
know where I'd be without your help.'

He took her in his arms, stroking her shoulder.

"Which reminds me," she said softly, "let me see how
those stitches are doing."

Orient dutifully unbuttoned his shirt. "My arm feels good."

Hanna lightly ran her fingers along the stitches. "Somebody
did an okay repair job."

"Prison doctor, when Klein had me arrested."

"Luckily, you heal fast. They're ready to come out—but not
before you go into the jungle." She bent closer and kissed his
shoulder. "I'll take care of this when you get back."

A sense of guilt clouded his smile and he quickly went into
his room to pack his gear.

Hannah stood at the door.

"The Bureau sent us the latest tech gadgets," he said, checking his knapsack.

"That machete looks pretty hi-tech,' she said drily.

"Apple doesn't have an App for cutting through jungle."

When he was finished he moved to bring his knapsack and suitcase into the outer room but she blocked his path. Orient understood what she needed. She was in pain. The rest could be sorted out later. He dropped his bags and gently kissed her.

It seemed to deflate the tension stiffening her body and she held him tightly. "It's so good to see you," she whispered.

Sybelle's voice at the door dissolved their embrace.

Relieved, Orient brought his gear into the living room.

"I brought something back from Marrakech for you Sybelle."

"For me? How did you ever have time to..."

She stopped and stared at the gold watch dangling from Orient's fingers.

"My watch. My grandmother's watch! The one you sold to the guide. You found it."

"I bought it back from him. Seems it refused to work until I arrived."

Klein stared at the watch with a mixture of suspicion and disbelief. "Your saying you sold this watch during your so-called vision, and now you bought it back?"

Orient smiled. "Hard evidence, Moe. Starting to believe us now?"

"I don't know what to believe," Klein grumbled.

"Well I'm overjoyed to have it back." Sybelle held the watch to her ear. "And it still works. Thank you, darling."

"We don't shove off for a few hours, I'm going out to see if our boat has arrived."

"Give me a few minutes to round up my things," Klein said. "I'll go with you. I'm sure the ladies would appreciate some privacy."

Sybelle beamed. "You are so thoughtful Morris. When we get back to New York I'm going to cook you a big dinner."

+ + +

"I haven't taken a walk for four days," Moe said, trying to keep up with Orient's long stride, "and I'm sure not used to this heat."

They hadn't reached the end of the block and his shirt was already soaked. He made a mental note to wear a T shirt and light pants on their upcoming cruise.

Orient slowed down. "How do you feel?"

"No worries. I jog regularly so I'm in fair shape. What's the name of this boat your lady friend found for us?"

Ignoring the dig, Orient read the note Alvira had given him.

"Name of the boat is Ondina. The captain is Martino Espada."

"How far is the dock?"

"A few blocks. Nothing here is very far from the river."

The morning heat slowed their pace, giving Klein a chance to take in the exotic market at the edge of the Amazon. "My god, this is wonderful," he blurted.

"We've got time if you want to explore a bit," Orient said. "I can go look for our boat."

Klein grinned. "Just a few minutes. I'll catch up.'

Orient waved and walked toward the line of boats further along the dock.

He returned almost immediately.

Klein was intently inspecting a necklace purported to be made of jaguar teeth, when he saw Orient beckoning to him.

Klein followed a few steps behind. "What's up?"

Orient stopped at the edge of a small building.

"Look who's here."

Klein peered around the corner.

A battered ship, with the name Ondina painted on the prow in faded blue script was docked nearby. A crew member was talking to a lanky young man on shore.

He recognized the young man immediately.
Malik.

Chapter 44

Hans had been anticipating his reunion with the Spear of Destiny.

When the hour came, he was prepared, having fasted and anointed his body with purifying oils.

Since his transgressions in New York, he had been denied contact with the precious relic. However the Architect deemed that he had served long enough in purgatory.

Now that the time was at hand he would assume his rightful place in the hierarchy of the Grand Design. The high priest would sit at the right hand of the Architect, and Hans at the left.

Tonight would be a simple affair, only him and the Architect conducting the mass of consecration. Early in life, when he had been naïve, he had been ordained as a priest. His consecrated fingers held the power to transform the communion wafer into the body and blood of Christ.

He had left the church to become the complete man; scholar, scientist and warrior, with access to all the weapons of angel and demon. And he had used them well—if indiscriminately at times.

Now their careful plans were about to come to fruition. The elements were moving inexorably toward the apocalyptic confluence at the hour of the solstice. The hour of the New Reich—when they would rise up as one and take their rightful place as the absolute monarchs of mankind....

His priestly vestments felt light on his body despite the humidity inside the windowless chapel.

The Spear and the Book were on either side of the chalice on the small altar. He was properly attired to say mass, save for the ceremonial SS dagger hanging from his rosary beads.

At the signal he began. The Architect assisted, opening the missal, handing him the cruets containing water and wine, responding to the prayers.

"Dominus non sum dignus..."

"E cum spiritu tuo..."

He lifted the sacred wafer and performed the miracle of transubstantiation, transforming the wafer into the body and blood of Christ. Then he dropped it into the wine in the chalice and watched it dissolve.

The consecration completed Hans turned his attention to the book on the altar. It lay open to a page inscribed with arcane symbols, forbidden names, and long forgotten gods. It was the Grimoire of Honorious, the secret book of spells and rituals compiled by the Roman Pope who was a magus.

With great pleasure he fitted the missing piece to the Grimoire's cover. The triangular swatch bearing the image of the goddess Antu, lost years ago, and returned in time to fuel their ascendance.

"Iah..." he began. As intoned the ancient words he lifted the Spear and lowered it gently into the chalice. The moment the tip touched the wine, the Spear became hot, forcing him to drop it.

"...Chameron, Oriet..." He felt the intensity rising with each syllable and stared at the chalice which was becoming red hot. The Spear stood half submerged in the steaming wine.

"...Ouyar." As he completed the invocation he watched the Spear begin to glow.

At first he was fearful the gold and silver casings would melt—but it wasn't heat. The Spear was *radiating*.

The Architect inhaled sharply, visibly impressed.

Hans bathed in the Spear's radiant energy, absorbing it through his pores. He exulted in its vibrant promise.

Like Yeats' rough beast, his hour had come round at last.

+ + +

Although exhausted, Hannah Wylde couldn't sleep.

Ever since Owen and Agent Klein left, she felt empty. She was grateful they were risking their lives to find Savana. But Owen had been distant. Supportive but remote, she reflected, not that it was his fault. She had done her best to drive him away, even blamed the poor guy. What did she expect?

Unconditional love might be nice, Hannah mused, rummaging for her cigarettes. One of the minor evils of this ordeal was her readdiction to tobacco. She paced the floor, unable to take her mind off Savana, in a cage, in the jungle, alone. Her thoughts jumped back to Owen. At this point she knew she'd made the right choice. He would make an excellent trauma physician. However their personal history might complicate matters.

Your personal history, Hanna noted ruefully, Owen's ship seems to have sailed. Anyway her life at the hospital seemed long in the past. She wondered if she would ever resume her work again.

It was approaching dawn when she finally fell asleep She awoke to the sound of Sybelle's voice in the other room.

"Have you heard anything at all? Do you know where they are now? Alright, Sam, thank you."

Hannah threw on a robe and went into the living room. Sybelle sat behind the lap top Klein had left for them

"Any news from Agent Klein?"

Sybelle heaved a sigh. "No darling, not a word. But that lovely Sam Jacobi promised to contact as soon as he knows something. The good news is his GPS system can track them... more or less. He did mention it was spotty in the jungle."

Hannah nodded. "I'm going to take a shower and get some food."

"I ordered breakfast at ten and luckily for you it arrived fifteen minutes ago. Coffee's still hot. I'm famished aren't you?"

"I'll shower later, where's the food?"

As Hannah poured a second coffee she noticed that Sybelle's frizzy red hair was pulled back and wrapped in a blue kerchief, a look she had never seen.

"Where did you get the head scarf?"

"This weather *destroys* my hair, it hangs like octopus tentacles. This morning I went out and bought this kerchief on the street. Then I came right back, in case Owen called."

Hannah's emotions stirred at the mention of his name. She wanted to light a cigarette but knew her aunt would disapprove. Instead she took a tepid shower.

Like Sybelle, Hannah was reluctant to stray too far from their suite in case someone called in with news.

After a few hours they became restless and decided to take turns going out. But Sybelle tired easily in the wilting heat and Hannah was too distracted for tourism. Hannah was also uncomfortably aware that a woman wandering about alone was vulnerable. She took refuge in the Hilton's cramped, pool area and ordered a fruit drink.

A young blonde girl sat at a nearby table engrossed in a book. She's about Savana's age Hannah thought. The girl looked up from her book and smiled at Hannah.

Hannah smiled back and looked away. The swimming pool was crowded, and samba music drifted from the bar. She wished she had brought her cigarettes and something to read. She wondered if Owen had sent an e-mail or left a phone message. He did have a satellite phone.

"Excuse me, do you speak English?"

Hannah looked up and saw the blonde girl standing next to her. "Why yes."

"Perhaps you'd like this book. I just finished it."

Hannah looked at the cover: *Pride and Prejudice* by Jane Austen.

"That's very kind of you but I couldn't..."

"Oh please, I'd only throw it away. Books get heavy when you travel.'

"Thank you. I could use something to read."

"I know how boring it can get. Our father is an engineer and he parks us here while he goes off to build stuff."

"Us?"

"Me and my twin brother Gunther. I'm Julia by the way."

She took Julia's extended hand. "Hannah Wylde."

"Are you a tourist?"

"Uh, yes, my friend and I decided to see the Amazon."

"It's really beautiful... and scary too."

Hannah smiled. Julia's blue eyes were wide and she looked like a little girl.

"Do you mind it I sit a minute? I just want a cigarette and my brother disapproves." She held out the pack. "Do you smoke?"

"Thank you, I forgot mine upstairs."

They chatted for a few minutes. Both Julia and her brother went to private school in France. Julia found Belem too primitive, she preferred Paris, but her twin brother was a birdwatcher.

"I'm bored silly but Gunther's in heaven," Julia laughed.

"I suppose it is difficult with your father away."

Julia wrinkled her nose. "There are perks. Daddy let's use the company car and his driver when he's away. So we get to see the town. There's a few good restaurants here."

"I hope so. The hotel food is good but..." she winked at Julia. "...boring."

They laughed. Julia stubbed out her cigarette. "I'd better get going. Gunther gets worried if I'm gone to long. You have to be careful out here."

"Better safe than sorry. Thanks for the book and the smoke."

Hannah watched her skip away. The girl was so young, so free of care, Hanna thought with a tinge of envy.

No message was waiting when she got back.

"Jane Austen, my favorite," Sybelle said, preparing to take her break. "Did you run across a bookstore?"

"No a charming young girl I met poolside let me have it."

"Well let me read it too, I'm getting tired of watching CNN."

After Sybelle went out, Hannah curled up in a chair and began to read, keeping one eye on the laptop for messages. There were none.

Sybelle came back early. "This heat is sapping my energy, not to mention my hair,' she declared. "I desperately need the AC."

Hannah read while Sybelle checked in with Sam Jacobi. The agent told her they were tracking Klein's progress, but there was nothing to report.

"Shall we go downstairs for dinner?" Sybelle said when she was finished.

"Fine,' Hannah said without enthusiasm. "At least it's cool in the dining room."

The buzzer sounded.

It was Julia. She stood shyly in the doorway. A young man with the same blue eyes and bland features stood behind her.

"I hope we're not disturbing," the girl said, "but Gunther and I are going to this cute place for dinner. And we thought maybe you'd like to go with us. We have a driver and car so it's no trouble. "

Hannah looked at Sybelle. "What do you think?"

"Well darling my hair..."

"The car has air conditioning," Julia said.

Sybelle gave her a grateful smile. "In that case I'm in. Lord knows we need a little adventure."

Hannah went along without protest, but she wondered how Julia found their suite.

Chapter 45

Moe wasn't fond of boats.

Just the thought of five days on the Amazon made him queasy. However, despite his bout of flu in Salvador, he felt better than he had in years. Maybe it was the tincture Orient gave him, or maybe because he was off his ass and on the job. Either way he was ready to brave the jungle.

Earlier, they had waited for Malik to finish his conversation and move on before boarding the *Ondina* and introducing themselves to the Captain, who spoke little English. Orient showed him the map and negotiated a price for the week. It was agreed they would shove off at noon.

There were only two crew members, the Captain and his mate. The boat was larger than most, with a proper bridge and cockpit. The galley was beneath the bridge and a fabric roof shaded two hammocks strung across the stern. Moe found that lying in the hammock helped disperse his mild seasickness as the boat wended its way upriver.

Orient, who spoke Portuguese, spent a good deal of time with the Captain, going over their route. Moe tried the satellite phone but had trouble making a connection.

He kept his eye on the mate, whose name was Le Mond. Orient had spoken to Le Mond who claimed he did not know Malik. He told Orient the young man had inquired about leasing the boat. The lunar eclipse had attracted a great many visitors and boats were scarce.

Moe had to admit that if Jake and the FBI couldn't scrounge up a boat, the mate was probably telling the truth. But there was still a connection between Malik and the mysterious lady who helped them get this ride. However when he mentioned it, Orient downplayed the coincidence.

Sexual chemistry always trumps the intellect, Moe reflected, swatting at a tiny swarm of insects. *And there's no such thing as coincidence.*

Orient was a cool customer otherwise, Moe thought, watching him on the bridge. Captain Espada was letting him try his hand at the wheel. Reluctantly he rolled off his hammock and went to the cooler for a beer.

The Amazon River was a muddy brown color that cleared slightly as Belem receded in the distance. There was brisk traffic on the waterway. Occasionally they passed beneath power lines strung over the river from steel grid poles on either side. Wood shacks on stilts dotted both banks, with children staring gravely from open doors or cavorting in the water.

The beer helped settle Moe's sensitive stomach. In fact he was getting used to the gentle swell until a passing tour boat threw up a huge wake which caused the *Ondina* to rock and roll—and Moe's belly to flip over.

He held on to the railing until he noticed Le Mond watching him. Clutching his beer Moe stiffly made his way back to the stern. He could have joined Orient on the bridge but knew the elevation would upset an extremely queasy situation. He sat on his hammock, feet on the floor, sucking at the bottle in an effort to steady his stomach.

Orient appeared, holding a cup. Without a word he took the beer from Moe's hand and gave him the cup. "Tincture in water," he said, "might help you feel better."

Moe nodded thanks and drank.

"You'll be over this by tomorrow," Orient assured.

Moe squinted at him. "Tomorrow's a long time when you're seasick."

But soon his belly stopped churning and he was able to stand. In fact he was able to join Orient at the rail.

"That tincture of yours really did the trick doc, thanks."

Orient scanned the river bank. "You can thank Alvira. It's one of her herbal remedies."

Moe frowned, but he couldn't deny the stuff was good. He took a deep breath. There was less humidity on the river and the air was heavy with oxygen steaming from the tangled jungle.

He looked at Orient. "How far are we?"

"We've gone about fifteen miles, only sixty to go."

"Hope you don't run out of tincture."

"That was the last. You go cold turkey from now on."

"I should have brought something to read."

"You have a laptop and a satellite phone. Download some movies and books. Do you play chess?"

Moe lifted his head. He considered himself a pretty fair chess player and had won a few matches against the hustlers in Washington Square Park.

"A little," he said, "do you?"

For the next couple of hours Moe forgot he was on a boat in the jungle, his attention locked on the sixty four red and black squares on the chessboard. Orient was a good competitor and came up with inventive gambits.

"Checkmate," Orient said, moving his bishop.

Moe studied the board. "Son of a bitch. You owe me a rematch."

"It's almost time for dinner."

"That should be a treat," Moe grumbled sarcastically.

Happily he was wrong. Le Mond had whipped up a tasty meal that included a juicy river fish, spicy rice and beans, and sliced bananas and mangoes for dessert. He also made a mean cup of coffee. Moe found his appetite had returned.

Orient avoided the fish but seemed content with the rest. He spent time conferring with Captain Espada, then took a walk around the deck. Moe decided to join him.

There is no sunset on the equator. Without any foreplay the sun dropped abruptly and it became very dark. The boat's light scattered a gleaming path on the river ahead but Moe felt the night enclose him. Despite his liberal use of insect repellant the damp river air brought out the worst offenders.

"That DEET you're using won't do much good," Orient
said.

"Yeah what do you use?"

"Le Mond gave me a local repellant made from ant's nests.
The smell of the ants repels the mosquitoes."

"I'll try anything. These suckers seem to like kosher blood."

The powdery substance Moe rubbed over his bare arms,
neck, and ears, actually did its job. The bugs didn't stop completely but they approached cautiously. He got Le Mond's
attention and made a big show of putting it on. The crewman
responded with a slight nod.

Le Mond's features were more tribal than either African
or Spanish, the dominant strains in Brazil's multicultural family
tree. A short man with powerful shoulders and a wide chest, he
had the dark, tilted eyes and black, bowl cut hair of an Amazon
Indian.

In contrast Captain Espada could have been an heir of
the Spanish pirates who came in search of plunder. Despite his
slight build he had the swagger of authority. His craggy features
were set in a permanent scowl, but he was polite and quick to
laugh. With Orient anyway, Moe brooded. He didn't understand
most of what was said.

Moe went to the cabin he shared with Orient and tried the
phone again. To his amazement Jake's familiar chirp responded.

"Is that you Moe?"

"Can you believe it? I'm in the middle of the fucking
jungle."

"Not yet Moe. You're only about twenty five miles from
Belem. I've got you spotted on the big screen.'

"That's a comfort. I'm a city boy remember. I'm afraid of
snakes, spiders, bats and anything bigger than a cocker spaniel."

"You feeling better? You sound good."

"I'm becoming a convert to herbal medicine."

"You're preaching to the choir Moe. But listen up, I've got
big news."

"All ears."

"There's this rare artifact in Austria..."

"The Spear of Destiny?"

"Exactly. How did you know?"

"My doctor friend figured it. Something to do with the solstice, lunar eclipses, that kind of thing.

"I'm an android Moe. That psychic stuff spooks me."

"Try living with it."

"Anyway they're testing this Spear for authenticity. Rumor has it there was a switch. Inside job."

"Any other news?"

"You're the big news. Director Caldwell is creaming over this case. The heist in Austria put the cherry on it. You are the man. Top level budget."

Moe sighed. Out here office politics seemed the height of lunacy. "Listen Jake, do you have a more precise fix on that photo the girl sent?"

"Negative. Still got Maybelline working on it."

"It's top priority...'

"Breaking up... can't... you."

The phone cut off.

Moe went out on deck. Orient was at the stern looking up at the stars which were brilliant in the blackness.

"You were right about the Spear of Destiny. Jake just told me they made a switch at the museum."

"So now they have the Spear, and the fragment," Orient murmured, almost to himself.

"Goes a long way to proving your theory about the solstice."

"Not a theory anymore," Orient said, eyes still on the sky. He turned to Jake. "The bad news is we have less than five days to find Savana."

"Von Speer can tell us."

"If he's at home, I missed him in Marrakech, in Paris and in Salvador."

The boat passed a shack lit by candles. In the distance it looked like a paper lantern.

"Jake's still trying to pinpoint the origin of that photo she sent."

Orient turned back to the stars. "You ever read Cervantes?"

"Sure, which one of us is Sancho Panza?"

+ + +

Moe slept well that night. When he awoke there was no sign of the previous day's sea sickness. The river had narrowed and he could hear the chattering birds

Orient was already on deck, lean body ensconced in a hammock, eating a piece of fruit.

Moe went to the galley where Le Mond fixed him a breakfast of eggs, cheese, and coffee.

"Than man can cook," Moe said grudgingly, mounting the other hammock.

Orient swiveled his head to look at him. "Did you have the eggs?"

"Yeah, why?"

"They're parrot eggs."

Fucking vegetarians, Moe fumed, the eggs were damn good. He turned his attention to the satellite phone. When it didn't connect, he went to his laptop. It was slow but eventually he found something to amuse him.

After a day, the unchanging view of mud brown water hedged by thick green vegetation offered little diversion, even for a city boy. Every so often he would see a pair of tribesmen in a dugout, or a brightly feathered bird overhead. But no Caymans, cats or water snakes, thank God.

Le Mond trolled for fish and caught a fat catfish within minutes. Klein paced the deck and when he reached the stern he saw Orient setting up the chessboard. To his annoyance Orient won again using an unorthodox offense.

"Getting repetitious," he remarked, referring as much to the voyage as to the second loss.

Orient knew what he meant. "In a few hours it will get more interesting."

"What happens then?"

"We get off the main highway and go down a side road. Basically a tributary that eventually connects with the Negro River."

Time for an equipment check, Klein thought.

"How soon before we get to Von Speer's place?"

"Hard to say. Hopefully by midday tomorrow.'

Klein couldn't wait. He was tired of the sweating, the sameness, the bugs, the lack of mobility. On the other hand his stomach was fine.

The promise of imminent change boosted Moe's mood and he stood at the rail with a pair of binoculars. The sight of a white-faced monkey through a gap in the vegetation stirred his fascination and he scanned the shoreline for the better part of an hour. He was rewarded with glimpses of wildly plumed parrots parading their colors, two more monkeys, and what appeared to be a gnarly Cayman immersed in mud... or a tree log.

"Anything interesting?" Orient asked.

Moe lowered the glasses. "Less wild life than I imagined."

"The snakes and lizards are camouflaged, you can't detect the insects until they bite, and the big cats hide."

"Ideal spot for a condo. Von Speer likes remote places."

"I was told he's got a kind of trading post, where he buys Indian artifacts."

"Shrunken heads?"

"If he can find them. The Jivaro tribe is further up in the mountains."

It was mid-afternoon and the heat bore down heavily. Even the temperate effect of the water couldn't lighten its oppressive weight.

Moe noticed his shirt was soaked through. "I think I need to lie down for a few minutes,"

Orient nodded. "I'll let you know when we get to the interior."

The interior. It sounded a bit intimidating. Moe went to his hammock and promptly fell asleep.

"We're almost there."

Moe's eyes were momentarily blurred. They focused on a spectrum of green vegetation about thirty yards away.

"We're about to turn inland," Orient said, I'll be up on the bridge."

Moe rolled to his feet and saw Le Mond manning the tiller, responding to Captain Espada's audible commands. He went forward and saw the boat was angling for an entryway into the dense forest. The gap was narrow but Espada and his mate worked well together, guiding the boat through the arched trees at the mouth of the tributary.

The water widened considerably, but the jungle was no more than forty feet away on every side. Espada had cut their speed but the soft chug of the engine sounded loud in the dense silence.

Golden shafts of sunlight angled through the branches and vines overhead. Here the water had become a clear green mirror, reflecting their presence. No one spoke much beyond the call and response of their navigators.

Moe felt the rainforest closing over him. It made him uncomfortable. He went inside their cabin and looked for the weapons he had stashed.

He had no problem concealing the Ruger. The light pistol probably wouldn't stop a hungry jaguar but it definitely made him feel better. The jungle was kind of spooky. He slipped the tiny automatic in his belt. The .45 Jake had sent was difficult to conceal but a wise thought, Moe conceded. Finally he put it in the outside pocket of the padded case that housed his lap top. He doubted anyone would notice the bulge. .

He decided to try Jake on the satellite phone.

"Hey ,Moe, Still got you spotted on the big GPS. You're off the main stream as usual."

"Yeah, we're in serious jungle now and it scares the shit out of me."

"You can always turn back."

"Not likely."

"Well sire I checked out Alvira Charisma as you requested, and came up with the usual stats. Born in Rio, school in Italy, got a doctorate at Tulane, very impressive, has a small herbal remedy business out of Salvador."

"That's the one."

"She's clean, quite a looker too, considering."

"Considering what?"

"Considering she was born in nineteen forty-five."

"Come on Jake that must be her mother."

Moe heard an electronic beeping and the phone went dead.

The sun had begun to plummet when he came out on deck. The engine was shut off and the boat was drifting closer to the muddy bank. He expected Le Mond to be in the galley cooking up the fish but the crewman was on the bridge with Espada and Orient. Although he couldn't understand what they were saying, something about their body language alerted him.

The discussion continued for some minutes and ended with Orient walking away, his eyes and mouth pursed as if troubled. He fetched his backpack and took out his GPS.

"Are we lost?" Moe inquired mildly.

"Captain Espada refuses to stay on course. He claims this tributary leads to dangerous territory. Some men were killed by hostile natives a few months back."

"What are our options?"

"He wants us to take us on another route, right up ahead. But from what I calculate it will take us in the opposite direction."

"Think it's a trap?"

Orient looked at him. "Might be."

"I was thinking about Malik."

"Actually, so was I."

The soft chug of the engine resumed and the boat angled for a large gap in the vegetation on the opposite shore.

"Looks like we ran out of options," Orient said.

"Maybe we still have one.'

Moe reached into the padded case and drew the .45.

"That won't help."

"It will, if you tell him to stay on course."

Orient looked around as if seeking another opinion then called up to Espada.

"Stop. He's got a gun," Orient said in Portuguese.

"Get Le Mond to come down with his hands up," Moe said moving closer to the bridge.

He kept one eye on Le Mond and gestured to Espada.

"Tell him to keep on our original course, no side trips."

The request brought a torrent of protest from the captain. Moe pointed his gun.

"I'm crazy, and I'll shoot your ass."

Darkness was starting to settle over the tributary and Moe wanted to get going. As the passed the entrance to the connecting tributary, the Captain hurled what obviously were curses in Moe's direction.

Moe glanced at Orient. "What's he saying."

"He's saying we're both as stupid as chickens."

"Yeah, well, I'll play chicken with the bastard."

"Easy, cowboy."

They continued for twenty minutes. Orient consulted his map and scanned the river bank. "It'll be coming up soon."

A high, whining hum, like that of a giant insect, floated over the forest.

Everybody turned except Le Mond. He scooped up the knapsack Orient had left in the cabin doorway, and swung it at Moe, knocking him off balance.

Before Moe could recover Le Mond had hopped over the side and run into the jungle.

"My knapsack..." Orient leaped over the rail and sprinted after him.

"Wait," Moe yelled, but they both vanished into the thick vegetation.

Espada was saying something Moe couldn't understand. The humming sound became louder and Espada grew more agitated.

Beams of bright light cut through the gloom. Two large hovercrafts skidded around the bend and stopped, churning water around them.

A bullhorn voice crackled over the hum.

"Drop your weapons and raise your hands,"

Unfortunately Moe didn't know Portuguese.

Bullets ripped the deck, the flat shots setting off a chorus of bird cries.

Moe got the point.

He lowered the .45 and raised his hands high.

Chapter 46

Twenty yards into the jungle Orient realized he'd made a colossal mistake.

He could see Le Mond up ahead but darkness was fast descending and the crewman seemed to know his way. His long legged stride kept pace even if unable to gain any ground.

It became a test of endurance. Orient settled into a steady jog and soon the man ahead began to falter. When Orient came closer Le Mond tossed the backpack aside and put on a burst of speed.

Orient stopped and picked up the survival pack. The first thing he pulled out was the flashlight. The next was a small bottle of water. He stood in the gathering darkness, sucking down the water, his breath ragged in the quiet.

He shouldered the backpack and started back. Even with the flashlight he couldn't be sure of the path he'd taken. .

Orient tried the GPS but it wouldn't respond. He tried the satellite phone with the same result. He even tried the walkie talkie even though Moe probably had his switched off and tucked in his backpack.

Orient switched off the flashlight and let his eyes adjust to the dark. He stood listening for a few minutes. The dense jungle around him rustled.

A sense of expectancy hung over the quiet like a spider's web. Orient senses bristled as if something was stalking him.

He looked up at the stars, recalling their position from the night before. Using the Southern Cross as a guide, he slowly began to walk toward where he reckoned the tributary must be.

The vegetation was thicker than he remembered, and he paused again to align with the stars. The path Le Mond had chosen seemed more like a well worn trail, than the tall grass he now moved through.

Reluctantly he switched on the flashlight, scanning the ground for footprints, compressed grass, broken branches; anything that would mark his headlong chase.

He moved in a semi-circle as the light probed the area for signs. Abruptly he froze, senses quivering.

The light had stumbled across a human foot.

It vanished so quickly he couldn't be sure it had ever been there.

He stood for a long moment, uncertain of what to do. Then he took a long breath and charged his body for whatever was waiting. Instinctively his hand went to the pouch around his neck.

"Hello?"

His voice faded into the darkness. Using the narrow shaft of light as his cane he blindly edged through the forest, stopping every few yards to listen. He thought he heard a motor and veered in the direction of the sound. .

Had he really seen a human foot, he wondered. In the dark, roots and vines took strange shapes. Moving slowly through the thick grass, it occurred to him that his high-tech devices were proving useless. He decided to give the GPS another try. Nothing, Then he remembered the compass in his Swiss Army knife. He swung the knapsack off his shoulders and crouched over it, flashlight between his teeth.

The Swiss Army knife had a small compass. Although unreliable it at least would keep him from going in circles. He turned his head in the direction the needle pointed and the light almost fell from his mouth.

A naked man, face and body crossed with green and black tiger stripes, stood watching him.

An instant later he was gone

Taking the flashlight from his mouth Orient slowly straightened up.

"Ola... como vai."

The Brazilian greeting brought a response. They seemed to melt out of the shadows

Orient turned and four painted men, eyes shaded in black were behind him, another two stood in front. All were armed with spears and bows.

One of the pair in front motioned for him to follow. The other picked up his knapsack. When Orient hesitated, someone behind him prodded him with the blunt end of a spear. .

They hiked for a half hour through marshy, mosquito infested forest before coming to higher, drier ground. Here the trees were taller, forming an overhead canopy. The quiet was as solemn as a cathedral.

Earlier he had switched off the flashlight and when his eyes adjusted he could see the jungle was more evolved. Everything was bigger, thornier, starker, more aggressive as they pushed further into the rainforest.

The tribesmen made no sound, however in comparison Orient was thrashing about, his booted feet heavy and clumsy in the dark, unfamiliar terrain.

Abruptly they paused, seemingly listening for something. Moments later they resumed. Orient glimpsed a flicker of light ahead. The jungle seemed to give way to flat open ground and after a few yards they emerged into a large clearing.

The area was illuminated by three campfires in the middle of the area. Beyond the fires Orient could see a large circular lodge with a thatched roof. Two ranks of tribesmen, spears at attention, stood between the fires and the lodge. Crouched before them, a bearded man with a crimson headdress, tended to a pot suspended over the center flames. His beard was dark blue and. intricate tattoos dotted his upper arms and chest. A thick red stripe masked his eyes and against the flames his painted face took on a demonic quality.

No one spoke.

Someone tossed the knapsack into the firelight. It hit the ground with a loud thud. Orient turned and saw that the men who had escorted him were kneeling.

The man with the crimson head dress stood up. He gestured and said something that sparked a flurry of activity. One of the men near the lodge went inside and came out with two low stools which he placed near the fire. Another fetched a clay jar.

The tribal leader gestured for Orient to take one of the stools. Orient half bowed in respect and sat down. The leader sat across from him. He leaned closer and Orient gaped in stunned recognition.

The man beneath the face paint and feathered head dress was Dr. Borges.

Chapter 47

Klein cursed himself for not knowing the language. Captain Espada's usual scowl had escalated into a disgusted glower that said: *arrogant American asshole gets everybody in deep shit.*

Klein didn't need a translator for that one. What he did need was out of this hot, airless hold they had stuffed him in, along with Espada. To make things worse his sea sickness had returned.

There was one bright note in this botched affair, Klein thought, trying to avoid Espada's stare. The bastards didn't find the little Ruger automatic he'd pushed down his shorts in the excitement.

Klein had to endure another hour in the hold of the captured *Ondina*, before someone opened the hatch and pulled them on deck.

Their captors were six blond youths, armed with AK-47's. Two of them operated the *Ondina* while the hovercrafts led the way to a long dock, where three more hovercrafts and two cigarette boats were anchored, along with a small yacht. The area was illuminated by overhead lights.

A tall blond man met then when they debarked. He was smiling, but Klein's attention was drawn by the lightning bolt scar that ran from cheekbone to ear. .

"Finally we meet, Agent Klein."

"Do we know each other?"

The smile dimmed.

"I promise we will know each other quite well."

The man said something to his captors and they led Espada away.

"Don't worry, he will be well treated," the man said, "and so will you. You must be hungry after your trip. Please join me."

Two guards fell into place behind them. Klein noticed that the overhead lights went out when they left the dock. Their path through dense jungle was lit by torches placed at regular intervals. They came to a spacious clearing, dominated by a low, wooden building with a wide overhanging roof. He had the sense that there were other buildings nearby but in the darkness he couldn't really tell. What he could see were the lights in the building they were approaching.

The interior turned out to be an office complex with a cafeteria. The offices were staffed by blond young men and women who looked curiously similar; tall, athletic, regular features. The man with the scar escorted Klein to the cafeteria. The two guards from the boat remained at the entrance.

The kitchen workers were Indians, in stark contrast to the uniform whiteness of the people eating there. His captor led him to a rear table set apart from the rest. As soon as they sat down three waiters came to serve them. One brought the bread and olive oil. Another brought water and a third delivered a plate of cheese and cold cuts.

"White or red?"

Klein looked at his host. "White wine, thanks. But you have the advantage sir."

"Yes...?"

"Your name. Although you certainly know a lot about me, I don't know what to call you."

The man laughed. "Of course. Please pardon the oversight. I am Dr. Hans Kammler, but please call me Hans, and I will call you Morris."

The name was vaguely familiar but Klein couldn't place it.

"As you can see we too have computers. I must congratulate your skill in tracking me this far. I assume the photograph the girl sent was a significant clue. "

Klein ate, only half listening, and studied this square-jawed poster boy for the SS; cold eyes, blond buzz cut and all. He kept trying to retrieve a name from an old file.

"If you think your GPS can trace us, our engineers have seen to that."

Engineer... the word jostled his memory.

"Are you any relation to Dr. Hans Kammler, the man in charge of Hitler's secret weapons program?"

Hans lifted his glass. "You certainly know your military history, Morris. To answer your question, yes, I am a relation. A very close relation. In fact I *am* that man."

Klein snorted and dipped his bread in oil. "If that was true you would be at least ninety years old."

"I recently celebrated my hundredth. One full century."

The bread hovered in mid air, inches from his mouth.

"You're shitting me right?"

Hans threw his head back in a mirthless laugh and Klein saw the corded muscles in his neck. The man looked to be forty at most, a healthy forty.

"No, I am not, as you say, shitting you, Morris. Tomorrow, when you've had time to rest, I will personally show you around our research facility."

"Let me get this straight. You claim you're one hundred years old and you were the Third Reich's top scientist."

"Yes well, I wasn't the top scientist—I was the man in charge of the Reich's top scientists. We developed the V2 rocket among other things."

Klein was too exhausted to be amazed. A dark skinned waiter bought a tray of food.

"How did you end up here?' Klein asked, helping himself to a sausage.

"There was a plan in place. On May second, nineteen forty five, we left Norway on submarine U977, just as the Russians overran Berlin. Our most elite personnel were on board. Today many of your so called Nazi hunters believe our Fuhrer was on board. But he was already dead and his body on its way to a separate facility. It was preserved in hopes of bringing back to life, but sadly that was not to be."

Hans refilled his glass.

Klein had stopped eating and sat in rapt silence, half stunned and half fascinated. Along the way as the Bureau's art expert, he had become acquainted with Nazi artifacts and delved into the history behind them. And he knew about submarine U977.

"We were at sea for a hundred and twenty days, packed like canned fish, some sick, others simply unbearable, it was a grueling exodus."

Too bad you didn't drown, Klein thought vaguely. Despite the sensational revelations he was having difficulty staying awake.

"Forgive me Morris, you must be quite tired from the trip," Hans said. "Please let me show you to your quarters. "

Klein debated whether to shoot him now but quickly dismissed the idea. It won't help Savana with me dead he reflected, following Hans outside.

+ + +

It was not yet dawn when Klein awoke.

He lit the candle on his bedside table and took stock. Aside from the candle and a pack of matches there were few amenities. There was a small shower, with soap and towel which he used immediately. By the time he had dried himself things had changed. The candle was out, a breakfast tray was on the bedside table and light was leaking through the open door on the far side of his cell.

The first thing he did was check the place where he had stashed the small Ruger. It was still there, in a nook between the wall and bed.

The second thing he did was eat. Fresh fruit, yogurt, eggs, cheese, juice and coffee: not bad for jail food.

The previous evening's discourse with his ageless host hadn't diverted Klein from his mission. Savana Wylde was somewhere on this psycho farm and he needed to find her. Right now, Jake would be honing in on his position Moe told himself. A gnawing in his gut suggested otherwise.

He went outside and found himself in a cage, like the one housing young Savana. It was already light and he could hear the energetic chatter of wildlife from the nearby forest. The outdoor section had concrete walls on either side topped with barbed wire, and cyclone fencing in front. Like the Central Park Zoo, he observed.

"I trust you slept well, Morris?"

Hans was standing at the door to his cell. "I've come to give you a tour of our little community. How was breakfast?"

As Klein followed Hans through his cell he saw someone had removed his breakfast tray. He hoped no one came to make his bed.

Maybe it was the superior smirk on that chiseled face, or the sarcastic edge to his remarks, whatever it was, Hans annoyed Klein. However his current position required him to zip up his feelings.

"Long ago the founders of our community decided to mimic the jungle itself. The rainforest is an interconnecting web of small and large islands, so our community is too, a series of interconnected clearings with jungle between. In this way we avoid detection from the air."

Hans pointed out a few buildings nearby. They all had overhanging roofs which Klein assumed were for shade or rain. "The design of all our buildings also decreases the chances of our lights being seen, "Hans told him, "all roofs are painted in camouflage as well. Even more effective is the work of our brilliant computer engineers, who are able to scramble attempts to locate us from satellites. Like the creatures who inhabit this jungle we have protective coloration to foil predators."

"Clever," Klein said drily. They came to the edge of the clearing which was bordered with thick, tangled vegetation and tall trees.

"How far to your next rest area?"

"Very near, Morris, as I said protective coloration."

He led Klein to a path as wide as a golf cart that cut through the vegetation. Once inside the jungle it was as if a door closed behind him. The birds announced their presence as they walked. Two hundred yards later the path opened onto another clearing that accommodated three large wood buildings. They were painted side and top with green and brown stripes. Hans was right, Klein thought, he didn't spot anything until he was right on top of them. The huge electronic dishes were equally well disguised.

"Here we have our tech facilities," Hans said. The inside of the largest building was well air conditioned, and housed long banks of computers and some wall sized screens. The computers were manned by workers of both sexes who were uniformly fair, blue eyed youths.

Hans pointed to a red blip on one of the screens. "This is our actual location." He moved to another screen where the red blip was slightly to the right of the first. "This is where your friends at the FBI *think* you are."

"Very impressive," Klein said, wishing he had brought the Ruger along.

From there they entered another path through the bush which opened onto the camp's medical complex.

"Because of our superior diet and exercise regime, sickness rate is low. We have developed a vaccine to prevent malaria which is the main culprit here. As you might imagine our clinic rivals any in the world, however I'm sure you will be most interested in our research center."

Klein had the feeling he was being set up by this unctuous sociopath. He no choice but to string along.

The research building was longer than the others and when Klein entered he saw that everything seemed color coded. The medical staff wore white, the young male patients wore blue, the females red. The chief of staff was easily distinguished by his black scrubs.

Klein was immediately struck by the fact that all the young patients—ranging in age from seven to sixteen—looked alike. They sat in cubicles with their blue clad attendants undergoing various forms of testing, from flash cards to blindfolds.

The doctor in black was studiously avoiding them but Klein couldn't help glancing back. With his rimless glasses and blank, thin lipped features, the man looked very familiar. Like someone on a wanted poster he'd seen a hundred times. .

"This area is our most special," Hans was saying, "do you know why?"

"I'm sure you're about to tell me."

"For years we have been studying the human facility of telepathy."

He leaned back and looked at Klein as if expecting a reaction "Is the FBI involved in similar research?"

Klein almost laughed. "The Bureau would probably fire me if I brought up the idea. Maybe the CIA."

"Your friend, Doctor Orient, is certainly involved in this area."

"Yes that's true. But I work for the FBI, Doctor Orient is a free agent." It occurred to Klein that this was why Hans was so cozy. He wanted information about Orient's work.

"Do you mind if I ask you a personal question?" Klein asked, while Hans was still in a good mood.

"Of course, please."

"Why does everybody here look alike?"

It was Hans' turn to be amused. "Because they are twins. That's the nature of our research. We find that twins are naturally clairvoyant. However their abilities are still crude. Like children learning to walk. Soon we will have a small army of telepaths at our disposal.—The last bastion of true privacy in a digital world."

Twins.

Klein remembered... but it was impossible.

"Dr. Josef..."

"...Josef Mengele. Excellent Morris,"

"But Mengele died in Argentina years ago."

"Really Morris, grow up. A convenient corpse was provided."

"The live version hasn't aged much."

Hans beamed. "I've saved the best for last."

It was fortunate Klein had left the Ruger stashed because he surely would have used it when he visited the Life Enhancement Center. The antiseptic, polished marble interior was an air conditioned nightmare. In the first section were long rows of young native children lying on hospital tables, their blood dripping into glass jars. Their blond nurses went about their business methodically, collecting and labeling the jars.

The next section had at least a hundred tribal patients recovering from either accidents or deliberate mutilation. Some were missing limbs, others were being fed intravenously, still others were attached to rows of strange machines. One row seemed to be on artificial hearts, another row some sort of kidney pumps.

A dark haired physician came into the area closely followed by two male nurses. The doctor had a large head and strong jaw. His hair was combed straight back in the manner of a retro film hero but it was his dark, hooded eyes that caught Klein's attention. He recognized that cruel, superior gaze from photographs he had studied of wanted Nazis.

"Aribert Heim," Klein said, almost to himself, "Doctor Death."

Hans softly clapped his hands. "You are a trove of information, Morris!"

Klein didn't mention the years of pro bono work he did for Simon Wiesenthal and his group of Nazi hunters. But he couldn't take his eyes off the self-assured man in black scrubs. Doctor Death was responsible for hundreds of thousands of civilian executions. He performed inhuman experiments; surgery without anesthesia, injecting victims with various toxins to find more efficient means of mass extermination, removing and reattaching limbs, performing needless exploratory surgery, deliberately infecting victims with lethal diseases, inducing cancer cells... the list of atrocities went on.

"The man is a sack of shit," Klein spat.

Hans stiffened. "Aribert Heim is the victim of vile, Zionist propaganda Here he is known as Doctor Life. Thanks to him we are at the cutting edge of transplant procedures and the harvesting of healthy organs. It is here where we have developed the science of extended youth to its highest level."

"Is this why you brought the girl here?"

Hans seemed disappointed. "Halfway around the world? I don't think so Morris. We have all the healthy raw material we need right here. Come, I'll show you."

Klein was sweating profusely as they hiked through vegetation which seemed to be rougher, less manicured than the previous stretch. Then again he was sick of the heat, the constant gnawing of insects, the lizards everywhere, vines that resembled snakes and vice versa... most of all he was sick of Hans and his dead Nazis.

"We have found that these Amazon tribes have natural intuition, telepathy even, which aids them as hunters. We have also noted that the girl Savana has great potential in that area. Was she working with Doctor Orient?"

Hans should rethink his interrogation techniques, Klein thought. Subtle he wasn't.

"I wouldn't know. I came on when you murdered Henry Applegate. When you kidnapped Savana the FBI ramped up our investigation."

"What about his friend Sybelle Lean?"

"I know she's a professional psychic, so do you."

"My intuition says there's much you're not telling me Morris."

"Such as?"

"Did Doctor Orient ever show you a ring? A ring belonging to Savana?"

Klein thought back. Wasn't there a gold ring among his personal effects when he was arrested? He would have to check with Jake. Fat chance of that.

"Ring? I don't recall anything like that." he said.

"Recall? Interesting word Morris."

His coy tone irritated Klein. At the next clearing his irritation boiled into rage. Here he saw wooden barracks behind barbed wire fences, where Amazon tribesmen and Africans, were being herded by armed guards into work squads.

Hans walked past with bored detachment. "This is our talent pool, which is replenished periodically."

"Nothing's changed from the old days at Auschwitch, has it? Is this where you're holding Savana?"

"Of course not. She has the same private accommodations you enjoy. But you are a bit behind the times."

"Please enlighten me."

"Her mother and great aunt are guests as well."

"Hannah and Sybelle here? Can I see them?"

"I suppose. You are entitled to some last requests."

Klein's belly went into free fall.

"Last requests. As in... I'm being executed?"

Hans beamed. "You do have a wonderful sense of humor Morris. Yes. It will be your honor to be the first Jew exterminated by the New Reich. And it will be my honor to preside."

Chapter 48

"You have journeyed long to reach us."
Orient dimly heard the traditional words of recognition, but they failed to register.

Slowly he dragged the response from his rote memory. "The journey is like the flow of water."

"And water finds the thirsty man."

Orient stared at Borges, not certain. His reply had been correct but Orient didn't know if he was being manipulated by a wily magician. The Amazon jungle was a long way from the hidden monastery in Tibet where he had acquired the Serene Knowledge.

Borges seemed to know what he was thinking. "I wear many masks," he said.

He drank from the clay jar and gave it to Orient.

A silence fell over the clearing. Orient saw that more tribesmen had gathered around and were observing his every move.

"Here in the jungle my name is Atu, and I am Shaman to my people," Borges told him. "Drink."

Orient suspected that the liquid in the clay jar contained some sort of intoxicant, perhaps psychedelic, but he knew that to refuse would be taken as a discourtesy or worse, a sign of disrespect. He drank from the jar, a bitter oily liquid then gave it back, still in a state of partial shock to discover that Dr. Borges could be a monk of the Serene Knowledge. However the doubts remained.

"Your coming was foretold by Ku. But we could not be sure."

The name convinced Orient. Not even Sybelle knew it was the Master Ku who had taught him the telepathic technique and the occult arts.

"The journey is strewn with illusions." Orient said. He drank and passed the jar back.

Borges nodded. "Then the journey will take a long time to complete."

"The journey will complete itself in time."

Borges' sharp, steely eyes looked into his. "Welcome. You have already begun to learn those things which will fortify you in war."

Whatever was in the jar was beginning to take effect. Orient's exhaustion and fear were melting into a calm sense of awareness.

"I do not seek war."

"Yes, but war seeks you. Survival is the first law in our world."

He looked around, the firelight deepening his perspective. The phalanx of painted spectators around them was composed of different tribes. Some wore green and black stripes, others were tattooed, and still others wore feathers. Whether it was piercings, beads or even weapons; each clan had its distinctive colors. And they were all watching him with silent intensity.

Sitting across from him, Borges seemed concerned about something. Until then he had spoken in English. Now he spoke in a strange tongue which Orient took to be a tribal language. The words seemed to magnify and take shape.

"Will you journey with us?"

Orient nodded, his head enveloped by a rushing sound, as if giant seashells had been placed over both ears. Somewhere far away he heard drums and singsong voices. Everything was moving too fast, he needed everything to stop...

"You know how to slow time, use your skills..."

Orient no longer knew what language it was but he heard the message. He went into a deep breathing pattern, focusing all of his concentration on the rhythmic ascension of air from lungs to brain. Pure air... it cleared his skull of thought and

sound... He cast his being on the currents and found himself
floating slowly in timeless eternity.

Orient opened his eyes. He heard muffled drums and
chants in the background behind the silent throng of armed
Indians observing them.

Borges showed no effects of whatever potion was in the jar.
Orient wished he had some water.

Borges said something.

Immediately a young girl came from the lodge carrying a
clay bowl. Shyly she placed the bowl at Orient's feet. The water
cleansed the bitter taste in his mouth and cooled his skin. He
went into a fresh breathing pattern and his vision expanded.
He saw Borges resting calmly on his stool, arms crossed, Le
Mond exhausted from his run sitting on the ground, he was
even mildly surprised to see Malik standing nearby. But in razor
sharp focus he saw the tribesmen watching them with a vola-
tile mix of tension and expectancy. He saw their need, and he
saw the seething life that layered every inch of the surrounding
jungle.

Borges handed Orient the clay jar. "You are ready."

Orient wasn't so sure but he drank. The oily liquid tasted
worse after the cleansing water and he felt his stomach churning. He relaxed his abdomen and accepted the potion, determined to maintain balance.

His consciousness ascended to another level. He realized
he had been brought to this jungle outpost for a purpose.

Borges stood up and gestured. Orient gingerly got to his
feet and followed him into the lodge. Made of wood, with a
straw roof woven in a circular pattern, the lodge was as quiet
as a church. A line of warriors stood outside to make sure they
remained undisturbed.

Borges led him to a fire in a pit dug into the earth. A crude
table laden with water bowls, fruit, flowers and tobacco was
nearby.

There were two empty mats in front of the fire. Borges sat
cross legged on one. Orient eased down onto the other mat.

"You do not wish to kill, nor do I. And yet we must eat to
survive. Which means something will die." Borges' steely eyes
seemed to grow in the firelight. "Our existence is a cycle of
death and rebirth. The universe is eating itself."

Orient met his stare. "Death is one thing, violence another."

"Death, violence, hatred, love, they're all facets of our nature—and nature itself."

"Compassion, empathy, they too are part of nature.'

Borges nodded and stroked his braided beard. "All true.
Every being must find balance within themselves, while juggling
contradictory truths."

"And parallel realities," Orient said.

Borges beamed. "Exactly. And it is parallel reality we will
explore." He removed his headdress and set it aside. "We are
about to undergo a transformation of body and soul."

A gentle probe at the base of his brain signaled Orient that
Borges was linking with his consciousness. Instantly he understood the primal technique Borges intended to teach him—
metamorphosis—the ability to transform his body into that of an
animal.

Orient had lost track of time... but it didn't take long.

Primal chemical sockets for channeling bestial power,
techniques gleaned from the first edge of evolution. Pre dawn
wisdom transferred from mind to mind over ten millennia, all
imprinted his consciousness in seconds. And the knowledge
was made flesh...

It went from unpleasant to painful.

Wrenching spasms, the unrelenting torque of birth... joints
and muscle twisting, popping, enlarging... nails extending into
claws.... black fur sprouting on his forearms... thick calluses
padding his hairy palms... mandibles distorting... teeth grinding
as his jaw distended and reshaped... heart and lungs swelling

inside his spreading rib cage... an agonizing, spine-shattering shudder... and he *was*...

Unsteady for a moment he slunk to the water bowl nearby. As he bent to drink he glimpsed a black jaguar in the water. He drank and it disappeared.

A low, throaty rumble alerted him.

The firelight revealed a spotted jaguar, tail flicking nervously. Instinctively he knew it was not an enemy. A horde of scents crammed his nostrils. He heard the rustle of a sloth in the trees outside, the scuttle of a spider in the shadows.

His muscles strained for action. He started to move and stopped. Just out of the light, the tawny jaguar waited, silver eyes shining. Something prodded him to follow when the spotted cat turned and padded outside.

A collective moan of awe rose up as they loped through a parting sea of humans and vanished into the protective cloak of the rain forest.

+ + +

Running free. He reveled in his powerful form, the coiled strength in his limbs, his acute senses. He ran alongside the spotted jaguar who showed him the hidden drinking stream. His teacher also marked where serpents nested, and which trees housed venomous ants.

He heard the jungle breathing and distinguished hundreds of smells. The scents provided a path as he padded swiftly beside the spotted cat. His vision cut through the darkness. Shining droplets of water highlighted vines and tree trunks, the small creatures moving to cover as they sensed predators nearby.

He bathed in the fecund stench of the jungle, a mixture of ancient rot and oozing afterbirth.

Then another combination of scents; fear, flesh, lust, blood, feces and other things—things not of the earth... The spotted jaguar slowed, then slunk low to the ground in a hunting crouch. He did the same, eyes prowling the darkness.

There was an obstacle, a metallic fence. Beyond it were dim lights.

He saw the jaguar jump onto a low hanging tree limb. The spotted cat turned and looked at him, silver eyes blazing. Do as I do, they said. A moment later he leaped high over the fence and landed soundlessly on the other side.

He followed. They stayed in the shadows circling the large clearing. Neat rows of darkened dwellings beside a large one, which was lit and guarded by armed men. He caught a musty scent coming from the large building, but couldn't place it. The spotted jaguar circled to the rear of the building and then ran along the metal fence. He followed and caught the scent of many humans inside the dwellings.

There was an opening in the fence that led into the jungle. But soon they came to another clearing. Here the scent was of death. Decayed flesh and fear wafted over the large dwellings. These too were guarded.

They went from clearing to clearing, the spotted jaguar sniffing where he could, pausing occasionally to lie close to the ground and scan the area around them.

In one of the clearings humans were penned together, guarded by other men. In another, humans lived in separate dwellings scented with meat, milk and honey.

They came to a clearing that had a venomous scent, poisons not from nature. He had no particular feeling about any of the places he had seen. None of it was his world.

But he was becoming hungry.

While circling back to where they'd entered, they encountered human hunters.

In the forest they easily eluded detection, but the low lights in the clearings cast moving shadows. The stillness told him they were being stalked.

He followed the jaguar closely, moving cautiously between the shadows of the buildings. They followed their own scent along the fence until they arrived where they had started.

"Ya!"

Startled by the sudden shout the jaguar skipped aside and came eye to eye with a guard. As the man lifted his weapon the jaguar pounced. He sprang directly at the guard and clamped his jaws on the man's neck, cutting off any sound.

The jaguar stood over his kill and turned.

Never feed, the silver eyes said. *Never.*

Then the jaguar leaped over the fence into the waiting jungle.

He paused, his senses drenched with blood and his body singing with an urge to kill and feed. Afraid, he turned and bounded over the fence.

Peppered with human blood, the jaguar's scent was easily followed. He knew the spotted cat would be waiting for him deeper in the forest, where the hunters couldn't easily track them. He heard barking dogs in the distance.

He came to a stream and swam across. On the other side he stopped to regain the jaguar's scent. But it was faint, overpowered by another, more compelling scent, familiar and insistent.

A female in heat.

Without hesitation he loped through the darkness in search of the source.

When he found her she was tearing flesh from the bones of a fresh kill.

A sensual hiss greeted his arrival. She lifted her bloody maw, fangs bared, a black jaguar, like him. Her eyes were yellow flames in the gloom.

Mate...

Her imperative loosed a swollen river of elemental need. She lifted her haunches and the stink of the universe flooded his senses. He pounced, sharp teeth biting the nape of her neck, claws raking her shoulders. Their loins collided, interlocking in a furious embrace. Her screeching yowl of pleasure—and triumph— unleashed a raging tide that lifted them both and flung them down on a distant shore where they lay panting for breath.

With a warning growl she shook him off.

She turned back to her kill, straddling the carcass. She looked at him, eyes yellow moons illuminating his instincts.

Feed with me...

The steaming scent of blood, sex and raw flesh drew him close. Exposed organs gleamed darkly beneath white bone. Hunger and lust boiled up in his belly, He opened his drooling jaws.

A dog barked and he lifted his head. She roared in frustration. The barking became an excited chorus and he knew they had picked up his trail. He turned to run but she remained where she was.

Feed with me...

Torn between need and survival, he hesitated. Then fear lanced his instincts and he bolted into the darkness. He sprinted blindly for a long time, unable to find the spotted jaguar's scent, senses besotted with the cloying female odor.

He became lost.

Finally it was his ears that pointed the direction. He heard the faint sound of drums and let the beckoning throb guide him home...

Chapter 49

It wasn't until they visited the training camp, that Klein comprehended the scope of Hans' master plan. There were at least a thousand young shock troops going through their various routines: obstacle course, shooting range, advanced weapons, explosives, hand to hand combat—the works. They were male and female, all blond, all over six feet, divided into squads of ten.

"This is the day shift," Hans said. "We also train at night."

"Where did you get these people? They look like Stepford Children"

Hans looked puzzled. "They are the result of superior breeding. Not only are they superior physical specimens but they are proficient in science, engineering and medicine. They also speak five languages which will enable us to infiltrate countries and work from within. The shooting war comes later. There are already groups around the world who would fall on their knees to join us."

Klein wasn't listening. He was gaping at a corpulent figure lecturing one of the squads.

"Son of a bitch... that's him isn't it? The short guy—Martin Bormann."

"General Bormann is Chancellor of Economics, as well as one of our most expert military tacticians."

"As I recall he didn't do too well the first time around."

"He did not have the Architect's power."

"Architect?"

Hans shrugged. "You will see, Morris. You will see all."

"When's the big day?'

"The day after tomorrow, eighteen hundred hours.'

Klein cleared his throat. "Is that when I'm due to be...?"

"Oh no, Morris. The day following our inauguration is soon enough for all of you."

"Who's all of us?"

"The girl's mother, Miss Lean, Doctor Orient and you." He made it sound like a dinner invitation.

"Doctor Orient is here too?"

Hans smile was cat like. "No. But he will come for the girl. That's why you're here isn't it?"

"Actually we were looking for your friend Von Speer."

"You people know nothing. Von Speer? He is no friend. The man is a supplier, a profiteer. He could even be a Jew like you. Within forty eight hours both of you will be eliminated."

Klein calculated how long it would take to pull the Ruger, smoke Hans and kill Bormann before they got him. He looked out at the young troops training with silent precision. How many of their cadre were resuscitated war criminals from the Nazi death camps he speculated, suddenly depressed. What made him think that one FBI agent and a psychic doctor could waltz into the middle of the Amazon and free Savana?

Because you believed you were dealing with a serial killer, possibly two, not a goddamn army of blond zombies, he told himself. It didn't make him feel any better. Wearily he followed Hans back into the jungle.

+ + +

As promised Hans brought Klein around to the interment area, which consisted or rows of stucco shacks surrounded by wire cages. Hannah and Sybelle occupied adjoining cages, but Savana was being held in another section.

"Sybelle, are you okay?" Klein asked, standing outside her cage

"As well as could be expected, though I feel rather stupid. I allowed myself and Hannah to be kidnapped by what I thought was a nice young couple."

"They got thousands of them here," Klein said, "don't beat yourself up. I made our captain sail into this flytrap. He tried to warn me."

"Where's Owen?"

"I think he got away chasing after some guy who stole his backpack.'

Sybelle took a deep breath. "I hope he's alright."

"How's Hannah holding up?"

"They won't let her see Savana and it's destroying her emotionally."

"Bastards." Klein noticed a stout woman with thick legs, positioned behind Sybelle at the entrance to her cell. She stood glowering at them.

"Who's the concentration camp commandant back there?"

"Her name is Valka and she worked for Henry Applegate."

The name jogged his memory. "Jesus. What does she do here?"

"She's a horrible creature. Stomps around like some prison guard in a B movie. Total control freak. She seems to be *simpatico* with this Von Speer character you were looking for. They're always huddling in a corner, like pigeons"

"Von Speer is here?"

"Of course. In fact he's right over there talking to Hans."

Klein half turned and saw a pale, paunchy man of perhaps fifty talking rapidly to Hans. He was dressed in white shorts and a yellow tank top that revealed all of his flabby body's shortcomings. In the midst of the cookie cutter perfection that set the local standard, he stood out like a pimple on prom night.

Then he noticed Valka in the background. She no longer had her eye on him but stood staring at Von Speer and Hans intently. As if she could hear their conversation from thirty yards away.

"They're pals huh?"

"I suppose. Obviously she had something to do with Henry's murder."

"I'll arrest her right away."

Sybelle blinked. A moment later she guffawed. "You are a cool customer, Morris. It's the first time I've laughed since I let them take us."

"Welcome to the club. I blundered my way in here myself."

Sybelle's mood wilted. "Oh, Morris... Do we have any hope?"

"Owen is still out there," he said in a tone that fell well short of reassuring.

Hans came up behind them.. "Say goodbye Morris."

Klein took a few steps back and lowered his voice. "Do they know?"

"Not yet."

"At least allow them a chance to prepare."

Hans gave him a bemused smile. "I think you have feelings for her. Quite romantic, Morris. However juvenile emotions are not part of our belief system. Let's go, now."

+ + +

Valka shooed Sybelle back into her cell, then slowly walked to the wire fence where Von Speer stood waiting.

"Did you tell him?" Valka hissed.

"I tried, I told him but he hardly listened. I can't understand. I told him twice that I located a gold dealer in New York who has the ring. He seemed distracted. The ceremony..."

Valka dismissed the idea with a brusque wave. "I spoke to Bormann. He is committed."

"What about Mengele?"

"He is a snake. I never trusted him. He claims to be with us meanwhile he commands his own little cadre of special students."

"We need funds to do this. What about the Architect?"

"Are you serious? The Architect is firmly allied with Hans... until such time we are able to demonstrate our own power."

"What are you saying?"

Valka's broad features hardened. "When you locate the ring, do not sell it—*use it.*"

"There you are, Uncle Dieter, are you preparing for the Solstice?"

Both of them turned their faces impassive. They had long since learned that any betrayal of emotion made them suspect.

"Alvira," Von Speer said with forced enthusiasm, "we were just talking about the ceremony. It's unfortunate we still don't have the ring. However I have an excellent source.'

Alvira looked at them, her eyes like solar flares. Then she smiled. "Dear Dieter, all of us were so impressed when you produced the Spear. No doubt you'll impress us again." She kissed his cheek. "See you both soon.'

Valka's smile faded as she walked away. She hated Alvira's sense of entitlement. "Alvira and Hans are as thick as thieves," she said quietly. "They have the Spear. We must have the ring."

+ + +

While walking back to his stockade, Klein saw a blonde woman of perhaps fifty, leading a group of girls in calisthenics. He was struck first by her age, since everyone with the exception of Hans seemed to be between fifteen and twenty five. Then he was taken by her familiar features, like those of a vintage screen star.

Klein stopped short. "Leni Riefenstahl? Can't be, the bitch was almost a hundred when she died."

"One hundred and one, to be exact," Hans said. "We engineered her death, cremated the fake corpse then brought her here for a complete rejuvenation. Our plastic surgeons outdid themselves. After all, the so called 'bitch' is a film genius, a pioneer. Actress, director, writer, still photographer, Leni Riefenstahl did it all."

"She also did Adolf, and most of the Gestapo."

"Always the petty moralist, aren't you Morris? You disappoint me. You've seen first hand the scientific miracles we have achieved here. And yet you still don't seem able to see the big picture, the... grand design."

"Your design isn't so grand for those slaves in your work camps, or those mutilated children in your hospitals."

Hans' scar flared red and Klein knew he'd touched a nerve.

"Take a look around Morris," he said, teeth clenched. "For the past hundred years it's been one mass murder after another. World wars in Europe and Asia, mass murders in Cambodia, Serbia, Sudan, the Congo, Mexico, oil wars, drug wars—we will restore order to an ignorant, overpopulated world. And create a functioning paradise for all."

"Except for Jewish people, and the darker races."

"Don't whine Morris, you are beginning to annoy me. I'll let you in on a little secret, the Grand Design wasn't planned—it was *ordained*."

"You make it sound like a religion."

"Finally you're beginning to get it." He pushed Klein forward, ending the conversation.

Back in his cell, Klein was comforted by the proximity of his concealed Ruger.

He wondered if Orient was on his way into a trap, or already dead somewhere in the jungle. No matter how it went down, Klein intended to take somebody with him, preferably Hans.

Chapter 50

The return was as painful as the change.

As soon as he awoke, Orient's body felt the aftereffects. His joints and muscles were sore and rolling off the hammock to his feet was difficult and graceless.

There was also a nasty skin burn around his neck, where the leather thong had dug in. Apparently the pouch had accompanied his jaguar.

A half naked female brought him a cup of fruit juice, her eyes lowered.

He realized he was naked. He drank thirstily.

"You are certain you did not feed?"

Still somewhat groggy Orient looked at Borges. He didn't ask how the Shaman knew what happened after they separated. Their minds were linked in their bestial journey.

"I'm certain."

"Had you eaten the kill your path would be forever altered. You would belong to the beast."

Orient nodded. He was still tired and hungry. His skin and hair felt oily, as if he hadn't bathed in days. And he carried a faint animal scent, like a wet dog.

"Come," Borges said, "we will go to the Ancient Pool."

To Orient's surprise when they left the lodge he saw that hundreds more tribesmen had arrived at the compound. As they had the night before, they parted to let Borges and Orient pass.

Orient's tender feet were still not used to walking barefoot. Fortunately the Ancient Pool was a short distance from the clearing. The crystal clear water was cool and washed away the soiled residue of his transformation. In truth, he felt reborn.

He was at one with the jungle, its rhythms, and its teeming life. Orient closed his eyes and breathed deep.

An unpleasant probe at the base of his brain vibrated with tension.

"What was it?" Borges asked lazily.

"My friend Sybelle is being held prisoner at that camp we visited last night. Most likely they have Hannah as well."

"There is nothing we can do before tomorrow night. Until then we prepare."

They lingered in the pool for a long time, as Borges recounted the history behind this historic uniting of the tribes.

"In the past they were at war with one another. But this evil has brought them together against a common enemy. The Kayapo tribe from near the Xingo River with tattoos that describe the birth of the world, the fierce Kamayura in red and black colors, the Kawahip with their long blowguns, the Kofan also blowgun fighters, the Suya, the Zuruaha, even the Jivaro are traveling a thousand miles to join their brothers. All have known for years what happens here."

Borges told him how the foreign encampment had grown and prospered over the decades, taking over land, and enslaving whole tribes. They drained children of their blood and stole their organs. It was these atrocities, and Borges enormous influence as Shaman, that finally convinced the warring tribes to unite.

"We know both the sun's solstice and eclipse of the moon are crucial for their rite. Our intelligence tells us the sun ceremony is a semi-annual affair" Borges said. "This eclipse is something new. However I do know these people generate enormous power. And it is getting stronger."

Orient realized Savana's abduction was a small cog in this cosmic wheel and he'd been led here for a reason. But he still didn't know how he could help.

"The ring is your weapon in this war," Borges said quietly. "Tonight after you're rested, we will channel its energy."

They talked for some time, floating in the pristine pool, letting the water heal the wounds of the previous night. Just scratches compared to what would happen tomorrow Orient mused, listening to the birds gossiping in the trees above.

The heat descended the moment they emerged, and after only a few paces into the jungle he was perspiring. Orient blinked as the vegetation ahead of them shifted and took human shape.

A man painted with now familiar green and black tiger stripes, hailed Borges and spoke rapidly.

"He is one of the Invisible People from the upper Amazon. He says the Jivaro have arrived and they want to attack immediately. I must go stop them."

The endless political discussions among the tribes diverted attention away from Orient. Back inside the lodge he found fresh shorts and a tee shirt in his back pack. He also found his satellite phone but knew any attempt to use it might pinpoint their location. Instead he ate, crawled into a hammock and took a long nap.

The drums woke him.

He went outside and saw that it was dark. Cooking fires dotted the clearing, and the tribes gathered in great circles eating and drinking. Some were dancing others singing. He saw a dark man with red blond curls seated on the ground, being painted with red war stripes across his face and chest.

It was Malik. He gave Orient a rueful shrug. "I told Le Mond and Espada the river route to avoid a take down when they were docked in Belem. But I hear Mr. FBI decided he knew better. Now your boy is sittin' in a damn death camp, and I have to get him out. Ain't that a bitch?"

Orient smiled. "You're not going in there by yourself are you? Anyway why didn't you tell me the route?"

"Would you have believed me?"

"Probably not. But I won't make that mistake again."

Malik grinned. "We're cool, Doc. You be careful when it hits the fan."

Borges was seated near the lodge with a group of men who wore yellow and red feathered headbands across their chopped black hair. Orient recognized the distinctive red stripe across their faces as belonging to the Jivaro tribe. Their bows and curare tipped arrows were on the ground beside them.

Borges waved him over. As Orient joined the one of the warriors said something. The others laughed. "He says you sleep by day, come out at night like the jaguar."

Orient smiled sheepishly. The men gathered around Borges were solemnly listening to what Borges was saying. The bearded shaman pointed to the sky and they nodded.

Later the Jivaro joined the other tribes in a pre battle celebration.

"In a few hours we go by boat and make camp in the jungle. We wait there until tomorrow night when we strike." Borges told Orient. "Let us concentrate on the ring."

Orient explained that his friend had made a duplicate.

"Very wise. You must wear it from now on."

There, in the firelight, accompanied by tribal drums and chants, Orient and Borges channeled the energy of the ancient ring, forged in the cradle of civilization. From the dark arts of the Sumerians, to the advanced wisdom of the Egyptians; all condensed to a tiny gold circle, like the dense, pulsing nucleus of a dead star.

Then it was time for stage one.

Tribe by tribe they left the compound, some by boat others overland, to the appointed meeting place. Their celebrations over, the warriors went about their business in deep silence.

Orient accompanied Borges in one of the small boats.

Under cover of darkness they were able to make the journey in three hours. It was understood the warriors circling by land would reach them much later. This to ensure there was no contact with the enemy until everything was in place. Otherwise they would surely be slaughtered by a superior force with advanced weapons.

A warrior in the lead boat proudly brandished a pole bearing a human head.

Wearing feathers and a war mask, Borges looked as fierce as any of the Jivaro headhunters.

The Jivaro had heard what happened the previous night, and insisted on endowing Orient with the red facial stripe of their tribe, to honor the black jaguar. Tonight he ran with them.

Lights appeared as they neared their objective.

They steered to the river bank and pulled their boats ashore. Without word or sound they melted into the forest.

+ + +

The leader of the Jivaro tribe had taken a liking to Orient.

Tupo had a barrel chest, thick arms and legs like tree trunks. When he smiled, which was seldom, he revealed fang-like teeth. Normally his face was set in a suspicious glower but it relaxed when communicating with Orient—which was often. Apparently Tupo was very concerned Orient might be injured in the jungle.

"They believe you are a great shaman," Borges explained, "a human with the soul of a black jaguar."

"News travels fast in the Amazon."

Borges grinned. "Don't need e-mail out here."

It was still dark and they had paused to regroup. There were hundreds of men concealed throughout the surrounding jungle. Borges took the time to outline his basic plan.

They would wait out the day and strike during the lunar eclipse. Borges would again use his shape shifting power to leap over the electrified fence as a jaguar, and take care of the guards at the power center. He intended to shut down the generators which would enable the warriors to get inside the compound. From there they would proceed to the armory where they would take what weapons they needed and blow up the rest.

After that it would be hand to hand combat but their enemy would be at a disadvantage without electrical power or adequate weapons. Their first objective after the armory would be to free the prisoners in the work camps and medical center.

"My only concern is preventing a bloodbath," Borges said. "Many of us have lost wives, children, whole families to these strangers." He gave Orient a sad smile. "We must learn to kill without hate."

Orient nodded. He knew many of the warriors were imbibing Ayahuasca, the same psychedelic potion he had shared with Borges the night he was initiated into the art of metamorphosis. .

Tupo joined them. He said something to Borges and showed him a bright yellow feather.

"Tupo would like you to wear this feather. He says it belonged to his father and will keep you safe in battle. It is a great honor," he added.

Orient pressed his palms together and bowed.

Without a word Tupo moved behind Orient, braided a few strands of his now long hair, and attached the feather.

"It is customary..." Borges stopped when he saw Orient rummage through his knapsack and presented Tupo with his hunting knife.

The fierce Jivaro chief didn't quite smile but Orient could see he was pleased with the gift.

"In the Amazon a knife is more valuable than a Cadillac." Borges said.

The most difficult part of the plan was staying concealed during the day.

Their scouts reported that most of the inhabitants of the great village were preparing for a ceremony and guards were few. Still the heat, insects and pent up anxieties made waiting a strain.

Borges moved carefully to his side, holding a jar. At first Orient thought it might be the Ayahuasca potion but it was actually purple dye.

"Tupo gave you a gift, now I'm giving you one. The mark of Dambala, the serpent spirit. Will you accept?"

Orient knew Dambala was of the Macumba hierarchy. His mind went back to Ganwi in Marrakech and his queen cobra.

"Yes," he said.

Borges traced a symbol on his arm and forehead, using a shaved stick dipped in the purple dye. When it was done Orient reached into his knapsack but the shaman shook his head. "We are brothers." He said.

As the sun rose in the sky they heard an amplified voice drifting through the jungle. At the same time two of Tupo's scouts reported they had found a way inside the camp. Tupo decided to investigate and motioned for Orient to accompany them.

Orient looked at Borges who shrugged.

Orient followed Tupo and his scouts. He did his best to keep pace with the warriors who moved easily and soundlessly through the dense forest. Coming closer to the camp Orient clearly heard what was being chanted over the loudspeakers and realized it was an occult invocation He could see groups of people dressed in white.

A low, droning hum cut through the jungle. Tupo and his warriors stiffened. They fitted their arrows and stood perfectly still as the ominous sound deepened. Orient wondered if their night attack would come too late.

Static electricity filled the forest like a swarm of invisible flies, scattering wildlife. After long minutes the droning subsided and it was quiet.

A man's voice came over the loudspeakers exhorting his followers. The warriors relaxed a notch, lowering their bows. They began moving closer.

A flat *crack* alarmed the birds and they fluttered in swift circles above them.

Tupo looked at Orient who mimed pulling a trigger. At the same time he felt a familiar probe at the base of his brain.

Sybelle. And she was terrified.

Without hesitation Orient started running in the direction of the gunshot.

Chapter 51

For years Moe had to endure snide comments and out-right ridicule for his choice of a small weapon. Today he was totally vindicated.

The light Ruger had been tucked securely in his shorts since breakfast. Hardly knew it was there, he gloated, pacing back and forth inside his cage. Not that it would change anything. Either way he was history.

It was clear from all the activity going on that today was important. Everyone was dressed in white shorts, shirts and socks. Usually they went about their duties with stolid determination. But today the young clones seemed animated, excited even, Moe noted.

An hour or so before the sun ascended to its Solstice, two guards came to fetch him. They escorted him to a town square as large as a small stadium. A covered stage built on high ground commanded a sweeping view of the sloping land below—and of the thousands of young, blond, men and women massed there, in precise groups of one hundred.

The glare from their white uniforms shimmered in the heat. There was an altar on the stage, draped in white. Emblazoned on the altar cloth and on the flags lining the clearing was a black swastika. Just like the old days, Moe observed glumly. .

His guards led him to a bench at the side of the stage. Within minutes he saw Hans approaching, accompanied by an incredibly beautiful woman. Slim, with deep gold hair and tawny skin, she moved with earthy grace, white robe clinging to her body. Hans pointed at him and she turned to look.

Moe was unable to turn away from her yellow eyes. Inanely, he realized his blue, sweat stained shirt must seem out of place in the sea of white. Gaze still on him, the woman nodded knowingly, and for a moment he thought she could see the weapon in his shorts. She shrugged and turned away.

Hans walked over to greet him. He was carrying a terry cloth roll.

"Morris, how good of you to join us. This afternoon's celebration is a joyous occasion. The sun at its zenith will mark the rebirth of earth—and of our crusade." He unrolled the cloth and showed Moe the object inside. "Today we will charge the potential of the Spear of Destiny."

Moe glanced at the gold sheathed spear head, then a Hans. "Von Speer stole it for you didn't he? Nice job. I heard they replaced it with an excellent copy."

"For once you have it right, Morris. That is exactly how we acquired it. And today Dietrich Von Speer will receive his reward."

Moe saw Sybelle Lean and Hannah Wylde being led into the clearing by the sturdy Valka. They were seated on the opposite side of the stage.

"But it is tonight—during the eclipse—that our full power will be unleashed by the Architect." Hans was saying.

Promises, promises, Moe thought, but he was really worried. He'd seen that flat glint in Hans' icy eyes before. It was the same pitiless stare that marked sociopathic killers. It was clear people would die today.

Hans carefully rewrapped the Spear.

"See how obediently they all wait," he said almost to himself.

Moe didn't know if he met the massed audience or the prisoners. Either way he was right. As Hans mounted the stage, Moe managed a halfhearted wave at Sybelle.

She didn't wave back. Valka glowered at him menacingly.

The altar evidently had an audio system. Hans' amplified voice echoed in the quiet as he began his ritual. A large volume lay open on the altar and Hans referred to it during the ceremony. Some of the words he chanted were in Hebrew, others in Latin, much of it in languages Moe didn't understand. But he did sense the voltage in the air rising.

Finally the words had a familiar sound, not German but definitely Teutonic. Then something happened that made the hair on Moe's neck stand on end.

A thousand voices answered Hans' chant with a deep *hum*. The wordless drone penetrated Moe's core and he became very afraid. He struggled to subdue his panic as the drone grew louder.

Hans' voice rose and he lifted his arms high, the Spear of Destiny in his hands.

The sun was at its apex now, its glaring heat poured over the white-clad throng as their throaty hum rose in volume. Its deep, ominous vibration shook the jungle around them

Stunned, Moe watched the uplifted Spear begin to glow.

It couldn't be the sun, the stage is covered, Moe reasoned. However he couldn't find a reason for the gold-sheathed spear head *radiating*. Hans triumphantly turned to the crowd and held it high for some time, walking back and forth across the stage as if to bless everyone assembled there.

As if on cue the humming tapered off. Moe heard his rapid heart beat in the quiet. Hans reverently placed the Spear of Destiny on top of the large volume. Then he turned and began to speak. Moe had acquired a working knowledge of German during his years with the Bureau and with Simon Weisenthal's group, so he was able to follow most of it. And it scared him.

"Children of the New Reich," Hans intoned, "your hour has come. But you must be ever vigilant of corruption in our ranks. Traitors are everywhere. We must insure that the blood of our enemies blesses our crusade for world order."

He lifted his hand and pointed toward the area where Sybelle and Hannah were seated.

"Bring him here to be judged!"

Moe saw two young guards roughly shove a portly man into view. It was Von Speer, his puffy features slack. He was sweating heavily, large dark patches drenching his white shirt. And he was shaking uncontrollably.

"Dietrich Von Speer, you are guilty of violating the sacred trust of the New Reich. You wanted to profit for cheap, personal gain. Not only did you delay the acquisition of some priceless artifacts, and not only did you almost lose the most precious of them all—you brought serious outside attention to our activities. These prisoners you see today are here only because of Dietrich Von Speer's Greed. He broke our code, violated our trust, and now he must pay."

"Let me speak," Von Speer cried looking about wildly, "I have been loyal since the beginning. He extended his arms to the golden haired girl standing nearby. "I was a close friend to your father... the Fuhrer himself. Please you know me," he went on, voice rising in pitch, "I'm your Uncle Dietrich... I was at your baptism."

The girl smiled and nodded. "Dear Uncle."

Von Speer fell to his knees sobbing. "Thank you... thank you."

She was still smiling but Moe saw something in her yellow eyes. The empty stare of a sociopath.

She glanced up at Hans who remained on stage, arms crossed. He nodded slowly.

Without preamble she lifted the pistol she had concealed behind her back and fired.

The sharp crack spurred a hurried flight of chattering birds. Then it was quiet again.

Von Speer lay on the ground, blood streaming from his shattered skull.

Moe could see Hannah sobbing. Sybelle sat stiffly, her face set as if determined to stay calm. In contrast Valka's composure seemed to disintegrate. Visibly shaken, she turned her face away.

It was over. The throng quietly dispersed. The guards took Hannah and Sybelle away but Hans left Moe broiling in the sun for some time. Still in a state of mild shock Moe watched them roll Von Speer into a body bag and haul him away on a stretcher. That pool of blood left behind was black with flies. He closed his eyes.

"I see you were properly impressed, Morris."

Moe saw Hans standing before him, the terry cloth roll cradled in his arms like a new born child. His eyes were bright and his face was flush with preternatural energy.

Moe glared stubbornly, refusing to give in.

"Who the hell is that scary bitch?"

Pain exploded against his skull.

The next time it will be more than a slap," Hans promised. "I will kill you slowly, do you understand Jew pig?"

Moe nodded, ear ringing and jaw numb.

"We are very proud of Alvira Charisma. She is the New Reich's Virgin Mary. Alvira is the prodigy of our Lebensborn Society."

"Lebensborn..." Moe searched his memory, "...wellspring of life. The Aryan breeding farms started by Heinrich Himmler."

"Crudely put, but accurate. We have continued the original policies here. Our youth is the result of superior genetics, scientifically engineered."

"What makes..." Moe half expected another blow. "...*Lady* Charisma a prodigy?" Besides being a natural born killer, he added silently.

Hans beamed "Alvira is the daughter of Adolf Hitler."

Moe gaped in disbelief.

"Her mother was an Olympic athlete selected from a thousand applicants and inseminated with the Fuhrer's sperm. There were other children but they failed the stringent requirements of their heritage. Alvira was the best and brightest. And she will rule beside me for the next two hundred years."

"Hitler's daughter but she's so..."

"So young? You forget Morris, we are at the cutting edge of science in our laboratories. You saw how well Leni looks lately."

"What did Von Speer do exactly? I thought he procured the Spear."

Hans hugged the terry cloth roll in his arms. "Yes, but he double crossed me and it cost me my ring."

"What ring?"

Hans' lips stretched in a ghastly smile, devoid of all humor.

"The ring your friend is about to return to me right now."

Moe followed his gaze. He squinted unsure of what he saw.

A trio of guards was escorting a man who looked like an Indian. A red stripe ran across the bridge of his nose and a yellow feather hung from his long dark hair,

Moe's belly sagged. It was Orient.

Chapter 52

Orient realized he'd been duped by his emotions. But he couldn't stand by if Sybelle called for help. He saw Klein's resigned scowl but didn't know if was sympathy, or disappointment.

Both Orient and Klein were taken to a building that was empty of furniture except for a few steel folding chairs, a decrepit pool table and a couch in one corner.

Hans regarded Orient with mock bemusement.

"Finally we meet face to face, Doctor. You frustrated me in New York, repulsed me in Marrakech and tracked me to my remote jungle lair. Well done."

Hans winked at Klein. "I told you he'd come didn't I? He couldn't help himself."

His smile faded and he extended his hand. "Give it to me now."

Orient hesitated. Hans nodded to one of the guards who drew a knife from his belt.

Orient slipped the heavy gold ring from his finger and dropped it into Hans' waiting palm. He looked at Klein and shook his head, completely drained from lack of sleep and failure. He had let base impulse drive him. He could only hope Tupo and his scouts had avoided capture.

Hans took the ring greedily and held it up to the window. "Ahh exquisite, the fine work, the pallasites." He glanced at Orient. "Better this way. You with the ring is like a child with a nuclear weapon."

The remark roused Orient. "It's a sacred trust, not a weapon."

But Hans wasn't listening. His eyes were on something behind Orient.

Even before Orient turned he caught her spiced scent. "Alvira...?"

"I'm so sorry it had to be this way, Owen."

Orient's brain rocked between shock and anger. In that moment he realized how easily he had been manipulated.

Her yellow eyes searched his face. "Why the Jivaro mark Owen?" She turned to the guards. "Who was with him?"

They shook their heads. "He ran right into us," one of them said, "there was no one else."

She turned to Hans. "Perhaps we should send out some patrols."

He continued to admire the ring. "He probably met some friendly natives after he ran off the boat."

Klein looked puzzled. "You two know each other?"

Orient tried to regain his composure. "Alvira is the friend who arranged for our boat, and provided the maps."

Klein snorted. "A real Venus fly trap."

"And I'm the fly," Orient said, meeting her gaze.

"It doesn't have to end this way," she said, soft voice massaging his anger. You and I together could create a new man—an enlightened being endowed with our special powers."

"Lebensborn..." Klein said. "You can work on the breeding farm."

Hans lazily lifted his arm and chopped Klein across the windpipe. The burly agent collapsed, gasping for air.

"Take the Jew back to his cell." As the guards dragged him away Hans put the ring on his finger and admired it. "I'll leave you with Doctor Orient my dear Alvira. I'm sure you have much to discuss. Meanwhile, I have important matters to prepare with the Architect."

Alone with her, Orient's anger wavered. Her sheer white robe clung to her body and her yellow eyes were smoky, like lights in a mist. She came closer and he caught the spiced scent of her breath. .

His body roused itself from exhaustion and defeat and met her lips when she kissed him.

"I know you're the one," she said, voice husky. "You do too."

"Problem is, I don't know who you are."

"Of course not," she said mouth coming close to his ear, "but you will come to know everything. We were connected long before we met. You were in my dreams."

Her closeness enveloped him. Orient remembered the dark creature haunting his dreams and realized it was her animal spirit stalking him. He focused on the ring at his neck, and felt raw energy charge his tired brain, waking his defenses. It evaporated his emotions and rebalanced his consciousness.

"Thanks but I know too much already,"

The fury that flared in her eyes quickly cooled behind a feline smile.

"Too bad, Owen, I really will miss you. No one else ever shared my deeper nature like you. Still I expect that over the next century I'll meet someone."

"The next century?"

"Hans will explain it to you I'm sure. Goodbye, Owen, I'll see you tonight, but it won't be the same." She kissed him lightly and left him alone in the room.

+ + +

Two guards stood outside the door, another at the window.

Orient went to the couch and stretched out. He closed his eyes and went into a breathing pattern. He reached out and found Sybelle.

A brief picture of a cage. But he sensed that she was alright. He wondered what had frightened her.

"Enjoying a nap or deep in meditation?" Hans said as he stepped into the room. "I see your conversation with Alvira was brief."

"Long enough to know who she is."

Hans suppressed a laugh. "Actually you really don't know who she is. Your soon to be deceased friend Morris knows. Maybe he'll let you in on our little secret."

Orient understood Hans was trying to rattle his focus. And he knew it was a sign of uncertainty. Hans was still unsure of the range of his psychic powers, having been stopped twice at the threshold. He looked away. "Who can guess a woman's secrets?"

"Well put," Hans said, obviously disappointed. "Now please let me show you a bit of our community here. My time is short, though not so short as yours, so I'll give you the broad strokes so to speak."

As Orient followed Hans through the forest that connected the separate areas he knew hidden tribal warriors were somewhere near. The sun was starting to drop and the hour of the eclipse would begin.

Hans did manage to unsettle Orient after all.

He took Orient on a tour of the facility for clairvoyant development where clone-like children joylessly performed common extra sensory experiments. Without any spiritual compass Orient knew that their psychic abilities would soon destroy them. However Hans cared little for their future. He was grooming them for a takeover no matter what it cost.

But their next visit proved beyond his worst fears. The Aibert Heim center for eternal youth was an extension of the grotesque medical atrocities performed by the Nazi doctor in his death camps. Orient knew of the horrific experiments but was under the impression that Heim died in Cairo. To find him alive-and thriving—was an obscenity

"And you can observe the unparalleled success of Dr. Heim's work." Hans said smugly. "I myself am the beneficiary of his genius. As is our lovely Alvira."

Orient wasn't quite ready for that. He shoved it aside and got to the point. "How many children have their blood drained, organs removed, glands milked—for you and your elite few to extend your existence for a few years?"

"You don't understand the bigger picture. At best our Fuhrer might have lived another thirty years and another less qualified leader would step in his place. And at that point the disintegration of all he had built would begin. Now the Architect can rule over the New Reich for two hundred years. Our vision will remain carved in man's consciousness the way the Ten Commandments were carved in stone."

"The reality is that the Fuhrer's vision lasted only a dozen years before it collapsed."

"But the vision lives on. The recent massacre in tiny peace loving Norway proves that we are everywhere. All it will take to ignite our followers is the ascension of the Architect."

"Who is this almighty Architect of yours?"

"You'll meet tonight, "Hans assured. "Come—our little tour is over and you must be starved."

Hans took Orient back to the internment camp and told the guards to put him in Klein's cage.

"It will be easier to collect you later," Hans explained. "After all, you are both guests of honor."

There was a food tray waiting for Orient when he entered the cell. Klein was both surprised and dismayed to see him.

"I was hoping you'd get away," he said, "maybe get help."

Orient didn't reveal anything about Borges, certain the cell was bugged. Why else would Hans put them together? He put a finger to his lips and motioned Klein outside.

"Chances are Hans rigged outdoor surveillance as well," Orient said.

Klein shrugged. "Who cares? We're going to die anyway." As he spoke he lifted the butt of his Ruger.

"Not now, I hope," Orient said, pointing to the weapon. "Much later. I think Hans wants to keep us under wraps for a while."

Klein nodded to show Orient he understood. It was not yet time to use the gun.

"That ain't the way I heard it," Klein said. "Hans personally assured me I'm on death row. They already offed Von Speer. Your friend Alvira actually."

"Alvira... killed Von Speer?"

"Cool as ice cream. I watched her do it. So did Sybelle and Dr. Wylde. What do you expect, look who her father was."

He told Orient that Alvira's mother had been inseminated with Hitler's sperm, and had been born just after the war. "She definitely qualifies for Social Security," Klein said, "but you'd never know it looking at her. The woman's a knockout."

"Certainly put me on the canvas," Orient said ruefully. He understood why Sybelle had reached out in terror during Von Speer's execution.

Klein also told Orient everything he'd seen that day, including the long list of undead Nazis still pursuing their totalitarian nightmare.

Orient half listened, still reeling from what he'd learned about Alvira.

"Everybody looks busy again," Klein observed as young men and women hurried past on their way to their various assignments. Some carried large wooden posts wrapped in rags that trailed the faint odor of kerosene.

"I'd better get busy myself," Orient said, moving inside.

He lay on the hard wood floor and began to stretch his knotted muscles and stiff limbs. Slowly he entered a deep meditative state, focusing on charging the Key of Solomon. In essence the ring's potential was far greater than any firearm. The question was did he have sufficient psychic prowess to pull the trigger?

Orient remained in a state of concentration for a long time. When he finally emerged it was night.

Chapter 53

Hans arrived with four guards in tow. All of them including Hans wore black military uniforms. Hans' shirt bore the SS insignia, the Sig runes.

"Tonight you are privileged to witness the second coming," Hans announced, eyes bright with anticipation.

More like the last hurrah Klein thought, wearily getting to his feet. The afternoon's solstice celebration had been enough for one day. He couldn't stand another killing. Especially if it was Savana.

Two guards in front, two behind, they were marched out of their cells into the tropical night. It was dead quiet as they walked, the sound of their feet muffled by the humid air. Every so often the shrill cry of some animal drifted from the jungle. Although quite dark their path was lit by flashlights, and the diffuse glow of a full moon.

Klein hadn't stopped sweating since he arrived in the Amazon but he noticed Orient seemed oddly cool. As if he was in control of his body thermostat. Hans paused to give the guards orders and Orient leaned closer. "Don't make a move until it happens," he whispered.

Klein half understood something was up. He wished he knew the other half.

They were taken to the community square where the solstice ceremony had taken place. Along with Von Speer's public execution. But tonight they had outdone themselves.

There were hundreds of torches illuminating legion after legion of tall, fair haired young people, as far as he could see, all wearing identical black uniforms. Perhaps three thousand, maybe more, they stood silently waiting beneath a hot, swollen moon. At measured intervals were Nazi flags.

The torch lit throng of zealous soldiers resembled the Rise of Hitler documentaries they ran on the History Channel, Klein thought, somewhat intimidated by the eerie scene. He wondered what Orient planned to do against these thousands of young shock troops.

The guards took them to a small house behind the stage. Unlike most of the living areas in the camp which had basic cookie cutter dwellings, this one had touches of style, including a garden, veranda and a large carved wood door.

"Wait outside," Hans told the guards

Klein glanced at Orient. He shook his head. Not yet.

Hans ushered them inside the house which was lit by large candles.

"Please make our guests comfortable, we'll be out in a minute," a man said from an inner room.

They all remained standing. Some minutes later a tall, black haired man, with a broad chest and cherubic features stepped into the room. He wore the purple vestments of a clergyman and a black pointed hat with a swastika in place of a cross.

From the corner of his eye Klein saw Orient's cool demeanor waver.

"Bishop Navarro," Orient said, obviously surprised.

It was Klein's turn to be surprised. He had never actually met the bishop.

"Hello, Doctor, I was hoping we could talk. We still have time before the celestial event that will alter man's destiny. Please gentleman, both of you sit down."

They both sat on the couch. Navarro sat across from them.

"I'm honored to announce that a month from now I will be elevated to Cardinal," Navarro said, "and if our plan proceeds as scheduled within three years I will be elected Pope."

Klein and Orient stared at him, overwhelmed by the news.

"Congratulations, Bishop," Orient said, "when I saw your miter I thought you had changed religions."

Klein couldn't stop starring at the bishop's ceremonial headgear. Navarro gave them a benevolent smile. "I think of it as the evolution of the church. We are merging two profound forms of enlightenment; one spiritual, one political. Think of the benefit to mankind."

"And little benefit to God," Orient said.

"Open your eyes Doctor, civilization is sinking and begging for salvation. As Pope, I can deliver a global message—and direct the hearts and minds of a billion people to a make a better world."

"For the elite few perhaps. But you're right, Bishop, as Pope you'll be absolute monarch of your own country, the Vatican. Free of any law save your own."

"I've had the Grimoire of Honorious in my arsenal for years. When I was sent to Bahia and met Hans, saw what he had built, what he *would build* I conceived of the Grand Design. By fusing the entrenched political structure of the Church, with the loyal young soldiers of the New Reich we could consolidate absolute power over a lost mankind. Hans has managed to secure the Spear of Destiny and tonight I will channel the Seal of Solomon. You of all people understand what that means."

"Yes, it means you intend to sacrifice the life of a young girl."

Navarro sat back and removed his miter. He regarded the swastika on his hat and shook his head sadly. "I've told you all this because you can still join us and save your life. You would be a most welcome addition. Think of it as Werner Von Braun lending his brilliance to help America reach the moon."

"What about Sybelle and Hannah?"

"What about me?" Klein growled.

"You'll take part in our youth extension program," Navarro said, as if he hadn't heard. "Think, Doctor, you can expand you exceptional talents for another hundred years at least."

"The soul is eternal, Bishop."

Klein's thoughts were on the gun in his pocket. He could get Navarro and maybe Hans before the guards cut him in half.

"You know the Grimoire alone is sufficient," Navarro said. "It contains all the occult knowledge culled by man over seven thousand years."

"It was written by another Pope," Orient reminded. "Honorious III was a pious proponent of human sacrifice. He had the knowledge of millenniums at his fingertips. All that power, all that blood, and yet his reign lasted only eleven years."

"But his great work lives on. Through his Gimoire— and through me."

He stood up and carefully replaced the pointed miter on his head. Klein was struck by how tall and robust he looked. Like a professional wrestler, he thought. Then he saw the bright glaze over Navarro's coal black eyes and realized the bishop was either highly medicated, or totally psychotic.

"So, Doctor, if you prefer an ignoble death here in the jungle—perhaps as the subject of Dr. Mengele's experiments or those of Dr. Heims—so be it. I wash my hands."

"I'm ready, Bishop," Hans said, stepping into the room. He'd exchanged his uniform for the black robe and purple edged vestments of a priest.

Klein had gone to a funeral mass for an FBI colleague and taken an interest in the ceremony. The purple vestments were worn to say a mass for the dead.

When the guards came to take them away Klein cursed himself for missing the opportunity to gun down Hans and Navarro before they harmed Savana. He hoped Orient knew what he wasn't talking about.

+ + +

The moon's bright yellow surface had deepened to gold in anticipation of the eclipse.

The guards assigned Klein to the same seat he had for the afternoon execution. They placed Orient beside him then stood on either side, automatic rifles slung over their shoulders.

Across the stage area he could see Sybelle and Hannah. Unlike Hannah who sat slumped to one side, Sybelle seemed alert. Valka stood behind them, her face pale and rigid in the flickering light.

The uniformed legions remained eerily quiet, standing shoulder to shoulder beneath the light of hundreds of torches. The stage itself was lit by large black candles. An altar had been assembled there, complete with a white granite altar stone, and tabernacle. There was a chalice and cruets for vinegar and wine.

Klein couldn't see if there were five crosses in an X pattern carved into the altar stone, but he was sure they were there. A black cross stood above the tabernacle. All that was missing were the altar cloths, linens that covered the stone. In a sense they were table cloths since the Holy Mass was a celebration of Christ's last supper at Passover—as well as a sacrifice.

But there was no altar cloth. It wasn't an oversight Klein speculated.

He heard a bell chime. Head bowed, Bishop Navarro ascended the stage, followed by Hans.

After the Salutation, which was in Latin, Navarro began interjecting phrases in a strange tongue between the traditional Latin prayers echoing over the speaker system. Klein had developed a working knowledge of Latin and Catholic ritual during his years as an art investigator, but the guttural phrases meant nothing to him.

Hans acted as altar boy; assisting the priest, pouring the wine. Klein looked out over the thousands of uniformed worshippers, all kneeling at the same time as Bishop Navarro began the consecration of the host—the miracle of Transubstantiation in which the Eucharist wafer is transformed into the body and blood of Christ.

It was then the entire congregation, thousands of disciples, emitted a low humming drone that shook Klein's bones.

It was then that Alvira appeared, attired in a black gown that accentuated her yellow eyes— holding Savana by the arm.

And it was then the eclipse began.

Klein watched Hannah's reaction when she saw her daughter. She sat up and tried to rise, but Valka pushed her back. Surprisingly, Sybelle seemed to ignore the scuffle, staring at the crowd.

To Klein, Savana's slow, careful movements as Alvira led her onto the stage signaled she was drugged. In stark contrast to everyone else Savana wore a white gown, which made her seem even younger and more innocent than her years. Alvira assisted her onto the altar stone where she lay eyes closed, while Navarro continued his mass.

The humming drone intensified as the darkness nibbled away the edge of the moon and Navarro lifted the chalice and drank the blood of Christ.

Spooked, Klein started to go for his piece. One shot for each guard, pick up one of their AK-47s, and go postal. He glanced at Orient and hesitated.

Orient was staring out at the crowd, his expression a mirror of Sybelle's. He appeared to be calm, almost oblivious.

Something flared in the corner of his eye. Klein turned and saw that one of the torches nearby topple, igniting a small fire. The humming drone wavered.

At the altar on stage, Bishop Navarro placed a communion wafer in Savana's listless mouth. Then he reached into the tabernacle and took out a gold ring.

He lifted the ring high then put it on his finger and began chanting in a language Klein didn't understand.

Oddly, Navarro's voice rose in pitch, as if he was straining. Hans moved to the altar where Savana lay motionless and presented the Spear of Destiny to the bishop.

Hannah screamed.

Another torch fell to the ground.

Chapter 54

The Pope is infallible.

It is one of the immutable tenets of the Holy Roman Catholic Church.

This means that whatever a Pope decrees—especially in matters concerning the church— comes directly from God.

The Pope's word is sacred.

He can institute new codes or do away with existing beliefs at will. He can transform the papacy into Satan's throne.

And over the course of history a few have tried, Orient reflected.

He was impressed by the pomp and discipline of Hans' minions and apprehensive as well. If Borges failed to secure the arsenal they'd be slaughtered. Except for their guards Orient could see very few armed personnel in the crowd. He could feel Klein's anxiety and hoped the FBI agent would restrain himself from pulling his gun.

As the strange droning hum lifted from the gathered disciples Orient focused his consciousness and reached out to Sybelle. Having spent the past couple of hours in telepathic contact with her, reconnecting was relatively easy.

Once his consciousness merged with hers, he felt a surge of energy. He carefully swung their momentum to an experimental target—a nearby torch—and pushed...

The torch toppled over.

The mass continued but the droning sound subsided for a moment. Orient fingered the pouch at his neck, channeling the energy of the ring inside. He could feel resistance, a barrier, and realized it was the Spear. He swung their combined energy to the altar and heard Navarro stumble over his words.

Orienr watched Navarro give Savana the consecrated host and put on the replica ring. Hannah screamed when Hans produced the Spear of Destiny. Above them a giant black maw devoured the moon.

Buttressed by Sybelle, Orient intensified his concentration causing another torch to fall. Then another. He felt their momentum gather intensity with each one and again swung the energy to the altar, like turning a ten wheel truck at high speed. They crashed through the Spear's dominant energy shielding the altar and skidded into Navarro's concentration.

The loudspeakers amplified the change in Navarro's tone. Hesitation, then an uncertain stutter tripped the measured cadence of his mass. He glanced at the gold ring on his finger as one might check the speedometer while driving. He didn't know his tank was empty. Orient felt the Seal of Solomon burn hot against his chest and gathered the energy.

The dim electric lights that fringed the compound blinked out, leaving only the flickering torches in the darkness

Navarro didn't notice. He raised the Spear above Savana's chest.

The first explosion got his attention.

When Navarro saw the red glow lighting the distant trees and the small fires from the overturned torches, he stopped and glared angrily at Hans. "Rally them—now!" he rasped impatiently. His voice carried over the loudspeakers.

Hans turned to the shuffling crowd. "All units report to your stations in full combat gear. This is not a drill, repeat, this is not a drill."

Another blast shook the earth and he heard the sound of distant gunfire. Their guards looked at each other then raised their AK-47s and walked quickly toward the sound of the explosions.

Orient saw Hans take the Spear of Destiny from Navarro's hands. He started running to the stage as Hans attempted to complete the sacrificial mass. But he wasn't fast enough.

Two shots blew a cloud of granite splinters from the altar. Hans ducked and backed away, searching for the shooter.

Klein moved past Orient, thick body in a combat crouch. The pistol looked tiny in his hand. He fired another round and Hans jumped to the front of the stage, the Spear clutched in his fist.

"Kill them!" he shouted over the loudspeaker, his sweeping gesture including all prisoners.

The two guards with Sybelle and Hannah aimed in Orient's direction and fired. The ground erupted, spraying dirt and dust at his feet. Orient dove aside but Klein kept moving forward, firing his automatic. One of the guards went down, hit in the chest. The other guard kept shooting until Sybelle threw a body block that knocked him to the ground. Klein shot him point blank in the shoulder and grabbed his fallen AK-47.

Klein shoved the Ruger into his shorts.He lifted the rifle, and swept it clockwise. Their guards were running back to the stage, spraying bullets as they came.

"Get behind the stage," Klein yelled returning fire.

Orient put his arm around Hannah and half carried her behind the stage. Sybelle was right behind him.

The sky was completely dark and the crowd was in disarray. Their black uniforms made their bodies invisible in the torchlight. All Orient could see were bobbing heads moving in different directions, milling wildly.

"Where's Savana?" Hannah said weakly.

Another explosion spewed flame and black smoke like a minor volcano. By the flaring light Orient saw why the crowds were panicked. Hordes of tribesmen armed with arrows, blowguns, machetes and automatic rifles looted from the arsenal were descending on them. Fighting alongside them were prisoners freed from the death camps, hollow eyed and thirsting for revenge.

Still holding Hannah he led them behind the stage. As he motioned for them to get down, Hannah cried out.

"Owen, over there!"

A guard knelt a few yards away, his rifle fixed on Orient. There was no placed to hide. Orient braced himself.

Abruptly, the guard half stood one arm behind his back, as if desperately scratching an itch. He twisted and fell. A powerfully built warrior came out of the shadows. He bent over the fallen guard and yanked a knife out of his back. He held it high and waved.

Orient recognized Tupo—and the knife he had given him.

"I'll get Savana," Orient yelled. Klein covered him as he mounted the stage and lifted the girl's limp body from the altar. He hefted her over his shoulder and hauled Savana to the rear of the stage where her mother was waiting. He carefully lowered the girl into Hannah's arms then jumped to the ground.

As he herded Sybelle and Hannah further away from the chaotic battle, Orient saw Hans leave the bishop's house, carrying something under his arm like a football. Divested of his robes he began sprinting for the jungle. Without hesitating Orient went after him.

Hans had the advantage. He knew the area, had a head start and was a fast runner. Within minutes Orient had lost him. He could hear the cries and screams of battle behind him.

Orient knew what he had to do but wasn't sure if he was up to the challenge.

He ran a short distance and came to a high, metal fence. No doubt Hans had an escape route that skirted the fence. But he had no time to find it...

+ + +

Orient moved into a shadowed area and dropped to the ground. He gripped the pouch at his neck and channeled the Key of Solomon. A surge of energy bolted through his senses as he dove deep into the core of his existence and connected with the dormant chemical sockets of his primal origins.

He roared in pain as muscle and bone twisted, stretched, and reformed, popping and grinding, seething with relentless agony. Black fur pricked his skin like thousands of hot needles. His heart and lungs expanded past the bursting point. Iron fingers squeezed his brain and his eyes filled with blood.

Then it was over and he was at one with the darkness.

Everything in the forest had its place and he knew his responsibility as alpha predator of the night. Burning powder and human blood scented the humid air as he leaped over the fence and bounded into the jungle.

Chapter 55

Adrenaline streaked through Klein's veins.

He hadn't been prepared for the swiftness of the attack and froze at the first explosion. But when Hans lifted the Spear to carve Savana, he yanked his Ruger and fired blindly. The stray bullets backed Hans away. .

"Kill them!" Hans yelled, voice echoing over the speakers.

Their guards had been running toward the explosions but now they turned. Klein saw them but kept moving after Hans. The men guarding Sybelle and Hannah came at him and for an instant he was caught in a perfect crossfire. Then Klein hit one and he went down. Sybelle took the other one out with a body block that would have done the NFL proud giving him time to scoop up an AK-47 and put a round in the guard's shooting arm.

The attackers had overrun the square, hemming in the assembled legions. Most of the people in the compound had gathered for the ceremony as they had that afternoon. Security was light leaving them unarmed and helpless against the sudden onslaught. Within minutes the battle became a massacre. A large explosion rocked the ground and Klein saw painted warriors armed with arrows and machetes swarming the square, their skin glistening in the fiery glare.

As if to salute the returning moon a series of explosions went off in ragged sequence, lighting the distant forest. The bloodbath in the square did not subside and Klein could hear the terrible screams of the dead and dying. He gathered Hannah, Sybelle and Savana to a place of relative safety behind the stage and took a defensive position. At this point the attackers didn't know friend from foe.

He had yet to fire the assault rifle on full automatic and hoped he could handle it. He had trained with an M-16 at the FBI shooting range many years ago, maybe too many.

Through the smoke clouded chaos Klein could see that most people were running away from the stage area. It was the bunch running towards them that worried him. He didn't want to kill their saviors but there was a real danger getting smoked by friendly fire.

The attacking warriors were going about their work with frenzied concentration, taking no prisoners. From what little he had seen of the atrocities Klein understood their rage. He also knew blood lust was blind—and indiscriminate.

For that reason he fired a test burst over the heads of the group of people running headlong toward him. The AK-47 had an unexpected kick but the warning shots failed to deter anyone.

There were five of them, two in front and three hunting them down.

The two in front were losing ground. A few yards from the stage one of them whirled and fired, downing one of the hunters and slowing down the other two. He fired again then turned and headed directly at Klein. When he came within a yard Klein recognized the man in black waving a pistol at him.

Martin Bormann, his features contorted with fear, was again running for his life. And he was coming right at him.

Klein lifted his weapon. Bormann ducked but his momentum was carrying him closer. It was like shooting one of those metal figures in an amusement park. But this was real and he wasn't a cold blooded killer. He let Bormann run past him no more than ten feet away. Frustration put him on adrenaline overdrive and Klein turned the AK-47 on the other runner but he too was well past him. Klein caught a glimpse of his face and remembered the square jawed man in black scrubs from his guided tour. Aibert Heims, Doctor Death, had increased his lead on his pursuers and was heading for the jungle.

One of the warriors drew his bow and buried an arrow in the back of his leg.

Heims fell on his chest, gibbering in fear. He vomited, his breath coming in wheezing squeals as he frantically tried to crawl away from the two men descending on him. A machete chopped into his arm but he lunged forward, blood pumping from his exposed veins. With a triumphant shriek the warrior straddled Heim, pulled him back by his hair, and slit his throat. Swimming in his own blood Heims kept trying to escape until another stroke of the blade severed his head.

Klein heard Sybelle moan behind him.

A moment later four more warriors came into view carrying assault rifles instead of machetes. When they saw Klein they shouldered their weapons. Klein lifted his AK-47 over his head. He could tell they were a nanosecond away from cutting him in half.

"Kai!"

At the command they lowered their guns.

A burly warrior with red masked eyes and dark blue beard, stepped forward. "Get the women over to the house, my men will stand guard," he said hoarsely.

Dumbfounded, Klein stared at him. Beneath the painted face and feathered headband was a man he knew, Dr. Borges.

"Did you hear?" Borges rasped, coming closer, "take the women to the house now."

Without answering Klein helped Savana stand up and half carried her to the bishop's house.

Inside the sound of battle was muffled Hannah and Sybelle attended to Savana, putting her on a couch. As promised, Borges left two men outside their door before going back to try to prevent total slaughter.

The house was lit by candles that cast shadows across the still rooms. Klein took a deep breath and sat on a nearby chair, the rifle across his legs. The only sound was Hannah's low murmur as she bent over her daughter. Sybelle sat on the floor beside her, eyes closed.

Klein leaned back, thankful to be alive.

An odd creaking noise at the rear of the house pulled him to his feet. Adrenaline spiking he took another deep breath before moving into the shadows. He stepped into a dining room, table set with plates, crystal and silver all polished and glinting in the candlelight. It was empty.

The next room was dark. The only light came from a glowing kerosene lamp beyond. Klein saw it was some sort of pantry and assumed the light was coming from the kitchen. He took a step inside and heard another creak.

It was a large kitchen and the single lamp created a small circle of illumination. The rest was darkness. Rifle held at high port Klein edged inside. He peered past the lamp and saw something move.

He took a quick step and his skull ignited with pain. He fell to one side, fingers gripping the rifle like an oar in a rushing current. He saw the flash of metal and rolled. The weapon warded off a second blow

Brain ringing Klein pulled the rifle up to fire.

There was nobody there.

He hauled himself to his feet and shuffled into the shadows. He saw an open door and found himself outside.

The moon had emerged and its orange glow lit the garden behind the house. About thirty yards ahead, Klein could see someone running. Or more properly, jogging heavily like someone not used to it.

Despite a blaring headache Klein gave chase. The figure ahead had a good jump on him but Klein was a runner and his quarry wasn't. He was only about ten yards behind when one foot caught a rock and he fell. Very slowly, Klein pushed himself erect, ready to give it up. You don't even know who the bastard is, he told himself.

Then the figure paused and looked back, hands on his
knees. In the moonlight Klein saw the man clearly. It was
Bishop Navarro. He had a black satchel at his feet.

Navarro picked up the bag and started running.

Groaning Klein got up and found his ankle was sore and
tight. He ran gingerly for a few yards until the pain subsided to
a dull ache and picked up his pace. Navarro was heading for a
patch of vines and flowers covering part of the high, barred
fence enclosing the encampment.

For a moment Klein thought Navarro was going to climb
over the fence and he slowed down. His ankle was throbbing
but he knew that if he stopped it would swell up.

A high pitched whine like a giant mosquito zipped past his
ear. Ten yards in front of him a feathered arrow pierced the
ground.

Klein glanced back and saw two warriors coming after him.
Instinctively he fired a warning shot and started sprinting as
best he could on his injured ankle.

When he neared the fence he saw that Navarro had
vanished.

The warriors who stopped when he fired, had resumed the
chase. Climbing over the fence was out, even if he could, which
was doubtful, he'd end up a dartboard for his pursuers. Chest
heaving he dove for the protection of the flowered vegetation,
hoping he could fire another warning shot from minimum
concealment.

To his surprise the large patch of vegetation was actually a
narrow path through the fence, leading into the jungle. Navarro
had his escape route all worked out.

There was nothing but darkness in front of him but his
other option was a shoot out so he plowed ahead into the dense
forest. He heard Navarro grunting somewhere in the distance
and followed the sound even though he knew it was a lost
cause. The warriors behind him knew the jungle, and he knew

bupkis as in nothing. His best bet was to find some kind of concealment.

A large orange moon lit the path through the thick vines. Pausing to take stock he heard another short grunting sound. As if someone had run into a tree trunk. He glanced back and saw something move in the shadows. Hefting the AK-47 he started trotting toward the sound.

"Kai!"

The distant voice cut through the stillness. He started running faster, ignoring the pain in his ankle.

Abruptly something clenched his foot and would let go. Something cool and thick was oozing up his leg. Klein tried to kick it off but he couldn't. The ooze had wrapped itself around his calves and was rising.

His blood froze.

The ooze wasn't rising... *he was sinking.*

He gaped at the gleaming scum of leaves and debris that appeared to be solid ground and realized he had stumbled into a bed of quicksand.

Chapter 56

A red sliver of moon sliced the blackness above but he was intent on the mosaic of smells below. The odor of human was distinctive. Sickly sweet, like a rotted flower. And hovering over everything was the stench of death.

He followed the human odor deep into the forest, his night eyes probing the shadows. The human was moving swiftly but he controlled his easy pace, belly close to the ground. Too often a predator became prey.

Rodents and lizards scurried out of his way but they needn't have worried. He didn't feed. It was his only law.

The expanding moon made him more vulnerable to being seen so he slunk low, moving along the edge of the scent, not directly behind it. The odor became stronger and he paused. His ears pricked up and he lifted his head, green eyes cutting the darkness apart.

Footsteps vibrated along the ground and he knew his prey was still running. The trail was heavy with human sweat, a mixture of fear and naked aggression. A frightened human was extremely lethal and struck without warning. He stayed well to the side of the trail as the moon became the color of fire.

The hair along his spine prickled and his tail stiffened. He paused, muscles tensed to leap at the slightest threat. The human was very close now but another, muskier scent smothered his. The female jaguar was nearby, circling the trail just as he was.

Except it wasn't the human she was stalking—it was him.

He could make himself invisible in the forest but his own scent would ultimately betray him. Lifting his head he sniffed the air. The human was doubling back and the female cat was circling closer. They intended to trap him in a vise.

Nearby was a growth of night blooms, their cloying odor hovering like a thick mist. Cautiously, one limb at a time he crawled under the protective cloak of flowers. However what he gained in masking his scent he lost in visibility.

Humans had the ability to strike from a long distance which was a great advantage. Even before he heard the loud *crack*, hot pain lanced his shoulder. He rolled over and leaped as a second *crack* snapped past his ear. Instinct took over his limbs and he sprang high. He hit the ground running aware that the female had picked up his trail.

The smell of his own blood told him he was in danger. Once again they had him trapped. The wind shifted bringing a familiar spiced odor. She was up ahead, waiting to pounce. Behind him was the human and his killing stick. He decided to circle back toward the human who couldn't sense him coming.

It was a mistake.

Even a human with limited faculties could follow a blood track. And he was bleeding badly. Between the sharp smell and oily drippings streaking the leaves he was totally exposed. All he could do is try to make a break for it. He could outrun the human, but he knew he couldn't elude the female. Fresh blood would only make her more eager to find him.

He circled away from the human, intending to go past him. The rustle of his hunter moving through the forest was clear but he knew the female crept soundlessly. Hot pain seared his shoulder as he quickly made his way, trying to avoid the moon's growing brightness.

A sudden *crack* sprayed wood and leaves everywhere. The human had sighted him. He bounded for the darkness. As he ran the female's scent drifted from somewhere ahead. She was lying in wait.

He saw a fallen tree trunk leaning on another tree. It formed a ramp to the higher branches where he could hide or attack. But the moment his claws dug into the soft wood the tree trunk exploded. Whirling he stretched his great muscles for

an attempt at a high branch and saw the human advancing with
his stick.

Fire spat from the stick. Something hard and heavy
smacked him to the ground. Pain speared his lungs when he
tried to roll to his feet, He lay there, each breath an agonized
rasp. The human was coming closer, hair gleaming white in the
moonlight and teeth drawn back in a savage grin.

As the human raised his stick the shadows moved. A thick
branch lazily unfolded, twisted, and fell, draping itself around
the human's shoulders without a sound. Its weight drove the
human to one knee.

Swiftly the branch dropped and he realized it was a giant
snake, black scales glistening wetly. He saw its flat eyes and the
red pattern edged with yellow that marked its huge head.

A deafening *crack* left his ears ringing. The stick had
wounded the snake. He could see the bloody gash in its body.
But the snake was already coiling around the human's chest,
pinning one arm. The stick fell to the ground.

A coughing roar of anger drew his attention. The female
was nearby, crouched and poised to strike, her sharp white teeth
bared in the moonlight. She slunk closer as the giant snake
wound tight around the human, who groaned. The female
pounced, clawing at the snake's thick body.

Arching its neck the reptile struck as swiftly as the wind and
raked its curved fangs into the female's haunch. With a terrified
shriek the female leaped back and paced back and forth out
of range as the huge snake continued to squeeze. Each time
the human took a quick, frantic breath and exhaled, the snake
squeezed harder.

He saw the human's eyes pop wide and his mouth open and
close like a landed fish.

The female roared in frustration when the snake flexed its
long neck and opened its huge white maw. Then its head eased
closer to its prey.

The human's eyes were rolling in terror as the snake's open jaw *unhinged* and became as wide as his crushed chest. He kicked his legs as if trying to run but the serpent lifted him off the ground. Most of the reptile's rippling black body was wound around an upper branch and he pulled the human up as if cradling a child.

Instinct warned him to get on his feet. Despite the agony gripping his lungs he heaved himself erect and loped into the shadows. The female remained where she was, nervously moving back and forth. She roared as the serpent's enlarged jaw dropped over the human's head.

The giant snake worked its gaping maw around the lifeless shoulders and began to swallow its prey.

He turned and ran toward the stench of fire and death to make it difficult for the female to track him. But she didn't follow.

As his instincts dragged his bloody, pain wrenched body to some safe lair, the female's anguished yowl echoed across the moon.

Chapter 57

Klein had always thought quicksand was something of a myth.

Now, knee deep in spongy slime and sinking deeper, he was a believer.

At first he tried to lift one leg high to see if he could find purchase with his freed foot. He discovered that as soon as he tried to pull up one leg, he tipped over sideways pulling him deeper.

He tried to remember do's and don'ts he had read about how to survive in quicksand. It was either be very still or try to float. At the moment he was in the very still camp.

"Yo, help!"

His cry faded into the jungle. Then he heard a voice.

"Help!"

I said it first, he thought, peering in the direction of the sound. There was nothing but the orange moon overhead and the occasional croaks and chirps of the creatures in the swampy forest. Funny, he thought, a New York City boy ending up in the middle of the jungle, knee deep in quicksand.

At thigh deep, it wasn't funny anymore. While keeping still slowed the process, he was sinking surely and inexorably. At the rate he was going down he didn't have more than fifteen minutes.

He suppressed a surge of panic and tried to think. He was holding the rifle like a life line attached to nothing. The warriors hunting him were somewhere out there, either way he was dead so he had nothing to lose. He set the automatic on single and fired three shots about ten seconds apart.

"Oya!" the voice called.

"Over here," Klein yelled. There was no response.

When the slime reached his crotch he got nervous. He looked around for something he could grab; a vine, a branch, anything at all. All he saw was leaves and pond scum glistening in the empty darkness. He fired three more shots.

Again he heard the voice.

He cursed his stupidity at blundering through a strange jungle at night. Borges had told him to remain in the house. Why didn't he just stay put with Hannah and Sybelle instead of playing the goddamn hero. Klein quickly apologized for any blasphemy he may have committed against a god he barely understood. It was no time to make enemies.

Now waist deep and sinking fast he fired three quick rounds.

Someone yelled. Then silence.

Heart thumping he took a deep breath and held it, hoping it would make him more buoyant. It seemed to work but he had to exhale sometime. Every time he did he lost ground.

When it reached his abdomen Klein swung his rifle around like a cane, hoping to find a stray tree limb. All he succeeded in doing was to get the rifle muddy. Sucker will probably blow up, he speculated dourly. But the AK-47 was built for lousy conditions. He fired another trio of shots.

The answering yell seemed louder but not any closer.

Nobody will even know what happened, Klein reflected. He'll just vanish without a trace in this remote shithole. Biggest case of his career and Jake would get all the credit.

Chest deep he considered trying to swim for it. In desperation he pulled the trigger and heard a click. He was out of bullets.

Taking a deep breath he started to try for shore and stopped immediately. Still was better. But not much.

Something moved a few yards away. A man emerged from the shadows. It was one of the warriors.

"Hey!" Klein called.

The man came nearer and pushed something at Klein. It was a spear.

Instinctively Klein lifted his empty gun. The man shook the spear impatiently.

"Take it fool."

Klein blinked, tossed the gun at his feet and grabbed the wooden shank. Slowly he felt his chest lifting out of the muck The man pulled him in hand over hand until his knees hit bottom.

Gratefully, Klein crawled onto firm ground. He crouched there for a few moments like a dog about to shake water from his coat.

"Thanks, thanks a lot," he managed. "You speak English?" Someone yelled.

He lifted his head. The warrior was staring into the darkness with an expression of deep concern. Klein pushed himself to his feet and followed his gaze.

There was someone in the quicksand about thirty yards away. He held a black satchel over his head as if to protect it from immersion. But he was already chest deep.

"Help me, for God's sake!" The man yelled.

An acid pang of guilt pierced Klein's belly when he recognized Bishop Navarro.

"Can't we do something?" he asked hoarsely.

The man turned. "I had to make a choice—him or you."

Klein watched Navarro sink to his armpits, still holding the satchel.

At the last moment Navarro threw the satchel toward firm ground. It landed on the quicksand and floated.

Unfortunately Navarro did not. The effort of heaving the satchel hastened his descent.

"Help me, Lord!" he yelled, straining to raise his chin above the surface.

Klein sickened as he watched Navarro's face disappear beneath the thick, oily scum. One hand remained above the surface, thick gold ring shining in the moonlight. Then it winked out.

Klein took a deep breath and nodded at the warrior who had saved him from the same end. The man had moved closer to the bed of quicksand and held out his hand to Klein. "Grab my wrist and hold on."

Using his spear the warrior nudged the satchel closer and pulled it out of the muck.

When he stood up and turned, the moonlight hit his painted face. Klein realized he knew that face.

"Malik... how the hell... what are you doing here?"

Malik shrugged. "Savin' your sorry ass. Come on, my friends are waiting. We've been tryin' to find you. They tried to warn you back there but you just kept runnin'."

"Warn me how?"

"They were yellin' 'Kai' at you. That's the Indian word for stop."

"Now you tell me. But you haven't said what you're doing here."

"I'm an apprentice of Dr. Borges. The forest people call him Atu, the master shaman. He organized the tribes for this attack. It's been on the calendar for almost a year."

A sudden wave of exhaustion washed over Klein. He paused, hands on his knees, and took a deep breath. He'd been through a fucking war. That was nearly him under that slime. Missing in action. Except nobody would have ever known it happened.

"You alright?" Malik asked.

Klein snorted. He was running on empty. He picked up the empty rifle.

"I'll be fine. Let's go."

They started walking, Klein careful where he put his feet. His wet, slimy clothes stuck to his body and attracted hordes of insects. After they'd gone a hundred yards he stopped and looked at the moon, shaking his head.

"You sure you're okay?"

"Not really," Klein said quietly, "I owe you my life."

Malik squinted at him. "Always wanted the FBI on my payroll."

Laughing they began walking towards the flame colored tree line. Abruptly Malik spun and gaped at Klein, blood exploding from his chest. At the same time, Klein heard the shots.

He tried to catch Malik but he fell through his arms to the ground.

"Throw it here!"

Klein looked up. A short man with a large head was approaching, pistol trained on him. "Throw me the bag now!" he demanded.

"Why not come get it?" Klein growled.

"Throw it and I will not shoot."

Like I believe you, Klein thought. "Sure, okay..."

"Stop! Drop your weapon."

Klein tossed his empty rifle in the man's direction. The man took a few steps closer.

"Now the bag."

It was then saw the man clearly. It was *Bormann*, Martin Bormann himself, holding a Luger.

Arms half raised he moved over, picked up the satchel, and tossed it very high.

"Careful, you fool!" Bormann shouted. He hurried over to where it landed, intent on his prize.

When he bent to pick it up Klein snatched his Ruger and fired. Surprised, Bormann lifted his pistol. He managed two shots but Klein paid no attention. Slowly walking toward Bormann, he kept shooting until the gun was empty.

Bormann spun and jerked from side to side in a grisly parody of dance. His intestines gleamed wetly in the moonlight as they slowly spilled from his belly. Hands frantically trying to push them back, he collapsed.

For a long time Klein sat beside Malik's body, swatting away the flies and ants that seemed to materialize at the first whiff of blood. Finally he started back to the camp, guided only by the firelight. He almost threw the satchel into the quicksand until he remembered Malik had died for it.

Whatever was inside felt as heavy as a tombstone.

Chapter 58

Tupo and some of his Jivaro warriors found Orient lying unconscious in the crook of a tree. He was naked and had suffered a two minor bullet wounds as well as three broken ribs. The tribesmen seemed to know Orient had undergone a metamorphosis and made a litter to carry him back.

The compound was in smoldering ruins and bodies were strewn everywhere. Dr. Borges, still in tribal dress had set up a field clinic to treat the wounded. He attended to Orient personally, applying an herbal salve to his wounds and taping his cracked ribs.

There was much to do in the aftermath of the attack. Borges enlisted Hannah's help and provided medical treatment to the surviving residents of the compound. His intervention as tribal Shaman had prevented a bloodbath.

Orient recovered quickly and within twenty four hours he was up and about, helping Hannah and Borges at the clinic.

"Are you sure you should be doing this?" Hannah asked half joking, as they worked side by side in the surgery room.

Orient plucked a bulled from a young girl's leg. "It only hurts when I breathe." Then he lowered his voice. "Physically I'm okay but I'm still kind of stunned."

Hannah glanced at him over her mask. "So am I. Right now performing emergency surgery is a way to come down."

"How is Savana?'

"Sybelle is with her. Whatever they gave her kept Savana out for hours. When she woke up it was all over, thank God. I don't think I'll ever forget that man's execution. That woman, so cold..."

Orient said nothing, also unable to push Alvira from his memory. As far as anyone knew she had vanished somewhere during the battle. He wondered if she was still in the rain forest.

Hannah finished stitching up a warrior's tattooed arm. "I'm going to have a serious sit down with Sybelle and catch up on our family history. She never mentioned my wicked grandmother before."

"I just met her briefly but she looked a lot like you."

"I believe you—but it still scares me." She signaled the nurse. "Next patient..."

Later while they were all sharing a communal meal Klein confided that Navarro's satchel contained the Spear of Destiny and two gold bricks. "We still haven't located the Grimoire or Hans for that matter. Bastard is still out there."

Borges glanced at Orient. They had discussed what happened during their journey through metamorphosis. However it would be difficult to explain.

"The good news is that Hans Kammler and company kept meticulous records," Borges said. He had exchanged his tribal dress for surgical scrubs.

"Everything was backed up on CD and flash drives and stored in fireproof file cabinets. We have medical records, names, splinter groups, moles, political cronies, payoffs; everything. The FBI is welcome to share them."

Klein nodded gravely. "Believe me I'm going to need something to back up my report or they'll ship me to rehab. Oh yeah, now that their scramblers are knocked out I finally got hold of Jake. He's sending a boat for us. Should be here in less than forty eight hours."

"Thank heavens," Sybelle said, "I'm going to spend a month on Fire Island recovering."

Hannah put her arm around her daughter. "I'm taking Savana to New York and try to get back to our boring little routine."

Orient looked surprised. "I wouldn't call trauma surgery boring."

"You will after six months or so. The paperwork will turn you into a zombie."

Orient smiled and nodded, avoiding eye contact with Klein and Borges. They still hadn't revealed the extent of the Nazi's human experiments in their quest for extended life. The revelations would do no good except to inspire others to attempt the same. The medical compound, children's 'clinics', computer systems, arsenal, work camps—everything had been sacked and destroyed. Many of the residents had run into the jungle or took small boats downriver. A few, very few, had been taken prisoner.

Orient could feel Borges' pain. Malik had been his student for years and although he had limited psychic powers, the young expatriate's intuition was unerring.

"It's almost like he had some interior GPS," Borges said, as they basked in the Ancient Pool. The boat Jake sent was delayed due to a flurry of unusual lightning storms, and the two of them met at the pool for an hour of meditation.

"Malik found us as soon as we left Navarro's church. Lucky he did, or Moe's flu would have turned critical."

"That was him, right place right time. I never had to tell him anything twice. He was loyal and brave. We prayed over him for hours before cremation. "

Orient nodded. He had been recovering from his injuries during the ceremony.

"Malik told Moe Klein that you had planned the raid for over a year."

"Yes. I knew the confluence of solstice and eclipse would generate a ritual ceremony and Bishop Novarro would likely preside. For years we watched the bishop extend his hold on politicians. His endorsement in the pulpit was a winning vote. The media loved him and he appeared frequently on TV. The humble healer you saw that day had a public relations staff.

Hans Kammler was funding his church and Navarro used that money to become a global religious figure. For all those reasons he was slated for elevation to cardinal. After that there'd be little hope of stopping him. Especially with the Grimoire's power fused with the Nazi occult machine. "

"You managed to keep your clinic and your church going.'

"Yes, but it was small potatoes compared to Navarro's operation. He used formulas from that Gimoire to heal the sick. Everyone thought he was a saint. But Saint Navarro never told his patients that their magical recovery was temporary. As you know every action..."

"...has an opposite and equal reaction." Orient said. Floating in the clear water relieved the stress on his cracked ribs.

"Exactly. Malik hadn't learned that yet. He was impetuous."

"I've been there," Orient said, recalling his headlong rush to help Sybelle that ended with his capture by two very surprised guards.

"We all have. My strategy could easily have backfired. But there was no choice."

"And Navarro never suspected what you were doing?"

"In Bahia the people see me as a lay doctor and a spiritual priest. That is something very common in Brazil. Teachers, engineers, judges; all practice one form of Macumba or another. To the renowned bishop I was a neighborhood medic of no consequence."

"So how did you pull it off?"

"What Navarro didn't know is that I was born in the Amazon and in the jungle, the shaman Atu has power over all the tribes. Uniting them all was my greatest feat of magic."

Orient's laugh was cut short by the pain in his side.

"I would like to ask a favor of you," Borges said gravely, his grey eyes moist.

"Anything."

"Merge minds with me while I spread Malik's ashes on the water."

"Yes, I'm ready.'

Solemnly, the bearded shaman took a clay jar that he had left at the edge of the pool and held it in both hands as they both slipped into deep meditation.

Orient let his ego dissolve, allowing his consciousness to connect with the pure cosmos. When it merged with Borges he felt the shaman's deep loss and his total commitment to the evolution of man's soul.

A wind came up as Borges tipped the jar, and Malik's ashes spread over the pool like white butterflies, Along with Borges, he directed his energy to Malk's safe transition. He clasped the pouch at his neck and felt the ring's power bathe them all. From now on it would serve as compass for his own journey.

+ + +

The weather cleared and the boat finally arrived.

One night after dinner Orient asked Klein to take a walk.

Along the way Klein lit a cigarette. "I found out the smoke helps keep mosquitoes away. You want to tell me something?"

"Hans is dead. I watched him die."

"You were there?"

"During the battle I followed him into the jungle. He stopped under a tree to shoot at me. A huge anaconda dropped down on him and killed him."

"Killed him? how?"

"Just like any Anaconda would, crushed him and swallowed him,"

"Did you try to save him?"

"I was unarmed."

"You chased him without a gun?"

"Followed, not chased."

Klein blew a reflective smoke ring and watched it hang in the humid air. "Looks like you're just as dumb as I am. Swallowed you say, you mean *whole?*

"The snake unhinges its jaw and..."

"That's too much information for me. So Hans is lunch, and Bishop Navarro is deep sixed. No bodies, no evidence. What the hell do I say in my report?"

+ + +

In the end the official version was that Von Speer was the mastermind behind the museum theft. Von Speer was murdered by a man named Hans Kammler suspected in multiple homicides and who had abducted Savana Wylde from New York to a Neo-Nazi encampment in Brazil. Agent Morris Klein had freed Savana and recovered the Spear of Destiny, but Hans Kammler escaped into the jungle and was presumed dead.

No mention was made of Alvira Charisma, Aibert Heims, Josef Mengele, or any of the other fugitive Nazis in residence. Or the grisly science behind their extraordinary life span.

"They never found Josef Mengele," Klein said unhappily. "I hope he ran into a crocodile."

Jake took a healthy bite of his pastrami and swiss. "Like they say, only the good die young."

He studied Klein for a few moments then set aside his sandwich. "Look, Moe, you did real good with this case. Safe recovery of a kidnap victim, recovery of a priceless artifact, new office upstairs, bigger budget, commendation... maybe you should keep this Nazi fugitive thing between us, know what I mean? You've been on a hardcore case. You know when you walked in I hardly recognized you with all the weight you lost."

"And I'm going to keep it off," Klein growled, eying Jake's sandwich.

"Of course, no question, but you've gone through a lot of stress, the Amazon jungle for chrissakes... so take a little vacation. You deserve it Moe."

Klein appreciated Jake's attempts at diplomacy but he knew what he was getting at. Bottom line, Jake thought he was nuts.

He's right about one thing Klein reflected sadly, the only people who would believe him were Orient and Borges. Sybelle and Hannah never visited the grotesque medical facilities created by Mengele and Heim, nor did they see any supposedly dead Nazis. And after a few weeks back in New York, he hardly believed it himself. But he hadn't forgotten what Malik did for him. That memory remained painfully clear. And it put things in perspective.

Klein sighed. "You know what Jake, I believe you're right. I will take a vacation, if you don't mind covering for me."

Jake flashed a brilliant grin. If there was anything he liked better than food it was being told he was right.

"No worries, consider your ass covered. So where are you going?"

"Back to my office I guess."

"Your vacation. Where are you going?"

Klein got out of his chair. "A lady friend invited me to visit her on Fire Island. I may take her up on it."

"Very nice." He gave Klein a lewd wink. "Be sure to tell me all about it."

"It's not like that Jake, but I will tell you one thing—just between us."

"What's that, Moe?"

"I fucking shot Martin Bormann."

Chapter 59

Savana began her recovery on the boat back to Belem. Fortunately she didn't remember anything about the sacrificial ceremony. They had given her something that put her out. Even the big battle that freed her was just a haze of noise and light.

When they returned to New York her mother took her to see Dr. Walter Jaffe, a therapist who specialized in war trauma and terrorist victims. Walter was very nice, and helped her but Owen was the person who helped the most. Just taking a long walk through Central Park was like some sort of yoga meditation. They didn't talk much and when they did it was about something ordinary—and funny. Owen had a cool sense of humor and made her laugh. He was cool in other ways too, Savana observed.

She had never seen her mother so happy. Owen had a nice gentle way about him, but he was strong underneath. That fact that Owen, her mother and her aunt had gone to Brazil to find her, made Savana feel protected somehow. Which is how she felt when her mom and Owen were together, protected. She knew that no matter what happened Owen would be there for her.

Not only that, he was handsome, Savana mused. A few of her girlfriends had seen them together in the park and freaked. They thought he was an actor. They groaned when Savana told them he was her mother's boyfriend.

Savana didn't remember certain things but she did recall being kidnapped. Worst of all she remembered Bumpy and what she saw that day. Once in a while she had bad nightmares.

Owen really helped her there, she reflected. He taught her breathing patterns that enabled her to control her fear. He also taught her how to empty her mind and channel universal energy.

The bad news was she hadn't been able to resume school. In a way her classmates seemed younger—and shallow. So she was doing home study for a semester. Savana had thrown herself into her schoolwork determined to catch up, or possibly qualify for her senior year. .

"Who was Pythagoras?" she asked one night while doing her math assignment.

Orient looked up from his book. "He was said to be of Greek origin. He went to Egypt and studied with the high priests for twenty years. However they refused to grant him access to their inner secrets, the final degree of initiation. He returned to Italy and there gave the world the laws of geometry. Pythagoras founded a school outside of Naples and his students took a vow of silence. Eventually superstitious Neapolitans burned out his camp. Pythagoras disappeared..."

"Wow, that gives me a whole new slant on math. How do you know that stuff?"

Orient smiled. "I collect odd facts and weird theories."

"Anyone for some nice normal ice cream?" Hanna suggested.

"I'm in," Orient said.

Savana grinned, "Me too." It was nights like these when she forgot about what happened. As the weeks stretched into months the nightmares came less frequently, but a certain wariness lingered...

+ + +

It took Orient two weeks to recover from the wounds and psychological residue of battle. It took Hannah three, giving him time to prepare for his new career. On the fourth week he began training at St. Luke's trauma center.

The work was demanding and Orient threw himself into it, knowing he needed to build stability in his life. Along the way he rediscovered his love of medicine. And his friendship with Hannah grew into a real relationship He hadn't told her about Alvira. That might come later if things became serious... or if he figured out how to explain it.

Some weeks later Klein called him.

"I thought you'd like to know the esteemed Bishop Navarro, has been reported missing while on a mission of mercy in the Amazon jungle. The buzz at the Vatican is he might be nominated for sainthood. Can you believe it... Saint Navarro?"

"He'll make a great statue," Orient said wearily. He knew illusion was the way of the world but it never failed to surprise him.

When he told Hannah she became angry. "That bloody saint tried to murder my daughter. I feel like contacting Agent Klein and..."

"He's the one who told me," Orient said quietly. "If we decide to open this can of worms it will affect your professional credibility. The establishment will come at you with everything they have. Not to mention the media. Do you really want to put Savana through all that?"

Hannah snuggled closer. "How come you know so much?"

"Years of experience at avoiding attention."

"Well you've certainly have mine," she purred. "I've been getting compliments on your work."

"From who?"

"Your patients doctor. Or more specifically the lady you patched up after she OD'd and totaled her Corvette."

"Dani Hayden?"

"So you do remember."

"Hard to forget a heart stoppage *and* a punctured lung. I couldn't even use opiates for the wounds."

"She said you diagnosed her soul or something like that."

"I saw she was on drugs so I gave her adrenaline before...."

"The girl has a crush on you Owen. She told me you're like a doctor on TV."

Orient lifted his head off the pillow and looked at her. "Are you jealous?"

"A little, wouldn't you be?"

He considered the question. "A little."

"Good." She drew him closer and kissed him. "What's this pouch you wear around your neck?"

"Something a good friend gave me in Marrakech." He nuzzled her ear. "You were up late last night, Are you okay?"

"Do you dream a lot?"

"Off and on, why?"

"The last few nights I've been having odd dreams. They're not exactly nightmares but they are kind of creepy."

Orient smiled. "You can tell Dr. Jung."

"They're nothing special. I'm walking somewhere and I see this black shadow, it seems to be some sort of big cat, but it isn't. I can't explain it. It probably has something to do with that horrible incident with Jillian."

"Probably," Orient said. But he knew better.

"I still haven't been able to tell Savana how her cat disappeared."

Orient sighed. This wasn't the way he would have planned it.

"Look, about your dreams." He fingered the pouch around his neck. "Something happened while I was in Bahia looking for Savana..."

The author would like to express his gratitude to his wife Ellen Smith for her enduring love and support, and his thanks to Keith Deutsch, Larry Townsend, Christine Roth and Rob Cohen for their friendship, faith and enthusiasm.

42653512R00260

Made in the USA
Charleston, SC
05 June 2015